Lemon Blossoms

Lemon Blossoms

Nina Romano

TURNER

Turner Publishing Company
424 Church Street • Suite 2240 • Nashville, Tennessee 37219
445 Park Avenue • 9th Floor • New York, New York 10022

www.turnerpublishing.com

Lemon Blossoms, A Novel

This is a work of fiction. All the characters and events portrayed in this book are either products of the author's imagination or are used fictitiously.

Cover design: Kristen Ingebretson and Maddie Cothren
Book design: Kym Whitley

Library of Congress Cataloging-in-Publication Data

Romano, Nina, 1942-
 Lemon blossoms / Nina Romano.
  pages ; cm. — (Wayfarer trilogy ; Book Two)
 ISBN 978-1-63026-909-8 (pbk.)
 I. Title.
 PS3568.O549L46 2016
 813'.54--dc23
                                        2015030457

Printed in the United States of America
14 15 16 17 18 19 0 9 8 7 6 5 4 3 2 1

For
John Dufresne

Life is a series of natural and spontaneous changes,
Don't resist them—that only creates sorrow.
Let reality be reality. Let things flow naturally
Forward in whatever way they like.

—Lao Tzu

Love looks not with the eyes,
But with the mind, and therefore
Is winged Cupid painted blind.

—William Shakespeare

Lemon Blossoms

CHAPTER I

Angelica

THE WINE SHED
VILLAGGIO PACE 1895

I WAS BORN IN A lemon grove, the scent of blossoms everywhere. Mamma told me it was paradise on earth, and so she named me Angelica, whispering in my ear that life, like the lemon tree, houses both the bitter and the sweet. A breeze had brought to earth a cover of white blossoms, and Mamma said she imagined a far-off winter playground. The day I was born she removed a veil from my face while lying in a bosk of flowering trees and looked up to see tiny white *zagarelle* frame an ocean of sky that mirrored the straits of Messina.

Mamma insisted we speak Italian—the language of angels, she called it—but sometimes we'd slip into Sicilian. After she had my brother Peppe, Mamma lost four children before I arrived, followed by two sisters. Mamma prayed her guardian angel would send her a celestial being, but instead she got me. Mamma had a thing about angels, saying we are born with a host of eleven thousand watching over us. She had promised that if I were born and lived, she'd make sure that I would be devoted to my own patron and, with God's help, the seraphim could choose amongst themselves who would guide me. That poor angel didn't have an inkling of what he'd be getting into.

Angelica—a name that caused me difficulty right from the beginning. Angels are listed in God's Chain of Being as below God but above man. And man is above animals and animals are above plant life. This always troubled me because I knew I was human and humans suffered just like animals. And in my life on the farm I had learned to love animals.

⋯⋯⋯

ON AN OCTOBER DAY, EIGHT years after my birth, I started thinking about the heavenly trust with which Mamma had encumbered me. I couldn't be an angel all the time, nor did I want to be. The sun warmed, yet the air was cool. Autumn announced itself with the acrid fragrance of burning leaves and the sweet scents from Mamma's kitchen. Mamma asked me to pick up twelve eggs from the chickens so we could make ricotta cheesecake. I loved helping her.

I had a special chicken, Cluck, a true prize that laid the best eggs. On this day, I hunted all over but couldn't find the egg she'd have laid, not a pure white nor a blood-stained one. I couldn't find her either. But when I finally found her near an abandoned stone cottage, she was dead. I looked at her outstretched body and open eyes staring back at me, unseeing. I swooshed my hand at the flies around her eyes and picked up her limp body, her neck hanging slack. She was lost to me forever, and there was nothing I could do about it. I put her in my apron and ran, my chest heaving, all the way to Mamma, who was waiting for me in the kitchen.

"Did a fox get her, Mamma?"

"I'm afraid not," Mamma said.

I laid the chicken on the sideboard.

Mamma sat at the table sewing. She set her work aside, pulled me close, and placed her arms around me. She looked right up into my face. I knew by the set of her mouth that whatever she was going to tell me was not only going to be the truth but was also going to be one of those awful lessons about life that I didn't want to hear. Why couldn't I have been born a for-real angel?

Mamma told me how life was paradise on earth. But I was beginning to learn that an earthly paradise is a canvas splotched with the color of sadness.

"Listen, sweet one."

Oh, now I knew for sure it was going to be hurtful.

"Sometimes life doesn't turn out the way we want. It has a way of presenting us with trials to deal with right then and there."

"Mamma!"

"That chicken has given us many healthy eggs, and we are grateful to her, but now her time of egg-bearing has finished."

"For good."

"She died because she wasn't supposed to have any more. She's what we call egg-bound. The egg was either too big and she was too tired to push it out, or it might have been twisted or even cracked and the yolk . . ."

Mamma looked at me the way she did when I was supposed to have understood what she was saying, only I wasn't quite sure if I had.

"Do you understand, Angelica?"

She shook me gently by the shoulders and I answered, "Maybe, except for the breaking . . . Could this happen to a woman?"

She smiled and hugged me.

I'd gotten it right, but it vexed me all the same, Mamma pointing out life's cheerless possibilities. My throat burned and clogged with something that felt egg-sized. I wriggled out of her grasp and ran out, grabbing my chicken from the sideboard.

I didn't stop running until I passed Papà's wine shed. I fell to my knees and cried, venting the sorrow that overcame me, shedding tears I couldn't when I'd first discovered my chicken—perhaps because I'd been so shocked by her death. I cried and rocked my dead chicken till I heard my mother's voice call me for supper. If I buried my chicken, Mamma might get angry. She never wasted anything, and probably had intentions of using that chicken, stuck egg and all, for soup. But I knew I could never eat Cluck, and the thought of cooking her was so horrific to me that I chanced Mamma's anger and dug a deep hole with a shovel from the shed. Good or bad behavior? I tried not to think about it.

Mamma always said I was good, but that didn't mean I didn't love to play hard and take risks. Somehow knowing I had such a strong presence around me made me, well, not quite invincible, but able to take chances because I knew I was safe and protected. This invisible shield felt marvelous. I did things—some of them crazy and wild—with a sense that there was no danger. In fact, to me, there was little peril in doing things like jumping from the hayloft and landing smack on the mule's back.

Our property was extensive, not quite a *latifondo*. Fenced in from the road, the land could have been mistaken for a monastery. One hundred meters from our house, built into the side of a cliff, was a barn where we stabled horses, a donkey, and a mule. There was a pigpen, a chicken coop, and a hutch for rabbits, whose cages were always filthy. The day before, I'd cleaned them, but hated the task because of one fierce buck. He looked sweet but was mean as a snapping crab in a tide pool.

The arbor was a short walk of a few meters from the house. That's where Mamma canned tomatoes, though I don't know why it was called canning because we always used bottles. In the arbor was a huge stone sink and a marble table big enough for twenty people. One summer we went through one hundred kilos of tomatoes. About half were conserved whole and peeled in widemouthed glass jars while the rest we passed through a sieve. We poured the smashed pulp and juice through a funnel into wine or beer bottles. Even though it was summer, we made huge fires and wrapped the bottles in old newspapers, cooking them in boiling water. We couldn't touch the cooked bottles till the next morning. We always lost some. A few broke in the water; others burst when we took them out, especially if the morning air was cool and the bottle still hot.

Our land was covered with fruit trees. We had a mandarin tree and other trees like walnut and cork, the bark of which had many uses. Our lemon, orange, and almond groves were far from the house, and so was Papà's olive orchard, which some years he would rent out. Even the alley down the orto was lined with wild asparagus. But the figs were my favorite. Sometimes when picking figs I could see raspberry apricot cloudlets perched between other trees, overspread and dense. Whenever my father found a ripe black fig pinched off at the honeyed end, he'd ask, "Angelica, who could have done this?" As I opened my mouth to answer, he'd say, "A bird perhaps?" He would then pick the fruit and bring his arm way back over his head, ready to hurl it, and say, "Shall we let the birds have it?" Then I'd grab it from his fingers and shove it in my mouth. When I finished chewing I'd say, "No use wasting a good fig, Papà." I was the little bird, but he always played the game.

That night Mamma saw how upset I was at supper. I wouldn't eat a thing, so she asked me what was wrong. I told her I buried my chicken. She said, "Of course. Did you think I'd cook it?" All I could do was lower my head. "It might be poisoned," she said ever so quietly.

AFTER THE EVENING MEAL I paid a visit to the burial site of Cluck. When I got back I said to Mamma that burying my chicken made me decide to take extra good care of my little donkey, Pupa. Everyone made fun of me because I called her Doll, but that's what she was to me. By then it was late, but Mamma gave me permission to make sure my pet was all right.

As I neared my donkey, I spoke softly, "Pupa," and watched her prick up her ears. She knew me, knew the sound of my voice and touch. She hated my brother, who sometimes played mean tricks on her. Walking back to the house, I passed the carob tree and thought about how I loved to climb it and pick long brown pods to feed the horses and my donkey. I would even chew the pods when Papà wasn't looking.

❦

THE NEXT DAY AFTER LUNCH Mamma told me to clean the stable, but I didn't muck out the stalls right away. Instead, I led Nero d'Avola, Papà's black horse named for a grape, out by his mane, climbed up on the dead tree log in front of the stable, and mounted the horse. He took off at a trot, and at once we were cantering. Then he began to gallop, and soon I was bouncing hard up and down and all over and had a difficult time keeping my balance. I yanked his head back with all my might and he slowed somewhat, but it was then I realized he was going to jump the fence. I didn't think he had enough speed to manage the jump, but he soared over it as I flew right over his head and landed with such force I thought I saw stars.

It wasn't just the feeling of the wind being knocked out of me; it was as if I'd run for kilometers and was hyperventilating. I couldn't slow down enough to catch my breath. I remembered Mamma always putting a bag over my mouth when this happened, so I cupped my hands in front of my face and tried to breathe. Slowly, my breath came back to me. I was shaken, but knew I'd live, although I felt terribly sore in my private parts. I checked my body—no bones broken. The horse was content, munching on some high grass. I took him by the mane and we walked all the way back to the stable. He was gentle as a lamb most of the time. What made him think he'd suddenly become a racehorse?

Still hurting after I deposited the horse back to his stall, I had no energy to muck out anything. I would have done it later, but my nosiness won out and my feet wandered into Papà's wine shed. I was preparing to receive my First Holy Communion. My uncle Don Ruggero, Mamma's brother, who was a priest, said we only got the bread, which is both body and blood. But I'd never tasted wine, though I did think about sipping some on Sundays when everyone was napping. Something tempted me, so I decided to try some.

Bougainvillea, bay leaf hedge, and oleander blocked the view of the wine outbuilding from the house. Somehow I understood the importance of being out of sight, hidden by shrubbery, though I never had before. I entered the storehouse and felt a difference in temperature from outside. I nosed around, sticking my fingers into demijohns of this and that, sometimes forgetting which cork went where.

I walked around inspecting hoses and funnels. There were many wooden barrels on their sides. Everything seemed hazy and musty. The smell of fermented wine made me marvel at so many other things in nature, like how the sun rose or why a dappled pony stood in what shade he could find out of the sun.

I put my mouth to a spigot and trickled in some wine, sweeter than grapes. How was that possible? I took another sip. I wasn't fast enough in turning the nozzle and splashed my feet, like rain. I liked to watch rain, how it gave me that magical feeling of knowing life through generations. Mamma said we have an inner voice, an inner knowledge passed down through the genes. She was right, because sometimes I've known things before they happened. I swallowed some more wine and felt my cheeks warm, my head become airy.

I closed the door. A shaft of light poured in from a high window, now the only source of light. I sampled another of my father's wines. I began to think of my life as if I were seeing it from outside of myself. Sometimes I pictured it running next to me—like how a shadow moves along the wall. I owned up that life was a mystery. Why was there blood at birth? Why did females have to endure all that waiting like long-suffering saints before the baby came? But there was nothing in the world that seemed more wondrous and natural than the life my mamma led. I wanted that same life surrounded by children and love when I grew up.

A ladybug landed on my hand, and I wished for the promise of paradise on earth, which to me spelled family. Birds twittered in the eaves. A three-note call, the cooing of the doves. I glanced upward, saw nothing, but heard another trill of two staccato and one extended beat. I listened again to two unstressed and one stressed warble. Then silence.

Demijohns, bottles of a liter, a liter and a half, and two liters, and all of them had small necks and were fragile. Mamma was constantly telling me to take care with them, except for the stout demijohns. The bottles were spaced out and lined the floor, maze-like. I stepped gingerly around and in between them. They were scattered in a narrow space like a corridor between two walls full of rickety old shelving that almost met. I leaned back on one wall and reached to touch the other with both hands and arms extended. I looked at the opposite wall from where a ladder leaned and saw the faint outline of an archway, pleased to discover the secret that there once was a door that had been sealed shut. How odd. Life cradles so many secrets, so many lie ahead waiting to be discovered. The ladder rested upon the wall to my left.

Curiosity got the better of me, and I wanted a better look at the archway. There seemed to have been a window on top of it. I lifted my skirt and petticoat, tucking them into my waistband. I began to climb. I climbed with slow, careful steps up the wooden rungs, higher and higher, my steps unsure. "Whoops, I slipped," I said, thinking it couldn't be the wine—I drank so little. *Better stop.* I reached shelving, skipped the first, and decided on the second. Then I sat balanced, though some-what precariously, on a ledge. A lemon-yellow butterfly flitted by, the distraction underscoring what I already knew: I shouldn't be here. The air stilled. The same peace that ushers in a storm reigned within the shed, and soon thoughts of my donkey crammed in on me. She would have to go through the rigors of birthing someday, Mamma said. And as I hoped to be like my mother, I trusted Pupa's jennet would be like her. I'd made Mamma promise I could be there to help when the time came. All she said was, "We'll see."

I looked all around, down at the bottles below me, and then followed the flight of the butterfly. So lost in thought was I that when Mamma called me from the garden to gather tomatoes, her shrill voice startled me and I slipped from the shoulder-level shelf that my father had built for his convenience. I grappled to keep my balance, but then everything dipped and pitched out of kilter, as if time had slowed. My arms flailed, a bird, a butterfly in flight. I screamed, a wail that seemed to wake the dead. Reaching across for the opposite shelf, I grabbed for it but it gave way. Falling forward, I scraped my hands against the rough, opposing wall. I slid down it, crashing through planking that broke some momentum but did not stop or save me as bottles and wood shattered around me.

It was a bad day for falls. I stood painfully and pulled out my skirt and petticoat, dusting myself off, the glass falling and tinkling onto the floor. Smashed glass was all around me and on me, and I even had to pull a sliver of glass out of me, moaning as I did so, a trickle of blood oozing onto the legs of my knickers. I hurt all over. Where had my angel flown off to when I needed the divine creature now? Poor cherub. How I wished so that he'd caught me. Probably crying somewhere in a tree because I'd disobeyed. My thoughts were cut off by pain. I hoped my insides were all right. I felt strange, but didn't think I was dying. All the same, I needed assurance. I'd ask Mamma. She always had answers to my questions. I unwadded a handkerchief I had in my apron pocket and folded it across the inside of my ripped knickers.

My knees were scraped, but I offered this up to Jesus who died on the cross, suffering so much for me and for reparation of man's sins. Although I wasn't quite sure what *reparation* meant, Don Ruggero said it often enough, so I thought I should include it.

Blood on my hands. I wished I had been sewing so I could wipe my hands on a piece of cloth. I must have cut them before protecting them with my skirt when I pushed myself off the ground. I was about to clean my palms on my skirt, but thought better of it and wiped them on my knickers. Funny, I didn't hear them rip when I fell. How could I, in the soaring waves of broken glass and the sea of splintering wood?

I had never disobeyed Mamma before. Now I had sinned, broken God's commandment and at least five of Papà's bottles. I began to cry from shame and fear. I brushed the tears away when I reached the house, but something kept me from telling Mamma. Why? I stood there for a moment in shock before she sent me into the yard to pick enough tomatoes to make *picchi-pacchi,* her name for tomato sauce. I usually scampered about, but I hurt too much to run around and wondered how I could tell her about the horse accident and my fall in the shed. My body was cramping and my insides throbbed uncomfortably. I slowed to a turtle's pace because I was still bleeding. Hiking up my long skirt to keep it from dragging in the dirt, I washed my scraped knees and cut legs at the fountain near the vegetable garden. Then I collected a basket of plum tomatoes.

In the kitchen I started to say with urgency in my voice, "Mamma, I've something to tell you—"

"Not now, Angelica," she said, rushing about, cutting me off with her don't-bother-me-now tone. "Watch your little sisters. Prepare the *picchi-pacchi*. Heaven knows I'll have enough to do when I get back from Zia Concetta's."

"Must you go?" I hoped Mamma wouldn't chat a lot with my uncle Nino's wife.

"Zu Nino went clamming in Acireale. He promised me some."

As she spoke, I felt a throbbing dullness where I'd never felt anything like this before. A twinging. Pain, yet not quite pain. I decided it could wait until she returned, knowing I had to confess. I was ashamed. How could I tell her that I'd been in Papà's wine shed when I was supposed to have been mucking out the stalls? I was terrified to explain what had happened—all those broken bottles—and glad that I didn't get a chance to tell her before she left. I heard Mamma's voice instructing me to mind my sisters.

Not long after Mamma left for my uncle Nino's, I remembered something that only last week Papà had told me about his brother. Nino used to be a great fisherman in the *mattanza*—the killing when the blue fin tuna ran. The thrashing fish were trapped in a vast water chamber of heavy nets, where they were harpooned and truncheoned to death in a chanted ritual dating back to Santa Rosalia in the eleventh century. I thought of Zu Nino, so skinny yet strong, clubbing a tuna ten times his size, of my father telling me that the massacre bloodies the sea for kilometers. A red sea of dead fish. Recalling the tuna killing, I quaked inside.

Still shivering, I watched Mamma take off her apron, hook a sennit of palms basket on her arm, and set off down toward the dirt road that led to my uncle's farm. She glanced back to see me in the doorway. Mamma set down the basket and semaphored her arms. Waving back with one hand, I closed the door with the other.

Which should I do first? Clean up the mess in the shed or make the sauce? When would I clean the stable? Or groom my donkey? I couldn't even ask my little sister Rina, who was napping with baby Nunziata. I dashed to the shed, nauseated by the run. With a twig broom, I swept up the shards of broken bottles.

As soon as I got back, I changed my messy undergarments. I sewed the ripped ones where they'd been torn, and washed and hung them to dry along with the handkerchief. Dark shadows started to appear in the yard, and with the absence of light I felt two disappointments creep into my heart—one for me because I couldn't clean the stable till tomorrow and one for Mamma because I hadn't.

⚜

I KEPT FEELING SICK, AND Mamma came back shortly after I retched. She entered the kitchen and put the dripping basket of clams that she'd gotten from Zia Concetta in the sink. She sent Rina into the yard to pick basil and parsley near the rosemary hedges and leaned over the crib, picking up baby Nunziata, who had begun to cry.

Seated comfortably, Mamma unbuttoned her blouse and suckled the child. I watched her switch breasts and thought of the *Maternità*, a painting of the Madonna and Christ child in one of the side altars of our church. Mamma was more beautiful than the painting of Mary.

The baby dozed off. Mamma looked content. Rina came in from the yard, and Mamma told us that she herself was an excellent clammer and next summer she would teach us how to dig with our feet in the muddy shoals and pull up *vongole veraci*. She even told us on some beaches it was possible just to move the sand where the waves break and tiny purple and green and gold *tellini*, thumbnail-size clams, would come to the surface.

"Your father calls them 'fool's food' because they are so small. You need to eat a basket worth to get full," she said.

I went to pass water in a chamber pot that Mamma kept in the back of the pantry for emergencies. I noticed there was still blood. When I returned, I wanted to tell Mamma I'd messed myself, but how to begin? Mamma looked at me as if I were someone else. I felt embarrassed when she asked what was wrong.

"Angelica, you're so pale."

"I've soiled myself . . ."

She didn't seem overly concerned and said, "Angelica, speak up, you're whispering."

"I've sullied my bloomers, but not in back. In front. It's blood, but honest, Mamma—"

She slapped me across the face. Maybe I said it wrong. I didn't mean to frighten her.

"Mamma, you've never slapped me before. I'm sorry."

"Oh, my love." Her hand flew to her mouth. "It's an old custom that means you're a young lady now. Don't be afraid."

"I'm not. I just wanted to hear my innards wouldn't fall out."

"They won't. The slap's a tradition, not because you were bad. You didn't do anything wrong." She hugged me to her.

"Then why?"

She released me. "To bring back color to your cheek because of losing blood."

Mamma brushed hair out of my eyes. "This is natural. It's just that you're only eight . . . It usually happens later."

"What does?"

The baby woke and Mamma said, "Rina, sit here." Mamma put the infant into her arms. "Now rock gently, but stay put. I'm taking Angelica to her room."

"Is she naughty, Mamma?" Rina asked.

"Never—she's an angel."

Mamma showed me how to attach cut diaper cloths for the bleeding. She pinned them to my bloomers. She was so patient with me, not at all like when she washed and combed my long chestnut hair, which sometimes snarled; if ever I'd start to cry, Mamma in her haste yanked my tresses free. But now she looked like the Madonna in the painting above her bed. Calmly she cautioned me to wash the strips immediately with brown soap and hang them on the far side of the pigpen away from the rest of the wash where no one could see.

"Where are your other bloomers? The ones you wore today?"

I told her I'd washed them, and she caressed my cheek saying, "You'll blossom into a fine woman." She told me to lie down.

"But who'll help you set and clear away?"

"Tonight, little one, you're excused. Rest before supper."

She sat next to me and explained that when the time came, the bleeding was necessary to make a cushion for the baby, like the one Zia Concetta was carrying inside her.

I imagined a baby pillowed on blood, squinted my eyes tight shut, and hoped with all my heart that the baby could swim like my brother, Peppe, who had taught me over the summer.

Mamma said the bleeding would come every month now, and questions in my brain darted left and right. Forever? Did the same thing happen to boys? Would it interfere with play? Somehow I knew things would be different. I had the feeling this was going to crimp my climbing and jumping for sure.

"Why am I bleeding? I won't be old enough for babies for a long time."

"Your body wants to be prepared."

My head felt like it was trying to swim somewhere. I needed to ask more, tell more, but I couldn't.

"I wish you'd sing me a *canzone* now." I seemed not quite myself.

She began to hum, and I said, "Maybe the bleeding won't come every month." But what I didn't say was that I thought the bottle might have caused the bleeding.

Now pain was all I could think about.

"Oh, this hurts. This is my punishment for drinking wine," I said.

Mamma was talking, but I could barely hear her because my head was floating around the ceiling. She seemed to be asking me about the wine. The last thing I remembered was her telling me that the walk to my aunt's farm had been hot and dusty and dark clouds had appeared without rain. My eyes felt hooded. As I looked toward the window where the dusk light poured in and as Mamma closed the shutters, she said something like, "Penumbra. Twilight. Time of dreamy dreams."

CHAPTER II

Rosalia

SHATTERED TABLEAU

ABOUT AN HOUR AFTER SHE had put Angelica to bed, Rosalia felt chilled. The day had been sunny and hot, but now the October evening cooled the house. She shut windows and dead bolted doors against the coming night's fog and frost. She hummed a lullaby as she went about her tasks. Her voice broke into song and her six-year-old, Rina, standing by her side, giggled. Rosalia understood the laughter was because her hard, stretched *Parlemitano* accent differed from the softer *Messinese* the child heard everyone else speaking. Rosalia had lived all of her married life in Villaggio Pace, a suburb of Messina, but accents are hard to lose, and somehow stigmas are attached to them. That was why she insisted they speak Italian.

Rina sat next to her mother, who was thinking that all too soon this child would also be having her menses. Her next thought was that she hoped she'd allayed Angelica's preoccupation concerning it, intending to talk to her again after she had rested. Rosalia got up, and as she washed the clams in cool water, she remembered her own first period and her mother's slap—and the shock of both—when she was thirteen and had been walking in the market with her mother, her embarrassment washing off her legs at the running fountain where even dogs relieved their thirst.

Rosalia had grown up in the butcher's section of Capo Market in faraway Palermo. Her mother had thanked God that day that they lived nearby and whisked Rosalia home immediately after the birth her mother had been assisting. One thought triggered another and Rosalia pictured a huge, headless swordfish, sprawled on a bed of seaweed, ready to be cut and sold. As a girl, she loved to go to Piazza Croci where the street vendors sold grilled intestines; small eggplants called "quails" because on both sides they are cut with slits that, when fried, resembled tiny quails, tasting slightly of anise; fried artichokes; and delicious beef spleen served on a bun and sometimes offered with a slice of fresh ricotta. And who could forget the taste of *sarde a beccafico*, sardines rolled up and stuffed with raisins and *pinoli.*

The last time she had been at that market was with her husband, Nicola. He had cried to the street vendor with a handlebar mustache, "Signor Baffone, *sempre scarsu d'ogghiu.*" As always, the food lacked oil.

ROSALIA PUT THE CLAMS INTO a terracotta pot smeared with virgin olive oil, and placed it on the stove so the clams would peep open. To finish the cooking, she added four smashed garlic cloves still in their sheaths and some garden herbs Rina had gathered. She covered and removed the pot, placing it on the windowsill to cool. She listened to Rina imitate the soft cooing noises of the baby. In order to change the baby's diaper, Rosalia positioned the infant on the square, thick chestnut table centered in the middle of the room. It concealed three leaves that, when set in place, seated as many as eighteen—all the members of Nicola's and her family.

Ironing was laid to one side with a piece of paper on top of it— her forgotten list—articles scratched in lead pencil she had asked her husband to bring back from Messina.

Rosalia bent over the baby while Rina, undaunted by her long dress, climbed out of her sitting position and kneeled upon the chair with webbed backing to get a better view.

No light streamed in from the window. This warned Rosalia that the evening chores had not been finished. Little time remained for night to settle. Before she could think more on it, a wild scream in another part of the house cleaved the air. Frozen, Rosalia stood as if nailed to the spot. Nothing moved. She thought of her husband gone away to the city, traveling with their son, Peppe, by horse and cart, bringing demijohns of oil and wine to hawk in Messina. The draw of kilometers leading Nicola cityward was strenuous, the roads rocky; some treacherous stretches, deep ravines, ravished by nature and time. Time. *How long before he gets back?*

Then in a whirl of motion, she helped Rina down from the chair and picked up baby Nunziata, wrapping her in the soft handmade blanket she was lying on. Rosalia grabbed the hand of the older child and ran frantically out of the kitchen, stumbling when she caught her toe on one of the uneven tiles. She bolted through the hall yelling, "My angel Angelica!"

Rosalia flew up the narrow stairwell with Rina in tow and lunged against the heavy wooden door left ajar. She found Angelica on the lamb's wool mattress sullied with blood.

Salve, Regina, Mater misericordiae, vita, dulcédo, et spes nostra, salve, she prayed in Latin. Hail, holy queen, Mother of mercy, our life, our sweetness and our hope.

A dog barked, stunning her into action. Her eyes, riveted to the bed, began to seek a safe place to put the babe.

Alone. *What in God's name shall I do?* Laying Nunziata on the floor far from the bed, she cautioned Rina to watch the baby.

Rosalia grabbed Angelica's legs, held them high in the air as she rolled, and scrunched the mattress under the child. The girl was pale and crying softly. "I am bad, Mamma, I did wrong."

"You did nothing. Hush now. Don't speak." Rosalia ran to the washstand, poured water from the pitcher into the basin, and soaked a linen towel. She washed the girl's legs and wadded up the wet towel, swaddling her with it, thinking, *So much blood for the first time. Something's not right.* "I'm going downstairs."

"Mamma, I'm cold." Angelica was shaking.

"Here," she said as she pulled the coverlet over her and rushed out of the room. *Ora pro nobis, sancta Dei Génitrix.* Pray for us O, holy Mother of God.

She looked over her shoulder and said, "Rina, attend your baby sister." And to Angelica: "Rest. I'll be right back."

Rosalia hurried to the kitchen where the fresh ironing lay, took several of the baby's diapers in hand, and pulled them apart. She looked for her kitchen scissors, but they were not in their usual place hanging on the wall by the dry sink. She rummaged around in the silverware drawer and then looked in her sewing basket. She took the tiny scissors and, feeling time escaping her, cut a little of the material and ripped long, thin strips. Rosalia rolled them tightly, counting seven. These she placed in a small basket with a handle used for bread.

She went back upstairs. Angelica opened her frightened eyes. Rina was humming her mother's song to the baby. Rosalia whirled about, *un vortice*, a vortex in a cyclone. She took hold of Angelica's pillow from behind her head, pitched it to the floor, and straightened out the mattress.

"Rina, put your head down and close your eyes and think beautiful things." She moved closer to the bed. "And, Rina, if you're very still, I'll let you hold the baby again after supper. Angelica, close your eyes." As she spoke she was already ministering to Angelica, stripping her of the swaddling and rewashing her. She glanced furtively to assure herself that Rina couldn't see. Rosalia sat on the bed. Angelica's bleeding had not diminished. If anything, it had increased. "More," she said aloud. *How can this be?* Rosalia feared doing what she knew she must.

"Forgive me," she prayed of God, begged of her daughter whom she knew didn't hear her. A doctor? *A priest. I must get a priest. But how?* "God help me!" she murmured, realizing the girl seemed weak from loss of blood. She thought of sending Rina into the dark night to get her sister-in-law Concetta. Impossible. Slowly she began to insert one of the wadded-up rolls into Angelica's vagina. Rosalia's hands shook; she could barely steady them. As soon as she felt the cloth was well up into the cervix, she tugged at a loose end and tied it to the next roll, repeating the process. Rosalia thought, *My poor baby, this isn't right. What was she telling me when I left for Concetta's?*

"Rina, do you know if Angelica hurt herself?"

"When, Mamma?"

"In the barn? Rina, did she fall? On the rake perhaps?"

Rina started to cry.

"Good God, what? Tell me!"

"She took the black horse for a ride. He jumped the fence, but she wasn't ready and he threw her. It was an accident, Mamma. She told me."

"*Cristo mio.*" Rosalia took a sheet and bound Angelica, wrapping her as if she were a mummy. Then she covered her, got up, and washed her hands. She put her finger over her mouth just as Rina looked up and said, "What's wrong, Mamma?"

Rosalia squatted. "Rina, what were Angelica's exact words?"

Rina told her mother how Angelica had sipped wine and played in the wine shed, fell, and cut herself. When Rina finished, she took a breath and added, "But she was good, Mamma. When you went for clams, she swept it up so you wouldn't be angry. I minded Nunziata. She said she'd clean out the stable tomorrow."

"Good girl. Hush now. Stay quiet."

Rosalia stood and pinched her lips between thumb and pointer finger. She made a quick decision. Carefully, she removed the packing she had so gingerly attended not minutes before. It appeared to her that the flow had increased, or was it only because she'd removed the bandage?

Wiping tears from her eyes with her shirtsleeve, she splayed Angelica's legs and examined her for cut glass. Her stomach lurched and she thought she'd be sick. Finding no shards, she rewashed her bloody hands and repacked her child. When she finished, she said to Rina, "I'll be right back." Again she washed her hands, then raced down the stairwell into the kitchen where she opened her work drawer and took out a hammer along with a sharp knife. Sliding the bolt across the door, she ran with a lantern into the garden. Past the vegetable patch she set the lantern down, unlooped a hasp, and entered the pig's pen. Closing the gate, she put the hammer and knife deep inside her apron pocket.

Her eyes darted furiously until she located the sow she wanted. She sidestepped a farrow. With unbridled strength, she dragged the squealing pig by the ears into the light of the full moon. She cinched it around the neck with her left arm, wet her thumb, and pressed it hard between the pig's eyes. Removing her thumb, she took careful aim. With one sharp blow, she bludgeoned the pig with the hammer, rendering it dazed. Rosalia yanked it upward by the snout, exposing its throat. She slaughtered the pig, slitting its jugular with the kitchen knife. Blood spurted onto her apron, mingling with Angelica's. Rosalia dropped the pig's head to the ground. Then she disemboweled it, slicing open its belly. She reached in and took out a completely formed piglet embryo, its heart barely palpitating. After suffocating it with the warm, moist placenta, she cut the umbilical cord and left the dead sow where it lay. Placing the tiny corpse, cushioned by the placenta, into her apron, she retraced her steps to the kitchen. There she put the placenta into a ceramic bowl, thinking she'd have to bury it later. At the sink, she washed the embryo, slit its throat, and poured the blood into a cup. She left the lifeless corpse in the sink and, with dripping hands, carried the cup to the wood-burning stove where she melted cocoa and sugar in a small pot, and added the piglet's blood. She stirred the mixture, then poured it into the cup and stirred it again. Rosalia caught a glimpse of herself in the upper glass portion of a door, and was horrified to see she was covered with blood. She ripped off her apron, drying her hands with it, and grasped the middle of the laundry pile, taking out a freshly ironed one, upsetting the rest of the clothes. They tumbled to the floor. In her haste, she left them, tied the clean apron around her, picked up the cup, and carried it upstairs to where her Angelica lay bathed in sweat.

Rosalia sat next to Angelica and cradled her head. Rosalia's bosom ached with the fullness of milk while she spooned liquid from the cup into her daughter's mouth. The girl sputtered, but after a while she sipped from the spoon. When she opened her eyes, her mother said, "You must swallow all of this. You have lost much blood and this will help you replenish it."

Angelica sighed. "I'm tired, Mamma."

"Feeling better?"

Rosalia saw that color had returned to her daughter's cheeks and kissed her forehead, more a check of her temperature than a sign of affection.

"Here," Rosalia said, "finish this," holding the cup to Angelica's lips, pleased the girl sipped on her own.

"What is this, Mamma?"

"*Sanguinaccio.*"

"Why is it called blood pudding? It tastes like chocolate."

CHAPTER III

Rosalia

A BLESSING

ROSALIA DOZED FITFULLY IN A chair beside Angelica's bed. Toward morning after her chores, and while Angelica slept, Rosalia started to change the packing and saw that the bleeding had ceased. Rosalia spoke soothingly, explaining that perhaps the monthly bleeding had not started and this flow of blood was caused by the horse-jumping accident.

Angelica asked, "Are you angry, Mamma?"

Rosalia reassured her daughter, adjusting and primping pillows. When Angelica drifted back to sleep, Rosalia paced the floor. She attended to the infant and dressed Rina, enlisting her help in some of Angelica's usual duties.

That morning Concetta was expected to stop by to see if there were any essentials that Rosalia needed from the local market.

Even before Concetta knocked on the kitchen door, Rosalia opened it. Rosalia's nervousness caused Concetta to wring her hands and cry with her sister-in-law before she'd even asked what was the matter. Rosalia sat down, calmed herself. Concetta joined her at the table. The smell of baking bread made Concetta look toward the oven.

"It's almost done," Rosalia said, and then explained what had happened the night before and how much she'd wished for the doctor and Don Ruggero. When she was less agitated, Rosalia stood to open the window and said, "This is serious, Concetta. Angelica was so frightened. I thought she'd begun her cycle. Now I'll have to explain—no, she probably knows—that she may not begin and the bleeding was due to the trauma." Rosalia checked on the bread and then sat down again.

Concetta pulled a chair closer to Rosalia. "You've always been able to explain things to her. Don't let this upset you."

"It's not just that. Oh, Concetta, don't you understand? She must have disturbed the maidenhead, and if not, I did. There will be repercussions."

"Are you sure?"

"I'm certain," Rosalia said and, knowing she was short with her dear Concetta, apologized.

"I'll get Don Ruggero. You'll explain everything to him so that if and when a situation arises in the future, you'll have a priest's word," Concetta said, fanning her face with a lace-trimmed fan.

"Your face is flushed. Shall I open the door?"

Concetta shook her head.

"When she marries, you think her spouse will accept this priest's word? He's my brother."

"I think you're inventing problems before they arise, and that serves no purpose. You've said that to me a hundred times since I told you I was expecting again."

Rosalia nodded slowly. "How can you go for him?" Rosalia indicated Concetta's stomach. "Absolutely not. You're only a few months and already you're starting to show." She placed an open hand on Concetta's breasts. Rosalia took care of everyone awaiting a baby in the neighborhood. "You're already swollen with milk, thank God. But you're not bouncing around on a cart to town. Bad enough you came here. God forbid an accident. You stay put. I'll go."

"Perhaps it's better if we both stay. What if you're needed for a birth? Two of your neighbors are close to delivering, aren't they?" Concetta asked and, not waiting for an answer, continued, "I'll send Nino when he comes in, and when he's finished all his errands, he'll pick me up. I can help you prepare something for dinner."

"You're right. I hadn't thought about it."

LATER, DON RUGGERO ENTERED THE house with an acolyte ringing a bell and holding a candle. The priest took off his beret and kissed his sister, Rosalia, who waved the altar boy away. She told Ruggero what had happened to Angelica, then whispered, "I want to confess." Since there was no sin involved, he refused, but said he would bless the child. As they climbed the stairs, Ruggero leafed through a book. The altar boy carried an intricate silver thurible. Before they entered Angelica's room, Rosalia asked, "Which blessing will you use?"

"I've looked in my *Collectio Rituum* for a special prayer and found blessings for first building stones, a house, a school, any kind of food, and only here"—he pointed to his black leather-bound book—"on page 541, did I find, sandwiched in between a blessing for a vehicle and one for a sacred statue or painting, this blessing for all things . . . to give her strength to heal."

The priest nodded to Concetta, asked if he could begin, and said, "All kneel."

He prayed in Latin. "Our help is in the name of the Lord."

The acolyte responded, "Who made heaven and earth."

"The Lord be with you."

"And with your spirit."

"Let us pray. O God, by whose word all things are made holy, pour down Your blessing on this child, Angelica, whom You created. Grant that whomsoever, giving thanks to You, uses Your name in accordance with Your law and Your will may, by calling upon Your holy name, receive through Your aid health of body and protection of soul. Through Christ our Lord." He moved closer to Angelica's bed.

"Amen." Don Ruggero placed his hands on Angelica's head. He held a crucifix reliquary with which he made the sign of the cross over her. He faced Concetta and was about to hallow her next, when Angelica said, "Mamma, I heard an owl."

Rosalia's hand flew to her mouth. "Oh, my Lord, forbid it."

Concetta said, "Bad luck to come."

Rosalia knew it meant far worse. "Hush, Angelica," Rosalia said in a muffled voice.

The priest shook his head. Rosalia read the annoyance spreading across his face at her fear of the superstition. She ignored the look. He finished his blessing over Concetta, who Rosalia thought looked puzzled, probably because neither of them had heard the owl. Then he sprinkled holy water on Angelica and her bedclothes, continuing to scatter sacred water all the way down the stairs. The altar boy followed. The boy extinguished the candle, juggling it with the thurible containing burning incense. From time to time, he tapped the censer with its attached chain, emitting an exotic aroma. Mid-stairs, he switched the candle to the bell-occupied hand, almost overturning everything. Incense filled the house like a church. Ruggero sent the boy ahead. At the door, exchanging farewells, Rosalia and Ruggero decided it was unnecessary to get Dr. Amorosi now that Angelica's bleeding had stopped and she was on the mend.

Ruggero hailed Nicola near the gate as Rosalia ran to greet him. Ruggero departed and the couple sat on a roughhewn bench under the kitchen window. Rosalia felt Nicola study her face, draw its contours. She wondered if he noticed crow's feet at the corners of her eyes. Rivulets of tears began to wash her cheeks.

Peppe kissed his mother. Nicola sent him for water.

"What is it?" Nicola put his arm around his wife.

"A-Angelica . . ." she stuttered.

"Is she all right? What happened?"

"It turns my stomach to think about it."

"For the love of God, tell me."

And so she did, until Peppe returned with the glass, turned milky with a splash of anise, and handed it to his father. "What's wrong with Angelica?"

"At times, your sister just plays too rough and . . . Go see her, dear. Bring her the ricotta I prepared. Spread it on bread, dust it with sugar. Go now."

Rosalia continued saying to Nicola how Concetta came, and how Nino had summoned Don Ruggero. "I wanted to confess, but Ruggero said there was no need for absolution, blessed Angelica, and anointed Concetta. Maybe I should have insisted on telling him only in the seal of Confession."

CHAPTER IV

Angelica

GRANDFATHER'S VISIT

ONE MORNING A FEW MONTHS after my accident, I was in the kitchen washing tomatoes and throwing boiling hot water over them in the sink so the skins would loosen and I could peel them. Then I fried garlic and hot pepper and added the chopped tomatoes, minus as many seeds as possible. While they simmered, my little sister Rina came bounding into the kitchen—she always moved so fast, my father sometimes called her a tornado. The red tomatoes must have prompted a recollection because I started to tell Rina what had happened to me months ago, but she cut me short with an exasperated, "You already told me. I'll be more careful." I made her promise not to run all the time, not to take so many chances, and definitely not to climb the ledges—now repaired—in the wine shed. I took the sauce off the stove and covered it and told her not to touch it.

Our house had a huge kitchen with a marble-topped *piattaia*, which held our plates and stood next to the door. It had two drawers. The one on the right held Mamma's wooden clothespins. I yanked the drawer too hard and out spilled a cascade of wooden pegs. I gave two to Rina to dress as dolls. On top of the wooden *ammadia* that Papà had made, which was used to store flour and roll out pasta, Mamma had left *biscotti*. I stood near the large furnace oven built into the rock wall; the space in front of it radiated warmth, yet the rest of the floor was cold. The uneven rectangular brick tiles formed a pattern, each born from the middle of the other. I gave one cookie to Rina and ate two myself, feeling fine after eating the dry, sweet cookies. But soon after, the warmth of the kitchen made me sick to my stomach and I stepped outside for some fresh air.

Rina handed me a glass of water. I drank some and felt more like myself. After returning the glass to the kitchen, Rina dashed outside to play just as Mamma came in to prepare *sfincione*, a thick, spongy pizza topped with the tomato sauce I'd cooked, onions, salted sardines, and *caciocavallo* cheese. She placed all the ingredients into a large rectangular pan and put it in the oven to bake. It was then she told me I'd be going to stay with Zia Concetta for a while to help with housework and chores.

"But who'll help you, Mamma?"

"I'll manage. Besides, your papà says you should go, and he's right."

Before long the pizza-like bread perfumed the warm air, a sense of well-being along with it. After dinner, Mamma packed me a bag since I was going to stay with Zia Concetta until her baby came. I was thinking of the excitement of holding an infant as I lugged an overstuffed bag down the staircase. I stopped on the landing and looked out the window. In the sky a formation of gray clouds shaped a funeral carriage, white horses with white plumes pulling it. A sudden chill made me shiver. In that instant, I knew my aunt had lost the baby. I dropped the bag and went screaming down to the kitchen, begging Mamma to hurry over to Zia Concetta's. I told Mamma what I saw in the sky and, bless her, though at first she doubted me, she believed me. I guess she saw the fear in my face.

<hr />

WHEN IT WAS OVER, I watched Mamma console my aunt, saying in no time at all she'd be awaiting another one, after all, isn't that the way of married life? I kept reliving my accident in my mind, some of Mamma's words about babies and where they came from hopping about my head. I forced most of these to the rear, like poor relatives in the last pew at a church wedding.

I stayed for two months helping my aunt during her convalescence. There were many things I thought about while I attended her, but I tried not to dwell on anything in particular because my aunt was too unwell to discuss the things that filled my mind. Often when I said my prayers my brain would lose concentration and head in another direction, completely opposite of where I wanted it to go. Women endured such awful things. First they had to suffer all that monthly bleeding, way in advance of when they needed it. Then they got married and tried to have babies who were never born or babies who died during the birth.

I left my aunt's house when my father's father came to visit Zu Nino. It was the late summer when my grandpa vacationed with us. My nonno was ninety-three years old and still shaved. One morning he propped a small mirror in the crook of a fig tree for the best light. I brought him a pitcher of warm water and a big bowl. He left some lathered soap on his face that I wiped away with a long, fringed linen cloth. While I waited for him to finish rinsing his face, I braided and unbraided the towel fringe. I couldn't understand why Papà had such an old father, or why he let him shave himself. Nonno's hands shook, and I thought for sure he'd slit his throat like a lamb. Nonno Giuliano slicked back his long hair, grinning a toothless smile at me. That's what the Bible Methuselah looked like for sure.

ON A PICNIC THREE WEEKS later, my nonno and I got tar on our feet at the beach. We sat on a lava boulder cleaning it off with olive oil. He said that fuel oil made the tar and came from ships; the ships somehow brought his mind to docking up someplace in England where there was a coal mining town. The people there didn't use olive oil, but lard and butter.

PEPPE GOT TO SLEEP WITH Nonno and told me he snored like the trumpet of a processional band. So every night my brother went to bed early, hoping to fall asleep before our grandfather. I couldn't believe I got to stay up later than Peppe. After days of kitchen cleaning I knew— Peppe had outsmarted me. Again.

THE NEXT TO THE LAST day of my nonno's two-month visit, Peppe came into the kitchen and yanked my long wavy hair.

"Ouch. Why are you so mean to me?"

"Just want your attention," he said. "I slept on the rug."

I smoothed my hair. "In front of the fireplace? Why?"

"Grandpa's old legs are like octopus tentacles."

I conjured up an image of Nonno's slithering legs.

"He kicked me out of bed and clear across the room."

I considered this. Nonno's skinny legs were fast, but hadn't the strength for that. I sighed, "Pinocchio nose."

His hand flew to his face to see if it were true and he giggled. "Even," he said, sticking out his hand to shake.

"Meet you in the *orto* in ten minutes," I said and began to stack dishes.

Mamma was making Nonno Giuliano's favorite meal of pasta with sardines. When she told him what the menu would be for lunch, he thanked her and kissed the top of her head. That was the only kiss I'd ever seen him bestow on Mamma. He had to bend to reach her head. Nonno seemed as tall as the lintel of the kitchen door. I held my breath as he walked outside, but he missed it by several centimeters.

I set the table for lunch under the sprawling apricot tree in the grape arbor. Mamma gave permission to Peppe and me to watch Papà kill a rabbit and dress and hang it for tomorrow.

In the orchard, Papà asked if I wanted to participate rather than just watch the slaying. He offered me the knife.

I recoiled. "I couldn't cut its throat." A cloud cast a shadow as I wondered if I would ever be able to defend myself from danger if my life were threatened and had to use a knife to stab a living creature.

Peppe said, "I'll do it," and he did.

Wincing, I asked for the paw. Papà hacked it off and set it to dry in the blistering heat of August's sun. Flies buzzed. "It's a cruel gesture," Papà said, and added, "even a little barbaric on both our parts, yours for asking and mine for rendering, but that's part of life sometimes." I felt a twinge of sadness like a lurch in the pit of my stomach, but I knew my father wasn't being mean. As for me, I only wanted a remembrance of my pet while his soul flew through the heavens, circling the planet.

"When the paw's thoroughly cured, I'll make you a key chain," Papà said. I thought that was strange as I owned no keys, kept no locks. But I didn't say anything, for fear he'd change his mind and give it to Peppe.

After the rabbit killing, Nonno said to me, "Don't worry, rabbits are prolific—they make big families. There'll be many more before long." He chucked my chin, just like he did Peppe's. "When you grow up, Angel, be sure to have many children. There's nothing more precious than family."

Peppe went to pour wine into demijohns with Papà. I steered clear of the shed, volunteering to help Mamma in the kitchen. I put on an apron and stood at the sink, cleaning guts out of sardines Uncle Nino brought over for the pasta *con le sarde*. I tried to make sense of what exactly he'd told me about sardines swimming in schools and rabbits and families. Maybe it all had something to do with same groups living together. Fish. Animals. People.

The making of this traditional Sicilian platter was complicated. Even though the combination sounded strange, it all blended together in what my mother called a perfect marriage. What she meant was it all went together well—the way a man and a woman should.

Peppe came inside and pulled the strings of my apron.

"Just look," I said, pushing my blood-and-guts fingers almost into his face. "How am I supposed to retie it?"

"Enough," Mamma said.

I could have sworn Peppe had grown another head high. "You may have gained in height, but your brains don't match," I said, thinking how much he favored Grandpa and guessed how handsome Nonno must have been at that age. And just as all my thoughts about Peppe and Nonno came together, my brother did the oddest thing—he kissed the top of my head and scuttled out the door. The way Nonno kissed Mamma. I smiled at that, realizing there are all sorts of relationships in a family.

Mamma bowed the apron strings in back of me while I wondered about that kiss.

"Are all boys wild yet sweet when you least expect it?" I asked Mamma, who gave me a gentle shove.

"Here," she said, setting an onion on a cutting board. "Chop this fine." Close to the onion she placed a handful of tiny dried raisins, not really all that sweet. Next to the board, Mamma stacked a bunch of feathery tops from wild fennel. This anise-tasting herb grew on a ridge under umbrella pine trees at our property's border. I'd picked these, always leaving the root, with Nonno early that morning. They'd been wet with dew.

"Mamma, this morning I found a wild plant that looks like parsley, but wasn't sure if it's good to eat or not." I took a small bunch of pinnate leaves with small white and greenish flowers from my apron pocket and showed them to her.

"Angelica," she said.

"What?"

"Angelica—that's the name of this herb."

"You mean it's named after me?"

"Not quite. I think it was originally Greek." Mamma touched a stray strand of my hair and tucked it behind my ear.

"What's it used for?" I asked as I watched her wash her hands at the pump.

"I've tasted wine and liqueur made from it, and these—" She stopped herself, dried her hands on a tea towel, and on tiptoe reached overhead to a high cupboard shelf that I would have needed a chair to reach. She rummaged around and pulled down a canister, popped the top, and offered me a taste of the candied leaves that I recognized as garnish for desserts. At the bottom of the tin were seeds I'd seen her add to pastries.

I was thrilled I had such a delightful herbsake. Mamma said it showed in my smile.

"Where are the anchovies? And the pine nuts I collected?" I asked, pleased I knew the names of some other ingredients for the sauce.

"*Brava*, you remembered. I didn't hull them. You can," she said. These few words were a big compliment from my mother, who always stinted on praise, lest we be spoiled.

I finished cutting, dicing, and chopping. Next I sat down to husk those tiny *pinoli* that turn the pods of your fingers black like soot. With gentleness in mind, I tapped them with a hammer and culled the sweet meat inside. When I had a handful, I asked Mamma if it was enough. "*Va bene?*"

She looked over my shoulder and said, "Husk another handful and I'll make ricotta pie." I busied myself, a squirrel storing and laying away for winter.

Seated at the table, my father, who always said grace, ceded his place to his father, who said a prayer in a dialect that Papà defined "dense as spartina along salt marshes and with as many panicled spikelets." It was hard not to laugh, but then Mamma said that Papà sure could sling a heap of words together and make them sound like poetry. I thought to myself, *Maybe that's why she married him.* I knew then I wanted to marry a man as strong, handsome, and smart as my father.

Mamma told Nonno I had helped prepare the lunch. He smiled, bent over, and with both hands, pinched my cheeks so hard I thought he'd kept chunks between his fingers. Mamma opened her eyes, round as saucers. I knew not to yelp. Papà caught Mamma's look, whispering that pinching was a sign of affection.

I whispered back, "I wish he'd be affectionate at Peppe."

"Affectionate with," Papà corrected.

CHAPTER V

Angelica

THE CLIFF STRUGGLE

IN THE FALL OF MY twelfth year, I tried to convince my father to take me to the Messina market. I knew he loved company when he traveled, so I had hinted left, right, and in between for weeks that he should take me instead of Peppe. "Just this once," I pleaded when I kissed him good night before I went upstairs. I think I would've promised anything. Papà almost weakened but was determined to take Peppe.

"Have I ever gone back on my word?" Papà asked at the foot of the stairs, me at the top.

I shook my head. And he gave his word to me, "Next time."

‹⸻›

I HAD A PREMONITION THAT next time would be now and that somehow it tied in with a fox I'd found trapped in mesh wire by the chicken coop that afternoon. I was afraid to let the animal go, but more afraid to let it suffer and die, so I wrapped my hands tightly with old rags Papà used to clean his hunting rifles. With a stick to wedge open a slot big enough for him to pass through, I pried and jimmied the fence until the animal felt the air of freedom fill his lungs. I saw in his eyes that he was grateful and wouldn't hurt me; he was gone quicker than flash lightning. When he reached a high ridge, he turned to face me, his shape a silhouette in the sunset.

SURE ENOUGH, MY BROTHER CAME down with influenza. Papà postponed the journey till Peppe was better. However, when that time came, Mamma declared my brother was still convalescing and not strong enough to go. My father almost decided to go alone.

"But, Papà, you promised." I thought my heart would burst.

"After this trip," he said.

I felt the fire-dart of an angel piercing me—just as surely as did Saint Teresa—and knew I'd have to bear this small torture and offer it up as sacrifice. But my heart couldn't reconcile itself with my head. I felt tears, hot behind my eyes, brim the rims. I willed them not to cascade down my cheeks just when Mamma suggested that a change would do me good. "After all, Nicola," she continued as she dished out pasta *con le melanzane* at the dining room table, "while I tended Peppe, Angelica has had complete charge of the little ones. She's done the wash and ironing and fed the animals."

"I cooked too," I boasted and, because I shook my head, a truant tear escaped. I blotted it away with my napkin.

Papà smiled and said he was pleased with my behavior.

That night I prayed on my knees in my goffered nightshirt. Mamma came to say good night, and I stood up to hug her and tell her I felt guilty. "I prayed to be forgiven, Mamma, in case Peppe got sick on my account." Then I told Mamma about the fox and implored her to tell me it wasn't my fault. She assured me it was God's design and I had nothing to do with it, yet I found it hard to believe. "But beware of hurt animals, Angelica. Like angry men, they can turn on you."

Mamma got that faraway look. I asked her if she remembered something.

"Oh, nothing."

"What?" I pleaded and got into bed.

She adjusted my covers. "Just that Papà once helped a hunted man. Your father gave him work in the groves, but when Papà tried to help the thief make amends for the wrong he'd done, he turned vicious. He left your papà to finish his own work and the hired man's as well. His name was Ciccio Batalamente."

"What happened to him?" I asked, curious and wanting to hear more.

"He and two others were going to be tried, but they were freed . . .

bought lawyers and judges—with *bustarelle*—" I must have shown recognition of this—payment with fat envelopes—because Mamma gave me a look, signifying she'd said too much. "Never mind." She kissed me. "That was long ago and not the discussion at hand. Now Destiny will have its way. For some reason, you're meant to go with your father."

I fell asleep with the image of the fox on the rise, realizing he had saluted me just as surely as if he'd spoken. I wondered if he'd see me in dreams the way I was seeing him.

THE NEXT DAY AS MY father and I approached the market, I felt the air change into a living thing. The hair on my arms stood up. Not only was the air warmer, it was tinged with spices, some I recognized and others I didn't. We passed a square umbrella, braids of garlic, bundles of tomatoes, strings of peppers, bunches of dried oregano, rosemary, and sage dangling from spines.

Papà brought the cart to the rear of the fish stalls, but I couldn't imagine why. "Papà," I complained, sounding just like Peppe said I did when I got pesky, "it stinks here."

He reined in my donkey Pupa, burdened with the weight of her third foal, and I could tell he intended to leave the cart.

"Why leave it here?" I asked.

"Because no one else does and there's plenty of space and we only have to walk a short distance to the stalls we need."

Without a word spoken between them, I watched Papà ask an old man to keep an eye on our cart by pulling down the bottom lid of his right eye with his index finger.

A FAT LADY WITH ROSY cheeks wearing a checkered apron arranged a table of lace, materials, ribbons, and threads. There were other items like crocheted doilies the lady had made to sell. She sang one of Mamma's favorite melancholy songs: a love story about someone who was left behind waiting for a letter, begging for even just a line. Mamma sang it much better, her accent not so pronounced when she sang.

The woman screeched at me as we walked in front of her table, "Eh, girlie, want to buy a brocade doily for your mother?"

I tugged at Papà's arm to stop and look. Again, I shook him for attention. He bent down so I could whisper in his ear, "Mamma needs ribbon thread for the mattresses. Does this lady sell it?"

He nudged me closer to the lady's pudgy middle. I almost bounced off it. Papà laughed, probably thinking I didn't have the spunk to ask for it myself, but I did.

"Would you happen to have flat thread for mattress making?" I asked, politeness dripping from every word.

"How wide do you need it?"

I had an idea, so I showed her a tiny space of less than half a centimeter between my thumb and pointer finger. "Quite narrow."

"Perfect measurement," she announced loud enough for the entire market to hear, drawing an angled line with her thumb from cheekbone to chin, just the way Mamma does to signify excellent.

She dug into an old cigar box and scattered things about as if she were playing pick-up-sticks, moved on to a hat box where she found what she was looking for, held up the cording, and called to me, "Here's our treasure. How much are you willing to spend for your mammina?"

I almost answered, but then figured she might cheat me. Papà told me at an open-air market, anything can happen.

So I pretended to think and count on my fingers, then said, "How much do you want?"

"Well, I've had it for some time. I'd be willing to let it go for—"

"By the way," I quickly said, "how many meters long is it?"

"Ah! You're a crafty one," she said, and flung the ribbon like a long yo-yo across the table to where I stood. She picked up the end, measuring from the middle of her chest, the length of her extended arm. One meter. Two, I counted in silence, now certain the woman was authentic, because that's how Mamma measures.

"Ten meters," she said.

"Do you have more?" I asked, remembering that Mamma probably needed more than that.

"Let me see." She repeated her search.

"Here they are," she said, ticking off the meters without having been asked. "Almost eleven in this and twelve in this."

"Can you give me all of them but count them only as thirty?"

"What?" she asked in a voice high as the sky.

"Give me a better price because I'm buying so much."

She winked at Papà. "She's her father's daughter for sure!"

Papà put his thumbnail under a coin and flipped it to her. Then he introduced me to the ribbon lady and I curtsied. I couldn't believe my own dear papà had set me to a task when he'd already done business with her before. It was on my tongue to ask, "How'd I do?" But by the size of his grin-showing dimples, I knew.

The chubby lady gave me a gift of a tiny piece of lace for a doll baby; enough for Rina too. It had some stains on it, but when the lady saw me inspecting it, she told me to sew some pearl beads over the spot or cover it with some other material. The lady smoothed my hair, wishing me children with wide doe eyes, as deep and candid as mine. As we clinched the deal, the breeze picked up and the air filled with the smell of plump chestnuts roasting on a brazier two stalls down. A different nut, the biggest I'd ever seen, was cracked open to show a pure white inside.

After Papà and the lady exchanged some polite chatter, we walked in the direction of the chestnut hawker, bellowing about the quality of his wares. I asked Papà about the huge nut.

"Coconut. Your mamma says that the water from the inside of it cleans your kidneys. Want to try some white meat?"

"The inside? What's it taste like?"

"Mmm, like good, you'll see," he said, urging me onward.

ON THE CART RETURNING FROM Messina, I listened to my father hum and I congratulated him. He seemed satisfied with himself, having sold his olives for a good price in the market.

"Not only that, but I think we got most of what we were supposed to get," Papà said.

I knew by his tone that, even though my father had forgotten Mamma's list like always, he was pleased he'd remembered the flowered white-on-white damask cloth she needed to make the mattresses she would sell in Calabria.

"Thank the Lord, we also didn't forget the long needles with curved points—"

"Mamma said they're ten centimeters long—"

"And *fettuccia*—that flat ribbon thread your mamma needs."

Turning toward me, Papà asked me what I thought of my first trip to Messina. I told him I liked the fat lady who sold the notions, but for the rest, well, I was still a little shy, saying it was a bit confusing and I was glad to be returning home.

"Your mother will be happy with this many chicks," Papà said, holding the reins in one hand and making an expansive swing of his arm with the other over the back of the cart. "Even if the coop is full, she'll trade with them. Your mother bargains like a Gypsy."

My attention was elsewhere, though. I jumped in my seat, frightened by the movement of thrushes in the cork trees. The calling out of doves, the dirge of cicadas, made me turn around. A little later down the road, I looked backward a second time. I had a presentiment: danger was near.

Yet when Papà asked, "What's the matter?" I only answered with, "Nothing. Maybe the drone of *cigala.*"

How could I say I felt uneasy for no apparent reason along the dusty road where ancient umbrella pines stretched across the shadowy path as if a handshake were being offered? I felt fear for no cause. But somehow I knew that somewhere close, peril awaited us. Looking at the arbor of trees overhead—joined limbs in prayerful attitude—I was wary, yet excited at the unknown.

It was autumn now, and not a great deal of change could be noted in the tree leaves. Some were gold while others were mottled like the skin of old men. The evergreens and palms, still verdant, gave no indication that a quick frost could destroy them, or that the almond harvest was only weeks away. Something nearby prickled my skin. I rubbed my forearms briskly.

Time keeled in upon itself as we rode most of the way in silence, into the late afternoon. We would soon reach the turn for the trail that led to our peaceful village.

Papà began to reminisce, saying, "Less than twenty years ago King Umberto I passed on this same road."

My father told me that along this same hillside, the king had ridden on the way to Taormina and, a scant thirty years before, when Papà was a boy, Garibaldini red shirts had traveled this very route. He mentioned that shortly thereafter, Garibaldi handed over a unified Italy to Umberto's father, King Vittorio Emmanuele I. "A unified Italy that included our island," he said.

As he drew the boot of Italy on the dusty seat space between us, he ticked off the major cities and told me something to remember about each one. Assisi was the city of Saint Francis, Sienna the city of Saint Catherine, Saint Rita was from Cascia, but best of all was Venezia with Saint Mark's Square, a city made of canals where a Bridge of Sighs dwelled. I thought of the impossibility and wonder of it all. Next he sketched Sardinia. I traced our island.

I sensed danger's nearness. Even my soul's hair tingled. The thrum of blood gushed through my temples. Why hadn't I been aware of danger in the wine shed? Suddenly there were hooves thundering in the road ahead. With it came the realization that only after my accident did my talent of knowing things would happen before they did become acutely enhanced.

With this thought poised midair, the pounding earth spooked the *asino* pulling the cart. I saw the donkey's ears cock and freeze for an instant, listening for danger. I watched my father edge to the side of the path to avoid the horsemen. At first I couldn't tell how many there were. Then I counted. Three of the five men wore black berets and all of them wore *scapolare*—long black cloaks flowing over the haunches of their magnificent stallions. They cantered at a furious pace, almost an advancing gallop. Each man carried a *lupara*. The shotgun was either carried across the pommel or strapped to a rider's back. Only one stowed his in a sheath fastened to his saddle. The riders gave no leeway. I scanned the road ahead. My eyes took in the seemingly moving landscape—trees and brush to the cliff side, a wall of mountain to the other—calculating in that instant the least possible peril. There was no escape, but my father yanked hard on the reins toward the ridge's limit and yelled, "Jump!" before the inevitable crash, shoving me out of the cart. I sailed through the air, arms and legs flailing, bouncing into an alleyway of tall grass, thistle, and nettle. My shoulder slammed against the mountainside.

When I was finally able to stand, I saw that my father was nowhere on the road. Had he fallen down the cliff face? In the distance I spied the runaway cart just in time to see it topple over and crash on the road, crushing the donkey. My wail muffled the donkey's shriek. There was no sign of Papà. I looked out over the bluff and screamed, "Help!"

but no one heard my cry or came to aid me. Where was Papà? My eyes swept the road. I called out to him. No response. My head felt light as bamboo reeds on the roadside, whereas my heart plummeted—a lead weight—somewhere between my sore chest and stomach. I crumbled to the ground as the riders' dust settled, falling down as if I'd been socked in the jaw. I shook my head, staggered to an upright position, wiped blood from the scratches on my face. When my head cleared, I looked around, trying to make sense of two things: the donkey-driven cart had crashed, and my father no longer held reins.

I hobbled over to Pupa, whose breathing was labored, her upper torso pinned. I unhitched her halter and soothed her with talk as best I could. I squatted down with my back to the cart and hoisted it up onto my haunches and, taking baby steps, slowly moved it till it was off her. She breathed a little easier, but with a whistle sound Mamma had told me Nonno had. She called it a death rattle. Pupa's hind legs jerked as if she wanted to get up but couldn't. I felt so unsure of what I should or could do next. I knew she was broken inside. A gloom descended on me, like parts of my inner workings coming undone, unhinged. I nuzzled next to her and explained that I had to find Papà. With an unbroken flask, I wet her lips. Petting her, I told her to be calm and I'd be back. Papà must have been vaulted out of the cart, tumbling down the craggy butte, rolling to the bottom of the crevice. My body wobbled and lurched as I steadied myself and peered over the ravine, teetering on the edge, almost losing my balance.

Then I caught sight of him. He was dead. He had to be. I wondered if he'd hit his head on a log nearby. His body was twisted in a weird way. *My God!* My father's body at the cliff base. Eyes fixed on his contorted position, I felt all hope abandon me.

Instinct made me move. I climbed down. Salty tears stung my cheeks as I heard him moan. He was alive!

Papà came to, and I yelped when I saw his arm dangling from the place where it should have been attached to his shoulder.

He seemed dazed and said, "I don't understand what happened."

I pointed to his arm.

"You must be very brave, my child," he said, slurring his words some-what. "Strong." He breathed deeply as if he couldn't get enough breath to finish, then said, "Wipe your tears and steady yourself. Take hold of my arm. Pull it out as far as you can, then release it so it'll pop back into place. Can you do this for your father?"

"How can I?"

"You must."

I sat opposite but close to my father's left side. I readied myself, took a deep breath, and leaned back into the rocky wall of the cliff. I gripped his right forearm and elbow with my right hand, holding Papà's wrist with my left before yanking it. When pain registered on his face, I started to let go. He screamed in anguish, "Not yet! For the love of God, keep pulling."

Too late. I had already released my grasp.

I scooted my behind over the rough terrain away from the jagged wall to give myself more space. I tried to get a better grip, but my hands were sweating. I wiped my palms on my skirt. I made another attempt and failed a second time.

Papà begged me in garbled speech, "Don't stop, no matter what. Do you hear me?"

He sounded angry. I made a third try. It was only by jamming my laced boot into my father's armpit, pushing on the same side I was tugging, and leaning as far back as possible while pulling with all my strength that I managed some leverage. As I began to jerk the arm forward, Papà yelled. But I was resolved. Just when I thought my father would faint and I could no longer hold on, I heard a snap and released the arm, the ball popping back into its socket.

We just looked at each other, one tear-stained face mirroring the other.

I don't know how long we sat there, but after a while he and I started to scale the ravine, an impossible feat for Papà, who again sank down to the bottom. I was filled with hope because of what I'd just accomplished, so I said, "I'll go up and toss you the rope from the cart." My movements were quick and sure for the first few meters. Suddenly I was exhausted. After several other attempts I panted, breathing through my mouth. The crevice was a sleek climb I knew my father would not be able to negotiate without feeling great pain. What I didn't anticipate was the difficulty I was encountering due to my own loss of strength. My feet were caught in roots and my face was whipped and scratched by brush and twigs, the distance of which I'd misjudged. I thought, *If I am having this much trouble, how will Papà be able to make it?*

I reached the ridgetop and hurried to the cart. Pupa. I consoled her as best I could. Her breathing seemed steady. So I got hold of one of the wine-filled sheepskins that had not burst and tossed the skin down to my father, begging him to drink some quickly, hoping the effect would be numbing. I had already tied the rope around my waist and circled a plane tree. Then I climbed halfway down and threw the cord to my father. I miscalculated, and it fell short. I hauled it up and climbed farther down the cliff face and hurled it once more. With great difficulty, Papà slipped the knotted loop diagonally across his body. Slowly, I began to pull.

The next half hour proved to be not just a test of strength but of will and desire. Somehow I managed through false starts and slipups to pull my father up onto the dusty road from which he had been launched an interminable amount of time before. I helped my father sit and told him to rest while I got some of the supplies from the ruined cart.

The last trip back to the cart almost made me heave. I saw squashed chicks, feathers, blood, and guts. Why hadn't I seen them before? As I approached, I kissed my fingertips and touched them to my donkey's forehead. The poor beast. Then, about to place my shaking hands upon Pupa's eyes and pull down her lids, the eyelashes tickled the balls of my fingers. I saw light in her eyes. I placed an ear to her chest. "Papà!" I yelled. "She's still breathing. Pupa's alive!"

I took another wineskin that had not been crushed, crossed it over my chest, grabbed a burlap sack, and stuck in a few of the chicks that had not wandered off or been killed. I gawked in disbelief at the carnage as I dragged out one bolt of the fabric meant for my mother's mattress making. I unwound it, folded it narrowly, and placed it over my shoulder like a blanket.

The rest of our belongings will have to remain, I thought. How could we ever retrieve this mess of splintered wood and soiled goods? I ran and placed the things I carried next to Papà.

"What should I do about Pupa? She was caught beneath the cart, but I freed her."

"Push her over the side."

"But she's not dead! Didn't you hear me? Her upper body is hurt."

Something registered in his glazed eyes. He said, "She might not be dead yet, but if her ribs are broken and her lungs or liver punctured, she's dying."

"Oh, Papà. The baby will die too."

Papà hesitated a second, then thrust his hand into his pocket and pulled out his knife. He tossed it to me. "If you love her, cut her. Save the foal—her baby—you must."

Somehow he made it to his feet, and I got him near enough to Pupa so that he could tell me what to do. I washed my hands with wine, and they stung. I shook the excess off but did not dry my hands. I washed the knife, handle and all. I rolled my donkey a little more and braced her back.

I screamed, "I can't! I can't!"

Papà beckoned me to come near him and when I did, his face screwed up. I bent close. With his good hand, he pulled me closer by my shoulder. He squeezed so hard it was like a vise. Where did he get this strength? Was this foal that important to him?

"You must. You will," he groaned. "Save her baby, if you love her. It's what she wants now. That's why she's holding on to life. Hurry."

Slumped against a tree, Papà gave me instructions again and I did what he told me. I made a T cut and a stream gushed out. I dropped the knife.

"Pull it out!" Papà shrieked.

With two hands, I yanked the jennet out, warm and bloody, fur matted with fluids, a swollen rope like an intestine Papà called a *riata* still holding her to Pupa. I placed her on my mamma's mattress material. The inflated cord followed. Papà hollered for me to cut the umbilical cord. Listening to my father, I didn't have time to get sick or think. I did what he said. I wiped the knife on my skirt and trickled the last of the wine over it. My father shouted where to cut and make a knot. I was thankful I'd handled animal guts before or I'd have been squeamish touching all that slimy juice.

When it was over, I knew Pupa would suffer no more once she stopped breathing, but I wondered if she was pleased at the miracle of the baby I presented her. I nestled the bloody, matted infant, who didn't weigh so much because she wasn't full term, next to her.

The hardest thing, harder than even pulling out that foal, was leaving her dying mamma there on that dusty, lonesome road. Was birth always connected in some way with death and vice versa? I thought of Zia Concetta. She had lost a baby and cried for days. Mamma comforted her, saying, "There'll be other babies." To me she'd said, "We must be thankful. We could have lost your aunt instead of the baby." Those words set a fear in me, greater than any goblin story on the Feast of All Souls.

Papà said we must bring the foal home with us. When he said it, I realized just how tired I felt. How could we carry this animal? What a pair we made—my father, with his injured arm and loss of strength, and me, weighing all of thirty-five kilos dripping wet in every stitch of clothing.

"How can we, Papà?"

He told me to lash the small back panel from the cart onto three poles—two long side ones and a shorter middle one.

I pulled down lean, supple branches from saplings. With all my weight dangling from them and the dry heat that had persisted for so long with lack of rain, they snapped instantly. I leaned the three poles on the wrecked cart for support, mounted the back panel, and next added the squirming foal, swaddling her down, her eyes unsure and luminous. I spoke gently to her, trying to calm her. I stroked the soft spot behind her ears.

"Have faith, little one," I whispered. She seemed to relax.

When I'd finished constructing, I thought, *How will this help? How can I carry this? It's even more weight?* But I didn't ask Papà because as I looked at the leaning contraption, it came to me that I would rest the long poles on my shoulders and drag it.

Struggling homeward, Papà said, "Hopefully someone will come back and dress out the animal. Maybe bring it to the *mattatoio* to make *mortadella*. If . . ." he started to say with a shaky voice. "When Zu Nino comes, he'll bring the carcass back on a travois—the device you just built—to the butcher . . ." He was too tired to finish. I was thankful I never heard the condemning words that would turn my pet and friend into a family delicacy.

Years later, I would think that when life challenges us with something never attempted, perhaps never even thought of before, the feat can only be met if the person challenged will risk enormously. Maybe one doesn't know herself well enough yet, or her own capabilities, until she is put to a trial.

CHAPTER VI

Rosalia

THE HOMECOMING

ROSALIA SANG, BUT HER VOICE broke in the middle of the melody and burst into a shout of joy when she saw her husband and daughter approach. She had been taking in the wash when Nicola whistled, then called her name. Always the same, she dropped whatever she was doing and ran to him.

But where is the cart? They're on foot? What's Angelica dragging?

When Rosalia noticed his arm in a rough sling, she badgered Nicola with questions and at the same time hugged and kissed Angelica, who seemed embarrassed at the display.

Rosalia saw how grateful Nicola was to his daughter, in the way he looked at her, smoothed her hair, touched her cheek. He told his wife he would remember this as the day of distance.

Nicola said, "The girl is growing quickly. And this incident catapulting me—she acted well, she's maturing."

"Sit, my husband," Rosalia said to Nicola, indicating a place next to her while Angelica took the foal to the barn.

Nicola sat beside his wife and started to narrate the details of the accident.

"Accident?" Rosalia said.

Anger smoldered in his eyes. "I was helpless to prevent it." He softened then, and told Rosalia how Angelica had served as a midwife for Pupa and how he'd walked beside his daughter, comfortable in the knowledge that Angelica was capable of so much more than he'd ever credited her. The walk along the dusty road was hot, but finally some autumn rain had begun to fall, taking the bite out of the heat. Nicola thanked God the accident had occurred near the village.

"You keep saying 'accident' as if you really believe it was."

Nicola ignored her words, and Rosalia could do nothing but listen as he explained that the evening's cool breeze had helped refresh them. They had stopped many times on the route home—once near an ancient ever-running fountain covered with moss and bracken on the outskirts of town. They bypassed the center of the village, taking the shorter, more direct route. After a while, they rested again under a chestnut tree in a grove of clover, wild mint, and rughetta.

"I shouldn't have drunk the wine. My legs feel shaky," Nicola said, but Rosalia knew it was also due to the trauma he had sustained and the shock of seeing the riders.

"Did you recognize them?"

"Of course, 'men of honor,'" he said to Rosalia. "Lawless men, creating chaos, bound by secretiveness and a code of silence. *Omertà*." Nicola spat. "They rode hell-bent, horses lathered. We're sure to hear of some dastardly deed they were escaping from."

"Or going to?" Rosalia asked, hoping for an answer.

"Too coincidental," Nicola said, "that Ciccio would've been among them, or that he'd have known I'd be on that road . . ."

"Thinking out loud?" Rosalia said, wishing for more of an explanation, but none came.

Peppe approached his father and kissed him. "I helped Angelica in the barn and sent her inside to clean up and eat. She's exhausted. What else can I do?"

Rosalia noticed the look of terror on her son's face as he gazed at his father's appearance.

Nicola said, "Peppe, ride to your Zu Nino's now. Tell him about the crash and the animal in the road. Tell him to set out at first light; there's nothing to be done tonight."

"*Certo*, Papà," Peppe said.

THE NEXT DAY AFTER THE midday meal, Nicola sat down on a wooden bench and leaned against the wall of the house.

"Some more *vino*, please," Nicola said to Angelica. He turned toward Rosalia and said, "I think it was Ciccio's band ran us down, though I'm not sure." Then he gulped the last swig of wine. When the girl was out of earshot, he told Rosalia, "Angelica is no longer a child, Lia, she must be treated with esteem." This was the second time he had said this in two days. Rosalia knew he meant to do something about their daughter's new station in the family. But she couldn't guess what. She waited until late in the day when they walked in the garden and sat under a large apricot tree whose fruitless branches spread to a trellis of clustering strawberry grapes.

Peppe joined them under the arbor. Rosalia saw immediately how displeased the boy was to have missed all of what his father had to say. She was glad in a way he hadn't heard and hoped he wouldn't bear a grudge against his sister.

Nicola said, "Peppe, check on the foal."

With his uninjured arm, Nicola slapped at a fly, but the jarring motion made him grimace. He leaned back against the stone wall and said, "You should take the girl with you when it's Concetta's time for this third baby. Angelica should learn all in that regard."

Rosalia objected. "She's young yet. She has a lifetime, and besides—"

Nicola turned his head to look Rosalia in the eyes.

"Concetta was mistaken."

He cocked an eyebrow. "Then next time."

There was nothing left to say. The discussion was over.

Rosalia didn't even bother to hedge. Not now. She pointed to his arm. "Always something. Look at you. What about the almond harvest?"

"When you return from Calabria, Peppe will assist me. Then I'll be well enough to take him with me to repurchase all the things we lost. For now you'll have to make do, or I'll go with Nino to market."

CHAPTER VII

Rosalia

CALABRIAN DAYS

EVERY YEAR WHEN ROSALIA BEGAN the wool harvest, her mind summoned up images of herself with her mother, who had been incapable of explaining things of nature and life. Rosalia wanted to be different, to be able to teach and guide Angelica. It was difficult for Rosalia, not having had a good example herself.

Rosalia wanted to instruct her daughter as to the ways of midwifery and the world. She did not want Angelica growing up fearful. The girl demonstrated courage in so many things, yet when it came to herself, her body, and the functions required of it to enter an adult world, Angelica seemed reticent.

Nicola favored Angelica following in her mother's footsteps and learning to be a midwife. Rosalia was less convinced that Angelica should be channeled in that direction. Did the girl possess the substance and stamina for it? Rosalia was determined to devise a test.

She gave her daughter more and more responsibilities. Instead of hiring Giuseppina, a neighbor, whom Rosalia always suspected possessed sticky fingers, she designated new and different tasks and labor to Angelica.

One evening Rosalia sent Angelica into the yard to hunt for the chicken, telling her daughter to hike up her long skirt when she scurried about. "Find me the chicken. Call out to me and I'll come to show you how to kill it and then you can pluck it clean. I want to pot it for supper."

Rosalia watched Angelica run into the yard.

Twenty minutes had lapsed. Angelica, breathless, returned and said, "Mamma, there's no chicken. She's disappeared."

At first Rosalia thought it was because the girl didn't want to kill the chicken, but then she realized by the look on the child's face that she was in earnest and really couldn't locate it.

"What are you saying, girl? It was the last one in the coop when your father left this morning for the lemon groves. He'll be back for dinner, and he wants to eat chicken with olives and fennel. In a few days, he'll be going to Messina and then we'll have a yardful again, but right now I need that one."

Rosalia wiped her hands on her apron and said to Angelica, "You watch the young ones. I'm going to hunt for that chicken."

To her surprise, Rosalia couldn't find the chicken either. She went back to the house, took off her apron, and left Angelica to pit ripe black olives. Shortly afterward, Rosalia ambled down the road. The day blistered with heat. As she walked she kicked up squalls of dust.

The odor of chicken soup reached Rosalia's nose before she rapped on her neighbor Giuseppina's open window. Giuseppina opened the door. Rosalia did not greet her, but simply sauntered into the woman's kitchen as if she were the owner of the house, lifted the pot cover of the stewing chicken, and without a word, scooped it up and plopped it into her mapina-lined basket. The crocheted fringe of the tea towel hung out of the basket, and Rosalia used it to cover the half-cooked fowl. Rosalia felt Giuseppina's eyes, wide with terror, follow every gesture, but she made no objection to the hostile action.

"I've promised Nicola a chicken dinner and I don't intend to disappoint him," Rosalia said. She hesitated. "You've seen him get cross, yet I would have faced his wrath if only you'd asked me . . . I'd have given you this last *gallina*, but not now . . ." She sighed. "When Nicola gets back from Messina I'll try to convince him to give you two chicks plus a day's wages if you send your son Gaetano to help prune the olive trees next week."

Shame colored Giuseppina's face scarlet, but she agreed.

"Enjoy my chicken broth."

On the way home, Rosalia thought about Gaetano as a possible match for Angelica when the time came. Though she wanted to see if he had hands like his mother's that adhered to things that didn't belong to him. She and Nicola would have opportunities to observe his behavior. So she decided to think on this for a long while before she mentioned it to Nicola, lest he make a hasty decision and begin to formulate a plan for the girl that all might later regret.

The sound of a tinkling bell and sheep bleating in a field nearby caused Rosalia's mind to skip back to early spring when she had superintended the wool collection from Nicola's sheared flock.

THE GATHERING HAD BEEN DONE before the weather was too warm. The shearing took two days to accomplish and was the work of men. Nicola had hired extras. The mountain of wool was then stored till the beginning of June.

Rosalia's mother and her mother before her had been mattress makers. Rosalia had jotted down a recipe for wool gathering in preparation for Angelica's birthday and brought it to the nuns of the convent to write it in beautiful calligraphy on decorated parchment paper. Knowing her daughter would treasure it, Rosalia had it framed by a local *falegname*, a woodworker who ran a hardware store. The word *Lana* stood at the top of the page in gold lettering.

WOOL
1. Shear sheep in March.
2. Gather wool.
3. Store it covered with tarpaulins until June.
4. Wash wool with brown soap in aqueduct water.
5. Dry it on hot sand.
6. Comb it with the ripple.
7. Store for summertime mattress making.

In June, Rosalia and Angelica had hauled the wool to the public fountain where they washed it with caustic soap. They sang a song about "many hands making light work." It was a full day's worth of labor no matter how many worked alongside. The wool, even partially wrung out by strong hands, doubled in weight. This wet wool, heaped upon the wagon again, was carted home and covered again with a tarp. Rosalia rejoiced that Nicola had invested in a new donkey.

The next day before dawn, Rosalia and the children had collected fat land snails. These she placed into a large basket with scattered bits of bread and fastened a linen cover over it. She left the basket in the shade for three days until the *lumache* had eaten only bread and eliminated everything in their systems. These purified snails were then ready to be washed, cooked, and eaten. If cooked improperly, they became hard and rubbery. The secret Rosalia discovered was to put the snails in cool water, heating slowly until the "sleepy" snails relaxed enough to come out of their shells. Nicola loved this specialty with garlic and hot *peperoncino*. The children rejoiced in capturing them.

Then Concetta joined Rosalia before they set out for the beach. The two women packed up the children on one wagon, and the wool-laden wagon, driven by Peppe, followed behind. They ate breakfast en route. Angelica opened a parasol and placed it over her newest baby sister, Beatrice. When they arrived at the beach, Rosalia and the children affixed the tarp to the back of the wagon like an open tent in order to shade the baby. The family carded, stretched, and spread the wool upon the sand to dry. Rosalia thought it looked strange to see the hot sand covered by wool, her thoughts carrying her, like the warm, dulcet breeze, back to her youth when she, her mother, and grandmother did the same. Pangs of nostalgia struck Rosalia. She wondered if this life would be of Angelica's choosing—did she really have a choice at all?

The weather was so pleasant the children convinced the adults that a swim was in order. After the wool had been laid to dry, the children ran into the surf and splashed in the waves. By the time the picnic lunch was laid out, Nicola and his brother Nino arrived and spent the rest of their time enjoying the day. While the women rested, the men and children gathered green, leafy seaweed into baskets. They fished off the rocks and pulled in a few small fish.

Rosalia and Nicola sprawled under a large square umbrella. She said to him, "They'll think we're lovers. Go fish with your son. Peppe is thrilled to be with you and Nino."

Nicola took hold of Rosalia's wrist and kissed the crossing veins at the heel of her hand. She pulled his hand toward her, creeping hers into his.

"We're done fishing," Nicola said. "Now we'll scavenge around the rocks. The children delight most in this."

"Look how Angelica adores Concetta, hanging on her every word. So many things she needs to know, but I can't always talk to her," Rosalia said.

"Maybe you're too much alike. Besides, you worry too much."

They subsided into silence, locked for an instant in each other's eyes. He got up from the blanket, stretched, and went to join the others where they trapped octopus and calamari in a squirt of black ink among the natural jetty boulders in the shallows. The children's jubilation could not be stymied for an instant as they squealed in their bliss and ran toward the jetty to garner mussels.

Rosalia heard Nicola cry out to the children, "And remember to pick only the *cozze* underwater, never exposed ones." Then his voice trailed off and was lost to her.

Concetta returned without Angelica, and Rosalia asked where her daughter had dashed off to. Concetta said that she'd gone to a pool of water hemmed by a lacy tracing of dried salt where she hoped to snag a few small, almost transparent shrimp. As she sat down Concetta said, "Angelica adores children. She's such a little mother hen."

"But she's fanatical when it comes to prayer—reminds me of my father. I hope she doesn't want to make it her life's work."

"Why would she?" Concetta said, pouring water onto a hanky, patting her hands and wrists, daubing her neck and cheeks.

"Mmm. Certainly Ruggero isn't a stellar example of piety," Rosalia said, and both women laughed.

Before the evening dampness settled, when the quilted sea was the color of cobalt, they began to collect the wool. By the time the waves were silver and the sun had almost reached the horizon, the gathered wool—dried, lighter, shaken free of sand—had been combed through with ripples to remove any seeds that had remained. Nicola devised the handy, comb-like ripples that Peppe helped make. They were rounds of wood hammered through with long nails, the spikes acting like the teeth of a comb.

Afterward, they pitched the wool into the wagon for the trip home. The family spent the night on the beach. With the dawn light they would leave for home.

Rosalia was pensive. *This is how darkness descends: the sky loses luminescence and light is drawn to another part of the world.* She looked at Nino as he made a roaring fire. She steamed open the mussels in a huge iron skillet, skewering pieces of calamari, octopus, and a few of the larger shrimp that Angelica had retrieved from the salty, seaweed-filled pool.

After dinner Nicola took out his guitar and Nino held his mandolino and the brothers played poignant Sicilian songs whose melodies sundered the night.

Angelica said, "Mamma, are the dreams of the little ones fringed with lyrics and rhapsody?"

This was her moment. Rosalia decided to speak as openly as she could with her daughter.

"Come walk by the shore with me, Angelica."

As they walked, Rosalia said nothing for a long time, then her foot touched something that made her recoil and lose balance. She had to lean on Angelica. They continued walking arm in arm.

"I saw you talking to Concetta. You have so much to say to each other, yet so many times with me you are silent."

"She told me what it's like to lose someone you love in death. How you hold fast to their memory and their spirit hovers near. Then she told me of the joy of carrying an infant within."

"What did she say about carrying a baby?"

"That sometimes they kick or splash. Sometimes they turn like a fish in a tank of water."

"Very true. Let's sit here and watch the stars. What else did she tell you?"

"That you know as much, if not more, about bringing babies into the world than a doctor who studies at a university."

Rosalia dug wells in the sand at her side. "Now your father wants me to teach you what I know if you're willing to learn."

"It's not that I'm not curious, but I don't know if I'm ready or if I'll be good at it."

Rosalia glanced at the sky, and it seemed as though in that split second the stars swept earthward in a quick, inexplicable spiraling that left them almost within reach. So much so that Rosalia raised her hands upward.

"Why did you do that, Mamma?" Angelica asked.

Rosalia brought down her arms. "We must always reach for the stars, for even if we fall short we might catch a moonbeam."

"I wouldn't mind helping, if it'll please Papà and you."

"There will come a day when women won't always do their father's and husband's bidding, but that time, I fear, is far away." Rosalia heaved a sigh. "But I'd like you to have knowledge of your own body and to help other women . . . Angelica, I was so ill-prepared when I married. I don't want you to be ignorant of—"

"Mamma, I see farm animals, I think I understand more . . ."

Rosalia played the tips of her fingers over her lips in concentration. She wondered if it was worth Angelica's sacrificing her innocence to become a midwife. Would this alter the girl? Change her completely and make her afraid of normal female functions? She'd already suffered a traumatic physical experience, along with the emotional trauma of delivering the donkey's jennet. Would midwifing help or hinder her emotionally? Rosalia thought back to her own experiences and how she had had nightmares in the beginning. But she'd overcome it, and so would her daughter.

Angelica took hold of her mother's hand and said, "But I wonder if the pain and heavy bleeding is for everyone—"

"You have your monthly visit? And you didn't tell me?"

"Mmm. Zia Concetta knows, but I made her promise not to tell you—I didn't want you to worry. You were so upset when I had the horse accident, and cut myself in the shed."

"God constructed us all the same, but sometimes there are deviates, variations in nature."

"Like Zia Concetta?"

"How do you mean?"

"She told me she thought she was pregnant, but it was a false alarm. She also said you and Papà are disputing whether I should become a midwife."

"The next time it won't be a false alarm for your auntie."

"How do you know?"

"Her body's preparing the way. We'll think about midwifing then, eh, pigeon?"

"I like being called 'angel' better."

"Now why is that?"

"Oh, pigeons squawk too much and soil everything. Angels don't." Angelica rested her head on her mother's shoulder. "Mamma, I don't ever want to grow up. I never want to leave you and Papà."

Rosalia put her arm around her daughter, drew her close, and kissed her forehead. Rosalia thought of herself as a girl, telling her mother the same thing before Nicola had come to propose. A burst of falling light swished earthward across the sky, spectacular as fireworks.

"Mamma, look, a shooting star."

Rosalia looked up to see the last of the star fishtail into nothingness. "Someone dies, someone is born." Mother and daughter sat for a long time. A breeze ruffled their hair, the breaking of the waves the only sound.

Angelica drew an angel in the sand. "Are you afraid to die?"

"I don't dwell on it, or plan on it. Not now, not for a long time to come. I've got too much to do. In a way, I think we cause our life to take different tracks—like deer sniffing for water or foraging in the woods. When we need things we hunt for them; when we're finished needing, we die."

Once home, Rosalia saw to the wool being stored in the barn. Afterward, she cleaned seaweed, chopped it with onion and pieces of octopus and calamari, and added the mixture to a batter. She spooned these plump rounds into hot olive oil, and fried and served them with homemade *limoncello*—a liquor infused with lemon skins gleaned and prepared at every harvest.

BY THE TIME ROSALIA RETURNED home with the chicken, all thoughts of Giuseppina and her son Gaetano had vanished, along with the remembrances of sheep shearing. After dinner she made a list of the things that she needed from market.

THAT WEEK WHEN NICOLA BROUGHT back the damask, needles, and thread from Messina, Rosalia stored them wrapped in dense brown paper in a cupboard where she had laid small sacks of cheesecloth filled with lavender.

All summer long, when she was done with her normal chores of the day, she would sit outside in the evening air and stuff and tuft the damask with the wool she had recarded again after the beach drying. Although Angelica had learned to sew when she was young, watching her mother's deft hands taught her to craft.

When Rosalia finished making a mattress, Peppe, Angelica, and Rina helped her roll and store it, covered by the tarp. Every once in a while, on warm, sunny days, these were unfurled and laid out to prevent them from an attack of *muffa*, mold that grows from dampness. Barefoot, little Nunziata would jump and tumble all over them. When Rosalia was ready to travel with these, Nicola and Peppe stacked them on the wagon to be hauled to Calabria. Usually it was done in the beautiful month of September, but this year it was October.

———

ROSALIA HAD WEANED FRAIL BEATRICE, well past toddling, over the summer so she would be able to travel, unburdened, to the mainland. It was the first time she ever remembered being glad to be going away from her family, from her village, from her island. She realized the memory of Nicola's accident still weighed heavily on her and, feeling somewhat fatigued, welcomed the trip as a diversion.

Nicola and his wife made the mutual decision that it was time for Angelica to make the trip with her mother. It was the perfect opportunity to teach Angelica to travel, to sell, and, more importantly, to begin her debut tending to the business of midwifing. Rosalia's cousin Silvana was about due.

Concetta would take Beatrice and Nunziata home with her and offered to look in on Nicola, Peppe, and Rina from time to time. Giuseppina was hired to take care of the rest of Nicola Domenico's household, laundry, and cooking.

The trip on the *traghetto* made Rosalia feel nauseous and unwell. She had booked passage for a below-deck berth, even though it was only about an hour ride. Now she was sorry for having spent the extra money on herself. At least Angelica slept while Rosalia paced the upper deck with the cold, fresh air of the Messina straits blowing full force in her face. The last time she was sick overboard she thought for sure she'd lose her stomach. How she wished she could control the nausea. A sailor who had swabbed the decks was now heaving ropes from a mass of tangles into orderly loops. He took pity on her and offered to get her some food to quell the nausea.

"You must eat, *signora*, or the churning of your stomach will not settle. Let me bring you some bread."

Rosalia sat leaning against a life raft, not having the strength to refuse. When he returned he said, "I've never seen anyone as sick as you. And the boat is hardly rocking."

"I've never been seasick. Not ever. Perhaps I'm sick for a different reason. But it couldn't be influenza. I'm not the least bit feverish. I thank you for your kindness. God will reward you." Rosalia added the boy's face to the many others on her list for prayers.

When the ferryboat docked up in Reggio Calabria it was 6:00 a.m. The nausea had finally subsided once Rosalia had eaten the bread. She even slept a little in the same leaning position as before. With the brisk morning air she found herself sniffing freshly brewed coffee.

"How can I ever thank you?" she asked the sailor holding the demitasse cup.

"No need. I put a little too much sugar in it, but it can't hurt."

Again Rosalia thanked him.

"Someday a stranger might help me if I'm in dire straits, or help my mother," he said.

Rosalia handed back the cup and collected her belongings. She trekked downstairs with her bundles to collect Angelica and then they headed toward the loaded wagon; the smell of the horses and dung assailed Rosalia, and once again she thought she would heave.

"Mamma, what's wrong?"

"Just a little *mal di mare.*"

Luckily the sailor, now in civilian clothes, came to Rosalia's assistance, offering to drive the wagon. She told Angelica to mount the wagon and said to the sailor, "This is my daughter." He told Rosalia to walk across the lowered gangway, that it would be quite some time before all the wagons and carts would be able to debark.

"I'll meet you on the other side with the wagon and your little girl." She knew Angelica would bristle at that, but Rosalia was so ill she didn't need much prodding.

⚓

AN HOUR LATER ROSALIA, SEATED under an *hostaria* awning and fanning herself, watched the sailor drive her wagon onto land, calling, "Where're you headed?"

"To market," Rosalia raised her voice. "To sell my mattresses."

When Rosalia caught up, he said, "If I may be so bold as to suggest it, I'd like to drive you. My home is minutes away."

"I could never repay you," she said. She saw her daughter's eyes wary.

He stuck out his hand and introduced himself. "My name is Domenico Balsamo."

"And I am Signora Domenico."

"What a coincidence, my first name is your last."

"My husband's." Rosalia patted Angelica's hand to reassure her.

They drove on in silence. After a long way, he said, "My mother's booth is nearby. She'll be setting up by now. I'll present you to her. You don't have an umbrella. My mother will share hers with you, I'm sure."

"What does she peddle?"

"*Merceria*, notions of all sorts."

"Oh, this is too good to be true."

"Why?" he asked.

"Someone who sells threads and needles, buttons and ribbons is just the person I need to make contact with."

"Ah, no wonder," said Domenico as Rosalia uncovered a section of a rolled mattress.

Rosalia felt her daughter's tension ease.

"It'd be lovely for us to have some female companionship," Rosalia said to the young man.

After the introduction, Domenico left the women alone to get acquainted. Rosalia took one look at the woman and knew she would do business with her for a long time to come. Gina Balsamo's face was open and her eyes honest, though tired from hard work. The vendor asked Rosalia to share her umbrella and market space. Rosalia settled her belongings while Angelica got down a light wicker chair for her mother, laid a cloth for herself, and sat on the ground.

When they were seated, Gina said to Rosalia, "There's something in your eyes. Ah, there it is. You're expecting."

"You're mistaken, I assure you."

"No mistake. Shall I read the cards for you?"

Rosalia instinctively clutched her abdomen. She thought for a fleeting instant that maybe it wasn't the sea that had made her ill after all, but new life in her womb. How foolish. She never dreamed she could become pregnant because she'd been nursing until a month ago when she weaned the little one. She had not even had her monthly period. She realized now for sure that the sickness on the boat was not a thalassic reaction.

"What could the tarot tell me that I don't already know?"

"Cross my hand with a coin and I'll tell you."

"There's nothing you could say to pique my interest," Rosalia answered with false bravado. Against her better judgement, she dug into her pocket and pulled out a coin.

The woman cackled and handed her back the coin. "I was just joking. It's a gift. I do it for fun. No cards then, give me your hand."

Rosalia hesitated, then gave in. Angelica, silent, looked on as Gina laid a red thread across the hand. "Your husband will be kicked in the head by a horse."

Rosalia scoffed, knowing how docile the stallion was and how expertly Nicola handled the horse.

"And it will be difficult, if not impossible for your girl here— Angelica, that's your name?—to conceive and bear a child. She is fearful."

Angelica sat up straighter.

Rosalia pulled her hand away. "Nonsense. She's brave, and she'll marry and have many children." Rosalia spat three times on the ground. But how did Gina know her daughter's name? Had Rosalia possibly mentioned it to Gina? Surely she hadn't.

"Your second daughter is willful and lucky, but this girl"—she indicated Angelica—"is narrow in the hips, isn't she?"

"What of it?"

"Slim-hipped and devoted to religion. Better so for her."

Rosalia felt a chill and drew her shawl tighter around her shoulders. Gina took hold of Rosalia's hand again, but she jerked it away and made horns behind her back. She'd thought she would like Gina, but now she wasn't so sure. Her doubting led her to other thoughts. If it were possible, she'd return home tonight. Rosalia knew Nicola would make a celebration for her whether or not she'd sold her mattresses or gotten orders for more. But pride made her stay. That and the fact that she was scheduled to visit her cousin Silvana, which she would do in a few days.

As if Gina read her mind, she said, "Even if you returned now, your husband's destiny is written, as is yours, Angelica's, and even mine.

Sometimes there are choices to be made even though the events that shape our lives are cosmic."

"I wonder . . . but I must stay to sell these." Rosalia motioned toward the cart stacked with rolled mattresses.

Gina appraised Rosalia's handiwork. "You have a gift, but I see this is not your only talent. You're a shrewd bargainer and will make an excellent vendor."

Rosalia smiled in spite of herself. "Angelica helped me, she has hands of gold."

"Yes, but your hands own another genius your daughter lacks till now. You help women in grave situations."

Gina took both of Rosalia's hands and flipped them. "Of course," Gina said, "your hands are marked by blood and water catching babies."

Rosalia pulled away her hands and looked at their cleanliness.

"Wait a minute," Gina said, "give me your hand."

Hesitantly, Rosalia proffered her hand again.

"Not you." Gina looked at Angelica. "You. Your hand."

Angelica timidly produced her hand.

"There." Gina pointed. "See?"

Angelica and Rosalia looked at the lined palm.

Gina said to Rosalia, "No blood, no birth slime yet. Soon, though. Ah, and there. See? Someone's in your daughter's future. It's a bit hazy. A man and his shadow. He is dark and strong like my Domenico. Rosalia, you'll have moments of despair with this girl. But wait, perhaps it is a man concealed in his cloth, or not one man, but two . . . or one man of two minds."

What did all this mean? Rosalia looked at the query lines forming on her daughter's face and said, "Never mind, Angelica. The future is in God's hands. The good book says we must try to perform acts of love and kindness. Six hundred and something in a lifetime, right, Gina?"

"I never heard that. What book is that?"

Gina and Rosalia fanned themselves as the heat of late morning declared itself. They sat in the shade chatting about family when two nuns walking arm in arm approached them.

"We need new mattresses for the infirmary," said one to the other.

At first Rosalia thought they were twins.

She heard another snippet of their conversation.

"Indeed, but these are far too fine and won't do for our purse," the tall nun with square shoulders said.

"Very fine. Look here at the cloth and the tiny stitches," Rosalia interjected, indicating with a pat her merchandise of exceptional quality.

The smaller nun shook her head. "We've a limited budget, I'm afraid."

"Perhaps we can work something out," Rosalia said. "After all, it's for the community . . . Make me an offer, and we might yet conclude."

Rosalia knew she must be shrewd in order to clinch the deal. She let the nuns speak first, hinting as to the sum they might be able to afford, and in hopes of raising the proposed ante. Rosalia adroitly indicated the exquisite handcrafted bed cushions without being too obvious. She complimented the sisters on their beautifully sewn habits. In that instant she was convinced she had the nuns in her pocket. Sure enough, she saw a gesture of acquiescence pass between them.

❦

ROSALIA SOLD ALL OF HER mattresses in less time than she'd imagined. She thanked Gina and her son, and started off on the wagon to Bagnara Calabra. Along the way mother explained some important midwife considerations to her daughter. "Never forget, if there's been a previous birth, it facilitates matters for the mother. Even if the baby was not full term."

Angelica's face looked puzzled. "Even if the mother didn't carry the baby nine months?"

"Exactly."

Rosalia handed the reins to Angelica. "Labor is usually long when it's the first time. And there is a surge of liquids to help the baby swim out. But they leave no mark like Gina said. Here, look for yourself." She showed her hands to Angelica.

Rosalia then stretched and rubbed the small of her back. "Stop a minute."

"Whoa, hold up there, Beauty," Angelica said quietly as she pulled back on the reins.

Rosalia took her daughter's chin in her hand and said, "This first time will be the worst. It's like shaming yourself, taking a mirror in hand and looking at someone's private parts to figure out how they work. But it is not sinful in any way, child. This has been passed on to us from God. He decreed this strange and mysterious female nature and has given us birthing as our life's assignment. You're young and you'll be strong about this, because it's your nature to be so; and I need your help, for I am not myself this time." Rosalia seized her stomach.

"Mamma, are you ill?"

"Gina's right. I didn't want to admit it, but I may be expecting." She wiped her hand across her brow. Rosalia saw surprise register on Angelica's face. Now they shared a secret. "And something else. You must think, even pretend, you know and understand the birthing process, for the mother delivering, but also for me as well as you. Somehow God will see your spirit through with knowledge that comes from other lives passed on to us, or perhaps at the moment of our birth. Since we come from God's realm, we're already equipped with this knowledge, forgetting it at our birth and relearning it throughout life. Forgive me," she said, leaned over the side of the wagon, and vomited.

<hr>

ROSALIA THANKED GOD IN SILENT prayer for His goodness because everything had gone well at Silvana's. Angelica acted as if she were already a seasoned midwife. Rosalia was amazed that her daughter hadn't even flinched the first time she saw a woman's legs spread for Rosalia to confirm that the pregnancy was progressing well. Anything Rosalia did she defined nonchalantly as if mother and daughter normally discussed these things every waking hour of the day, like the decision to have Silvana take a crouched, almost-sitting position to ease the child out. "After all, Silvana," Rosalia assured her, "this is your fourth. It'll go quicker this way."

<hr>

THEY LEFT HER COUSIN'S HOUSE early the next morning. Rosalia was glad Angelica had seemed more curious than appalled during the delivery and now laughed aloud when Angelica asked, "Does anyone ever break bones delivering?"

"Never," the midwife answered. "It's muscle contraction and relaxation—no bones involved. The birth canal stretches as far as needed."

"Always?"

"No, sometimes there are . . . abnormalities."

Rosalia said this was the first of many lessons and Angelica must be attentive always.

"Observation and understanding help the practice," Rosalia said.

❦

ROSALIA'S WELCOME HOME WAS SWEET and rewarding. Nicola's smile was proof that he was more than happy to see her and hear of the successful mattress venture and Angelica's assistance with Silvana's *parto*.

The third day after their arrival, when everything seemed to be back in order and under Rosalia's control, she was shocked into action when Angelica ran into her arms and breathlessly cried, "Papà had an accident in the stall cleaning the frog of the horse's rear hoof. She jerked her leg out of his hands. I was standing nearby with Beatrice in my arms—the horse must have smelled the baby and made the mare jumpy. Then the cat meowed and the horse reared and kicked Papà in the head." Angelica started to cry, mumbling, "I pushed Nunziata and jumped out of the way, but—"

Rosalia gathered her in her arms.

When Angelica composed herself, she told her mother that he lay unconscious. "I screamed for Peppe and gave the baby to Rina. Then Peppe and I dragged him out of the stall to another part of the barn and made a pillow of hay for him."

Rosalia ran toward the barn to see how seriously Nicola was hurt, Gina's words coming back to her. A shiver went through Rosalia's core, even though she was running in the hot midday sun.

CHAPTER VIII

Rosalia

CONCETTA'S VISIT

TWO WEEKS LATER, NICOLA SAID he was recovered well enough to return to supervising the vineyards and cultivating the lemons. One year to the day after Nicola returned to work, Rosalia received a visit from her dearest friend and confidant Concetta. In the interim, Rosalia had given birth to another baby girl, who was sickly. She named the child Giovanna, after Saint John the Baptist.

Rosalia prepared espresso and positioned the cups gently on the tabletop. She had made cannoli early that morning, frying the dough mixed with wine into crisp shells of toffee brown. She had taken sheep's milk and made it into ricotta, covered it with cheesecloth, and set it out on the windowsill. In the afternoon she diced into tiny pieces lemon skins she had candied at the last harvest. She combined them with chocolate shavings and set them aside. She added sugar to the ricotta, then mixed it with the citron and chocolate for the filling of the cannoli shells.

"Concetta," she called out through the window, happy as always to see her sister-in-law. Concetta waddled toward the kitchen, and Rosalia suppressed a smile at her duck-like approach. Rosalia kissed her on both cheeks, then made a fist and with it measured the space between Concetta's breast and extremely large belly. "Still not yet." A crease spread across her brow. *She's overdue.*

"I'm as big as a cow. Are you sure I'm not carrying twins or maybe a little calf this time?"

"You look radiant. And what's more, it'll all be over soon." Rosalia placed the coffee pot on the stove.

Concetta struggled to pull a chair away from the kitchen table. She sat down heavily.

"You're also glowing. But you're strong. I'm so tired. My legs won't carry me through half my daily chores," she said.

"Stay the night. I'll have Peppe ride over and tell Nino. You deserve a rest. Let me pamper you. Just once." Rosalia reached for the sugar.

"Oh, so tempting, Beelzebub in my ear. But I can't. I will, however, eat your delicious pastry and take some home. What difference can another kilo or so make now?"

"Nino loves you just the same, and before you know it you'll be a broomstick again with this baby."

Rosalia poured the frothy coffee and sat down. "Have you made arrangements for your little ones? Would you like to leave them here?"

"You have your own brood, and your Giovanna needs so much attention. Nino will take them to my mother's and on his way pass by here to let you know my time has come."

Before Rosalia could object, there was a weak cry from the cradle on the floor. She stooped to pick up the child, who seemed feverish. "I'll sponge her down and change her," she said.

"You see what I mean, dear. You have enough to concern you," Concetta said.

Rosalia thanked her, patting her hand.

CHAPTER IX

Angelica

TALE OF THE MIDWIFE'S DAUGHTER

I FELT VERY GROWN UP in the autumn of my thirteenth year with my long, wavy hair atop my head. It was beginning to be apparent to me that important occurrences happened every fall. On the beach in spring, Zia Concetta had shared her news with me that she was again pregnant and the baby was due late fall or early winter. Throughout those summer beach days I glimpsed her, not as an aunt or mother, but as a woman in love. I watched her stroll hand in hand with Zu Nino, as they whispered things to each other. He would kiss the back of her neck where the tendrils of her curly hair wouldn't stay put. She'd tuck her chin into her shoulder like a giggly schoolgirl. I realized they saw no one else seaside, seemingly devouring each other with their eyes.

❧

JUST BEFORE THE ALMOND HARVEST, Mamma asked me to assist her at Zia Concetta's birthing because she had been pleased at how I had handled myself so well with Papà and Pupa, her cousin in Calabria, and her when it was her time to deliver Giovanna. I was thrilled at the excitement of entering an adult world—a world secret even from men— yet I was apprehensive when a stray thought of what had happened with my donkey presented itself.

I was pleased I wouldn't have to babysit Rina, Nunziata, Beatrice, or Giovanna. Nor would I have to prepare the evening meal for Papà and Peppe. All of these attitudes about dodging work and supervision I supposed were not the most mature, but I had my heart set on going with Mamma.

I stood on tiptoes dusting the shelves in the pantry. When I finished, Mamma came in. I was so glad when my mother asked me "to attend Concetta's giving light to the infant." I said yes faster than a frog's tongue catching a gnat.

"Bring a shawl, it's chilly," Mamma said as she mounted the cart to drive to Zia Concetta's.

Peppe held the reins and, ever impatient, shouted, "Put a move on, snail."

I shot him a look but bit my tongue.

I ran back in the house and for some reason couldn't find my shawl, so I took Mamma's Sunday one. On the way to my aunt's house, I relived the experience of Mamma's physical examination of her cousin. There was nothing that my mind skipped. I recalled every breath, every recoiling movement, and every wince as Mamma touched her cousin's insides. I cringed with the memory of that observation, then flinched because it had jarred yet another. I looked at my hand and saw again the bloodied piece of the wine bottle I'd pulled out of me years ago.

❦

ZU NINO GREETED US AT the door. He was unkempt, unshaven, and smelled of wine. *How odd*, I thought, *because my uncle seldom drinks.* Mamma and my uncle exchanged glances. Something passed between them, a message I wasn't quick enough to intercept.

Mamma and I entered Zia Concetta's room to the sound of moaning. To Mamma, midwifing and birthing were natural, but delivering this baby added another factor: Mamma's emotions. I watched my mother straighten and tidy the nightstand, puff the pillow, all the while speaking quietly to my aunt as if to calm her. Then Mamma pulled down the sheet and raised my aunt's nightgown to examine her. I had never seen a completely naked pregnant woman before, not even Mamma. I was more curious than anything. I remembered Mamma's cousin; I couldn't see much then because Mamma had blocked my view and kept a sheet over Silvana, even though I tried to position myself closer. This time I was determined nothing would obscure my view.

My mother lingered at the bedside for some time. I watched her assess the situation. All seemed normal to me. Then I saw a frown register and, in place of serenity, panic spread across her face. Why was this? I couldn't even guess. Mamma approached me, confiding that this would be difficult, if not impossible. Her voice—her entire look—changed to despair and she implored me to leave.

"Go home with Peppe."

"He just left with the cart."

"Run after him. Go!" Her frantic look made me obey instantly.

I ran down the lane as fast as I could, yelling after him, but I couldn't catch up and he never heard my pleas for him to stop. I crumbled like an old sack on the dirt road and cried. How much I wanted to be helpful to Mamma, but I'd failed even my first test at taking instructions.

Slowly I started to walk back until I caught my breath, then ran again. In my aunt's house my mother shook her head and in an exasperated voice said, "Why did you come back?"

"He didn't hear me yelling for him to stop."

She closed the door and went in to Zia Concetta.

I had seen births before in the stable, around the yard, and even been through Pupa's ordeal, but this was different. I didn't count cousin Silvana's squat-birth, because I hardly saw a thing except the mucky baby afterward. And Mamma's having Giovanna was completely out of my hands until I had to wash the baby. So I thought of this as my first human baby. My heart raced with excitement. I opened the door partway.

I heard my mother say to Zia Concetta, "I'm here. It'll be all right. Try to stay calm, dear."

I stood in the doorway. "I couldn't catch up to him," I said, my voice apologetic. A baffled stare told me she was disappointed that I didn't go home, or was it that I'd eavesdropped?

After a time, she came to me and whispered, "This may be rough." She touched my cheek with her hand. Not too much later, with the same hand, Mamma took hold of Zia Concetta's and crooned to her.

I decided to clean up the mess Zu Nino had made in the kitchen. Another hour went by. I heard muffled sounds from my aunt's room. Zu Nino had gone to chop wood.

I looked in on Zia Concetta. Mamma walked over to me, and as she hugged me she muttered, "Almost twenty hours now and the water broke. This may be her third, but it won't be easy."

"What does it mean about the water?"

"A dry birth makes it difficult. No fluids to flush out the baby," she said, as if I understood exactly what she meant.

"What are you saying, Lia? Speak up. I can't hear you," Zia Concetta said.

As it sunk in that my mother's words were not meant for my aunt, Zia Concetta called out louder, "Lia. Lia. The contractions are coming closer," a pleading in her voice.

Mamma put up two fingers and held them sideward. "You're dilated only five centimeters."

"It can't be. The pressure is too much." Concetta groaned, then screamed.

Mamma sent me to the kitchen *armadio* for a clean sheet. "And bring hot water."

When I came back I thought how tired my mother looked, as well as my aunt. I watched Mamma wipe my aunt's forehead, soothing her with, "Hush now."

I remembered her saying that to Rina when I had my accident. Then I recalled the hurt feeling as if my insides were on fire. And the blood. Mamma had said we are all born in blood. My mind blocked out the noise of my aunt's scream with thoughts of uncertainty. What had I done to myself because of that accident? Would I be a normal woman? And here and now, with all these thoughts converging like swells of waves in a storm, I wasn't sure what my duties would be. But I wanted to do anything for Zia Concetta to save her pain. I went out and came back again, returning to the room once with a kettle and again with a darned and tattered but clean sheet.

"Now, precious girl, go to your cousins' room and rest till I call you," my mother said.

I hesitated, knowing my cousins had been sent to their grandmother's. "Go lie down."

"But, Mamma, it's lonesome without the children."

"I'll need you later. Please rest."

On my way to my cousins' room, I heard the kitchen door close and knew Zu Nino had returned with the firewood.

ALMOST TWO HOURS HAD PASSED before I got up from my nap. Still yawning, I passed Zu Nino playing solitaire with an old deck of Neapolitan cards at the kitchen table.

I watched Mamma comb her fingers through Zia Concetta's hair and again dry her brow. Mamma took out a bottle from her small kit of midwife things and poured hundred-proof alcohol—used for making liquor—on my aunt's stomach, mopping up the excess.

Suddenly I was wide-awake.

"Oh, so cold," Concetta murmured.

"I'm going to have to cut you," Mamma said in a church whisper. My stomach lurched. My eyes looked at my aunt but instead saw Pupa, lying cut in the road. I took hold of the doorjamb.

"Never," my aunt said. "I'll die if you do."

"You'll die if I don't."

"What's that? What're you doing?"

"This is your husband's razor." Mamma held it up and drew the blade lightly across her tongue, washing it with saliva, testing the edge. I wondered if she tasted blood. I froze, knowing she would cut the baby out, the way I had cut my Pupa. Something was so wrong. I heard a baby whimper. A minute passed before I realized the cry had been made by me.

Mamma paid me no mind, so intent was she on the work at hand. She took the blade from her mouth, signed an imaginary line from navel downward. She steadied her shaking hand by gripping the heel and wrist with the other. She was about to slice open the round belly when Concetta grabbed Mamma's arm.

"Wait just bit longer."

"I can't."

"I beg you," she groaned.

Mamma pulled her hand free and drew a make-believe line a second time and cringed. Her shoulders tensed. Her face became hard like stone. She bit her bottom lip and began to carve into the taut flesh. Its softness yielded, which surprised me.

"Stop—I implore you. Lia, Lia, Lia. It's too late. The baby's coming." Concetta grasped overhead, clutching the bronze bars of the bedstead.

I heard my mother call my name, but I was already standing there.

It was as if she didn't see me. I went closer, but was startled and jumped back when Zia Concetta pushed and screamed.

Mamma held the razor in her right hand and with her left measured her cousin's dilation and held up four fingers. "Ten centimeters open," she said, triumph in her voice.

Still with her left hand, I watched Mamma feel the abdomen and pelvic area. Mamma's words had been edged, framed with the sound of success. Yet I had a terrible feeling that all was not right, not as it should be. I prayed to the Infant Jesus I was wrong. I saw my mother shake her head to Zia Concetta and say, "The fetus hasn't turned."

My stomach felt queasy, like when I don't know an answer to my teacher's questions. What did that mean? Wasn't it good that she didn't have to finish cutting her?

An audible sound escaped my lips. I thought I saw tiny feet in between my aunt Concetta's bent knees. Wouldn't everything be fine now that the baby decided to come out?

As if she were talking to the saints on the wall or somebody else I didn't see in the room, Mamma said, "The head should be crowning. Instead of scrunched, crinkly skin and a mat of hair, the top of the head—" Mamma, all choked up, garbled in her throat, "Oh my God, my God."

Why did Mamma seem shocked? Surely she had witnessed every kind of birth. And then I knew—it was because this was her beloved Concetta. Mamma never dreamed this could happen to one so loved, so close to her.

Zu Nino rushed through the door, but Mamma gently pushed him away. "Go back to the kitchen, Nino. Help Angelica."

"To do what, Mamma?" I noticed she still clenched the razor.

I put out my hand and she dropped the razor into it. I placed it on the night table and dried the little blood off of my aunt's belly.

"Daughter, go and boil some more water."

Did she really need more water? Or did she want me out of the room? And if so, why? It was like my heart spoke: *pray for a miracle*. And though I tried to beg of God a special grace, I kept hearing other words in my ears. I had listened to many a tale when the women gathered in the kitchen after a holiday or Sunday dinner. I'd heard enough to understand that this was a particularly peculiar birth. I feared for Zia Concetta, feared for my mother who loved her, and feared for myself, not able to concentrate on my supplication to God, nor knowing the consequences of such a birth.

CHAPTER X

Rosalia

ADDIO AD UNA CARA AMICA

NO TIME LEFT, ROSALIA THOUGHT. *Almighty God.* Why had she hesitated?

Rosalia covered the tiny wound she had just inflicted with a clean piece of a diaper cloth. The position of the tiny feet she saw instead of a crowning head warned her the patient was doubly unlucky. Not only was the baby completely breeched, but also faceup. Normally the belly of the infant faced the mother's vertebra, but here, mother and child were layered spine upon spine.

The worst luck. Rosalia wrenched her hands and out of habit dried them upon her apron even though they weren't wet. The baby should have been at least slightly turned. Concetta's life was at risk, and now Rosalia encountered the possibility of losing the infant too.

Angelica returned with hot water and with eyes, her mother noticed, the size of chestnuts and, unfortunately, in time for Concetta's last exhausted push. The baby emerged, and Rosalia pulled a veil-like piece of amnion from the infant's face. Her mind traveled back to Angelica's birth. She too had been born with a caul. As the midwife turned the tiny girl upside down by her feet, slapping gently till the lungs filled with air to let out the first wail, she thought of stories of the ancient seamen and how they purchased, at great price, an infant's caul. It brought luck, and it was thought that the man who possessed it would never drown.

"Thank God," Rosalia said, cleaning the baby and placing her on her mother's stomach. Had the caul saved this baby from drowning in its mother's fluids? So strong had been the feeling that the infant couldn't survive birth. Rosalia shuddered. She had expected to find that the baby had choked on its own liquids or been strangled with the umbilical cord around its throat.

Concetta's voice broke into her thoughts.

"Rosalia. Lia, I feel like my arms and legs aren't attached to the rest of me," Concetta said.

"Sh-sh. Rest now. You did very well, and you're tired."

"Lia. Lia, don't go."

"I'm here."

"What'll we call her?"

"The baby. Like all the rest in their turn."

"No, you know what I mean. I thought this one would be a boy. I don't have a name—"

"Save your strength, Concetta."

"Lia. We'll call her Lia . . . after you."

"Not this one. We'll name her Concetta for her brave mother, my friend. The next one." Rosalia saw how weak Concetta was, how her shallow breathing came with effort. Exhaustion pooled into black circles underneath her eyes. She had become too fatigued in the long labor and, to make matters worse, it was a dry birth. Rosalia cut and knotted the umbilical cord. Then she checked the time. The afterbirth should be expelled in about four minutes. When ten minutes had elapsed, Rosalia knew that something was terribly wrong. She needed to remove the baby from the room. After she tested the water with her elbow she took the child from her perch on top of Concetta. Washing the newborn with the now tepid water, she swaddled her and handed her to Angelica. "Take the infant to her father."

"Wait," murmured Concetta. "Just a minute. Let me hold my baby. Once."

"You'll tire of holding her in a few months." Rosalia inclined her head toward the bed, and Angelica carried the infant to her mother. Angelica laid the baby in her aunt's arm. Concetta kissed the top of her head.

Rosalia observed Concetta's failing strength and understood that she was too weak even to hold the baby. "Take her now," Rosalia said to her daughter, handing over the infant.

Angelica started to walk out of the bedroom, cradling the soft bundle and cooing. She rocked the baby gently as she made her way, bearing the infant as if she'd been born to nurture. Her mother thought, *Ah, yes, this is her destiny: to marry and have children.* "Angelica," she called after her daughter softly, "no one remembers pain. Afterward—only joy at the sight of the newborn."

Twenty minutes later, Angelica entered the bedroom just as the placenta gushed forth, Concetta's uterine wall collapsing with it in a flowing hemorrhage Rosalia knew she could not staunch. All she saw was red. In her peripheral vision she caught sight of Angelica.

"Angelica, leave. Now, I said." The child stood frozen, a deer caught in the pale shadows of a gas lamp. Rosalia screamed, "Get out! Take the baby from Nino. Get him in here."

Concetta was still conscious. Rosalia sobbed at her sister-in-law's side.

"I beg you, forgive me. Why did I delay? I should've cut you like Caesar's mother."

"Emotions have a life of their own. Perhaps, Lia, you're part me."

"Forgive me," Rosalia whimpered.

"There's nothing to forgive."

Nino came in and knelt by the bedside. He cried out, "Why? Why? *Dio mio, perché?*" and burrowed his head, nuzzling Concetta's breast.

"You must absolve me, I beg you," insisted Rosalia.

"God's will." Concetta sighed. "Not yours or mine. I'm so tired."

"Then rest, but first forgive me."

"Lia, come close. Let me kiss you."

Rosalia bent near for Concetta's kiss. Concetta placed her hand in Rosalia's, who signed a cross.

"Bless you too. Now call a priest. Nino, get my mother."

Knowing Concetta could lose consciousness soon because she had lost too much blood, Rosalia said, "There's no time."

"Kiss my children—all my babies. Give my mother my love."

CHAPTER XI

Angelica

PREPARATION FOR A FUNERAL

AS I ROCKED THE INFANT in my arms, I thought of my aunt. *This is how a life ends. Quiet submission to God's will, but only if you're good.* I remembered a talk I'd had with Zia Concetta on the beach when she explained what it was like to lose a loved one. She'd said that death was like stepping off the edge of a skyline; the rest of the world's sphere was still beyond, but we couldn't see because our field of vision was limited.

I stopped rocking and nuzzled the baby. "When my life is over, I'll be at the junction of that horizon and see your *mammina.*"

Remembering what my mother had told me about the circumstances of my own birth, I thanked God I had not been left an orphan. I went to the children's room and laid the baby down in the center of the bed, blocking her into the middle of four cushions. She was so warm and pink, too beautiful to be real. I kissed her tiny hands and tucked them into the flannel bunting. Then I climbed up on the top bunk. Before I fell asleep, my mother came in and kissed me.

"Backward," my mother said in answer to my question of what went wrong—as if that were enough of an explanation for why the baby had killed her own mamma.

Exhausted, I slept.

DURING THE NIGHT, AT DIFFERENT intervals, Mamma and Zu Nino came in to check on the baby, and then I fell into a deep sleep. In the morning, before I was fully awake and in a half-veiled dream state, I couldn't believe that only yesterday I'd heard Zia Concetta's screams of labor.

With the sounds of a cock crowing and the light of dawn, I fully awoke. I heard my mother's sobs and Zu Nino's, thinking it strange the baby had not cried out for her mother's milk while I slept. I climbed down from the top bunk and touched my lips to the infant's forehead. Cold. So cold. A chill ran through my own body, although I was warmed by a woven blanket I'd used to cover myself like a cloak. I touched the baby all over and listened for a heartbeat. I cried with every action. Then I reached for a mirror and held it to the baby's mouth, and seeing no breath, cried as if my heart had burst.

I thought, *Now what bodily preparations wait for Zia Concetta?* I remembered certain Bible stories of Lazarus and of the women who had prepared Christ's body for burial in the tomb. I had heard about what was done for funerals. I made my way to the front of the house and found the adults in the kitchen.

"Make some coffee," Mamma said to me. "Is the baby still sleeping?" she asked, but didn't wait for an answer, adding, "Use the big pot."

I started to say something about the baby, but the words became jumbled in my head. How do I tell her? What do I say? "Mamma, the baby—"

"Don't fret. We're waiting for a wet nurse. I wonder what's keeping her," my mother said.

"But, Mamma, this can't—."

She covered her mouth to stifle a sob. "Not now."

I could almost feel her pain, but all I could do was obey. I put the water into the bottom of the coffee pot and filled the basket, then screwed on the top. Mamma said, "Go get some boughs of rosemary." Mamma picked up a jar of olive oil and carried it to the bedroom along with a sea sponge that Concetta hung near the large *bacinella*—the basin used to bathe the children.

I did everything my mother commanded, but felt I was moving through weeds and couldn't walk without something grasping around my ankles. When Concetta's body had been washed, I hunted high and low for cotton wool and finally found some in a kitchen cabinet. I gave this to my mother and stood in the doorway, watching her place the cotton. I don't think she was aware of me. That dream feeling of being present yet absent at a scene prevailed.

"In all the orifices," she repeated. A litany: "In all the orifices, my dearest friend, my sister." I could see her profile and the little rivers of tears flowing down her cheeks.

"Forgive me the lie," she continued, "telling you it would be all right." She sat down heavily. "All right for whom? Orphaned children, a widowed husband, myself left friendless?"

"Mamma," I whispered. She didn't answer. I said more insistently, "Mamma, listen to me."

She jumped with a start and turned around. "You're white as a ghost. Have some sugared milk and coffee. Were you here the whole time I prepared Concetta?"

"Mamma, the baby—" I couldn't finish speaking, my mind was reconstructing my mother's last embalming steps. I had seen her gently stuff the nostrils, ears, anus, and vagina the same way she stuffed the arms, legs, and body of cotton rag dolls she'd made my sisters last summer. This wasn't a doll. It was a flesh-and-blood human being who had been alive only a short while ago. I couldn't believe my darling aunt and her beautiful baby were dead.

Mamma had washed her hands in between each procedure. With every ablution, like a priest on the altar for Mass, Mamma prayed aloud for the soul of the faithful departed. Then she tied Zu Nino's neckerchief around Zia Concetta's head to keep the chin from dropping after she had wadded up the last of the cotton wool and put it in the dead woman's mouth. I felt as though I were gagging. And now, dressed as a bride, Zia Concetta was lying on the bed, seemingly asleep, where the baby had been born.

"What is it, Angelica?"

She looked at me as I stood with my palms open in supplication, and I knew I didn't need any words.

"Oh, my child, no. No, I beg you don't tell me—why didn't I keep the baby with me?"

"Mamma, I didn't kill the baby. She fell asleep and never woke up."

"Crib death," she said, and then repeated, "crib death. It's my fault. I was so upset last night I forgot to baptize the infant immediately."

I ran and picked up the baby, stiff and serene as any toy doll.

My mother wailed till she had no breath left inside her. Then sobs gushed out of her in torrents. She fell to her knees, rocking the infant to and fro, comforting only herself. "Oh, dear God, did You need the baby too?"

Mamma got up and sat down, still clutching the baby to her bosom. Then she held out the child and told me to baptize the infant in the kitchen sink. "I'll finish dressing Concetta," she said. "Be strong."

I felt my eyes go wide with fright. Why didn't she ask my uncle to do it?

I hesitated, afraid to ask how. Then I took the lifeless bundle and performed the ritual. I tried to push my aunt's brutal hemorrhage from my mind and remember the types of Baptism the priest had taught me. Baptism of water, Baptism of desire, Baptism of blood. I didn't remember all the words of the Sacrament, or what the salt and oil was used for, so I skipped that part, but I made the sign of the cross with my hand over the baby and then poured water over its infant forehead with my trembling hands.

"I baptize you, Concetta," I said. Had I the right? "In the name of the Father," *never will I be a mother*, "and of the Son," *never will I have a son*, "and of the Holy Ghost," *I'll never marry, but be the bride of the Trinity*, "Amen."

I brushed passed Zu Nino, sitting at the table, his face in his hands. "Never wed to become a mother and suffer this pain and lose a child," he said to me as if he'd read my mind.

Better to serve God another way and become a nun, I thought. How could I become a midwife like my mother?

I heard Zu Nino's pitiful plea, "What am I going to do without her?"

At first I was confused, then I understood he meant his wife, not the baby. I wanted to cradle him like the baby I held.

I walked into Concetta's room and, as tenderly as I could, laid the baby next to the woman who in death had assumed an even more youthful face.

I never before realized how precious life was—it took death to instruct me. I promised God I'd try never again to fight with Peppe and to be kinder to that little pest Rina.

"Mamma, can we go home now?" I asked, my lips quivering.

"'Last of all we must die,'" she said. "The words of San Filippo Neri . . ." Her voice trailed off. Then Mamma took my hands in hers and kissed them. "You'll make a fine midwife."

I pulled my hands away from her. "No, I won't. I didn't do anything. You didn't let me help you."

"We must wait till the priest comes to give her Extreme Unction," she said, looking toward my aunt and the baby nestled beside her. "The Last Sacrament." She picked up my hands again and I wrenched them from her.

"Mamma, I don't want to be a midwife. I want to be a nun."

Mamma ushered me into the kitchen. "Ah, you're just saying that today. You'll change your mind. Up until now I've not been convinced that this is for you. But your father is right, you should learn midwifery with me."

I sat down next to Mamma. "I don't want to watch women go through agony only to die at the end of their suffering—"

"You're upset and exaggerating—"

"Mamma! I'm not."

"You are because you're so close to this death, but you know, not everyone dies—"

"I don't want to marry and go through this—" I wanted to say, "Hell."

"We've all wanted to be nuns at one time," Mamma said with the voice of an angel, sweeping hair out of my moist eyes. "This is a decision for the future, and if it ever came to pass—why, there are many nuns who aid the sick or tend unmarried mothers. But I don't think you're cut out for the nunnery."

———

BEFORE THE PRIEST CAME TO give Zia Concetta Extreme Unction, I watched with fascination and horror as my mother plaited three thin braids of my dead aunt's hair. I asked what she was doing. She told me she was making neck circlets, one for Zu Nino, one for Zia Concetta's mother, and one for her.

"What are they for?"

"They are *memento mori*," she said as if I already understood.

Her hands stopped moving. She looked at me and must have seen my still puzzled expression. "Time ravages, leaving in its furious path death and decay. We all die someday, Angelica. This is a reminder of our dearest Concetta and the fact that we will one day join her in the *al di là* —the hereafter, in that other place."

"Why not make four? One for Letizia?" Mamma didn't answer me. I told her I could understand why she wouldn't make them for both my cousins, but why not make one for the eldest daughter who would most remember and miss her mother? Then I added, "And I too would like one."

"No, but I will give you each a snippet. You can put it in a locket or keep it in your missal."

"I don't have a locket."

"I do. It was a wedding gift. You may have it . . ." she said and hesitated a moment before continuing, "as a thank-you for your help tonight and also to serve as a reminder of your own mortality." My mother cried softly. I wanted to put my arms around her and comfort her, but her words had somehow distanced me from the present.

"I'd rather keep it in my missal. Why not give the locket to Letizia?"

"That would be such a lovely gesture, if you're sure you don't want it. It's very beautiful—silver filigree—made in Libia."

I shook my head, thinking, *All the more reason Letizia should have it. I won't need it in a convent.*

When Mamma finished intertwining the hair, she asked me for a candle; when I brought it to her, she cut off the twisted hair at the roots and sealed the ends with hot wax. I looked at the candle and remembered helping my aunt, who was much poorer than we, make candles from rendered animal fat. I never liked the smell of tallow. Our candles were made of beeswax. When Mamma molded candles, which was rare, it was always around Christmas.

I went back to the kitchen with the candle, scissors, and two curled snippets of my dear aunt's hair. I sat at the kitchen table and put my head onto my folded arms, like a rest period at school, and slumbered deeply. Before I awoke, I felt cold and was dreaming of a wind-swept valley with snow flurries dancing all around. Smoke billowed out of a small cabin. I looked out a windowpane and breathed half-moons into the corners. While I scrawled my name on the frosted spot, I saw a deer disappear into hillocks canopied with snow. His tracks vanished, so I knew he was magical. I wondered if he was a unicorn.

The next thing I knew in my dream I was making candles with

Mamma. Sticks were tied with wicks and threaded through tin molds. Mamma melted wax with bay leaves in a big tub, the last batch she colored with the juice of holly berries. I woke up just as she was saying I could ladle the wax into forms that rested suspended between two chairs.

Everything had seemed to be happening so slowly, but when I woke up, I realized it had really been speeding by, like a bird in flight or a squirrel you can chase but can never catch.

I'd fallen asleep with the hair in my hand. Mamma came in the room and I told her I had had a dream. Her face clouded when she saw that I still held the hair. "I hope you didn't dream of hair, because it means treachery."

I shook my head, but felt too tired to tell her about my dream. As it happened, I did tell her the next day—the day of the funeral—while we walked slowly behind a horse-drawn hearse to the cemetery from Zia Concetta's house.

There were four horses the color of pitch, and I was momentarily distracted, wondering where four such black horses had been found. The horses, sheathed with velvet caparison, seemed to know where they were going, for not once did I notice urging with the reins. The hearse itself was draped in crepe, and the elaborate fretwork on the roof reminded me of a country fence. The glass sides and back permitted one to see Zia Concetta's coffin cordoned off with low bronze pipes inside—it was festooned with flowers on top. As the horses clop-clopped along, the wheels of the carriage turned slowly over the hard-packed dirt road. I looked back once or twice and could see our village on the crest of the hill. I never realized the cemetery was so far away. But of course it wasn't the distance—it was the tortoise pace that made it seem so remote.

All of the children in the cortege ahead of the hearse were in double file and wore black mantels with hoods and black stockings. Many huge floral pieces on a flat-bedded cart preceded the hearse, and several men carried wreaths on wooden stands like painters' easels. The weighted part of the corona was supported by the man's neck like a winning horse after a race. Attached to the flowers were purple ribbons with gold lettering that made crinkly noises as they fluttered with the slightest breeze. Following the funerary florals came the priest holding a banner, as if the procession were a happy occasion and he was announcing a celebration.

We walked behind the hearse with all of our relatives, Zu Nino first. Mamma walked next to me and some of the women. The rest of the mourners followed us, with Papà and the men bringing up the rear. *Protectors from what?* I wondered. There were many questions I wanted to put to Mamma but knew they would have to wait. Mostly, I wanted her to confirm what I'd learned about death: that it has no respect for age, that it is the final step in growth, and at the end, if we are fortunate, we will master who we really are and what our life on earth has meant—even what our passing will mean to others, especially our loved ones. My brain prickled with these impatient inquiries. What I dearly needed to know for sure was if I had sought the right path by searching out the meaning of death.

I started speaking to Mamma, who seemed only mildly annoyed when I whispered to her along the beaten path. She didn't tell me to hush up, though, because so many other people were walking arm in arm and talking quietly. Mamma's strong face wore hurt and anxiety and the vestiges of a valiant warrior who'd lost the battle—it was then I determined what I was trying to accomplish with my incidental chatter. I sought to comfort my grief-stricken mother with soothing words, and it mattered not what those words were.

I heard drifts of speech and conversation between older folk. Not all of it was about Zia Concetta, and not all of it was kind. What outraged me was Giuseppina, the chicken thief, accusing my mother of negligence. My angel must have had to do penance for me, because I wanted to step on the old crone's ugly booted foot, and thought seriously of tripping her. But I let go the anger with a deep breath. I even forgave myself for being human.

After the internment, when the priest had blessed the casket and the gravesite, I approached him. Since I'd been asleep when Don Ruggero had given Zia Concetta the Last Rites, I thought he'd be pleased to hear that I'd baptized the baby. Instead, he chastised me, saying, "You baptized a dead baby? The baby was already dead."

"So was Zia Concetta, but you gave her the Last Sacrament."

"That's different. Her soul had not left her body."

"But neither had the baby's."

"Angelica," he said, heaving a sigh.

By the tone of his exasperated voice, I knew the discussion was over. I had done a wrongful deed and there was going to be no further satisfactory explanation as to what I had done wrong. I wanted to scream, "Not fair. Life and you and religion just aren't fair." Instead, I held my tongue because it was Mamma who had told me to do it and she knew better than this priest because her heart was pure. I stalked off after my mother.

When I reached Mamma at the huge black gates, she asked me what I'd said to Don Ruggero. I changed the subject and instead repeated one of the things I'd heard about Zu Nino, which was that he shouldn't have gotten my aunt pregnant because she was too weak from her last miscarriage.

All Mamma said was, "Don't pay attention—it's idle chatter. People always have to talk. Not everyone is as good or kind as your aunt."

I watched in silent fascination as my mother took hold of a clump of grass, rubbed it between her hands, and scattered it as she left the cemetery, saying, "'Man's days are like the grass. He blossoms like the flowers of the field, a wind passes over them and they cease to be—their place knows them no more . . .'"

I knew it was from a psalm, so I asked her which one. Mamma said that the Bible is not just a religious text; it holds many things applicable to life. For me, it was the stories I loved, the language, the poetry, the musicality. I'd never thought of it quite that way before.

We all went to a fountain. Mamma washed her hands with me, hers still sweetened by the grass, yet lemony. Walking through the intricate wrought-iron gates, I turned for a last, silent good-bye. I noticed the plumes on the horses' heads, black as a moonless night. Feathers remained, for the rest of my life, an adornment I detested.

CONSOLO WAS A WORD I heard often over the next several weeks. What best describes it was the care Zia Concetta's neighbors took of the bereaved family. I, my mother told me, was even a big part of it. I didn't sleep over at my uncle's house anymore, but I went often to clean or serve him.

Giuseppina sent over minestrone soup and kept my cousins for a week. Other acquaintances often stopped by with covered dishes, some delectable things, others strange. Neighbors stayed when they brought food. They spent time talking to my uncle, so I assumed that along with the food came succor and kindness.

Don Ruggero always brought fresh eggs from the convent or a bottle of wine made by the nuns. Sometimes he carried a box of pastries in the form of breasts; these were named for Saint Agata and were filled with sugared ricotta. As for the children, oh, how I delighted to watch them open their sweetmeats—a package of gelatines made of pistachio so fragrant to the taste it seemed as if you ate them twice, once in your mouth and once in your brain. His kindness was never overlooked, but I soon discovered he too had a sweet tooth.

If I had children of my own, I would set out dishes of them on all occasions. But the minute I thought of children, I clutched my abdomen in fear. I forced my thoughts to return to my uncle's kind gifts, or was it selfishness wrapped in a generous guise?

The mourning period following my aunt's death lasted forty days. I thought of the forty days following Christ's death when He ascended into heaven and wondered if my dear, sweet aunt had spent time in Purgatory to atone for her sins before making the trek to Eternal Paradise.

Right after my aunt died, Mamma covered all the mirrors in my uncle's house and ours too. My uncle stopped shaving and this made him look old and haggard, like one of the men who stood around the coffee bar after Mass on Sunday. My father didn't shave either.

My beautiful mother stopped arranging her hair. She barely combed it free of snarls. I knew then what a sainted hermit must look like.

My father wore a black shirt for the forty days and then switched to a black armband for a year. Everyone wore black except the children, but if it were up to my mother, even they would have worn it. I heard the adults arguing about it right after my aunt's death. Mamma was for it, but Zu Nino was adamant. "No mourning for the children. They are young for such a little time," he yelled, and then broke down and cried.

He, like a good grieving widower, would wear black for seven years, including an armband. From the time my aunt died I never again heard Zu Nino mention Zia Concetta's name. He would forever call her "that good soul."

CHAPTER XII

Rosalia

THE HERMITAGE

ROSALIA'S GRIEVING WAS MAGNIFIED BY her own loss of the consumptive Giovanna, laid to rest just days after Concetta and her baby. On the return home from Giovanna's burial, Angelica started to bleed. This time it was her menstruation. Though Rosalia had been told on the beach a year ago that Angelica had been menstruating for some time, the tradition had not been fulfilled. So Rosalia slapped her daughter as custom warranted, the joy cut short remembering the slap she'd given Angelica the day of her accident.

Nino had given Rosalia some of Concetta's silk-wrapped pots. Unpacking them, she thought of Concetta's absence. Rosalia touched the copper cauldron and kettle. Strange, she'd always admired Concetta's dishes. But now, hanging on Rosalia's kitchen wall, with others still boxed, "I don't want them at all," she said out loud with an urge to smash and break each and every one of them. She bit her bottom lip until it bled, sat down, and put her face in her hands and cried.

On February 2, the feast of Candlemas, Rosalia felt a quickening inside herself. She changed her black dress for gray and began to uncover the mirrors swathed in black, but thought better of it and decided to let them stay that way till after Lent. Something made her think of the fortune-telling Gina who had been right after all about Rosalia's last pregnancy.

Now Rosalia was glad she'd have the care of yet another infant to help her get over the loss of Giovanna and of her dearest Concetta. How Concetta had yearned for a boy. Now Rosalia herself prayed for a boy.

She decided to attend Mass and dedicate her child as Mary had done when she presented Jesus in the Temple. Only Rosalia's was still in the womb.

She called out for Angelica several times. Finally, she sent Rina, who ran helter-skelter all over the secluded property to find her elder sister.

When Rina returned without Angelica, Rosalia said they'd leave without her. Exasperated and running short of time, she went upstairs to finish dressing. She hadn't primped or fussed with her hair in such a long time that she'd almost forgotten how long it took, or how many pins were needed to make her chignon.

Soft crying sounds made her stop and listen. The one place Rosalia and Rina hadn't looked for Angelica was in her own room.

She heard Angelica's voice saying, "For love of You, sweet Jesus, and you, Blessed Mary, have I done this."

Rosalia was about to say, "You can pray in church. Now get ready," as she pushed open the door. There, standing in front of the dresser mirror was Angelica, shorn of her beautiful waist-length locks, the chestnut hair circling her bare feet, a halo in reverse.

Rosalia saw Angelica mugging in the mirror, first a sorrowful look, then a smile. As shock dissipated, Rosalia's anger surged to 9.999—the mark used on pure gold she'd read about in the *Corriere della Sicilia*.

Unable to contain her emotions any longer, the stress finally reaching the boiling point, she burst out, "Have you lost all your senses? *Sei pazza?* Look what you've done!"

Angelica turned to face her mother. "I know, but, Mamma—"

Rosalia felt the blood in her face. She looked in the mirror—a clown, her cheeks smeared the color of pomegranate juice. Rage enveloped her, and she fought for control.

"Why? Why have you committed this disgraceful act? And with my scissors?"

"Vanity and long, beautiful hair will not get me into Paradise," Angelica said, placing the scissors on the dresser, pushing her now shoulder-length tresses in back of her ears.

"Better to cut out your mother's heart than do this. *Disgraziata!*"

Rosalia's thoughts swirled in a wash of anxiety. The shame attached to a girl who had lost her maidenhead, if it were to be made public—even accidentally like Angelica's. Accidents happen, but now this . . . this haircut like a city strumpet, but oh, how saintly a one!

Rosalia bent down to pick up a ringlet and kissed it. Her sorrow evaporated, and she almost laughed out loud as she said, "I could speed up your trip and boot you heavenward with the tip of my foot. How would that suit you, *santa*?" That gave Angelica pause, thought Rosalia, and not waiting for an answer said, "You're just a mite and much too young to think about sainthood."

"Mamma, I'm practically a grown woman."

"Really, now? Well, woman, why don't you meditate on this little problem: tell me how in the name of God, all the choirs of angels, and saints am I going to take you out in public now? You look like a scarecrow."

"I'll build a hermitage of stones in the garden and live on scraps of food."

"Not on my land, you won't. And just what scraps had you in mind? *Cannoli* perhaps? Or almond cookies? You want to be a hermit in rags? Well then, my little saint, take off your pretty velvet dress." Rosalia scooped up the tresses around her daughter's feet and placed them on the dresser. She put her hands on her hips. "Do it, I said. Now."

Angelica removed the dress and stood rubbing her arms.

"Off with the petticoat."

"But, Mamma—" Angelica protested.

"No buts or ands. Saints don't argue. Off with it."

Angelica stood in chemise and bloomers. "How can I go out like this? You don't mean it?"

Rosalia pointed to her and said, "Oh, but I do, Blessed Angelica, ex-daughter of Rosalia Gennaro and Nicola Domenico, I most assuredly do. And you may keep the underclothes on. Now go kiss your family and leave to be a beggar."

With that, Rosalia turned on her heels and walked to her own room where she finished dressing. She called to Peppe, Rina, and Nunziata, who soon appeared. Dressed and readied, holding little Beatrice by the hand, flanked by her other two girls and Peppe behind, she paraded into Angelica's room once more.

"What? You're still here? Do you need a cup or bowl to collect alms? You have my permission to take one."

Angelica sat on the bed, her feet dangling. "Mamma, I have no shoes on."

"I'm not blind like Santa Lucia. I see you're barefoot."

Angelica pointed to her feet. "But, Mamma, I need something on my feet."

"Really? By whose say so? Not mine. Plenty of saints went about shoeless. Shall I name them? You're the one trying out for sainthood like a stage player. Act the part, little miss."

"Mamma, please—"

"Angelica, I'm locking the gates just as soon as you are on the outside of them. The family you relinquish as a saint is going to church without you. And afterward, I'm buying arancini and zuppli, your favorite rice specialties. I'm so sorry you'll be missing out, but one must sacrifice to attain Paradise. Now get moving." Rosalia marched Angelica out of her room and pointed in the direction of the stairs. "Write us, won't you?"

Angelica stood rooted on the landing. "At least let me stay on my terrace."

Rosalia turned toward Rina and in a loud voice for the benefit of all, but meant for one in particular, said, "Get Mamma's purse, Rina. I don't want to forget the money for ice-cream cones this afternoon."

"Mamma," said Rina, "are you really going to lock Angelica out?"

"No," she whispered, "but I don't want her opening her own barber shop ever again."

CHAPTER XIII

Angelica

THE SECRET PLACE

FOR AS GROWN UP AS I pretended to be, I was excited when the last day of Carnevale finally arrived. In Villaggio Pace, it was always a huge celebration, especially for the children. The lanes and thoroughfares were strewn with colorful paper *coriandoli* and confetti all the way to the piazza. On the afternoon of *martedì grasso*, the day before Ash Wednesday, Peppe decided to dress like one of the Garibaldini red shirts. Mamma had to sew a shirt from a cloth she had reserved for the kitchen table. So she extracted a promise that he would wear it often. Children dressed in all sorts of homemade costumes. Girls were often dressed as fairy godmothers carrying magic wands or as Pulcinella. Mamma had made over my confirmation dress, letting out seams, adding ruffles and false hems so that it fit again. I sauntered into the kitchen in my costume and a long veil that Mamma had also made to cover my shortened hair.

Peppe said, "You look like a bride."

"A bride," I snapped. "I'm a novice! I'll never marry." My mother looked at me as if I'd grown another head. I continued, "I'm going to be a nun, you foolish boy." How could he mistake my costume? Would anybody else? I hoped not.

SIX WEEKS LATER, AFTER CARNIVAL season and the Lenten period were over, we uncovered every saint's image and statue in the house. After we folded some black and purple cloths, we were free for the day. Peppe decided to take me to his secret place. He'd made the mistake of telling me about it and now all I did was pester him till I got my way. We hiked deep into a ravine. From there we mounted a ledge at the entrance to a cave. Along the way, Peppe found a dead dog putrefying among blackberry thorns. I wanted to bury it, but we were ill equipped. Our outing was meant for picking enough berries for Mamma to make jam and a *crostata*. So we covered the dog's yellow matted fur with leaves and branches, then Peppe seemed to consecrate the ground as if the place were a sacred burial. He crossed himself and bent his head in silent prayer. "Must have been mistakenly shot by a hunter."

I pinched my nose shut and ran ahead through the brambles, wild rosemary, and huge bushes of capers budding white with tiny flowers. When I stopped for Peppe near a coppice of bamboo, my head held a vision of my dead Pupa gasping her last breath and the cart-shaft frame I'd built to carry her jennet.

Peppe caught up to me and said, "I'll lead. You follow or else you'll get lost."

The day was hot, as were all late-spring days in Sicily. The scorching sun gave no surcease to the pounding heat that bounced off fallen scrub pines, reverberated from pitted black lava rocks.

As we started to climb, my long skirt was a hindrance. I bent and pulled the back hem up through my legs and tucked it in the waist of my bloomers. My pony legs, as Peppe called them, were covered by white lisle stockings held up by garters, and as I moved they snagged. "Wait up. Mamma will be so angry with me, Peppe, if I ruin my stockings."

Peppe turned around. "Well then?"

I sat down and unhitched my garters and stockings. I stuffed them in the pocket of my pinafore apron. Sudden cramps attacked the lower part of my belly and my right side. A warm, sticky feeling between my legs made me feel as if my insides were leaking out. Could I offer up this pain like a saint? Again the monthly curse women always talk about arrived on time with cramping. Were these spasms normal? If only I could ask Peppe.

"Come on, slow poke," Peppe urged.

In front of us was a ledge that reached past a cave entrance hidden by thick foliage and brush. Peppe must have seen the look of surprise on my face when he pushed the scrub and undergrowth away. The cavern smelled musty. Toward the back there were bones. I figured they were human, but Peppe didn't want to scare me so he said they probably were deer. He couldn't say a dog's because they were too big.

"Where are the antlers?" I asked, testing him. "Deer shed their horns once a year, don't you know?"

There were charred logs where fire upon fire had been made, and smooth rocks nearby where people had sat. There were level areas where makeshift beds of pine needles had been.

"They look like human bones to me."

"They're not."

"Mamma told me the story of Santa Rosalia. Her bones were found in a grotto like this. She had saved Palermo from the bubonic plague so they made her their patron saint. If we go there I'll make a pilgrimage to her sanctuary." *Oh, the incessant pain. Will it ever stop?* I clutched my stomach and wished I had a cachet to take to stop the ache. "Mamma says the saint is laden with the gold that people leave to thank her for working miracles."

"How'd she die?"

I felt a little woozy in the head and sat down on a rock. I would have to stuff something in my underwear in case the bleeding didn't stop or got worse. "She was a virgin. What exactly is a virgin, Peppe?"

Peppe sputtered, "Well, it's sort of . . . what it is, I think, is . . . someone pure, clean, like Mary, never touched by a man. But Mary's different—because virgins don't usually marry or have children. Virgin means a nun." His face was red as a cardinal's robe.

I finally got why they called them cardinals, named after fancy birds. I wondered if that wasn't some sort of heresy.

"Go on with the story," he pleaded. He walked over and sat opposite me, toying with a stick and scratching in the dirt.

I'd lost the thread and was stalled for a minute before I went on. "You see, Santa Rosalia went to live as a hermit maybe in the 1100s. They didn't discover her bones till the 1600s."

"All those years? Where?"

"Oh, near Palermo, but that's not where she went first." I picked up a stick and drew crossed bones and a skull.

"Where did she go?"

"Mount Coschina near Bivona. She wrote on the grotto walls," I said, pointing.

"Wrote?"

"In her own hand. In Latin."

"Are you sure?"

"'I, Rosalia, daughter of Sinibald, Lord of Quisquina and Rosae, decided to live in this cave for the love of my Lord Jesus Christ.'"

"Mamma told you that?"

"Maybe it was old Ding-don."

"You mean Ruggero?"

"Who else? Anyway, later the saint lived in the grotto of Monte Pellegrino where she died and these"—I pointed up at the stalactites—"covered her body."

"Really?" he asked and scratched his head.

"Mamma said the saint wouldn't surrender her virginity. Did that make her brave or a coward?"

CHAPTER XIV

Angelica

ANGEL ON MY SHOULDER

MY FOURTEENTH BIRTHDAY CAME AND went, almost like spring itself slipping by without a fuss. On a day during Easter season, a day that felt fat and oppressive, like summer, my short ringlets, bathed in sweat, outlined the day as well as my face. The warm wind from Africa, *lo scirocco*, blew across the northeastern coast of Sicily carrying sand. It seemed the rains would never fall.

I washed and dried and changed all the plates in the house. I cleaned out every scrap of bread, pasta, yeast, rice, and cookies like Mamma told me. She was the only woman of our acquaintance who did this every year, and she was scrupulous about it. I gave most of the foodstuffs to our neighbor Giuseppina, and everything else went to feed the animals. Our dogs loved the bread and pasta, which I cooked enough of to feed a regiment of Garibaldi. There was never a time that Papà didn't keep dogs, and I loved them. He said I spoiled them, but they too were creatures of God, and didn't Saint Francis of Assisi adore them? The rest of the food I burned outside.

When I'd put out the fire, I retied my boots and raised my skirt and apron so I could run free. If only I were allowed to wear pants like Peppe. *Lucky Peppe,* I thought. He and Papà were driving Mamma and the girls to Taormina for a week's vacation. Mamma was stout with a protruding belly leftover from a miscarriage. She needed the rest. The men of our house would be home late afternoon and I'd already prepared the dinner for them. I was bored beyond description. After I finished the rest of my house chores, I climbed the wooden rungs of the ladder in the barn up to the loft, stood and dove into the hay, and rolled around like I used to when I was a small tot. It was childish, but I felt like doing something silly and carefree.

Enough of this, I thought as I tugged off my skirt and blouse. I yanked off my petticoat and pranced around in my knickers and camisole. Unhampered and freely undressed, I piled hay higher and higher until it reached taller than my head. I climbed yet another ladder leaning against the wall to gain the elevation I desired. I turned and, like a cat, waited, poised and ready to pounce. Something tapped my shoulder. I recognized it as an angelic touch. I was being warned of danger, but somehow I also felt protected.

The hair on my arm bristled, and I had the odd sensation that I was being watched. I sprang forward, leaping off the ladder, flying through the air. I usually squealed with joy, the way I do that always annoys Peppe. But the cry I now uttered was not of glee and was cut short in my throat when I came up for air. How could there be anyone in the mansard of our barn? I shook off the feeling that danger lurked because it seemed impossible.

Abruptly I realized how misguided I was. I started to scream when a man clamped my mouth shut with his dirty hand. He whirled me around, and I stared into the eyes of a stranger whose clothes were ripped and tattered, filthy and rank. He reeked of bodily odors, like some of Papà's workers. Worse, actually. The look in his eyes was evil, the reflection of his soul blemished with the mark of Cain.

My eyes felt like they'd stretched into saucers and I struggled to be free of his grasp.

"If you promise not to scream I'll let you go," the man said. He handed me my clothes, his hand grazing my breasts. I flinched. "You're Angelica. I was at your baptism."

I thought this was an outright lie, but I nodded my head in agreement to keep my mouth stitched. I was embarrassed to dress in front of him, but more so to stay in the state of undress, so I turned my back and pulled on my things as fast as my quavering hands allowed.

"I'm hungry," he said while I was still buttoning my blouse. "Can you give me something to eat and drink?"

My mind raced with fear, the Beatitudes, Bible sayings, and the Gospels, until somehow my brain slowed so the fear quelled and words rushed in, filling up all the spaces with what I was supposed to do in Christian kindness. *For I was an hungred, and ye gave me no meat: I was thirsty, and ye gave me no drink. . . . Verily I say unto you, Inasmuch as ye did it not to one of the least of these, ye did it not to me.*

I thought about Christ's words, knew in my heart it was the right thing to do, but I was frightened all the same.

"I won't stay here long, if you feed me," he continued. "Just enough time to rest my leg. See, it's been hurt." He showed me a bloody leg. The wound had festered and oozed not only blood but also pus.

I was a stranger, and ye took me not in; naked, and ye clothed me not; sick, or in prison, and ye visited me not.

"It needs cleaning," I said, pointing to the open gash.

"What do you know about it?"

"My mother's a mid—I know a bad sore when I see one."

"Can you dress it?"

I answered yes and promised to bring lye soap, water, and a cloth to clean and bandage it.

"Remember," he cautioned as I climbed down the ladder, "say nothing about me."

He looked vaguely familiar. I tried to imagine where I'd seen him. In the piazza? Shearing sheep? Gathering olives? Harvesting the almonds on my father's land?

"I'll be back as soon as I can." I made a cross over my heart.

His lips curled back, a sneer more than a smile. It revolted me. He was almost toothless, and the few teeth he possessed were dark like the shell coverings of pine nuts.

⁂

RETRIEVING THE ARTICLES I NEEDED was a more arduous task than I thought it would be. I assembled all the materials, a bowl of water into which I put soap and a cloth, and then prepared a linen napkin with some bread and cheese. I would have taken a persimmon, but they squashed so easily. I took a bottle of raffia-wrapped wine with a handle and slipped it onto my wrist. It was heavier than I'd imagined. I slipped it off.

I looked for a kitchen knife to cut cheese, but instead took down Papà's bone-handled hunting knife. *What if the man is a dangerous criminal? Why am I thinking that?* I had said I wouldn't tell anybody. That was silly of me. But I hadn't promised. I'd crossed my heart only to hurry. Maybe I should alert someone? Hadn't Mamma always said to be wary and careful of strangers? But my folks wouldn't be back for Lord knows how long. I snatched hold of Rina's *quaderno* for writing essays and ripped out a piece of lined paper. I printed in my neatest hand that a man was in the barn. I knew when I returned to the barn, the man's hunger would be satiated and it was then I heard Peppe's voice in my head, saying a virgin was never touched by a man. Was I to fulfill this stranger's next hunger? His hand brushing against me I felt was not accidental. I thought of brave Santa Rosalia running away to save her virginity. But was I a virgin? I had now been touched. Dear God! With the clarity of scorching sunlight, I realized I was no longer a virgin, and never again could be considered immaculate and intact. What did it matter then if I were to be ravished by this hungry monster? Maybe I would die attempting to avoid his grasp and gain eternal life with Santa Rosalia.

I put the knife in my skirt's left pocket and retied my apron over the skirt. I took hold of the things I'd gathered and marched toward the barn. The hilt of the knife rested against my thigh, keeping time with each step.

The wine bottle dangled from my right wrist, the knotted napkin from my left, leaving my hands free to carry the bowl. Walking toward the barn, my mind played out a scene of what-if.

What if before I'd finished writing the note, Peppe had come into the kitchen looking for a small wooden cask? I handed him the note. He laughed. "Cat got your tongue?" His laugh changed when he read my script, looked at me with all seriousness, and asked me to describe the man. Peppe asked if the man wore a beret or a bandolier. Did he carry a *lupara*? Where was his horse? Peppe asked so many questions that he frightened me. I still didn't understand what he was getting at until he asked, "Is the man wearing a *scapolare*? Did you see anything else in the barn to make you think there's someone with him? Could he be one of the men who ran you and Papà off the road at the cliff?"

I hesitated, taking some time before answering. I closed my eyes to be sure. The blindness made me see within and I relived the crash. I opened my eyes and, scrutinizing my brother, said, "Right before Papà hollered and I jumped, I saw four riders approach. No, there were five. One of them had on a brown scratchy shirt made of sacking material like the man in the barn. He also had a beard like him."

"A beard can be grown or shaved. Is he one of the men, Angelica? Think."

As I thought, my mind's eye watched my brother take the *lupara* from its place above the lintel of the kitchen door.

"One of the men carried his *lupara* in a sheath. It was the man in the barn," I said.

Peppe loaded the rifle with two shells he took from a small wooden chest that rested on the *piattaio.*

As we stepped from the kitchen, a horse and rider came down from the gate along the path that led to the house.

"It's Papà," I cried.

We told my father about the man in the barn. I watched Papà take the *lupara* from Peppe's hand and put it aside. He told me he would go back to the barn himself and minister to the man. "There's no need for a gun," Papà said.

The game of what-if that my head had played helped me see clearly. As I walked toward the barn, I shifted the bowl to my right hand and with my left instinctively sought the knife beneath my apron. If he came at me, would I stick him and be branded not only as a non-virgin but also as a murderess?

I nudged the door with my shoulder to open it. It took a few seconds for my eyes to adjust from the bright daylight outside to the dusky inside. Something rustled the hay in the loft and a sprinkling fell through the cracks. I called for him to come down, but he said he needed more rest for his leg and that I should come up.

I struggled with the necessities he'd sent me for, juggling them up the ladder. When I reached the top, I set down the bundles.

He jerked my arm, pulling me to a kneeling position. "Tend my cut," he said. I felt revulsion as I tore his pant leg to expose the entire putrid laceration.

When I'd washed and bandaged his leg the best I could with the linen napkin, I started creeping backward. He swigged the wine and lunged for me. Why, if I knew this was going to happen, did I return to the barn unaided? Was I testing my angel, or myself? I should have brought the dogs that Peppe had penned in before leaving.

As his strong hands went around my neck, I knew I didn't want to die here and now. My brain blanked like a wall suddenly aflame with splattering light. Shadows played upon it, becoming a myriad of life and death images. Salvation in the Lord was guaranteed me if—but I must move. I gasped for air as his hands loosened. He threw me down, trying to pin my flailing arms, my hands scratching his face, yanking his beard. I swished my head back and forth. He thrust his mouth close enough to almost cover mine so I bit his disgusting nose hard and he reared off me slightly and backhanded me.

He started to unfasten his pants—time enough for me to reach, left-handed, with sure swiftness as though it were my right, and snatch the hilt of the knife, forcing the point upward without taking it from my pocket. He ripped at my undergarments as I drove the knife tip into the soft flesh of his thigh, the heel of my hand pushing with determination. He squealed like a pig, raised his body, and I rolled out from under him. He lunged for me as I reached the stairs and I sidestepped, seeing my way blocked. Some unseen force shoved me out of the way and, leaping like a stag, I ran for the open trap door and grabbed hold of the rope at the other side of the loft. I swung over the opening, letting go, dropping down into a pile of hay I knew awaited me at the bottom. I ran screaming from the barn, thanking God for saving me, and for allowing me to have missed stabbing him in his liver.

I ran toward the house and there were Peppe and Papà coming back from leaving Mamma and the girls at Taormina. I told them what happened. Papà stalked off to the barn. Peppe, shocked I'd used a knife on someone, stayed a moment to hear about the shove that came from my angel.

Then Peppe ran after Papà, and I followed.

I peeked through a slat opening in the barn. Loathing and rage filled my papà's eyes. I saw the muscles in his neck jerk from tension and the veins in his temples rise. I'd never seen such controlled anger before, but from then on I was sure my papà loved me more than his own life. I could see he wanted to kill the man. Papà held a handgun on the outlaw—kept it trained on him the whole time my brother tended the wound I'd inflicted. Maybe he wanted the man to react so he could shoot him, but something held Papà's hand in check, frozen, his thumb cocked on the hammer, his pointing finger on the trigger. I felt it. Maybe my angel was still on the lookout for us. So much for my daydream of Peppe using a rifle.

Then they sent him packing. My father threatened to kill him if he came near any of us or our property ever again. My father's usually soft voice, iron hard, poured through the air, the way God must have sounded to Moses; chills echoed through my core. I heard Papà say he wouldn't tell the authorities. We minded our own business.

With the man out of earshot, Papà said to Peppe, "He'll not retaliate. He was glad to have gotten off with his life and knows I keep my word."

I'm ashamed to say when we were back in the house afterward, I eavesdropped on Papà and Peppe again. But what could I do? If I didn't, I'd never be able to put the name Ciccio with the face I would carry with me all the days of my life. Peppe was getting as closemouthed as Papà. Men's matters. So I listened at the door as Papà confided that Ciccio was an outlaw and one of the men who had driven us off the road. But why didn't my father consult with me as to this Ciccio's identity? I knew why and it ruffled my feathers. Because I was a female. I felt like bursting in on their little eye-to-eye and telling them, but thought better of it.

Papà poured tobacco onto a paper, licked the seam, rolled and wet the whole cigarette, first one end and then the other. He struck a match, the smell of sulphur still in the air. Peppe said, "Did Ciccio know you'd crashed the cart?"

"He did, but couldn't help us because he was on a mission, riding with men of *la cosa nostra*."

Papà had heard from the itinerant worker Gaetano that Ciccio had now come upon hard times and wanted to start a new life someplace near Palermo. I heard my papà say that if Ciccio hadn't accosted me, he would've given him money and work again, like he'd done before. This piece of information fit the puzzle of who Ciccio was—the same corrupt man Mamma had told me my father had helped in the past.

From a distance I watched my father spit on the floor, making a cross, as if the man were as good as dead. I read my father's lips saying, "*Disonorato*."

When Mamma and the girls returned from the vacation, I told Rina every detail of what happened in the barn, warning her to beware of ever being alone with a strange man. Mamma looked haggard, deep opaque wells the color of charcoal dust beneath her eyes. Maybe the time at the beach had been too much for her. Rina wasn't always as helpful as me, this I knew for sure.

CHAPTER XV

Rosalia

DELIVERANCE

THE FOLLOWING YEAR ROSALIA HAD recuperated from the miscarriage and was now well advanced in another *dolce attesa.* The Ides of March had started out with spring promise. Rosalia went with Peppe to prune and cut in the lemon grove. By late morning a front of low pressure arrived, bringing with it warlike winds that lashed about, tearing fragile lemon blossoms off the trees in the grove. The littered earth, blanketed white, seemed to Rosalia like a wintry field in another time, another place. The heady perfume made her reel. She thought of how she'd given birth to Angelica in the grove. Alone. She'd been so much younger.

Now, again, she was heavy with child, and her brusque movements had brought on pressure pangs. She knew this signaled the beginning of labor, but the baby was early. Why had she moved so quickly while cutting branches and stacking dead brush and twigs? She, above all women, skilled at parturition, knew the consequences. At the first alarm, she had sent Peppe for help. The grove was a kilometer away from the house.

Nicola had gone to Messina to barter. Her dear sister-in-law Concetta was kilometers away, cold in her grave. Why, Rosalia asked herself, had she sent Peppe? Now, isolated, without him, abruptly she felt old. But how could she have exposed him to the reality of birth? How could she have coped afterward seeing the look in his eyes that would forever shame her if he'd seen her nakedness? Her son was no longer a child, but a man.

❧

BEFORE ROSALIA HAD SENT PEPPE for aid, she sat under a denuded grape arbor and rested her head on a speckled travertine table. The air weighed on her chest. Air she had breathed in a different season, though with similar mass, during last season's lemon harvest. Even the air abounded. Too much. Too rich. Too heavy. Rosalia's breathing increased to an almost pant.

The harvest was over except for some late-blooming fruit. She watched Peppe gather the last of the lemons into a huge braided basket. He hoisted it onto his shoulder and carried it to where she sat, her breathing now restored.

She stood, rubbed her back, and stretched; then took to weighing the rough, thick-skinned, lumpy lemons. These were less juicy than the smooth-skinned lemons, but were in demand as well for making liquor and citron. She separated the lemons into two cone-shaped baskets, woven for heft by women from Siracusa.

"Even the leftovers are a fabulous yield, eh, Mamma?" Peppe said, pride in his voice.

"Your father will be pleased," she said, her thoughts elsewhere. Seeing the baskets had thrust her memory back in time to Siracusa when she was a bride on her honeymoon with Nicola. There they had visited the Greek ruins where she had called Nicola's name with her hand cupped against the cave wall, and where the echo reverberated for the ear of Dionysus way on high. Then the honeymooners left the coolness of the inner chamber of the cave to walk beneath the pounding, merciless sun and where heat rose from the dusty lanes on a day with air abundantly thick as this one.

❧

ABUNDANCE, SHE THOUGHT. IN SICILY it means many things.

Her heart lightened as Angelica came galloping into sight on Peppe's horse straight through a field of bergamot trees. The small pear-shaped sour oranges would bloom soon and assistance would come to her after all. Like her mother before her, Rosalia had prayed for help, and here in front of her was solace, light, and comfort. Beneath her heart, she carried and was about to bring forth yet another daughter. She knew this because Angelica had told her. Rosalia had miscarried so many times and was fearful. Still, she felt sure God knew what He was doing even if she didn't understand His divine plan, or this late pregnancy. At little Giovanna's burial Rosalia had said, "*Uomo propone ma Dio dispone.*" Man proposes, but God disposes.

Alone no longer, nor abandoned, Rosalia knelt in the grove and, about to face her ordeal, she uplifted her hands toward heaven. "Almighty Lord, I call upon You in this hour of need."

"Mamma, pray later, come on," Angelica said.

"When I was delivering you, I consecrated you to God to battle against the enemy Satan, as His archangel did, all the days of—" A stabbing pain that took her breath smote Rosalia.

She sat back against a tree while Angelica chose a spot nearby and wielded a spade like a scepter striking the earth several times. The intervals between the constrictive pains grew shorter.

Rosalia's eyes followed Angelica's every movement. When the girl had finished loosening the earth, dirtying her hands, she knelt and scooped out an oval large enough to catch the infant. She crossed some meters to a rain barrel, and with each ablution murmured her mother's prayer, "Do not forsake me—the Lord is One, the Lord is my strength."

Rosalia watched her daughter twist her ankle on a stone, ignore it, and hobble back to the depressed spot she'd dug.

"Angelica, your ankle."

"Mamma, hush. I need to position you."

Rosalia motioned toward the earth. "It looks horribly like a shallow grave, doesn't it?"

"Mamma, be quiet. Save your strength. Let's think only of delivering this baby."

Angelica helped her mother remove her petticoat and undergarments, tossing them into the thrashed-out hollow near the tree.

"*Grazie,*" Rosalia said, and ripped off her own apron and threw it in with the other clothing. Then Angelica tamped the wadding, testing for softness, cushioning the cavity.

Sharp contractions buckled Rosalia to her knees. After a ragged sweep of seconds, the pain subsided to a dull ache. She nestled herself on top of the earthen cavity so that the depression was protected with the small of her back. Dark clouds clotted overhead. Lightning crackled and rent the sky in jagged white clefts. Pain again gripped Rosalia until her howl nearly drowned the thunder.

"Go ahead and scream, Mamma. No one's here but me." Angelica knelt on the ground by her mother's left side.

Rain slashed Rosalia's face and naked legs. Shivering, she felt rain turn to hail that pelted her at first, then raked her with cold.

"Mamma, bend your knees."

"*Ayii*," Rosalia wailed.

"Come on, Mamma, a little longer. You've done this so many times before—"

"Let me live to usher in this life—" The wet between her legs was warm and Rosalia felt the head of her newest daughter crowning.

"Remember Silvana, Mamma? Squat."

Rosalia held to the trunk for balance. She sucked in short gulps of air. "Push, Mamma."

Rosalia gripped the tree harder, this time interlocking her fingers. Her hands pulled forward while her feet pushed backward. And, as women have done since time immemorial, she wept and laughed, thrust and urged, forced, goaded, and coaxed the infant out of her.

CHAPTER XVI

Angelica

THE FEASTS OF ALL SOULS AND ALL SAINTS

MAMMA GAVE ME THE HONOR of naming the baby. I called the frail child Caterina Flaminia. Caterina, in honor of the great stigmatic saint because the baby was born with strawberry birthmarks on the tops of her feet, on her palms, and on her side. It was my first realization that no matter how much one desires sainthood, the Lord culls His saints. I prayed the marks would remain just skin blemishes and that she would not be a stigmatic because they suffered so much on earth. Soon enough the marks faded slightly. The baby's first name got dropped along with them after her baptism, three months after she was born. From then on, we called her Flaminia. My sister Rina was glad because her full name was Caterina Maria.

Languid summer days drifted slowly into fall. The baby gained weight and strength, so we decided to take her with us on an autumn day when spirits hover in the air. We went to the cemetery outside of the village the day before All Saints to avoid the crush of people on the Day of the Dead, which followed it. My father's mother, *la nonna*, and Zia Concetta were buried there. Mamma brought chrysanthemums, bigger than oranges, to all the tombs. She always laid a stone on them. She dusted, then scrubbed the lettering inscribed on my grandmother's headstone, which was covered with lichen and moss. I watched her tend to her chores. I weeded the beds of earth, some of which had sunken in, most of which were bumpy and uneven.

While Mamma cleaned she told me the story of her father, Giuseppe Croce, who was buried in Palermo. I thought it odd that everyone had called him by his middle name, Cross.

Mamma's voice had a faraway quality, almost as if she were speaking like someone in a dream. "Don Croce, my father, was a religious man, almost a fanatic—sometimes I think you take after him, Angelica. We had a chapel in our home and a priest came to say Mass every day."

Her voice took me back to her youth. I loved to hear her telling tales, so I stopped weeding and sat down, my knees bent and drawn to my chest. Mamma handed me a copper vase, green with weathering, and I knew I'd have to wait for more of the story.

"Scrub the outside with sand and a little of this," she said, giving me a small tin of Sidol to help remove the oxidation. I wondered how much copper color would return. But when I'd finished it was almost like new.

"Rina," Mamma called, "bring some water for the flowers. Here, fetch it in this vase." Mamma handed Rina the shiny vase.

"How old is the vase?" I asked.

"That was a wedding present from someone my mother told me gave the evil eye. It's been in this cemetery as long as I've been married. Gypsies made it. They're good at manufacturing pots and that sort of thing. The kettle and the cauldron at home were made by them."

"Papà says they rob and steal babies," I said.

"Some, but not all. Most are approachable, but watch out for your gold; they're clever. Most don't have to steal, but they'll swindle you."

"There's a caravan of painted wagons on the way to the sacristy I see for months at a stretch and then they disappear," I mused, thinking of a swarthy youth I'd seen, naked to the waist, bathing in front of a tub of water I knew to be frigid. A bird of passage.

"They go north in spring and summer and return in fall and winter. This year it's going to be cold. Look," she said, her hand pointing toward Etna, "that boiler pot's already snow-topped."

"Papà says it's 3,300 meters high," I said.

"Mmm. Have you ever heard the Gypsies sing?" Mamma sighed and rubbed her back with both hands.

"They make beautiful music. The other evening after Vespers I saw them dance around a campfire." Wild, majestic creatures celebrating their own kind of "all hallow mass."

"They've just returned, then." She stretched.

"They have blue-black hair and almond-shaped eyes. You could be a Gypsy, Mamma."

"When I was young, your papà said my hair was like raven's wings. What about your high cheeks and coffee color eyes? Are you a Gypsy too?"

The saucy wind picked up and hair blew in my eyes. I readjusted it with pins, thinking I'd distracted her with this talk of Gypsies. To get her back on track I said, "You were telling me of Nonno Croce."

"Your grandfather. Though I respected him in all that he said, I feared him more than most. My brother Ruggero called him a Prussian general behind his back. My father called me his sweetest child. I used to think it was because I ate sugar, but later learned it was because I never disobeyed him."

"What else?" I asked and nodded to Rina who had returned with the water.

"From the chapel downstairs, you could enter the vestibule of our house. And there was a groove in the large banister where he slid down coins to the beggars who came on Sunday and cried out, 'God bless you, Don Croce. Your goodness will be rewarded in heaven.'"

Rina was about to sit with us, but Mamma told her to supervise the others and off she went.

"And then?" I said.

"Oh, he did other things for the poor. All of our discarded clothes were sent to an orphanage. And he used to visit the sick in the hospital once a week. I told you about the priest coming to celebrate Mass every day in the chapel. Anyone was welcome to attend right off the road. On hot summer afternoons, he had servants set out a table of refreshments for transients and pilgrims." She paused for a second as if to remind herself of something. "And he himself recited the Rosary each and every night . . . on his knees." Mamma rubbed her arms briskly. "In winter, humidity seeped into bones. I'd cover his shoulders with a woolen shawl. I wonder what ever happened to it . . ."

"Mamma, please don't stop."

She looked toward the sea. "After Peppe arrived, I miscarried four times, and about the time I knew I was carrying an angel—you—my father decided to build a church in thanksgiving for this blessed grace. He wanted to dedicate it to Mary, *Stella Mattutina.*"

"The Morning Star, Star of the Sea, patroness of sailors, right, Mamma?"

She nodded. "*Scirocco,*" she murmured, as if I'd never heard the name before, and then proceeded to explain what everybody knows. "The wind that blows across North Africa was constant for a week. The foundation of the church my father was constructing did not set. Did not set," she repeated as if talking to a spirit. "He had a booming voice"—her words getting louder with each phrase—"and when he climbed the scaffold to christen the church"—here she stood up, her right hand lifted high toward the sky—"he raised the crucifix triumphantly and called out loudly, his voice resounding across the open fields. He faltered and the scaffolding crumbled, the cross piercing his temple."

"Oh, my God, Mamma, I'm so sorry. I didn't know." I listened carefully as her heart-sore story poured forth, a family wellspring that I felt succored and sustained her. I was grateful for this, although I felt like an outlander, unfamiliar with the soil and topography of her youth.

"All joys are reflected by sorrow," she said once again in her natural voice.

No wonder she'd never spoken of it. Thoughts of my accident melded with thoughts of my grandfather's. I wanted to tell her the things that plagued me—the insurmountable desire for children that had grown inside me over time and the fear attached to having them. Did I really want the convent, or was that my idea of "paradise on earth" because I wouldn't have to suffer the pains of giving birth or losing children? Visions of Zia Concetta on her deathbed haunted me the minute I daydreamed of motherhood. The idea of watching the children at play and worrying when they were reckless and didn't heed my admonitions made me anxious.

How could I broach any of these thoughts to Mamma as tears coursed down her face? "He was dead by the time I got there. I never received his last blessing. I was supposed to name your brother after your father's father, but your papà let me break tradition and name him after mine because my father never believed he'd live to old age. Peppe's name is Giuseppe Croce."

The weather had turned abruptly cold and the wind had driven leaves off the persimmon trees early. In the distance there were three leaf-less trees. Orange globes decorated them. They looked like someone had adorned them just for this occasion. They were Mamma's favorite fruit, almost tropical. There were a few straggly fruit on the tree next to the persimmon, and Mamma said, "Take some *bergamotti*. We'll perfume some olive oil with them to rub our hands." She looked at her hands. "Nature's last good-bye before winter."

There, in the background, already covered in snow, was Mount Etna—cold, distant, implacable.

Nearby lemon groves, thick with piles of discarded leaves, permeated the air with an acrid burning smell consigning an aura of sadness, a finishing touch to autumn and an introduction to the winter not long away.

"Angelica, gather the little ones. Send Rina to pick some persimmons—not too ripe or they'll squash before we get home. I'll lay them on the windowsills to ripen." She leaned behind the headstone, picked up a basket, and tossed it to me. "You and I will go for lemons."

❦

THE NEXT DAY STICK LIGHTNING raved north of the cemetery and Mamma, gazing out the window, said to me, "I'm glad we're not visiting the graves today." I thought again of my leaving her to become a nun. A separation is always a little like a death.

Mamma had already prepared little packages of sweets and small gifts for the children on this holiday that she called the "Celebration of the Dead." She left treats hidden all over the house, and the children squealed with hilarity upon discovering them. While the girls searched for their treasures, Mamma said this occasion is a holiday in Palermo and she didn't want any of us to forget our dead ancestors. She told me how her mother had put up a gravestone for her father a year after he died and then died shortly after herself.

Mamma and I were in the kitchen cooking. I looked out the window again and saw thunderheads amass and ink over the sky.

"Mamma, I've been visiting the sisters and talking to Don Ruggero about becoming a nun. I think I have a calling, a vocation—"

Mamma was skimming off the milk, ladling it into a ceramic jar. She stopped and whirled around and picked up two lemons in her hand.

"Here," she said, her voice a heart pierced, "here is your birthright. This fruit and our blood. Our holy men study and live with the Torah, our women make families. We don't adapt well to convent life. You'll never be a nun."

"Mamma, what are you saying? What does this mean?"

She took the lemons from my hands. "Someday . . . someday you'll understand." Then she grated the skins with a fury and put the zest in a small glass dish. She squeezed the lemons with a vengeance, their juice, like the last drops falling from the wound in Christ's side, went into a small bowl.

"Mamma, speak to me."

Her face wore a mask of hurt and betrayal, and she retreated into silence, mincing a small onion. Then with a flick of her wrist she tossed it in a skillet with one *etto*, a hundred grams, of butter, just as she flipped the argument with the next thing she said. "Good thing your nonno Giuliano isn't here for this dish; he hates butter," Mamma said, and I knew she wouldn't say another thing about my declaration or hers.

The flame was minimal from the burning coals. She stirred the onions, and when they wilted, she spilled in the lemon juice. With a delicate hand she turned the mixture with a wooden spoon Peppe had whittled from cherry wood. Next she arranged a pot of water to boil on a back burner, adding a fistful of salt.

When the lemon juice bubbled lightly, she pulled the pot from the burner, letting it cool slightly, then flecked some lemon zest in here and there. She looked at me and her face softened. At first I thought it was the diminishing light, but her eyes, which had seemed hooded just minutes before, were naked with truth. "The Torah is the ancient law written in Hebrew. Older than the Bible you read in Italian, because there isn't one in our spoken Italic tongue of Sicilian. For the rest, you'll have to see what's foreordained as life unfolds. There isn't a hair on your head that falls to earth that the Almighty doesn't know about." And without even *basta così*, the discussion ended. I was left with questions galore, impatient to know more, and salt in the corners of my mouth from tears I hadn't known I'd shed till Mamma dried them with her apron.

I helped her carry a tea towel laden with homemade *fettuccelle* from the table. She jiggled the cloth so the fresh pasta tumbled into the water. She forked the pasta up in bunches and let it fall again till all was immersed.

She told me to put the pot with the lemon sauce back on the flame and add pepper in large, freshly ground flakes. "The lemon is bitter, but it can be made sweet. See," she said and poured in fresh cream, whisking the sauce until it was evenly heated, velvety, but not quite boiled, "like mother's milk. In life, there's good and bad, joy and sorrow, *dolce ed amaro*—sweet and bitter."

"Like a sweet, wonderful baby, but only after bitter pain. You said you don't remember the pain, but I know I would." I drained the pasta into a large ceramic bowl and tossed in the mix. On top of the pasta, I spooned some grated pecorino, a cheese Mamma had made from sheep's milk to amalgamate the whole, allowing the sauce to adhere to the noodles.

Mamma shook her head. "What we strive to do in life is seek a balance, reconcile pain and joy." I wanted her to say more but she called out, "*A tavola!*" Everyone was hungry and already seated at the table when she and I arrived. She signed to Peppe who said the grace and then she tossed the pasta, sprinkled with curly parsley.

On cue, Papà and the rest of us took hold of the pressed napery. As Papà tucked the corner of his napkin into the collar of his shirt and Peppe followed suit, I frowned.

Mamma must have caught the scowl and reproached me. "Why, even your blessed Don Ruggero covers his shirtfront!"

"It looks like a bib," I muttered.

Mamma poured Papà a glass of wine and said, "No matter then, gentlemen." She nodded to my father and brother. "You may remove the napkins since Angelica doesn't mind doing the extra washing and ironing."

Why couldn't I keep still?

CHAPTER XVII

Angelica

MOUNT ETNA

FLAMINIA BEGAN TO TALK WHEN she was a year-and-a-half old, the same day Papà gathered itinerant pickers in the predawn light of the piazza of Villaggio Pace. He and I rode horses while the other men followed on mules or in groups on wagons painted with scenes of the coronation of Roger, the Norman, as king by Pope Alexander II in the year 1070. Still others traveled on carts with scenes from the Middle Ages of the legendary hero Roland, known as Orlando Furioso, a paladin of France and knight-errant of Charlemagne's Honor Guard and champion of liberty.

We passed the lemon groves, which were about ten kilometers from the house, arriving in what seemed like no time at all at Papà's orange groves a total of twenty kilometers away from the house. Riding closer to Randazzo, we began to see an angry Mount Etna. We came upon the almond groves, and as the men straggled in, we laid huge muslin sheets all around the trees, knowing we wouldn't get much work done due to the late hour. We shook the trees and down fell the nuts. Once in a while, though not at all ladylike, I'd offer to climb a tree. Inevitably, my father sent someone else up the trunk to knock down the nuts on the upper branches, making sure to get a greater yield. By the end of the day, most of the men made off, but some camped near the refuge where my father and I stayed. The weather was balmy. We retired early, knowing a full day of work was in store for us.

The next morning we drank coffee in the dark and began our work. Every so often, Papà looked up to see Mount Etna soaring above us. "The highest volcano in Europe," he said. Smoke and ashes had blown from its bowels since the day before. He explained to me that there had been a long period of calm inactivity before this new eruption of ash and lapillus.

We heard the sharp staccato of nearby pelting almonds, each sound punctuating a concern for the four girls and Mamma. Papà had prepared her, though, knowing it was highly unlikely that a lava flow of hot liquid rock would reach Messina and its environs before she'd have time to escape. Distance was on her side. But he'd taken the precaution and said to her, "At the sound of anything explosive, take the children on the wagon and head west."

At home he'd left the wagon hitched and packed with temporary supplies—nothing much and nothing heavy. Papà warned her nothing mattered to him except the family. They would go to Palermo to her people, maybe the place where they really belonged. At the breakfast table on the morning we'd left—over the last dregs of coffee—he told me a story of people trapped by rivers of lava who were trying to carry away their earthly belongings while escaping Pompeii.

My parents had stood in the doorway, electricity shooting from their eyes. They stood there looking at each other for a long time. No words could express their feelings. Then, just as we were about to leave, my father, a man of little demonstrativeness, took hold of Mamma and kissed her full on the mouth. I had never seen them kiss like that before. The hair on my arms stood up.

⁕

JUST BEFORE LUNCH, SOME MEN gathered close to a wagon, and as I passed them I overheard some of them complaining that they didn't want to work till dusk. I pretended not to hear and walked to where my father was sitting for the break, and said to him, "That mountainous heap is now spitting rocks."

I watched Papà cut a slice of bread and hand it to me. "Lava fragments the boulders. They break up and become more like small rocks.

Distance makes it hard to judge." He looked away from the mountain and right into my eyes. "You're the spit of your mother."

I took advantage of his high regard.

"Papà, pass me the cheese and wine." I thought about the last disastrous time I'd had a desire to taste wine so many years ago. This time I wanted permission.

"'Please' is the only word lacking, daughter." Papà looked at me until I lowered my eyes in shame.

"You'll grow in spite of me. Here," my father said and tossed me a sheepskin filled with wine.

I felt his eyes on me the whole time, so I didn't drink right away, but placed the skin beside me on the ground.

"Take this," he said and laid a thick slice of provolone on the piece of remaining bread I held like a plate. Mamma had smoked and aged the cheese. She was good at so many things, yet he never thanked her. If I were to marry—which I won't—I'd want my husband to thank me. My head and heart held a conversation of the things I couldn't say to my father. Like, "Papà, you're some example for Peppe. No wonder he's such a big boss."

"The smoke," I said, "it's blacker than this morning."

"Just as black, only more of it." He turned to look over his shoulder. While he looked the other way, I lifted the wineskin and squirted a steady stream of wine into my mouth like I'd seen him do.

"Easy, young one, I don't want you falling out of any trees."

I laughed. "Mamma says I'm part monkey. And you won't let me climb."

"I'd hate to set a broken arm or leg now."

"Papà," I whispered, "I heard the men grumbling."

"About what?"

"They don't want to work till dusk as agreed because they think she'll blow." I pointed to the volcano.

"Beh, we have time yet. Only when we see red lava start to snake its way down—when that liquid fire slips over the crater and down the mountain's face—then we go." I somehow felt that his voice belied the roiling emotion below the surface. I knew he'd seen devastation in the path of a volcanic eruption. He said, "I left Peppe as sentinel to watch for warnings, making him promise a secret oath not to panic." My father had told Peppe to hurry Mamma and the girls into the waiting wagon, to give charge of the infant to Rina so that he could manage ornery old Pupedda, the "little doll" who'd grown to replace my donkey Pupa.

Something in the way the wind shifted seized Papà's interest to another part of the grove. I saw a flash of color, heard a scrap of whistled tune.

"That brings me back to my youth," he said.

"The tune?"

"A *cantastoria*—"

"A ballad singer?"

"*Sì.* He'd come from far off Trappani. He sang the story of another time, a different volcano, erupting in Stromboli, one of the Eolie Islands."

I pictured the volcanic islands off Sicily's northeastern coast. Pieces of the story flowed through my mind bright and hot as lava. His resonant voice depicted images for me, clear and large, as seen through a magnifying lens.

"Red tongues of lava licked the hillside, sucked up homes, devoured farmland, and gorged on fishermen, their boats and nets spread with a catch—not unlike those cloths spread with almonds."

A rider approached, and before his steed had come to a halt, he jumped off the horse and ran toward my father. It was Gaetano, Giuseppina's son. I'd wondered why he wasn't with the men who came with us in the morning.

"Don Nicola, forgive me. I had to stay home today to pack for my mother, but we just got word that a wall of lava has reached the opposite side at the base and the flow has increased in speed. I urge you—" he said, his voice pleading in a harsh whisper.

My father hushed Gaetano and put his hands on his shoulders. He looked at the men.

I said, "What if, unlike you, these men haven't prepared their families for evacuation?"

He glanced again at the almonds. He dropped his hands from Gaetano. "Go. Go and help your family."

Gaetano turned and, at a running gait, took hold of the saddle and hurled himself up on his horse. He looked like what I'd always imagined a young Greek god of ancient times should be.

Then my father spoke more to himself than me. "I'll lose them anyway and for all their weight, could they be weighed against the value of a human life?"

I was frightened by the gravity of his tone.

He stood with the knife and cheese poised in his hand. "Pack it up," he called out to the men. "We're leaving now." The command sounded as if he wanted to encumber the men with the haul.

"Of what use is it to burden ourselves?" he mumbled. Then he said, "Tie the bundles and stack them under the trees."

Maybe he hoped to come back soon to retrieve them.

"Move quickly!" he shouted to the men.

Then to me, sitting on the ground next to him, he spoke in a gentler manner, almost a mutter, "Black lumps of petrified lava. Angelica, ride out now. I'll follow shortly."

When I tried to object, my father's eyes opened roundly and he arched an eyebrow. There was no arguing with my father. I unhitched my horse, passed the wineskin cord over my head across my chest, and mounted, grateful I had tasted only a sip. I was still in control of my legs. I trotted, moving the horse forward into a fast canter so I could catch up with Gaetano in order to ride the rest of the way home with him.

<hr />

MOUNT ETNA. ANYONE WHO'S EVER seen her majesty speaks with respect. The volcano scare lasted several weeks. We lived under its pressure. Will it blow or won't it? Then suddenly one day it stilled itself and, like a giant in a fable, fell into a deep, deep sleep.

CHAPTER XVIII

Angelica

VESTING PRAYERS AND THE COLOR RED

THOUGH PEACE SETTLED ON VILLAGGIO PACE and our family after the quasi-eruption, my father had suffered a huge financial loss. The lava flow had hungrily devoured land and groves, villages and town, districts and *contrade*. He was not the only one to have suffered from this tragedy, but it felt as if this were far worse because it happened to him.

To make matters worse, I was having a difficult emotional time and causing unpleasantness for everyone, most especially Mamma. I was sixteen. Everything was changing.

Mamma noticed an improvement in my vocabulary, and she was pleased that classical literature had found a place in my heart. She questioned me on my readings. I told her most things, but not everything, during this period of flux when my reading habits became voracious and eclectic. I read the Bible, of course, and the lives of the saints and Dante. I kept the modern passionate writings of D'Annunzio to myself, not to mention the perverted pessimism of Pirandello's "The Wake." These sentences especially haunted me: "I'm not suffering on my account, or on your account. I'm suffering because life is what it is."

When I wasn't reading, I became irascible and bossy with my sisters. To silence my prattle, Mamma convinced Papà to let me work for my uncle Don Ruggero.

Up until this point, Mamma kept me busy enough in the house. Now Rina was able to assume some of my chores. I was overjoyed, knowing I'd be in the sacristy every day.

The sacristy was to the side of the main chapel and housed cabinets and drawers of rich, polished wood. There were high, vaulted ceilings with carved beams. Two straight chairs flanked a small table beneath a crucifix, which was burdened with ecclesiastical texts, a chalice, a ciborium, and crystal cruets. There was a washstand to the right of the doorway in an alcove.

One day I washed and pressed vestments for Don Ruggero and placed all of the garments he would put on for Mass tenderly within a hand's reach. Then I stood in the sacristy and waited for his arrival.

When Don Ruggero came in, he took off his beret and laid it on a chair. "No, Don Ruggero, never place a hat on a chair," I told him, taking the hat gently and propping it onto a wooden counter.

"Angelica, how can you profess to be religious and then give me counsel about superstitions?"

I couldn't explain it, but my mother was superstitious, as was her mother before her, and I had no intention of changing something that had functioned so well in Sicily for thousands of years.

He was wearing his soutane and I noted that the hem needed sewing, but there was no time for that now. I prayed silently that he wouldn't trip ascending the altar.

I watched him take and kiss the amice, which protects the neck from soiling the other vestments. This piece of cloth had a symbolic purpose to ward off temptation, disengaging him from preoccupation. The priest meditated on the Incarnation, the Trinity, and the Redemption. The prayers were part of my heart, and when he mouthed them I said in a whisper, "Place a helmet of salvation on my head, O Lord, so that I may ward off the attacks of the devil."

Then he took hold of the alb in order to offer the sacred mysteries. The alb spurred my inner eye to form a picture of Don Ruggero in an outfit of the early Romans, bony knobs for knees, protruding beneath a pleated skirt. I forced myself to concentrate and soon again mimed the words, "Purify and cleanse my heart, O Lord, so that, redeemed by the blood of Jesus, I may enter Your glory."

But my voice was a little too loud and he shot me a glance. I saw him tie on the cincture, a corded belt. Having discussed the prayers, the vestments, and their meanings so many times, I knew the cleric was thinking, "Rope of the Crucifixion," his mind transported to the *Via Dolorosa*. I followed along, "Gird me with cincture of pure intention, O Lord, by which all evil desire is bound, so that continence and chastity may remain always with me."

Next Don Ruggero put on the stole, a reminder of the priestly office and administrating of sacraments. I heard the incantation: "Restore the stole of everlasting life to me, O Lord, lost by original sin. And although I am not worthy to celebrate the sacred mysteries, may I be found acceptable to share eternal joy."

I coughed.

"Don't distract me, woman," he snarled, which got my attention.

I tried to usher a throng of devout thoughts into my mind, yet it was no simple matter. In an effort to concentrate on a host of religious meditations, I fixed my eye on the color red. But instead of reflecting on church symbolism, my mind filled with the red of blood. Blood of my accident. Of birth and of death.

Different colors reflected the liturgical calendar. Red—the color of martyrs, feasts of the Passion, and of the Holy Ghost—was the indicated color of the day. The wall calendar showed the date was February 5, the feast of Saint Agatha, a Sicilian virgin and martyr, whose name appeared in the Canon of the Mass and who bravely, I thought, refused solicitations from a Roman senator at Catania in the year AD 251.

I wanted so much to think that there was no earthly pleasure that could compare to the benedictions and preparation for Holy Mass, but the reality was that the color red distracted me. I considered this an occasion of sin, but I couldn't help it. I felt no peace. In fact, I was awash in thoughts red as blood. Holy words that contained *red,* such as *sacred, redemption,* and *redeemed,* made me feel as if I were gagging on my own blood—drowning in it until I wanted to run from the room.

My stomach churned and I was sorry not to have breakfasted, but it would have disallowed my receiving Communion. As I gazed up at a statue of the Sacred Heart, whose red robe flowed about Him softly, I was comforted, my thoughts conducted once again to piety.

The long-sleeved chasuble was the same color as the stole and was worn over the alb. I remembered Don Ruggero telling me the Latin from which this word had sprung was *casubala*, a hooded garment from *casupula*, diminutive of *casa*, which meant house. The significance was obvious—to house the minister of the great mystery of transubstantiation, he who was left by Christ to change bread and wine into the body and blood of Jesus Christ. And there it was again—blood. My stomach lurched and I felt faint. As Don Ruggero donned the vestment, his entreaty, "O Lord, who said, 'My yoke is sweet and my burden light,' help me to carry every cross so as to win Your grace and blessing" could be heard in a singsong chant.

When Don Ruggero had finished dressing, he appealed for Eucharistic ministers. His supplication began, "Jesus, bless these hands You have chosen as Your tools. Jesus, always keep us aware and in awe of our sacred mission. Jesus, make us worthy of this great ministry we have humbly accepted. Jesus, send us out into the world to distribute Your love."

"Don Ruggero, I need to be excused," I said, my voice imploring, and I bolted from the sacristy. I dashed into a side chapel and sat in the first pew, fanning myself with a hymnal. A woman who looked very much like Mamma's dressmaker lit a candle. The woman tugged at her bodice as if to lengthen it, calling to mind again a gesture the dressmaker had made only yesterday.

⁕

MY MOTHER HAD BROUGHT ME to see her, asking her to sketch and design a dress that would be made of red taffeta with ecru lace trim. I thought at first that it was absolutely shocking. "I'll never appear in public in that," I'd snapped at Mamma.

Walking down the corridor to the anteroom of the dressmaker's, she pinched the soft part of my underarm, getting my complete attention as was her wont, and said, "My dearest girl, not only will you appear in it, you'll use it several times and thank your dear papà as well."

"What do you mean?" We sat down to wait for the dressmaker.

"You're going to wear this new dress to the opera next month and to cousin Lella's engagement party. She's Silvana's only sister and you know it's expected."

I was looking at three gilt-framed designs of ladies in ball gowns. "Lella to be married? When?"

"Only you, my stuck-up daughter, have decided to embrace Christ as your groom. Everybody else marries a man made of flesh and blood. Someone to hold you on cold nights and give you children."

I recoiled at the thought. I must have blanched, because my mother said, "What's wrong with you? Don't you want to have a family of your own? You positively smother your sisters with affection."

"When are the nuptials?"

She withdrew an envelope from her purse. She handed me the invitation.

"Open it," she said.

"I can't."

"You mean you don't want to." Her tone reeked facetiousness.

The dressmaker entered with an armload of material swatches and an artist's pad. These she placed on a round table with a pedestal base of three curved legs that ended in claws. I fanned myself with the invitation and let it drop in my lap. The dressmaker tugged at the bodice pinned to a model as she and my mother began to discuss my dress. I must have absently started to tap my fingers on the card.

"Lella—pu, pu—u fa—u fa," I stammered. "Mamma, not everyone is loved and adored, pampered and spoiled—the world isn't made of Lellas. Everybody despises me, but even Jesus had enemies," I muttered.

❦

SOMETIME LATER AT HOME IN our kitchen, Mamma said that no one glancing at my well-shaped hands—the lovely look of unbroken and recently buffed nails crowning my slender fingers tapping a quiet rhythm along the border of the wedding invitation that lay in my lap—and at the listless way my head moved, fidgeting from right to left, could imagine that in a matter of seconds such a stream of unbridled thoughts would flow in a current of words as to embarrass her beyond belief.

"Angelica, back at the dressmaker's, it was as if a jealous streak possessed you. You babbled until I shook you and you returned to your senses. I could only assume you were jealous. Were you?"

I could have said, "Ouch," for that certainly pinched my conscience, but I defended myself quickly with, "That's not true."

"Your exact words were, 'It should be me. Rina said I'd make a beautiful bride—I'm prettier and well suited for marriage, and I'm trying to be as humble as I can,' and then you added something about fruit pickers looking up your skirt when you climb trees and how men ogle you in the piazza near the fountain. You said, 'I can feel the men staring at me even in church when they're with their wives.'"

"I don't remember that," I said, sounding peevish even to me.

"Remember or not, I kept repeating, 'Angelica, Angelica, come out of it.'"

"Forgive me, Mamma, and all the saints in heaven! I guess I'm only human. I am jealous," I said, and fled from the room.

❦

"ANGELICA? ANGELICA?" DON RUGGERO'S VOICE reached me, as through a tunnel. "Are you all right, Angelica? You're staring at the wall." He handed me a glass of water. "Maybe you should go home."

Even though he was right, and knowing my attention would be diverted with thoughts of Lella and the upcoming event, I said, "I'll stay for Mass," and blessed myself with holy water from the mottled marble font. As my hand touched my breast, I visualized a man's hand brushing Lella's breasts, not unlike Ciccio's touch defiling me in the barn.

❦

LELLA'S ENGAGEMENT PARTY, A TRADITIONAL evening ball, began with enough glitter and gaiety to nauseate me. It was held in one of the most beautiful palazzos in Messina. The long, winding carriage paths were lined with cypresses hundreds of years old, and the shaded parks within the confines boasted many species of palms, gardens, and fountains.

I watched from an upper-story window as carriage after carriage arrived, transporting every imaginable bachelor and pastel-clad spinster for the circumference of sixty kilometers.

I thought I looked hideous in the red gown, as if I were playing dress-up in one of Mamma's newfangled hand-me-downs. Her dear friend, whose palazzo we were invading like Hannibal's hordes, had insisted on putting my hair up to go with the new Gibson girl, American style of my dress. She also insisted that I borrow her ruby and diamond pendant earbobs.

My sister Rina came to claim me from my perch at the window seat and said that I could dillydally no longer. All the gentlemen had almost completed the barbaric ritual of dance card signing. I thought of my mother's pinch under my arm, and as I got up to follow Rina, I caught sight of my womanly appearance in the windowpane. My new image stayed with me all the way down the circular stair through the candlelit, mirrored hallway, replete with enormous porcelain vases overflowing with magnificent floral arrangements.

When I entered the main ballroom, it had a dizzying effect—all the brightness reflected from the huge crystal chandelier. In a moment of clarity I was aware that I too dazzled the gathering. The music had stopped and the entire company looked my way. Rina entered as if a page before a princess. My hand flew to the bodice of my gown to steady myself, and I made a pretense at smoothing the soft folds of material. I concentrated on gliding, rather than walking, in my new satin slippers. The impact staggered the onlookers. Men stopped in the middle of their conversing to look my way while others moved to glimpse me better. I knew for certain I'd have to repent for the overpowering sin of pride I felt. For the first time in my life I understood beauty as a dominating force over men—frightening, yet awesome in its raw magnetism, and exhilarating. I savored every instant.

The orchestra began to play, and I found myself encircled by half the male population of Messina in frock coats, some bowing, others smiling and introducing themselves, while still more implored me to write their names on the card that hung like a tiny noose around my gloved wrist. Inexplicably, my penmanship regressed to an elementary pupil's, all but for one, Liborio Ranieri. When he asked me to pen his name, I said, "I've no room, but I'll write your name at the bottom of the list, in case of a cancellation," and turned quickly to avoid looking at his motley skin.

After several swirling waltzes, I sat on a velvet settee, catching my breath and observing the ceiling of the ballroom. Along the stuccoed borders were putti armed with bows and arrows. In the center was a huge Neptune riding a chariot in a sea of cockatrice, gargoyles, minotaur, satyrs, and ogres. Didn't anyone think to change it since the seventeenth century?

Every other second I was accosted by some eager young, dashing dandy asking me to dance, to walk, to talk, to bring me some punch, to escort me to the dining hall. Finally, in desperation, I walked toward doors thrown open to an enormous terrace. There I sat on an ironwork bench. Honeysuckle tinged the air.

I spied the spinning pink skirt of my sister Rina's gown, but before I had a chance to hail her to come outside, and with my breathing finally restored, I was again assaulted by a group of men, each and every one with a swagger, collectively missing cockscombs. I had to admit that I loved dancing and was grateful to Lella for having taught us before the party. I checked my card, relieved to see it was quite a gallant I would be twirling with next. I extended my hand, feeling the heat from his through my glove. He escorted me back to the ballroom where we swirled in three-quarter time, uncaring of the ceiling, the other dancers, or the slight pressure of his hand on my lower back as he whispered a compliment that made my cheeks match my dress. I smelled his Cerruti aftershave—no, too strong—it had to be cologne. I recognized it because Don Ruggero often used it.

I danced to dizzying spins and heights, humming along with music, but there wasn't a single person I cared to dance with. It was the art of the dance that fascinated me, the rhythms, the twirls and sways, the cadence of the om-pa-pa band, the delightful dips, hesitations, and starts. Until I saw a man I knew I wanted to dance with. A man so still, so straight, so serious, so utterly mine—How could I think that? He was standing near a Venetian door, light glancing off the many small panes of glass.

"Who is that man by the potted palm?" I asked my dancing partner.

"Where?" he asked.

Was he blind? "Over there." I indicated with my chin and then pointed so that he turned.

How could I dare to think possessively of a man I'd never seen till now? And yet the feeling persisted until the uniformed man was gone. But had he singled me out? Hadn't he smiled on my last turn? Where could he have disappeared to? I looked toward the heavy silk shantung curtains by the patio doors. Had I imagined him? Why wasn't he on the dance floor? He had never been on the dance floor—he'd held himself apart, an observer. Yet his eyes had been on me, of that I was sure. Certain. But now he was gone. Gone. The dance ended. My partner escorted me to where I had been seated before. I sat for a minute and fanned my face, opened my tiny purse, and took out a lemon pastille, placing it under my tongue, the taste accentuating the disappointment of the disappearance of the handsome man in uniform.

⸎

AFTER LELLA'S ENGAGEMENT PARTY IN late March, she came to Villaggio Pace in the beginning of April. Lent was finally over, and in just a few months she would wed. She stayed with us for two weeks. Rina was her favorite. They doted on one another and were practically inseparable except at night when we all retired to our rooms. Lella slept with me because Nunziata would have been too jealous if her dear Rina had to be shared with Lella. Beatrice and Flaminia shared the superatico, the floor above.

The last night of Lella's sojourn with us, I stroked my hair a hundred times with my tortoise-handled brush made with wild boar's bristles. My scalp prickled when I blew out the lamp and said good night to Lella, who was already in bed. We had talked for hours after one of the most elegant dinners we'd ever had in our home. Lella's fiancé, Marco, had left the party close to 2:00 a.m. We talked a while longer, and then she fell silent for a long time. I thought she'd fallen asleep. Then, as drowsiness began to overtake me, she got up. She could've been an apparition. I almost spoke to her, but didn't. Her movements were those of a sleep-walker. What was she up to? She probably thought I slumbered, but now I was quite awake. Lella looked back once in my direction. I faced the door, watched her open it and walk onto the terrace outside my room.

I got up quietly, crept to the door, and peeked out to see her standing in the moonlight. She was beautiful, like a statue of a Roman goddess I'd seen in the Museum of Messina. Her hair was piled on top of her head and loose tendrils framed her face. She advanced toward the limit of the portico, and I could see the outline of her body through her nightdress. A noise from the garden stopped me from talking to Lella, who stood at the edge and bent over the rock wall. At the other end of the terrace, I peered over the wall and saw a man climbing. He stopped for a minute and seemed to be hanging from the cliff's face. The young man caught a ridge, and in the cold predawn light, he continued to scale the rock. I wondered if his hands were scraped and bleeding, as his feet searched, in an upward climb, for a ledge, an outcropping, a small space, a firm shelf to support him.

I had been in such a peaceful mood, but now I felt anxious—for the man climbing, my cousin waiting, and me watching. The precipice fell from the terrace to the road into the nothingness of dark and depth below—an area I knew to be covered by forested patches of overgrown land.

Lightheadedness. A thrill stole into my soul, and I thought of a youth in ancient times, stealing into the garden of Allah to taste of forbidden fruit—or of someone's harem. I recalled my father talking to Uncle Nino about white slavery and abduction. I became afraid for Lella, but the disquiet abated when I realized it was Marco, her fiancé, and she was expecting him. I thought about the climber. He'd made a great decision sculpted of need and craving. Would a man ever risk like this for me? Is that what I wanted? The man moved as if in a dream state. My clouded mind boggled. I knew what he wanted. But had he considered the consequences? I believed he'd go after it anyway, though it was wholly improper!

Lella outstretched her arms, a pose of yearning. I wanted to yell to her, "Are you willing to jeopardize respect and reputation? Every standard we were raised with? For what quest? Each other's arms and kisses?" My lips parted.

Scaling the sheer cliff, he found bliss through reckless endangerment to his immortal soul. Did he care? No. Not even if he had to burn in hellfire for eternity. I backed into the rock wall, a chameleon, variegating with the landscape beyond the bougainvillea. Hidden in the shadows, a voyeur, a seeker of life's truths, I gambled my soul like the man and woman who cherished each other's touch.

They were breathless in encircled arms, and I sensed a tingling in every fiber of my body. My soul fired with their desire, longing to know what they felt in an embrace so close it was as if they were fused. His head covered her neck, her breasts with kisses. She moved like a cat into him, almost purring. Her chest heaved, and they were so rapt in each other's tender caress that they were unaware of me, my scarlet cheeks, my icy feet upon the terrace floor, my own hands crushing my heaving breasts. So this is love between a man and a woman, natural and splendid. "How unseemly!" cried my head. "How magnificent," my heart. The words of *The Magnificat* when Mary conceived of the Holy Spirit sprang to mind and my lips mouthed the words "my soul doth magnify the Lord, and my spirit rejoices in God."

Emotions churned within me. A chill blasted through me. I wanted to go back to my bed, to the darkened safety of my room, yet I stood fastened. I shut my eyes, but some curiosity invaded me and I opened them again to see the couple dancing, swaying, tottering. His arms engulfed her, sliding down from waist to hips, then cupping underneath her—she sat in his hands. She sprang up to ensnare him in a vice with her legs, grappling for a tighter grasp—a cat's desperate clawing to hold on to the tree that was his body. The white gossamer gown flowed out and swirled round her. He sat on the wall, still holding her, then slid, sinking to the ground, and she, like I had in the wine shed, fell. I couldn't wrench my eyes away. My hand would not cover my gaze and protect me.

While they were still in the throes of passion, I cowered back into the house, but like Lot's wife, I turned. Lella collapsed, spent upon him. I flung myself on the bed, pulled the covers over my head, but sleep wouldn't come. I uncovered my face. Time lapsed, all the while shadows on the wall reenacted the scene, over and over and over. I became three players at once. First the climber, then Lella, then me. Now Lella, then the climber, and me. Now me and the climber. Where was Lella? I was soaked and threw back the covers. I felt chilled. A blanket tug-of-war ensued, then the rustle of sheets, not mine, made me relax, knowing she was once again safely tucked in bed. I heard a voice not unlike my very own saying, "Angelica, how you handle yourself from now on is a matter between you and the Universe, you and God. Be noble."

I knew the lovers' sin was not mine, although I had been momentarily swept up in their rapture. Such a paradox. So confusing. Beautiful but sinful. If I were to confess, it would endanger them, and if I dwelt on this, it could destroy me. What had taken place was over and done. I whispered into my pillow, "Don't let the past corrode tomorrow."

CHAPTER XIX

Angelica

DON RUGGERO LEAVES FOR CARINI

MAMMA SENT ME WITH PEPPE to the church to bring Don Ruggero a package along with a note inviting him to dinner that evening. Children promenaded past the livery stable where the *carretierre* fired his tools and the anvil's din rang out. Peppe stopped the cart for a minute because he wanted to ask the wheel-maker if there were any odd jobs he could help with. I climbed down after Peppe and peered in to see if anyone was about. The forge's flame quivered from the distance where I stood. The smell of horses and dung mixed with the smelting ore made me gag and turn away. We didn't see the iron-welder anywhere, so we mounted the cart and drove to town.

We shopped for salt at the tobacco store and for the other items Mamma needed. After we bought all the necessaries, we headed for church. As we approached the rectory, I said to Peppe, "You go and deliver Mamma's message to Don Ruggero. I'm going to make a visit to the chapel and light a candle."

"Ah, the little saint. Just when will you be canonized?"

"You have to be beatified first."

"Oh, give over, Angelica. As if I didn't know, but in order to be blessed you have to die first."

I circled the church to enter from the chapel side and almost careened into a *zingara* nursing a baby. The Gypsy wore her hair in braids, tied with red satin ribbons. She was seated on the ground, her multicolored skirt flaring out like a cape. The woman spoke with a strange accent, never quite finishing her words. At first it was difficult to understand her speech, but as she kept talking, I began to comprehend her singsong tone and the words started to separate into a Sicilian dialect I could fathom, my ignorance decreasing with each word I understood. I felt myself relax, let down my guard.

She extended her palm. I shook my head. She yanked my skirt, as if to snatch it off me. Her insistence won me over. I also wanted to get a better look at her. Her coal-black hair shone with streaks of blue. I had only seen hair like hers at a distance. It fascinated me. I boldly sat down next to her and her child, a cherub with lips painted rose, golden ringlets on his forehead, almost reaching a button nose. His eyes matched the slate sky before a storm. He drifted off to sleep.

She took my hand. "Dragan," she said and pointed to herself. "My name. Yours?"

"Angelica."

She placed a red thread in my hand and snaked it away. Where had I seen that done before? "I see you are of God," she said.

"Of God?"

"Virgin, not married."

"I'm young."

"Gypsy marry young."

Why wasn't I scared? It didn't cross my mind to bolt or even think of running away. Could she steal me for a gypsy wedding? I'd heard that girls are spirited from their families, shipped to other countries, never to be seen again. But something in her eyes made me trust her, made me listen to what she had to say. I wanted to ask her about the mandolin music and dancing around autumn bonfires on nights when the inky sky, ocean deep, was clear. Nights when I'd reached to touch a froth of stars or beams dazzling bright as the ones now reflected in the billows of her raven eyes.

She dropped my hand as if it were aflame.

Just as quickly, she held out her own hand, and without thinking, I reached inside my pocket and handed her my mother's change from the shopping.

"You'll risk your life for babies." She stuffed the coins into the bodice of her blouse. Seizing my hand, she began to trace the lines of my palm with her long finger. Her hands were warm and tanned, her fingernails surprisingly clean. She curled my fingers and looked at the side of my bunched-up fist. I watched her count four lines, then squeeze my hand a little tighter and add two.

"Six what?"

She pointed to her baby.

"Babies?"

She shook her head. I watched her draw an imaginary round from underneath my breasts down to my navel. "Pregnancies?" I laughed.

She put her hand to her mouth so quickly it stopped my laugh.

Reopening my hand, she scanned the tiny lines, crossed the hills and valleys of my palm. Circling the ball of her pointing finger over certain spots, she closed her eyes.

I started to say I wanted to become a nun, but before I could she told me I would wed a man who loved the sea and who had been to the Orient. She tugged at her braid.

"An Oriental with braids?" I knew no such person. How could I believe such a rash statement? Yet I felt compelled to listen.

What she said was *nero*.

"A black man?" The words weren't out of my mouth yet when I realized she was telling me the man would have black hair. Ebony, like hers. I concluded she was dead wrong, supposing she was saying that because she thought I wanted to hear it. Didn't all girls my age think of marriage?

After she said I would cross the sea, she asked for more money. But I had none, so I got up and went to church. Now I had no money for an offering to pay for my candle. Saddened by what I'd done, I resolved anew to think before an impulsive act. I rationalized all the favors I'd done for Don Ruggero were worth one candle. In fact, I decided to light two.

~~~

WHEN PEPPE AND I RETURNED, we unloaded all the packages. The first thing Mamma had us bring to the outdoor sink was a sackful of cozze purchased from the fish vendor who owned the vasca—tanks of sea water—in the middle of town where the mussels were farmed.

Next came all the other goods. Peppe took a piece of paper from his breast pocket. This last item he handed to Mamma was Don Ruggero's acceptance for dinner. Mamma read quickly and stuffed the note into her pocket. Wordless, she extended her hand to me.

My cheeks went scarlet as the taffeta underskirt beneath my gown at Lella's engagement with the appalling realization that I'd given Mamma's change to the Gypsy.

"I . . . left Peppe and went round to the church—"

"Don't tell me the rest for I can well imagine that you probably lit ten candles."

"No, I really—"

"Out with it. Oh, never mind, tell me later."

WHILE I HELPED MAMMA LAY the cloth and arrange the dining room table, I flushed again because I hadn't told her I never paid for the church candles I lit with her money. I'd sinned by omission. But at least I told her what the Gypsy said.

"Nonsense," she said. "You'll have children like that," and snapped her fingers.

I argued that I wouldn't marry and then added sheepishly, "I'm afraid to even think of having a baby."

"Don't rush life. All in due time."

AT THE DINNER TABLE, MAMMA served *zuppa di cozze* doused in oil and vino and flecked with garlic cloves. This antipasto soup was served with thick slices of *casereccio* bread. The best part was to make a *scarpetta*. I watched Papà mop up the juices with a piece of bread, though I never quite figured out why it was called "a little shoe." This action was considered polite, even in the best company, but Mamma always made a face when he did it.

Mamma had also made exquisite spaghetti with mussels in a red sauce with crushed red pepper. Don Ruggero's favorite—stuffed pheasant—followed the pasta. Papà had been hunting a few days before and came home with six *tordi,* a grouse, two wild hares, and a male pheasant. "Dinner here is always wonderful, the pheasant exceptional, my dear sister," my uncle said to Mamma.

I looked at his stomach—a protrusion under his tunic like an over-stuffed bird. I wondered why a man of the cloth indulged so. Exceptional? Actually it tasted stringy and gamey, no matter how many hours she'd left the dressed bird hanging in order to make it more tender, nor how many times she rinsed it in wine vinegar. I guessed it was an old bird. And everyone except Don Ruggero knows that females are more succulent.

He reminded me a little bit of a pheasant himself—always puffing out his wings, a squawking male more beautiful than the female, always attired with the finest plumes.

"When will you be leaving for Carini, Ruggero?" Papà asked.

"The beginning of next week." Don Ruggero sipped his wine, and I thought of the chalice he sipped at Mass.

"Are you disappointed you weren't assigned to Palermo?" Peppe asked.

"Not really. I love the country, and Carini's only twenty-two kilometers from there."

"Will you be staying with our brother or at the rectory?" Mamma asked.

Mamma, the peacemaker. She'd already asked this question and knew the answer as we all did. There was bad blood between Zu Vanni and Don Ruggero due to my grandparents' inheritance.

"Please look in on Concetta's folks in Palermo," she added.

"Living under the threat of a volcano makes me glad about this transfer to the other side of the island. Nicola, have you ever considered moving?" Don Ruggero said.

"Perhaps one day," my father answered.

Burning wood splintered and crackled in the hearth, momentarily distracting him. Flames licked up and lit my father's ruddy face. He seemed hypnotized by the fire.

"Not now," he continued, "but who knows what the future holds?"

"Only God," Don Ruggero said.

Despite everything, I would miss him. Pompous bore that he was! *Mea culpa, mea culpa!* I already told Mama I had no intention of working for his replacement. I'd decided to work at the Monte Carmello Convent of discalced Carmelites where Mother Lucia, the sub-prioress, could become my spiritual mentor in Don Ruggero's absence.

CHAPTER XX

Angelica

AFTER LELLA'S WEDDING

THE WEEKS BEFORE EASTER PASSED by in a blur. I remembered Palm Sunday and the long gospel, the giving out of olive branches in church, and Papà weaving baskets and crosses for all of us from stripped palms. And the following Holy week, the Tenebrae—the office of matins and lauds sung the last three days. Spy Wednesday's ancient service of extinguishing candles dramatized the darkness enveloping the world at Christ's death. Then there was the glory of the resurrection—redemption awaited all who embraced it.

Easter had been celebrated with roast lamb and *pizza rustica*. Then Lella's fairy-tale wedding was over. I returned from my cousin's marriage and reception with a splitting headache, and my mother administered a cold compress and a cachet to relieve the pain. A few hours later, Mamma was about to give me another pain remedy. I realized that part of my anxiousness was due to the fact that I didn't know how Lella would get around showing her bridal sheet. Lella was clever, and somehow I knew she'd thought this out and would manage it.

Mamma asked me if I'd forgotten to put salt in my pocket like she'd told me. Next she asked me if at least I'd made horns behind my back. I admitted that I hadn't made horns, nor did I form a *figa* by crossing the pointing finger over my thumb when I entered the reception where guests gaped and gawked. I suppose they were in awe of my dress, or something else, perhaps my beauty. So taken by their stares and compliments was I that by the time I realized it, I'd committed yet another sin of pride and vanity and neglected Mamma's advice. I paid for this with Mamma's promised headache if I didn't use her superstitious precautions. Would I ever learn?

Mamma said, "Sit here, Angelica," and indicated the kitchen chair next to the *vassiliere*. I watched her reflection in the glass pane. She took a small bowl of water and placed it over my head, then took hold of the *oliera* and spilled in some olive oil. She put the *oliera* on the table, took a pinch of salt between her fingers, and sprinkled it into the bowl. She formed the sign of the cross, stray grains falling on my shoulders. As she did this, she said the prayer she'd learned as a girl at the stroke of midnight on Christmas Eve in Holy Cross Cathedral.

At the end of the prayer she said in a soft voice, barely audible, "*Caccia sta mal'occhio fouri.*" I knew she had faith that the evil eye would be cast from me.

As Mamma prayed over my head, I felt a drawing away from my eyes to the crown of my head. I smiled when she removed the bowl and asked how I felt. My voice had a quality of disbelief in my own ears, a hollow sound coming from a cave.

"Mamma, the evil's really gone."

She showed me the dish she'd held over my head. Oil and water had split into many eyes.

"Now do you believe me?"

"Undoubtedly the cachet taking effect," I said, stubbornness in my tone, anything not to admit she was yet again right. "And besides, I've never seen an eyeless dish after this Sicilian hocus pocus. Water and oil don't mix."

"Just wait. You'll be convinced yet, but only when it's your turn to do this for someone you love. You'll see, my doubting Tomasina, and then believe."

I didn't have to wait. I believed her. I just refused to give her the satisfaction. Shame on me. Where did this stubbornness stem from?

I went immediately to bed and finished reading Manzoni's *Promessi Sposi*. Putting the book down, I sighed. The plight of the poor betrothed characters Lucia and Renzo stayed with me. I read somewhere that a good book leaves you thinking about the characters days later; these were real, deep, consistent. I thought about love between a man and a woman. I traced the struggles the young couple had gone through to be together. I recalled Lella and her climber on the terrace, and for the second time in my life, I glimpsed what happiness was in store for a couple who loved. Even through sacrifice they would do anything to be together. Not a minute passed before I again picked up and held the book, perusing the pages. I began rereading the beginning, those sentences that had first captured my curiosity and made me want to read on and never have it end. The opening seemed now so much a part of the end, but I never could have imagined that when I first started reading.

My lids were heavy. I stowed the book. I was glad Mamma had always insisted on our reading, ever prodding us with her, "We may not be rich, but we don't have to be ignorant." Yawning, I thought of her explications of opera, and how they made any kind of work we shared at the time lighter than thistledown.

I picked up the lamp to blow out the wick, but remembered the piece of Lella's wedding cake I'd stashed in my purse. I got up and padded barefoot to the dressing table. I emptied the black beaded bag fringed with jet, placing the contents next to the lorgnette still inside a demi-point embroidered case I had used for the opera. I opened the drawer and put away the tiny fishbone comb, a scapula of the Sacred Heart, and an *Agnus Dei* with a delicate, embroidered edge. I fingered a small pot of rouge that I'd bought in Palermo without Mamma's permission. Guilt engulfed me. Why had I purchased it if I hadn't the courage to use it? I thought of my entrances to Lella's engagement party and marriage reception and my cheeks flamed. Who needed rouge?

Sheathed in my linen handkerchief with a handmade lace border tatted by my aunt Concetta was the small piece of wedding cake. I unwrapped it and licked icing from my finger. I repacked and placed it under my pillow corner in hopes it wouldn't get squashed and that I'd dream of Christ, my future bridegroom, but with shameful misgivings. Did I already know in my heart that my fate was moving elsewhere?

I went to bed with the lines of a poem in my head. I awoke in the middle of the night. My nightgown had coiled around me and the covers tangled. I asked myself, *Who did you dream of? A mustachioed man in a sailor's uniform, hair the color of lava and eyes like jet.* I unwound my nightie, uncoiled the sheet and blanket, punched up the pillow beneath my head, covered my face with my hands, and cried myself to sleep, wondering if God had plans for me other than the calling I seemed to be inventing.

The following morning I rewrote the poem. Had the dream continued when I fell back to sleep? I couldn't remember, but I had the distinct feeling of annoyance with myself. Perhaps I'd gotten up too fast and the dream dissipated before I could grasp it or any of its meaning. It was so vague, yet I seemed to recall a loggia of a palazzo I've never seen with twisted trunks of *melograno*, covering stanchions of the same pomegranate color supporting an overhead balcony.

Had I dreamt someone had stolen my heart? I dipped the pen nib into the inkwell and wiped the excess from the tip against the side of the squat bottle. When I started writing, it seemed as if the poem were being dictated in my ear and I had nothing whatsoever to do with it. What a queer feeling.

"Icicles at Christmas"

We went to cut down our Christmas tree,
but fir trees aren't half as big as I remembered them to be.
And red is not the red of Christmas bows! nor tinsel bright,
nor does it shimmer like the brilliant stuff
we threw by fistfuls. And icicles! Daggers of ancient Siculi.
Props for the sword swallower at the circus.
I break a jagged stalactite, dangling from a slanted roof,
watch sun glitter through it in your eyes.
Enchantment. Magic. Alchemy.
You make me look inside deep within the icicle's heart
where snow castles soar in the sky and the winter court
of Princess Snowflake floats on clouds, and there!
Jesters cartwheeling, somersaulting, spinning round giant
fir trees sparkling with silver slivers and cranberry bows.
Harlequins pirouette, dizzying me till I shout,
Stop the earth!
Caught up in your arms, you twirl me slowly,
a top winding down.

You kiss my nose, cold as a puppy's,
calling me angel fallen from above and say,
Stay forever in these arms past icicle season, beyond
gifts wrapped with fabric, tied with satin ribbons
as you loose one from my hair and set me down.
In my ear, the whispered words,
Be my Christmas ever after.

CHAPTER XXI

Angelica

CHRISTMAS EVE

I LOVED TO ROAM THE countryside, despite my mamma's admonitions that I should be accompanied. I often wandered about a kilometer from my home to the monastery nestled away in the thickets of Villaggio Pace. I wanted to work for the cloistered nuns in the convent on the hill, but Mamma was against it. So I arranged and was granted an interview on Christmas Eve without telling her, though it was my intention to do so after the fact.

I felt torn because I wanted to be with my parents and brother and sisters, preparing for the feast day and celebrating with them. I loved this season of whispers, gifts wrapped with cloth remnants, packets tied with gauze streamers and satin bows, and the perfume of baked goods in our kitchen. Yet there at the convent gate I stood, the earth frozen beneath my feet. I glimpsed the garden walled within, winter twilight illuminating plump persimmons on a leafless tree. I thought of Chinese lanterns but couldn't say why. How did I know they existed? Where had I seen them?

Snowflakes began to fall upon the huge crèche below the fruit tree. Silence surrounded me with its own sound, only to be broken when voices from the cloister snaked their way to my ears in the rise and fall of rhythmic *Kyrie Eleison* chorales. For some reason I thought of the three wise men: Balthasar, Caspar, and Melchior. Perhaps because I inhaled incense, or did I only imagine it? I puzzled about what the scent of myrrh was like. I had heard that it was used in the anointing of the dead.

A cold wind glided round me, and suddenly I felt as if my soul didn't know its own mind. Why was I here instead of home with my family? I yearned for something and thought the answer was the solitude behind the convent walls. But deep within didn't I have a twinge of longing? Didn't I desire a family of my own where I would oversee the roost like my mamma?

The choir chanted the ancient liturgy—songs that soothed. I began to pray the Divine Office, feeling Christmas as a hymn that blessed.

I clanged the bell. The old doorkeeper approached. I awaited the unlatching click as the man, his cape flying in the wind, struggled with the hasp. My fingertips were so cold they hurt as they clung to the wrought-iron bars bathed in Vesper sun. Again, I thought of my family. Maybe I would never make a good nun if earthly things forever captured and entertained me, keeping me from total adoration of God.

Upon entering I was immediately struck by the resemblance of the *parlatorio* to the one described by Manzoni in his novel *Promessi Sposi*. There were oil paintings of nuns—mostly deathbed scenes, some framed, but others were not. The room was white stucco, recently painted, and the smell of cooking with grease permeated from the refectory.

I approached the grate and was stricken by the thought of the prioress having had a life before the convent like Manzoni's character the Signora. Come to think of it, she didn't want to be a nun at all, but was forced into it by her parents to save the family's wealth for her brother. My parents would never barter me away by such means, even if they had to scrimp and beg. So sure of these feelings was I that I shivered. Sell me into bondage behind high walls—never!

I was nervous for my interview with the Prioress Teresa Margherita. I offered her my credentials—a letter from Don Ruggero—and told her of my experience in the sacristy.

Mother Teresa and I spoke through a double grate. At first it was difficult to focus on her face through the black bars, but after a while it seemed normal. She was heavyset, her brows thick and coarse, almost mannish, and her cheeks were rosy with spidery veins while her jowls protruded from the tight guimpe that framed her face. We were both seated. She asked another nun, Sister Paola, to bring me coffee and almond cookies. These were situated on a small tray that she put into a rotating wheel and spun outward to me.

She told me that my duties would be limited to answering the inside door as well as cleaning the receiving room and entrance foyer where the packages and shopping were delivered to be passed through a larger rotating wheel in the foyer. I would also care for and change altar cloths and repair any tatters. Cleaning the priest's parlor, his chambers, and water closet were also to be my responsibility. I must have made a face at that because Mother Teresa said, "Humility above all else, my child."

Mother Teresa told me that another nun, Mother Lucia, who had previously been the prioress, was to be my spiritual counselor. Ruggero had all but gushed mentioning her to me, but the instant Lucia entered I knew immediately I could never subjugate my will to hers. She barely acknowledged me. She was rigid, unbending, and lacked every social grace. In plain words, she had the amenities of a peasant. God forgive me!

Mother Teresa introduced Lucia as the sister who would be my spiritual guardian.

I thought I'd choke, right then and there on the spot.

"Would you be my spiritual mentor, Mother Teresa, instead of Mother Lucia?" I rubbed my hands together and had a great urge to stamp my feet. I could feel the humidity penetrating. Mother Lucia moved toward the prioress, bending forward to whisper in her ear. As she did so, I realized that she was discalced. I wondered how the nun could stand to wear just simple sandals and no stockings in this miserably dank place during the winter.

"Why do you wish it, child?" Mother Superior asked. She waved away Lucia, who inclined her head, backed up several steps, and then turned and left.

I hesitated and then blurted out, "I think our personalities would clash, Mother."

"You don't even know each other." She glanced over her shoulder to see that Lucia had gone. "You must learn to get along with all the good sisters. Are you sure you wouldn't like to keep her as your guide? Perhaps you could be rewarded with a true humbling experience."

"Most certainly, if that is what you desire. It's just that I feel that I would be a more apt pupil under your tutelage."

"In that case, Angelica, I will allow it."

"I would like to enter the convent now, Mother." The lighting was so poor and came only from the high windows. The day was overcast so it seemed as if it were very late evening when, in reality, it was afternoon.

"What do your parents say?"

"They think I'm too young, that I'll change my mind if the right man makes an offer of marriage." I sipped the coffee. It was bitter and nothing like Mamma's delicious brew. I must have conveyed this by my expression because the nun said, "We use chicory instead of coffee beans, which are too expensive."

No wonder, I thought, *and sugar too must be used only for monsignors.* I could have bit my tongue on that unuttered unkindness. *Remember to bring some sugar after the feast of Saint Steven's,* I urged myself.

"And do you feel this is so? After all, your parents know you well."

"I don't think so. I've tried to discourage Mamma every time she mentions Domenico—he's the son of Mamma's friend from Reggio Calabria—" I abruptly remembered Domenico's sparse good looks and wondered what it would be like for him to hold me in his arms the way Lella's lover had held her. So real were these thoughts, I jumped up from my chair and began pacing the floor, looking around trying to focus.

"Sit down. What's wrong with you?"

"Nothing."

"But do you feel you could love a man the way you love God?"

"I know I love God and want to serve Him in all things." I hesitated and added, "I don't want to marry. I don't want to have children." This was the very first time I'd said this out loud, and it didn't ring true in my ears. I loved children, I was just petrified to carry and deliver one.

She smiled a toothy grin and said, "That's not what I asked you, child." *What awful stained teeth. Doesn't she brush them?* "I don't think I could ever love anyone more than God," I said, but the underlying question was much more difficult for me. Could I love a man enough to marry him? I clasped and unclasped my hands.

"We use only lye soap to wash our mouths. Does that satisfy your curiosity?"

I inclined my head and felt my cheeks getting hotter and more scarlet. I looked up at her and crimsoned. Could she have noticed I was judging her poor health habits?

"On my next visit I'll bring you some Pasta di Capitano if you'd like."

"Toothpaste is a vanity I can live without."

But can I?

She continued, nonplussed, "Does love of God supersede your love of parents?"

I hesitated and then said yes, but that my parents were representative of God on earth and worthy of more than just love. After all, they had given me life. I loved them as I did Don Ruggero, my confessor. But that wasn't completely true. What I couldn't concede was that I adored them. They were the spheres of my world and if I could, I'd pursue no other. Was this, then, a means to flee comfort and love? What was I proving and to whom? Maybe I loved my family more than the church and all its rituals. Why was I hesitant to acknowledge such love? Did this mean I was afraid of Don Ruggero and this nun? If not fearful, I was wary to say the truth. I loved God, but I was not convinced about the laws of the church because they were established by men—human beings like myself, imperfect people. There could be no holier perfect vision than the Holy Family, than my family, or a possible family I could be head of.

"Of course," she said, "God has given you life," shaking her head in disapproval of my words. "We'll have to introduce you to a new confessor at the earliest possible minute."

I didn't want to start all over with a new confessor. It was then I knew for certain I would never reveal in confession every thought that crossed my mind. Misdeeds, bad actions, maybe. Was I questioning confession? The beginning words of *The Creed* came to me. "I believe in God . . ." A man to take His place in a confessional on earth was a marvelous belief, but unexpectedly, I doubted it. What was I doing here?

Looking past Mother Teresa to the back wall, I noticed a frameless painting of a dying nun surrounded by angels. I thought how quickly Papà would be able to remedy a frame. His carpentry skills were formidable, and I could convince him easily enough, I was quite certain.

Mother Teresa caught me looking at the painting and told me the sister had been Princess Orsini before entering the convent. This was fodder for my soul: a young, rich princess leaving hearth and home to serve God in a contemplative order. Now, that was positive information to feed Mamma. Though wealth was nothing to me, my family I treasured.

How would I ever reconcile myself to leaving them for something I wasn't even sure I really wanted?

"There is one other serious matter I will have to discuss with your mother." She put her hands into the opposite sleeves. "Your virginal state is not intact," she said, almost preening.

I swallowed hard, trying to conceal my surprise, hurt, and anger at Ruggero, who had disclosed this family secret, and my loathing for this nun who'd slapped my face with it.

"Quite unusual," she said, adjusting her veil.

I bit my lower lip, tried to make my face a blank, but my cheeks flushed and I stammered to say something, but couldn't. Did that mean the priest had broken the seal of confession? I'd ask Mamma. Was the nun inferring that Papà would have to pay a higher dowry price for me?

"You look upset, dear. Didn't you know that your secret would be disclosed? You are not intact, are you?"

I felt ashamed. Not for myself, but for Ruggero, whose loose-flapping mouth had caused me this embarrassment, and even more for this *mischina* nun who gloated over my misfortune.

My indignation showed when I stood up, catching her off guard, deflating her ego, and usurping her of the opportunity to terminate the interview.

"I'm leaving," I said.

She stood with slow, deliberate movements. Mother Teresa took from her beaded belt a large hoop on which were attached many keys, some of them twenty centimeters in length. She fished about for the one she wanted, explained that I was to note it, and handed the key ring to me through the square bars on what looked like a long, narrow, wooded flour scoop with a handle.

"Go through this door and lock it, then turn right and go through the entrance. You'll come to a door. Open it with this key. It's the hallway that leads to the rear of the chapel. On your way back, just reverse your steps and lock the door. Then put the key ring in the large wheel. This short journey will familiarize you with the route you will take in four days when I'll see you again. Be prompt. Six o'clock."

I didn't answer or incline my head or curtsy. I thrust back my shoulders and left. How more dramatic it would have been had I just walked out of that *parlatorio* and into the courtyard. Instead, I did as she had commanded and came to a remarkable hallway. It was lined with plants of every kind imaginable—philodendra, wandering Jew, cactus—and it faced a courtyard that had a loggia and a well in the center. I must have stood transfixed for a long time, the simple beauty of it quite spellbinding, contrasting the nun's final revelation of my unworthy, irreversible state. I'd lost time so I had to rush, and when I returned the keys to the wheel, I was breathless.

I came away from the convent with the bitterness of chicory on my tongue, the image of what lye soap had done to Mother Teresa's teeth, and eyes blinded with tears of outrage. I shuddered. The gatekeeper opened, but I slammed the gate closed. I started to wend my way toward home when my ears were accosted by the music of the *zampognari*, piper shepherds, clad in thong-tied boots and sheepskin vests, knitted hats covering their long locks. They had left their flocks to other tenders' hands and come down from the hills, playing mournful songs. The twangs and breaths of the bagpipes, meant to brighten the December afternoon, instilled in me an indescribable loneliness. My soul would shrivel and die of starvation if it were not fed love. Melancholy would seep around my spirit to strangle it. I crammed the thought of convent life into a dusty corner of my brain, letting it fill instead with the wonderful season of Christ's birth and love for the world and everything in it.

I broke into a run and didn't stop until I was winded on the outskirts of town.

I hadn't taken a direct route toward home, as I deliberately wanted to pass the stalls and vendors to savor the sights and smells. Merchants and customers alike huddled in storefronts waiting to conclude a sale or for the cold to abate.

As I approached the town's heart, snippets of conversation and tidings from shopkeepers issued forth from stores surrounding the piazza. Musical piper sounds echoed in a miracle of notes and tongues, "Welcome!"

I couldn't help myself, and so I smiled at a very young shepherd boy who reminded me of Peppe. I could almost hear my papà saying I had a smile that angels envied. And I brushed my teeth three times a day with real toothpaste. God forgive me!

By the time I reached home, I still carried with me the image of the shy shepherd boy who'd made me smile. My thoughts were of the international language of children—love, a message of hope and peace for all who believed. A true Christmas blessing. I saw my mother's worried expression and realized I had been tardy and she was frantic. I ran to her, and she enveloped me in her outstretched arms, a refuge where I felt safe and secure. Then something strange happened. There was static in my clothes from the cold air outside that I'd carried in with me to her warm kitchen, which gave me little electric shocks as I removed my coat. In my mind, I had exchanged places with my mother and it was I who held out my arms to a daughter. This transformation was a foresight—I sensed it a long way off in the future—but it was real and present in the same way I had felt the coming of danger or death in the past, only this time I wasn't at all agitated, but rather peaceful and oddly content. What did it mean?

❦

MAMMA AND I SAT AT the kitchen table having our coffee. Real coffee. I told her about the interview with the prioress.

"Why did you go alone and without my permission?" she said, her voice tart.

"What kind of man is your brother?" I asked. The accusation hung in the air between us.

"Your uncle told the prioress about your accident?" she guessed.

I nodded.

"It means nothing."

"It means everything. The cruel way she said it. They can refuse me."

"Not if your papà makes a substantial enough—"

"Dowry gift—that's what I thought. But would he?"

"I doubt it—he won't hear anything about it. Be content for the time being, at least, with him letting you go there to work." She started to clear away the cups.

"For now," I said. "Mamma, sit down. I haven't finished."

"Do you want more coffee?"

"Not coffee. The discussion."

She sat down.

Next I asked whether Ruggero had broken the seal of confession. She assured me he hadn't, but was cross at the wretch. *"Sciaguratu.* Worse than an old woman gossiping."

Then I surprised myself and took my mother off guard when I asked, "What is love?"

Mamma took a long time to answer. I started to fidget, but I kept my eyes fixed so that she knew I wanted her answer, needed it.

She pursed her lips, pushed the sugar bowl away, and leaned her arms on the table. Mamma's face was close to mine. Her sweet breath, tinged with anise, warmed my cheek. "So many kinds of love." She sighed. "It's a feeling that you wish someone total well-being. You want them to be forever protected by an invisible cloud of light, as if the air of the saints surrounds them. The extent of human passion is beyond what any of us can possibly imagine or experience. I know this only because I've dreamt it, tasted it, but only in dreams." She brushed my cheek with an upward motion with the tops of her fingers. "*Bedda*. My mother instructed me on what she learned from her mother, and I pass that knowledge to you. This may not be enough; you'll go further."

Mamma sat up a little straighter, and I knew she saw more questions in my eyes because she continued in the sweetest way. "But what you're asking me is not this—it's romantic love, isn't it? When you love, you'll know, Angelica—the force of it is as explosive as a volcano, yet peaceful as a dove in flight, unaware that danger lurks at the next change of wind direction."

I felt the hair at the base of my neck raise. My frightened heart yielded erratic beats till I was aware of the movement of my chest. Wild and frantic, like wings of a bird caught indoors.

Bird of the wild.

Was I capable of owning such an experience?

As if to calm me, Mamma raised her hand, then took hold of mine. "Loving a man is contrary to all you think you now want, but if it's for you and in God's design, you'll be imprisoned by it and remain a slave to it, never seeking freedom, never wanting liberty."

We were still seated at the table when there was a loud knocking at the door. Two men who worked as pickers on my father's land brought us a pine tree. One of them was Gaetano. I was so overcome with emotion by what Mamma had said that I foolishly asked how they'd chopped it down. Mamma offered Marsala. Gaetano asked why we wanted the tree, and Mamma explained that it was Nonno who'd brought the tradition back from England. Then, as Gaetano began his tale, Peppe came in. Mamma asked him to get Papà and bring back a small axe. When he returned he immediately started hacking at the lower boughs, arranging them on the mantel, calling out orders for Rina to bring in some candles.

Papà came in, followed by my sisters. He thanked the men and gave them some coins and *un fiasco di vino* each, but instead of sending them on their way, he invited them to sit. Mamma poured another Marsala and served them almond cookies and large wedges of rum cake.

The boughs transported me back in time, and I remembered my dream about candle making when Zia Concetta died. In my head, I constructed a verse called "Christmas Keepsake," which I later wrote down in an old school copybook. Afterward, I made a finer version in my best hand to give to Zu Nino.

Mamma said, "Angelica, are you with us? You're so far away. Were you daydreaming?" The scent of pine permeated the air, and my head filled with notions and pieces of novels I'd read. I felt elated, willing to forgive the nun for her mean thrill at my expense. It seemed I traversed from my little village to every other part of the world that celebrated the birth of Christ.

Papà asked me to recite something for the men who had brought our tree. I remembered a poem I'd written and memorized for school. It came back to me line by line, image by image, succinctly. I cleared away the dishes and served the woodsman strong coffee laced with anisette, and then recited "The Christmas Market":

> As the sky's light dims to allow
> The dusk of eve to take its bow,
> The market bustles with an air
> Of Christmas business everywhere.
>
> The hawkers' cries do jar our ears
> As cold stings eyes that brim with tears.
> The brazier's chestnuts heat to steam
> Warming hands, giving hearts a dream.
>
> The old ones wrapped in shawls and muffs,
> With booted feet and fur-trimmed cuffs,
> Take refuge when the snowflakes fall
> Upon the large umbrella's stall.

Some carry bread beneath an arm.
Or juggle fir trees picked for charm.
A bell is rung to spread good cheer:
Joy, health and prosperous New Year!

Mamma, Peppe, Rina, the girls, and my papà applauded, saying, "*Brava*," all at the same time, like they had one voice only. I flushed red and went to do the dishes. I think I forgot to say thank you.

CHAPTER XXII

Rosalia

A TELEGRAM

ROSALIA ACCEPTED THE TELEGRAM ADDRESSED to Nicola from Carini. She held it for what seemed an interminable amount of time. She carried the envelope to the parlor and set it on a silver salver that had been a wedding present.

She started walking away, but something drew her back to the envelope and she opened it, reading the harsh black words: "Brother Giovanni gravely ill. Send Rosalia at once." It was signed "Ruggero."

Rosalia's shriek could be heard throughout the house. She now sat on the floor where she'd fallen in a heap. Angelica and Peppe came running toward her.

Peppe began to fan her face as Angelica went to the bureau where a pitcher of water and glasses were set on a tray. She poured Rosalia a glass of water, but Rosalia pushed away her daughter's hand with the glass.

"My God, Mamma, what's wrong?" asked Peppe.

"I felt weak, maybe I fainted," Rosalia answered. "The room turned suddenly dark."

"It's going to storm. Mamma, why do you think you fainted? You're not expecting again, are you?" asked Angelica, a note of agitation in her voice.

In reply Rosalia shook her head. "An ominous—" She looked around on the floor and reached for the telegram beneath the sofa. She held it up and Angelica read it aloud.

Peppe helped his mother to a chair.

"Oh, Mamma, maybe there's hope yet," said Angelica. "We can pray." She clutched her heart.

"What is it?" Rosalia asked.

"Nothing. Just blood passing through my heart." Angelica sat and unfolded the telegram. "It's addressed to Papà."

Rosalia said, "Telegrams are always emergencies and trouble. Are you questioning me?" Then in a softer tone added, "My darling girl, I fear my brother's already dead. I know it." She sobbed. "I knew the minute I took hold of the telegram."

"How can you say that? You don't know for sure. It says he's ill, so you have to hope," argued Peppe.

Rosalia was proud that Peppe assumed Nicola's place when he wasn't around. She smiled weakly. "I know. Here." She tapped her breast. She looked at Angelica. "You know it too, don't you?" Rosalia saw by the girl's expression that she did. "Later on today there'll be another telegram, saying he's taken a turn for the worse."

"But why would Don Ruggero play cat and mouse with your emotions like this? You must be wrong," Peppe countered. He pushed a stray curl off his mother's forehead.

"As I sit and breathe, it is as I say. Ruggero isn't toying with me. Believe me. It's just his way to ease me into the idea that our youngest brother is gone forever."

Rosalia broke into uncontrollable sobs. Angelica handed her a handkerchief. The room grew darker and the storm broke loose. Lightning illuminated the sky in a frenzied zigzag. A bestial thunder roared. The wind shook the windows. Its howling could be heard lashing about in the branches of trees near the house. Rain came in torrents, sheeting down the windows.

The three people in the room fell silent. Rosalia listened to nature playing havoc outside. Wind blustered about in the garden, ripping frail limbs from the trees. She turned toward the window. "It was like my heart splintered. Why did I open it?" Then she asked Angelica why she had gripped at her heart earlier.

"A sinking feeling in a furrow of my heart convinced me he was already dead. I'm so sorry, Mamma."

Rosalia watched as a tender look passed between her son and her daughter. Peppe got up and took hold of his mother's hands, kissed them, and left.

"I'll need some dresses altered. Angelica, work a miracle for your mother. There's no time to go to the *sarta*."

They went upstairs where Angelica immediately began to rip collars, change bodices, and sew black ribbons on some of her mother's dresses and hats so that she'd be properly attired for the funeral and mourning period. While she helped Rosalia pack, the second telegram arrived.

<hr />

ANGELICA CLOSED AND LOCKED THE suitcase, took it off the bed, and placed it on the floor.

"You're in charge of everything now, Angelica. You'll have to forego your convent visits and work solely for the family. I've sent Peppe to ask Mother Prioress for a novice to help you with the cleaning, washing, ironing, and cooking. We'll make a donation to the convent when I return. Please don't be a heroine, my darling girl; let the novice do the heavy work. I don't want you falling ill during my absence."

Rosalia looked at Angelica's dreamy expression and snapped, "Am I making myself clear?"

"Perfectly, Mamma."

Angelica handed her mother a tulle veil and a black lace mantilla.

Rosalia placed her tortoise comb along with a silver-handled brush and hand mirror into the leather traveling case and fastened it closed.

"I'll be gone at least a month."

Angelica sighed. "So long?"

She took her daughter by the shoulders and pulled her into an embrace. "I'm depending on you. Ruggero wants me to be sole inheritor of our brother's property. Law stipulates that we share equally, but since he's a priest and taken care of—we'll need legal counsel to arrange my becoming sole heir."

"Does Don Ruggero know a notary?" Angelica asked.

"I believe it's more complicated and we will have to see an advocate, someone who is not only schooled in the law, but also cognizant of inheritance taxes and the like. Your uncle knows someone who has an office in Palermo. It may involve a great deal of money . . ." Here she hesitated. "But also time. This may necessitate a possible move to Carini."

"Temporary?" Angelica asked.

By the look on her daughter's distraught face, Rosalia knew not to say any more. She kissed her cheeks and signed a blessing on her forehead.

ROSALIA RETURNED AS SHE HAD said she would in a month's time after all was settled. Don Ruggero had relinquished his inheritance share to his sister. Her brother Giovanni's house, groves, and shop in Carini were now her husband's.

CHAPTER XXIII

Angelica

MOVING TO CARINI

IT WAS WORSE THAN I feared. My parents made plans to move. I'd be celebrating my next birthday in an unfamiliar place—Carini. I had to give up my visits to the convent altogether in order to help Mamma organize Papà, Peppe, and the little ones for their journey to Carini. Papà's unmarried sister, Sofia, would act as housekeeper for them while Mamma and I stayed behind to close up the house, readying it for Zu Nino, who would move in just as soon as he sold his own house and property. He would now live in ours. Mamma wanted to finish selling the rest of her mattresses and to liquidate the salaries of the men who were in the middle of the harvest. Peppe yearned to stay to supervise, but Papà squelched that idea. He said he'd need Peppe to organize the groves and *enoteca*, our new wine shop in Carini. Papà asked Zu Nino to look out for Mamma and me.

AFTER PAPÀ AND THE CHILDREN were gone two months, I thought I'd die of loneliness. I missed them. Most of all, I yearned to hear laughter, but also voices overflowing with excitement. When Mamma had things on her mind she either shut up like a clam or snapped like a turtle. There was no pleasing her. She didn't like the way I packed some dishes and took every one out of the box.

"Redo them," she said, making a threatening gesture to break one over my head if I didn't do it right. Then she lapsed into silence again.

Whenever I lamented of this or that, the only thing Mamma said over and over like a litany was before long we'd all be together again. Lonesome thoughts nagged me, such as an alternative idea to convent life or marriage. I could remain an old-maid aunt like Papà's sister Sofia. As soon as it crossed my mind, I thought I'd gag. But Mamma had other problems. Her worries and *pensieri* appeared as new wrinkles on her forehead.

I complained again to Mamma, "Not even Lella will be visiting before we leave. Marriage has changed her. She's becoming a recluse." I said this just for something to say. I could have cut out my tongue because that kind of statement could lead to our visiting her.

"Wait. Your day and time will come and then you too will change."

"Mamma, I've no intention of marrying."

"For the time being."

I murmured, "Not ever," but not loud enough for Mamma's ears. I didn't want to enrage her. I'd tangled enough with her wrath for one day. "I even miss Don Ruggero. Seems like forever since he's gone."

I felt I couldn't wait to quit Villaggio Pace. Though the thought of moving to Carini frightened me, the prospect of living so close to Palermo intrigued me.

We had covered all the furniture with sheets. The house took on a spectral air. Mamma said that Papà would be back before we knew it to arrange the shipment of articles we needed and wanted. As I looked around I sensed that nothing would ever be the same. I didn't cry, but I pined for the gaiety of youth and carefree times I'd spent in this house and on this land. I had been reading Job of late and found myself reciting aloud: "My days are swifter than a weaver's shuttle, and are spent without hope. O remember that my life is wind: mine eye shall no more see good."

<hr>

AFTER ALL THE FURNITURE, I covered each and every painting, but no matter what I did or how carefully I did it, Mamma found fault with me. At one point when I felt like a kettle ready to blow, she apologized to me for her snappy behavior. "If you think you miss them," she said, looking at the curtains and yanking them down without sympathy, "can you imagine how I feel?" Her eyes glistened with tears.

"Let's take some time for ourselves," she said in a disembodied voice. I'd never heard anything like the tone or sentiment now in her voice.

"What can we do?"

"Perhaps . . ." she hesitated, "we could go to Messina for the day to see Papà's sister Margherita. Or to Taormina." Mamma was overwrought. She needed a holiday.

I answered, "Whatever you say, Mamma."

Not that I particularly wanted to go to Taormina, or see Zia Margherita. Lella's mother could be noisome with her inquisitiveness. In my ear I heard her chirpy little voice asking over and over, "And when will you be announcing your wedding plans, *mia cara?*" I especially wanted to avoid a visit to Lella. I summoned back Mamma's words when I held Lella's wedding invitation. Was I jealous of Lella, the married lady? Petrified to see her happily ensconced in a home decorated with new furnishings, exuding love fulfilled by understanding and mutual sexual desire? We never got a chance to speak privately again after Lella's two-week stay before her wedding. Feeling intimidated by the possibilities of such an encounter, I wasn't about to answer these self-imposed questions. I only knew I didn't want to face seeing Lella just yet.

⚜

MY MOTHER APPEARED NERVOUS. WHENEVER I asked her anything, she answered me but was either bewildered or short-tempered. I thought about what could be troubling her, and finally came up with the reason. It was she who had insisted on the move and convinced my father that we should attempt this new venture. Mamma's acquired property, through her brother's death, meant we were to become proprietors of a *bottega*, where we would sell wine, oil, salt, and become tobacco merchants. What did she know of this business?

Before Papà had left, I learned for sure he never would betray my mother's hopes. He buoyed her, telling her time and again that all would go well with the move. However, in his own heart, he wasn't convinced. I'd overheard him in the living room, telling Zu Nino about his uneasy feelings.

My father stood near the table where I'd just laid a fresh cloth. On my way out the door I turned in his direction and my heart went out to him.

"The choice made, but the mind divided," he said to his brother, tapping his chest. There was a hitch in his voice, and for a brief moment I thought my father was on the brink of crying. But he cleared his throat and continued, unruffled. "I don't want distance to put a wedge between us."

I closed the door quietly and walked out into a brilliant sun that blinded me temporarily. I shaded my eyes with my hand. I wondered if it shone as brightly in Carini, the place where we were headed. Of course it did. After all, sun is sun, and above all, Sicilian summer sun is merciless, east or west. Somehow I'd allowed my father's apprehension to creep into the crevices of my heart. I looked around and knew I was steeped by a nostalgic sense, which I wouldn't dismiss and couldn't deny. I would miss the piazza, my walks to town, the orchards and groves, my meanderings to the convent. I would miss the place of my birth, the earth upon which Zia Concetta's last steps trod. I didn't realize I was crying until I tasted salt at the corners of my mouth. Out loud I said, "I'll see you again, Villaggio Pace, land of volcanoes and earthquakes, that's a promise."

◦━⧸✦⧹━◦

IT WAS FINALLY TIME TO move and Mamma and I hadn't taken time off. Instead, we assembled our personal belongings, everything the family had left behind. We left the house, grounds, and everything else in the capable hands of Zu Nino. It was he who accompanied us to the train station.

CHAPTER XXIV

Rosalia

THE TRAIN DEPOT

THE TRAIN STATION BUSTLED WITH activity. The movements of the porters, splashed by mud from the unseasonable rain, were well timed and spaced. Rosalia was amazed at their fluidity and grace and the fact that they didn't constantly careen into other porters, passengers, or portmanteaux.

Rosalia negotiated the crowded station, Angelica shadowing her every step. Rosalia watched the workers' garrison posts. Then, as if a silent bugle sounded a command, they hefted luggage and baskets onto flat trolleys supported by low wheels. The porters were black-clad Druids with beards; others reminded her of country priests, berets jauntily covering bald pates. These men wended and weaved, snaking their way on the besmirched platform. Arriving at the proper car, they deposited baggage and parcels. Travelers followed luggage, close on the heels of porters.

Rosalia took Angelica by the hand and watched her daughter gingerly lift her skirt with the other.

"Won't do much good, I can assure you. That's why I told you to wear the black or gray instead of the beige."

"Mamma, when will Papà and Peppe meet up with us?"

"I'm not sure, but we'll be met at the Palermo train station by my brother."

Rosalia thought about her other children and couldn't wait to be reunited with them. Maneuvering toward the coach, she thought about how they must have grown over the summer. A twinge of yearning washed over her and she bit her lip to stave off tears.

A strong gust of foul wind made Rosalia drop Angelica's hand and raise the capuche of her cape. Rosalia thought about all the work that had brought her to this train station.

She had been determined to make one more trip to Calabria with her mattresses before the cold weather arrived. She didn't need the extra money since she was frugal, but the mattresses were ready, and they would make a good ploy for Angelica to remake the acquaintance of Domenico. Rosalia hoped that his good looks would change Angelica's fascination with the church and make her start thinking like a woman instead. But Rosalia's neat plan had been foiled. When mother and daughter arrived in Calabria, only Gina met them. Domenico had been promoted to *marisciallo* of the *Carabinieri* and was transferred to Naples. One night while Angelica slept, the two older comrades talked and planned a future meeting for their children in Carini where Gina too had *parenti* in nearby Palermo.

THE TRAIN STEPS LEADING TO the drafty platform were steep. *La Letterina* would be crowded, and aware of this, Rosalia made sure they'd arrived with plenty of time before their departure. Mother and daughter made their way to their compartment.

Rosalia closed the door behind them. Angelica placed her parcels down and began to sort them out, arranging the soft luggage bag overhead. The seats were plush and comfortable, although the red velvet was frayed in spots. Angelica sat down and patted the seat beside her for Rosalia, who said, "I prefer to sit opposite and look at you."

"There's always a feeling of excitement when one voyages to a new place, but you must feel quite at ease, Mamma. After all, this is your girlhood home."

"We'll only be in Palermo a little while. I'm not all that familiar with Carini. It must have changed a great deal since I was a girl."

Once they'd settled into the compartment, Angelica said, "Maybe we can plan a trip or two so you can show me around."

"Once we've organized the house and store, you mean."

"Of course. Mamma, there's something else I'd like to ask you," Angelica added.

Rosalia placed the basket lunch she carried on the seat next to her. "What is it, dear?"

"You should let me help in the store. I've been thinking about it ever since Papà left with his sister and the children."

"That's a wonderful idea, but—"

"But?"

"*But* is spelled P-a-p-à. How do we circumvent that obstacle?"

"Mamma, if you've a mind to, you can do it," Angelica said, a matter-of-fact tone underscoring her sentiments.

Rosalia laughed. "Observant, aren't you? The truth is you should take care of the house and children. I've got selling experience and need a change from housekeeping and diapers."

"I agree. Ever since Papà left you've had the energy of a nervous colt. However, don't discount it for the near future. After that . . . rather . . . well, until I can enter the convent."

Rosalia let this comment slide as if she'd never heard it. It was irksome to have to think of preparing *una ricca dote*, not for Angelica's marriage, but for the novitiate. They'd had this argument many times before, but now she saw Angelica becoming more insistent. She was coming to an age where it would be difficult to prevent it from happening. Rosalia was saddened and turned her head. She had a headache and chose not to discuss it right now. As the car began to fill, she closed her eyes. The train moved forward then lurched to a halt, but before it chugged out of the station, she'd fallen asleep.

SHE AWOKE TO THE SWIFT moving car on the rails as if her mind too were racing to remember something. What had Angelica been saying? *She's still thinking of entering the convent. Is it my fault she wants to hide away? Has midwifing made her lose her peace of mind? Does she believe that she'll be protected from life if she shuts herself away?*

Rosalia sat up erectly and rubbed her eyes.

"You hardly slept," Angelica said.

"I was thinking of what you said to me. Sometimes I forget just how impressionable you are. I shouldn't have listened to your papà—you were too young to begin midwifing—and now you think closing yourself in a convent will protect you from life. I doubt you'd thrive shut away behind the walls. You're dead wrong, child."

"I'm not wrong. Not in this." Angelica shrugged.

It was this slight movement that caused Rosalia to detect a possible admitted doubt, some inner turmoil.

"Life has a way of unearthing your each and every hiding place whether you want it to or not. We all have a destiny to fulfill, one that none of us can ignore. Fate finds us. Believe me."

Rosalia watched her daughter give a haughty toss of her head. "You'll learn just as I did," Rosalia said as Angelica took hold of her Rosary. Rosalia closed her eyes.

But Angelica interrupted her with, "Sometimes, Mamma, I just think you want to relive your life through me."

Rosalia's eyes opened wide. "Whatever do you mean?"

"Just what I said."

CHAPTER XXV

Angelica

THE TRAIN RIDE WEST

THE LONG TRAIN RIDE WAS not in the least bit boring for me. I studied other passengers, looked out the window, and then replayed the events of Lella's visit. I had dreaded seeing her, but then when she came to announce she was expecting a baby and asked me to be the godmother, it had shocked and surprised me, but I accepted without hesitation or any reserve.

Lella and I walked in the *orto* after she had given me this great honor. At one point she became very still, took hold of my hands, and looked me straight in the eyes.

"Angelica, when I came to stay with you before my wedding—" She broke off. "What I mean to say is, of course you know my secret, don't you?"

My face reddened, and I was glad of the dusk hour to shade my coloring. My angel spoke softly in my ear, "Now. Decide. Speak or carry Lella's secret with you to the grave."

"Why, Lella, whatever are you talking about? I know only that you and your husband are truly blessed by God in a unifying love. May it last forever." I squeezed Lella's hands, then dropped them. We sat on a rough-hewn bench Papà had made that used to sit under the kitchen window. I looked up to see new shoots and lemon blossoms bursting forth again. Their perfume was intense.

"That's precisely why I've chosen you, dearest cousin, as godmother for this child of love I carry."

"Oh, Lella, I'm so completely happy for you. Forgive me if I didn't come to visit you immediately. I think I was a teeny bit jealous, but my heart is full of joy for you. Please believe me. And I'm very proud you've chosen me. I thought surely it would have been Rina. I hope she won't be hurt."

"She's got a tougher hide than you think—more resilient than yours."

When Lella left I told Mamma, who wasn't at all amazed, only happy for me.

⌘

I HAD READING MATERIAL WITH me on the train, but I was more interested in the layette I was making for Lella's baby, my future godchild. I looked at the snowy soft blanket growing in length and thought, *I'll add pink or blue bows afterward.* As I continued knitting the delicate stitches, I became lost in thought and reminisced about the child's mother.

The wool tingled my fingers as I knitted the receiving blanket, the long wooden needles clacking every once in a while. I tried to use the wooden sheath my mother gave me to support the left-hand needle with the work, but found it difficult to use. Mamma said I'd learned to knit the wrong way with the needles floating in the air just like Zia Concetta, who had taught me. The sheath, a piece of carved wood, curved smoothly and was a whittled work of beauty, but I found it uncomfortable.

I placed the wool work and needles in my lap.

"Mamma, where did you get this?" I asked, indicating the sheath.

"Your father's father had been in England in 1820 when he worked as an officer on a freighter that picked up coal in Newcastle-Upon-Tyne."

"What a funny name." I thought of Nonno Giuliano, how afraid I was when he shaved himself. It was hard to imagine him young, virile, an officer of a ship.

"There are many castles in England just like the one we'll see in Carini, which has an interesting, bizarre history."

I was immediately struck by the thought of ghosts.

"And Tyne," my mother continued, "is the name of the river. In fact, the very same Normans who had settled in Sicily founded the castle in 1080. It was Robert Curthose, son of William the Conqueror."

How does she know this?

As if she read my thoughts, she said, "Your father has a book about it. Had I known you'd be so inquisitive, I would've given it to you."

"Tell me more, Mamma."

"The Romans had been there a thousand years before the Normans, your grandfather told me. They had bridged the River Tyne and built a fort on the very site where the castle was constructed later."

"Think of it, a thousand years before."

"You see how little we matter in the universe God created."

———

THERE WAS A FLURRY OF commotion. Passengers reached for bundles and corralled their children, buttoning up collars, taking hold of hands. I overheard one young mother giving instructions to her son about how to behave when greeting his father. As new passengers settled baggage, the train whistle blew and the conductor came by calling out the name of the next station.

Once more under way, I looked out the window. The country sped past in a blur. I began to fidget and fuss with the knitting needles and sheath.

Perplexed, I asked, "So Nonno purchased a sheath and brought it back for Nonna?"

"Oh, no. They were not objects one could buy in a shop, but rather had to be a labor of love—handmade—much as a woman knits a sweater for her true love. A man had to carve and embellish the sheath he would give as a much-prized gift to the girl of his dreams. Coal miners, sailors, and shepherds whittled them, just like the one you're holding."

"How romantic," I said in spite of myself and blushed. I couldn't possibly imagine any of the silly dolts I knew making such an exquisite gift for a girl. "How did Nonno come about this one, and how is it you have it?"

"Nonno carved on his sea journeys to and from England, and he gave one much more beautiful than this," she said, fondly touching the sheath, "to your papà's mother."

"Not this one?" I held up the sheath.

"That one was lost in a fire."

"Then whose is this?"

Mamma took the sheath in her hands and stroked it as she would a baby lamb. It seemed to me that her eyes were moist with tears of remembrance when she said, "Your father made this for me while he tended his sheep. I was just your age."

When Mamma handed the sheath back to me, I examined it. "What do these initials stand for?" I asked, pointing and tracing figure and letter intaglios in the wood.

"Forever," she murmured, her voice wistful yet somehow plaintive.

Would I ever consider marriage to someone like Papà, a man who would adore me the way he does Mamma?

Before I allowed myself to dwell on the taboo subject, I picked up the needles and yarn and fell silent. I cringed, thinking how every association with marriage and sex could lead to pain and death. I worked steadily, watching the threads grow into an intricate fabric. My fingers moved like precise machines following each knit and purl stitch without counting; I was pleased with my work.

Something outside whizzed by and caught my eye. I stopped knitting and looked out. I rested my forehead against the cold glass pane and then, like a child, exhaled warm breath. But a child would have written or drawn in the smoky circle. Instead, I was assailed by the thought that one's death breath must certainly be frosty. Suddenly I wondered what my last thought on earth would be. Would I be dreaming, lost in an artificial world, or cognizant that death approached?

I saw, in my mind's reflection, a priest bearing the pyx and heard the tinkling of bells, and realized my eyes were now closed and I was reliving the arrival of the host for Zia Concetta's Last Sacrament. Only, Zia Concetta was already dead and could no longer receive Communion, though the priest, whom I now recognized as Don Ruggero, did give her Extreme Unction.

I shuddered because I saw my brother Peppe's face appear so clearly, without priest or Sacramentals. Would my brother narrowly escape death? I opened my eyes. We were in a lowland copse, and in the distance I could see Monte Pellegrino and even far-off Punta Raisi.

"Look, Mamma."

Mamma said, "The word *rais* is Arabic for head. Centuries ago Arabs came looking for hideaways. Sicilians would say '*mafi*' in Arabic, which means *non c'è*, they're not here, and so one legend has it that the Mafia was born of men in hiding."

CHAPTER XXVI

Angelica

ARRIVAL AT PALERMO

PAPÀ HELD A BUNCH OF flowers as he rushed forward to greet Mamma. He whisked her up in his arms and spun her around. Then he crushed me in a bear hug that felt wonderful and warm. We were all laughing and crying and talking over each other's words, gesticulating madly with our hands as usual. Peppe hung back, observing the three of us with a grin that spread across his face from here to Roma. Finally he held Mamma and me, and the time apart was like a dream of long ago. Nothing mattered except that we were once again reunited.

I was as disappointed as Mamma that my younger sisters were not there to greet us, but Peppe assured us that they were planning a great surprise for us at home.

On the drive out of Palermo to Carini, there wasn't a moment's silence. Papà filled us in about the children's progress. His sister Sofia was sweet and had more patience than Mamma, although this was never mentioned. Sofia was a spinster with no ties and she loved children, especially her brother Nicola's. I thought she would stay with Zu Nino when Concetta died, but she didn't want to come back from Calabria and leave Zia Margherita's family. Zia Sofia didn't get along with my uncle the way she did with my father. Now, in the not-far-distant future, she would return again to Calabria. I remembered the story and odd circumstances of her betrothal and why she never married. Mamma had told me the man Sofia became engaged to had been a fortune seeker, and when my grandfather found out, he broke it off. Then, sadly, she met the love of her life, only to become engaged for a second time and have him succumb to a fatal illness one month before the wedding. I wanted to ask why Sofia hadn't entered the convent, but somehow I couldn't.

SOFIA HAD STAYED AT HOME with the girls to prepare our welcome. And what a welcome it was—we sounded like a gaggle of geese. After hugs and kisses galore we went into the marvelous garden festooned with crepe paper and buffet tables laden with every antipasto imaginable: tuna in olive oil, rolled stuffed eggplant, tiny meatballs, marinated baby squid, zucchini *gratinati*, a host of cold main dishes, and mouth-watering desserts.

The girls ushered Mamma and me directly into the shop even before we got a look at the house. The store was to be Mamma's new domain as she was retiring from midwifing. I would continue, if needed, but there were other women better known and more accepted in the area.

Every nook and cranny exhibited Papà's master carpentry work. There were huge casks of wine and drums of oil. The shelves were laden with sea salt packed in burlap sacks. There was a huge counter and a small cash register with beautiful, shiny porcelain buttons on top of which were etched numbers in black. When I punched the keys, pretending to make a sale, bells sounded and the drawer popped out. It startled me, but everybody laughed. From the shop there was an entrance into the house. I thought this was extremely clever. It was not the only entrance Mamma and I discovered as we inspected our new surroundings while Peppe took care of our luggage and belongings.

The house was filled with massive furniture. There was a roll-top desk of oak in Papà's study and a huge chestnut table not unlike the one we'd left behind in Villaggio Pace. The furniture in the bedrooms was all palisander and topped with gray stippled marble surfaces. There was a vanity with a mirror in my room and, although it was beautiful, I wished Papà had given it to Mamma. How could I suggest it without offending him or her? The one thing my room didn't have and that I immediately missed was a terrace. It had only a tiny balcony.

How could I pine for a missing terrace when in a short time I hoped to abandon all earthly possessions and take up the robes of a poor Carmelite? In my heart I believed I could convince Papà that this was right for me even though he was set against it. He reveled so in his family that if I dwelled upon it for any time, my faith in my plans was immediately shaken. Perhaps I wouldn't be able to persuade him. My jovial mood gave way. After dinner I fibbed, avoiding Papà's eyes and saying, "I must rest, I fear that the trip overexcited me."

My father said I looked flushed. I kissed my parents and said good night to my sisters and brother. I read Rina's disappointment on her face. She had wanted to hear all about the trip and, more importantly, Lella's decision to make me godmother to her child. I whispered, "Come to my room and we'll talk."

She smiled. Her face had taken on a more mature look since our separation, and what she'd always hoped for—friendship overtaking our sisterly relationship—was soon to develop between us.

⚜

I WALKED INTO MY ROOM and blessed myself with Sacramental holy water in my ceramic angel font that I'd received when I made my First Communion. How dear of my father to have put it up for me. I undressed quickly as the air was frigid. At first the sheets were like ice. I squirmed and moved but still didn't warm up. I tried reading but my lids were heavy and I couldn't concentrate. Images of the day's travel, still imprinted on my mind, disquieted me, especially the vision of Peppe in the window glass.

Rina knocked softly and came in. Her hair was almost waist length and she had a startling amount of red in it. Had I never seen it before? She carried a long-handled copper bed-warmer stocked with coals. She made me get up, then threw back the bed covers and swished and swiped the copper pot all over the sheets while I stood huddling with a wrap around me.

"Now," she said, "hop in and cuddle up." She laid the warmer on a rug. She sat on the edge of my bed, picked up a bunch of hair, and let it fall in front of her face. As she pushed it back, she said, "What do you think of it?"

"What have you done? Have you been drying it in the sun?"

"Mmm," she mused. "That and I rinse it with red wine vinegar and lemon juice. Papà knows there's something different about me, but still can't figure out what it is."

"You won't get away with that with Mamma, you know. She'll catch on and you'll be punished."

"I certainly hope my husband will be more observant than Papà."

"You're too young to think about such things."

"Maybe so, but you're not. When you left the table and I was clearing away the dishes, I overheard Mamma tell Papà and Peppe that she'd seen Gina and has arranged for her son Domenico to come and visit you. Sounds pretty official to me. What do you think?"

"Where do you get your ideas and language?"

"Beh, I'm modern and not contemplating sainthood. And while we're on the subject of canonization, tell me how you wrangled the godmother switch."

"Switch?"

"I thought surely I was going to be asked."

"It was Lella's idea."

"Why did you accept?" She worried the hem of the blanket.

"Are you upset?"

"Not really. There will be other babies, I'm sure. I'm curious as to why you accepted. After all, she and I were close—you two never really got on so well."

"True, but for some reason, it was meant to be."

"Will Lella come here for the christening, or are you going there?"

"I don't know."

"Will you show me the layette Mamma said you're working on?"

"Tomorrow. Promise. Rina, forgive me if you think I should have refused. I suppose it was selfish of me."

Rina flipped her hair off her neck and let it fall. "I understand. This may be the only time you'll ever have a chance to be any kind of mother, if you're really slated to be a nun. That's it, isn't it?"

"You do understand, don't you, dear?"

"In a way I'm glad I don't have to crochet booties and mittens and can work on my painting."

I thought, *How self-centered of me not to have even asked how her painting is coming along.* But the budding artist anticipated me and said, "I'll show you my progress tomorrow. I've graduated from pastels to oil on canvas. Peppe calls me Donatello!"

"And how are you two getting on?"

"He's in love, you know."

"With whom?"

"Ludovica Millati. Her mother's a dressmaker and her father is the best tailor around. She sews beautifully and sits at the shop-front window looking like a porcelain doll—so fragile she might break. Her skin is transparent."

"You exaggerate, as usual."

"Never."

"Do you like her?"

"Does it matter? She's a *mezzalingua!*"

"A half tongue. You mean a liar?"

She shook her head. "A stutterer, that's why she hardly ever speaks. It grates on me, like chalk on slate." She stood, picked up the warmer, and walked to the door.

"Kiss me good night, you little rascal, and try to be kinder. Rina—"

She blew me a kiss, turned at the door, and said, "Not another word till tomorrow. Have golden dreams. I must admit, I really missed you. The little ones fray my nerves and leave me only snatches of time to paint. Welcome home."

I blew out the light and waited until my eyes adjusted to the dark, the only light coming in from the gas street lamps outside the window. It was a stormy night. I listened to the wind and rain, every creaking, an unfamiliar noise. When the house was dead quiet and I still had not exhausted my brain enough for slumber, I realized how deftly and in so few words Rina had sketched out the reason why I'd accepted Lella's offer to be godmother.

I crept down the stairs to the kitchen and walked through the door-jamb lit up by flashes of lightning. I looked up to see a crucifix hung with a piece of blessed Easter palm.

In the kitchen there was a wood-burning stove and a granite sink. My father had pulled down all the old cabinets and built new ones. These were plain but full of character, just like him. I spent time rubbing surfaces and inhaling the beeswax he'd used to polish. What a shame he wouldn't be able to make such a kitchen for me, his favorite child, I thought smugly. I always loved things made of wood. Wood has soul. I liked the feel of the grain, the smell of it, the richness of color. A memory flooded in on me till I almost drowned in the sheer joy of it. I remembered once I helped Papà restore a small antique bureau he said was his when he was a boy. We had brought it to and from the beach to work on it. What ever happened to that piece of furniture? We sanded it all that summer, a little every day. Papà said there was no rush, it needed to be perfect. When it was ready we stained it with two coats, then polished it with beeswax. What had he done with it?

The rain stopped, and I looked out the window at a dull, weak moon squinting in the sky. I pulled out the deep bread drawer and cut a thick slice off a loaf inside it. Then I heaped on a generous spoonful of strawberry grape jam. My head felt better then. Almost. But now I was thirsty and wanted a cool glass of milk, so I padded out to the garden. The flagstones, moist from rain, were slippery beneath my feet as I walked to the well. Leaning over, I pulled up the bucket that held a bottle. I uncorked it and poured myself some milk, thick with cream. The glass was frosty in the moonlight. I gulped down the cool liquid and felt it leave a mustache, which I promptly wiped away with a piece of my nightshirt.

Though our new house and connecting store in Carini was large enough, it wasn't quite the *casa paterna*, nor did it have the enormous property that was ours in Villaggio Pace. But it did have a spectacular view of the *Conca D'Oro* at the back of the house. Through the closed window, I looked out to a sea in total blackness, wondering what God had destined for Peppe and Rina and me and the little ones. How would the sea look in the morning after a storm? How would we fare with our stormy emotions? Me in particular.

Unfamiliar with the stairwell and the landings, I crept slowly back up to my room where I dove between the covers once again. I slept fitfully and got up early. It was pointless to stay in bed, tossing and turning when I couldn't sleep anymore. I felt as excited as a child on Christmas.

I prepared the coffee pot and then opened the door to the garden. A blast of cool morning air smacked me in the face. If I wasn't fully awake, I certainly was now. My father's hunting jacket hung appended on a hook by the door. I slipped into it and went to listen to the birds' chirping. The sleeves of the jacket were so long they covered my hands.

My father's garden was a child's delight. It was obvious that he'd laid things out in an unmannerly fashion, and that's what I found most charming. There was a stone-flagged passage that led nowhere. No order or symmetry could be found anywhere as there would have been if executed and organized by Mamma.

Did this mean that in all unions one was orderly, the other not? Did God preordain that all couples He placed in each other's care to be basic opposites? Did this kind of thinking mean that I believed in predestination, that marriages were truly made in heaven? This sequence of thought was starting to make me fidget, so I went back into the house.

Shortly after, struggling with the jacket sleeves, I took my coffee back onto the terrace and placed it on a wrought-iron table with a wavy Venetian glass top. I sat with my feet tucked under me because I was cold and awaited sunrise. It came stealing over foliage, wet with dew. I inhaled deeply and felt immediately welcome and one with nature. There were lemon and orange groves nearby, but quite far from where I was sitting, although the slightest breeze wafted *le zagarelle* to my nose.

Not far from the house, Papà had planted string beans that in spring should be at least fifty centimeters long. I remembered as a child running past a similar vegetable patch, perhaps more orderly than this one, and snatching one long string bean, eating it raw right off the vine, moist and crisp. I had an urge to do that right now, but there were none to pick and my bare feet wouldn't permit a run.

Of course, there were fig trees, but these were far too old to have been planted by my papà. Apricot and peach trees had already given up their last yield months before. I felt badly about that, particularly as there was nothing I liked more than to watch Papà peel one long skin off a peach, then cut it and drop it into his last glass of wine at the dinner table.

There were many other trees. Not all were distinguishable from this great distance. Later on in the day I intended to walk the entire property.

I looked to my left. A sundial appeared to be sprouting out of a circle of shrubs cut in a hedge of stout pinnate leaves and scented cream-colored flowers. Farther along, there was a birdbath encircled by a bed of late-blooming purple iris. I never appreciated the beauty of these flowers before, but now that I'd seen them flourishing, growing wild on the hillsides on our train ride here, I knew I'd always have a fondness for them.

Along the wall of a rather unkempt storage building far to the left,

beyond lichen-blotched stones of various proportions, were the remnants
of what I knew in late spring and early summer would be delicate, pink
rambling roses. I guessed these also were vestiges of Mamma's brother's
green thumb.

I heard a rooting, snorting sound that pulled me from my reflection
and made me sit up with a start, my feet touching the cold cement paving
of the terrace floor. In the basil plants nearby, someone had left a trowel.
I instinctively reached for it and grabbed it by the hilt, and as soon as I
did, I relived my harrowing experience with Ciccio in the barn. I knew
now that I was capable of murder. I could kill.

A small wild boar foraged in the plot designated for cauliflowers.
He was enjoying himself and, though he was small, I knew he could be
dangerous if he decided to attack. I hoped he hadn't noticed my impetuous
movement. I sat very still and controlled my breathing. Pigs have notori-
ously bad eyesight so I counted on him being less curious about me and
more interested in feeding his plump belly. After a while he went away.

The gray skylight was becoming milky. The sun would rise while a
sliver of moon lingered, affixed to the nothingness of sky.

❧

IT SEEMS I TOOK A CHILL that morning, and it wasn't long after
that I fell ill with a high fever. I was no help whatsoever to Mamma in
organizing our new surroundings. Mamma was frantic, though I don't
recall much of it. Rina told me about it afterward. I certainly could
imagine the scene, because if anything happened to Mamma it didn't
matter, but just let one of us have a hair out of place and she convulsed
with fear.

I was still not used to our new environs—even my own room. Everything appeared bigger than life. It must have been the night that my fever
broke. I awakened to a thrashing noise at my window. Great shadows
were cast upon the wall, and an emerging image moved back and forth
in close proximity to my bed. For a minute I thought I had a ghostly
guest. My cheeks were hot, and it seemed that my body roasted upon live
coals. I knew then how Saint Lorenzo felt being martyred, never losing
his sense of humor, saying, "I'm done on this side, you can turn me over."
I threw off the covers.

After a long, howling wind, rain lashed against the window. Then nothing. Silence. A peaceful hush ensued, like the sound of snow falling. Serenity itself had entered my room, much as spring morning light steals in after a night of torrential rain. A small halo of light ignited spontaneously around a figure. A man with a long beard, rather unkempt and wearing a red garment, appeared to be standing close to my bed. Though I can't remember if he spoke or not, I felt he was there to assuage the heat that burned my body. He comforted me, yet I can't say how. I felt my illness was nothing to fear.

The next morning my fever had broken, and as Mamma sat on my bed stroking my forehead, I told her what happened during the night. She said I'd been delirious and kept calling out to Jesus.

"No wonder He could walk through the walls of my bedroom!" I said to Mamma.

She laughed, but I had the distinct feeling I'd been guided through what might have been a serious bout of fever.

"What are you so happy about?" Mamma asked as she covered me up to my chin.

"We must have prayed together."

"Who?"

"I dreamt Christ walked with me. He wore a long dress. I think He was soft-spoken like Papà, but I can't recall His voice."

"What did He tell you?"

"He spoke without words. Strange, isn't it? I was ill and felt hot. He took me—"

"You touched Him?"

"I think so. We went to a place where there was guitar music and coolness."

"Rest now. I'll bring you some tea and toasted bread later."

"Don't worry, Mamma, I'm not at all hungry, but I think I'll sleep."

"Quiet now," she said and kissed my forehead. "Cool. Thank You, God."

I wondered if she was talking to Jesus. My eyes were weighted. I couldn't open them to see Him, but I sensed or glimpsed Him on the inside of my eyes.

I spoke to Jesus in my head, my voice saying, "You're so young and beautiful."

CHAPTER XXVII

Angelica

TIME PASSAGES

BY THE TIME I WAS well again, house matters had formed the sameness of a daily routine. Autumn sidled into winter and winter slipped and muddied itself into spring. I was getting used to everything, including my poor aunt Sofia's fits of depression over the fact that she never married or had children of her own. I guess she hid it rather well. Why, then, did I spot it? Was my acumen so sharp, or did I feel that kind of dreaded loneliness myself? I wondered if anyone else in the house was aware of this poor dear's bouts, then having to pull herself up by her bootstraps and put on a happy face for the rest of the family. I cut some branches of pussy willow and arranged them in a vase Uncle Giovanni had bequeathed us. It was a beautiful Chinese porcelain with a rose and willow design. As I fussed about positioning these willows, it came to me that I'd pussy-footed enough around my father in regard to joining the convent. I'd gained footing on one score only when he gave me permission to do volunteer work again in the rectory for Don Ruggero. The only difference being we were located a kilometer away. I cleaned house regularly for the priest during my free time. I also sewed for him, but usually at home.

On one particular late afternoon when the weather was inclement, I stayed behind to sew for Don Ruggero, who was in the library browsing through his many texts, jotting down notes for yet another boring sermon.

A tap on the door surprised me. What was it? I'd been concentrating on making small, invisible stitches in an alb I worked on. I never could use a thimble and had stuck myself to the point of drawing blood several times—each drop from my fingers signifying love, care, and an attention to detail. How pagan!

Deeply involved in wiping blood and sewing neatly, I heard the wind roar with a vengeance. I dismissed the loud banging noise as just a loosened slat in the *persiane* being blown about. It wasn't the shutter, but rather my father rapping at the door.

His greeting, "Wasting time again, I see, Angelica, when you could do a real Christian thing and help your mother at home!" made me drop my sewing to the floor.

Don Ruggero came blustering in, but neither he nor I could convince my father that my vocation was sincere and I would not consider any thought of marriage.

"Family is the sweetest thing she's ever known, Ruggero," Papà said, red-faced.

Too true. I'd been cuddled, coddled, and cradled by it. How could I truly give up familial love? If I loved God enough, I would be able to. But did I? Does anyone? Weren't my parents God's substitutes on earth? How many times had Mamma said that Christ left apostles, not nuns? I'd been through all of this self-doubt and argument before. These thoughts flowed through my brain now like the forceful pull of a waterfall till I went under and believed I'd never surface again. Now or ever? How many times did I think this way in so many quiet hours?

"Soon she'll have another communal family of sisters," Ruggero said. His voice seemed out of synch with his mouth.

Papà paced back and forth, his arms tucked behind him. "Like hell she will," he stormed. "She'll marry or— Look at my sister Sofia, she's a perfect example of an unmarried woman—"

There are other alternatives to the convent, I thought to myself.

"Do, sit, Nicola," Don Ruggero said.

But Papà continued pacing. Then he stopped, turned, and in a booming voice said, "She's meant to raise children—her own, not foundlings in an orphanage run by nuns who hide from life. Or else . . . Sofia's content with her lot in life, isn't she?"

I wanted to screech at him, "No way in hell. She's miserable," but of course I remained valorless, speechless, in the same way I never confronted Ruggero for having told of my accident to the prioress. Mamma's advice on that front was to leave it be.

My father pulled me to my feet and said, "Go home."

To my uncle he said, "*Basta cosí.*"

DISCOURAGED WITH MYSELF FOR FENCE sitting, that night at home I tried a new tactic. After dinner I begged Papà to let me help in the shop, but he wouldn't hear of it. Mamma mouthed the words "I told you so!" I hated to eat crow, but a full serving of it was plopped on my plate. Maybe Mamma was right. Maybe I was too arrogant and proud to ever make a good nun. But concerning working in the store, I heard Mamma come to my defense the same eve of the discussion, saying maybe it was a good idea to let me be a shop girl to keep me home and help me forget about the convent.

Instead, I was housebound in an effort to keep me from Don Ruggero, and as if that weren't bad enough, not even the garden was accessible to me. That's when I began to miss my terrace and thought about running away. It crossed my mind to go back to Villaggio Pace.

I thought my parents didn't love me anymore, and what's worse, I resented their every command and excessive punishment. I called them jailers. After which I retired to my room and refused to eat for three days.

On the third day, we received a telegram from Domenico Balsamo who was coming to Palermo with the intention of visiting us for a two-week period.

Two whole weeks?

Every time Mamma asked me if I remembered how tall and handsome he was, my innards jumped. What was worse, Papà laid down the law that I was forbidden to help Don Ruggero during the time Domenico would spend with us. It was understood that I'd behave myself with Domenico so that I'd have access to Don Ruggero afterward.

To my utmost chagrin, my mother had the dressmaker come to the house, as I still was not allowed out. She fit me for a new linen suit, which I would don for Domenico's arrival. I had lost so much weight that I looked like a lead pencil. I told Rina I was glad, that way maybe he'd realize my parents were insane and become discouraged in his suit and totally disenchanted with the idea of securing me as a bride.

"I'll attach a ruffle to this simple blouse," the kind dressmaker said. I was sullen and refused to converse with her.

When the dressmaker left, Rina came into my room and said, "How did you like Peppe's quasi-mother-in-law?" She didn't wait for an answer. "What if Domenico's really nice and you like him? You don't have to say yes or no, just maybe. That way you could stall for years."

"Just the solution I need."

We both laughed at that and then I toyed with my hair. I always wore it long and pulled back with a bow at the nape of my neck. But my spiteful side threatened to cut my hair again and put on a sackcloth dress so that Domenico would think I was a mad recluse.

Unfortunately for me, my mother overheard me saying this to Rina and entered my room without so much as a "by your leave," walked over to where I stood, and backhanded me so quickly I hardly had time to realize I'd been slapped. But slapped I was. It stung so much I bit my lip. No way would I give her the satisfaction of crying. So I did the next best thing. I bunched up all my hair, prim and matronly, and slicked back at the sides, no bouffant for this *opera bouffe*. I was pleased to see how grossly unbecoming it looked. It served Mamma right.

❧

ON THE DAY DOMENICO ARRIVED, Mamma sent the girls on a picnic with Zia Sofia so that Rina could paint undisturbed and we could entertain our guest. Peppe accompanied the picnickers with his sweetheart, Ludovica. Mamma insisted I wear the cameo brooch Papà had given her on their engagement. I felt ridiculous. Since it was just the three of us, Mamma had set up in the sitting room. I walked in and had the bad timing to choose these unwelcome words to my parents: "If you won't let me join the convent or let me venture out of the house, at least let me do something constructive like work in the shop."

My father smoked a cheroot. He clenched it between his teeth and slammed his fist down so hard, I thought he'd broken it and the side table. A vase shimmied and toppled, crashing into a thousand fragments, a punctuation to his imperative. He stubbed out the cigar in Mamma's beautiful rose porcelain candy dish. Mamma started picking up the pieces of the vase.

"Sit down, Lia!" he shouted at her, and to me he said, "There will be no further discussion. You will leave this house on a bier before you leave it as a nun and that's final."

"But, Papà, why?" I punched a grosgrain pillow on the settee and sat down.

My father's voice lowered almost to a whisper; I could feel frost form around his words. "No more talk of you becoming a sales girl either. Is that understood?"

I could not speak. Hot tears stung my eyes, but if I shook my head in agreement, I knew the tears would fall. A sarcastic little voice that matched my own said in my ear, "Clearly." But I answered him, saying, "I'd rather be eaten by dogs than stay under your roof any longer. Watch out I don't marry this bag-of-bones marshal for spite and make him miserable and you'll be to blame and will have to pay for all eternity." It was a mouthful and I was breathless. I stood to run out of the room, but my father grabbed my wrist. "Sit."

I trounced on the chair and hurt my behind, but refused to eat, and Mamma, intimidated by my father's ill humor, got up, slapped me across the face, and said, "You'll not do penance for imaginary sins at my table, not in this house. Not while I live and breathe, you won't. You'll eat that food or you'll wear it."

I had never seen my mother's wrath like this before and it stung more than the slap. I was mortified because she did it in front of Papà, which increased my shame. I'd never felt such outrage—an innocent punished so severely. Oh, if I could have entered the convent immediately, to be cloistered from the world . . . "Yet still a part of it," uttered an unseen tempter of my thoughts. The grate of the cloister sprung to mind, and with it thoughts of the nuns imprisoned in the convent.

My mind's eye always perceived the sisters with a surrounding aura of otherworldliness that separated them from the laity. I beheld them crystalline, unbending as mirrors, a forecast of me. Terrifying. I'd have to submit, obey, ask permission for every crust of bread, beg to read a letter from my beloved family I kept trying to distance myself from, prostrate myself before the prioress for each corporal necessity. Could I do it? In honesty, I felt I'd balk. Knowing my current will and character? If a sister slighted me, would I not think of a cruel torture to get back at her? And I'd succeed—just the same way I took no nonsense from the girls. I struck my breast with a clenched fist, *mea maxima culpa.*

I ate a forkful of pasta and deliberately poured myself a goblet of wine full to the brim. At this my father laughed and said, "If that's what it takes, Angelica, for you to become civil when Domenico arrives, then so be it. Make sure you clean up that vase. Don't let your mother do it."

The rest of the meal was taken in silence. Papà took a little *pisolino* in the garden with his feet up and his mouth catching flies. Mamma sewed, and whenever Papà started to snore she'd shake him gently. I read some of Michelangelo's madrigals, including one I loved repeatedly that began, "How can it be that I'm no longer mine? O God, O God, O God! Who's snatched me from myself so that he might be closer to me?"

⟨━━⧓━━⟩

LATE AFTERNOON WE AWAITED SERGEANT Major Domenico Balsamo in the parlor. Papà, Mamma, and I were seated at a card table. We waited in silence that reeked of my displeasure.

Someone thumped the front door brass knocker.

I drummed my fingers on the table as I listened to mumbled garbling of salutations. I stopped tapping, crossed my hands in my lap, and sat up straighter. Footsteps approached. I turned.

There stood Pulcinella! Or his twin, to be sure. I knew at a glance his stockings didn't match and he never learned the function of a comb or brush.

My mind raked him over hot coals, and I hated him before he even opened his mouth to greet me. How could he come courting me when he'd only seen me when I was a child?

My mother coaxed and cajoled, trying to get me to say something, but not even "good afternoon" would shake itself from my lips. I stood up, stiff and straight as a maypole, minus the ribbons, mute and indifferent until, finally, I blurted out a question that even took me aback. I asked him if his trip was business or pleasure.

He stammered, but couldn't answer. Then his mouth went slack and his face crimsoned as if he'd been smeared with a harlot's lip rouge. Hadn't he been a sailor? Didn't they frequent women of ill repute? Here was living proof.

"In that case," I said, "I suppose you won't be staying long."

I watched him fidget with the hat in his hand for an answer. Seeing none forthcoming, I excused myself.

"*Con permesso*. I'm going to rest and put a cool cloth on my aching head."

While I lay sprawled across the bed in tears, Rina said to me, "How else could that scenario possibly go but tragically? Don't blame yourself. I wouldn't. You were a cornered rat, for pity's sake."

"Oh, I was beastly," I said in between sobs. "You should have heard what I said."

"Actually, I did. I listened at the door. Wasn't too bad."

I was so upset by my own ill behavior that at first I didn't realize what Rina had said. "That poor man has feelings, and I crushed them as if they were vermin underfoot. I can only pray he forgives me in his heart. And Mamma and Papà, will they ever speak to me again?"

"Guaranteed. Most likely tonight at dinner. Just thank your lucky stars you weren't in kicking or pinching distance from Mamma. You'll just have to put up a better front. Remember, Angelica, your guest is staying a fortnight. There'll be time enough for reparation. Ah," she sighed. "If only I wasn't so young," Rina paused dramatically, preening in the dresser mirror, "maybe he'd like a witty girl with a little spunk."

"Wherever do you learn these things?"

"Ludovica and I have become friends. She shows me her French magazines."

"Does Mamma know?"

"I don't steal them. I merely read them. It's not a crime."

"Maybe it's a sin."

"That depends, my dear sister, on the conscience of the person reading."

"You are positively incorrigible."

"Thank heavens one of us is. Just think how boring it would be in this household if we had five Angelicas. Speaking of which, before you become too Rubenesque for me, I've decided to paint a nude and want you as my model. Will you pose for me?" Rina hesitated, then said, "Angelica, dear, close your mouth."

PAPÀ GAVE HIS PERMISSION SO Domenico and I were permitted to walk in the garden. Papà even encouraged us to walk to the main piazza with him as an escort but, of course, I refused. Domenico stood up almost at attention every time I entered the room. He did this little inclination thing with his head that was sickeningly polite. Oh, Domenico was dear and sweet, and how much he informed my senses of Peppe. I certainly couldn't fall for my brother, or anyone like him. What were my parents pretending for me? The next two weeks I apologized several times for my rude comportment that first afternoon, but he didn't seem to mind.

⁕

THE DAY BEFORE HE LEFT, I wrapped a shawl around my shoulders. The wind had picked up, bringing the faint fragrance of sea mixed with wet earth after rain. Rina followed discreetly several steps in back. Domenico stopped in the lane, and we walked into a small hothouse. Rina stayed outside, unaware or uncaring of decorum. Domenico picked a gold and purple pansy and handed it to me. How apt. A pretty dandy, insipid, no perfume, no zest. I twirled the flower in my fingers, wanting to scream, "A perfect metaphor for you!" I shook my head before he'd even asked, knowing by the look on his face what he was going to say.

"Would you at least consider my offer of marriage? I'm afraid you'd have to be separated from your family for a year or two at best, but I could initiate a transfer immediately if—"

"*If* is such a little word with such a big inference, isn't it? A separation from my dear family—an entire year?" Of course I sensed he knew I was playing with him, not out of cruelness, but from a deeper sense of self-preservation. What could I do? I'd set my will against Papà and nothing short of the grave could move me. After all, I was Mamma's daughter.

We reached a slippery incline, and I had to stretch for his arm to break a fall. I knew I'd trespassed decorum and would somehow pay for such informality. Where was Rina? My instinct was right. Nevertheless, it shocked me when Domenico took me in his arms and forced his thin, unwelcomed lips on mine. The same lips that had fallen slack in my entranceway when I'd held him at bay with mere words the week before. Why didn't this physical act shatter my universe? I felt smothered, winded, revolted. A strong girl, I refused to swoon. Did it make a difference? I pushed free of him and wiped away his kiss with my hand, staggering backward. In so doing, I realized it wouldn't be as easy to erase the memory of it, or the passion he'd displayed in delivering it. And yet I felt sorrowful that such a physical experience had been so wretched for me. And for him? I cared nothing. Did this man merely seek a wife, or could it be possible he really loved me? Desired me? Was I laughing in the face of destiny by refusing?

Although it was early spring, I felt chilled—the air of winter still close. I scuffed my shoe as I kicked away some dried leaves in my haste to back away from him. My aunt Sofia had given me a copy of a poem called "At the Sun-rise in 1848" written by Dante Gabriele Rossetti and some of the words came to me as clearly as if they'd been written in the sky. "Then heard we sounds as though the Earth did sing / And the Earth's angel dried upon the wing." What if I were destined to love? Maybe because I was so afraid of marriage and its consequences, I negated it at present. Might this cause a permanent denial of a future destiny taking flight? Was I exasperating fate? Would my capacity for love dry up? What if I needed to call upon it at a later time and it had shriveled, parched, and curled like the leaves at my feet?

SPRING PASSED, AND I STILL had not completely washed away that kiss in the garden. And neither had I convinced my resolute father to allow me to enter the convent. I felt miserable and at such an impasse in my life that if it weren't for Rina's antics I thought I'd burst. I wanted to be swallowed by the earth.

CHAPTER XXVIII

Angelica

THE FEAST OF THE ASSUMPTION

THAT SUMMER ON FERRAGOSTO, THE Feast Day of Blessed Mary's Assumption into heaven, we attended Mass and then piled everything and everyone into a wagon and headed for the beach. As tradition warranted, Mamma insisted that we all swim on this day, and if for some reason we couldn't, then we had to at least wet our feet.

Of course, Mamma herself never swam, but she loved to sit at the shoreline and let the waves break and roll over her legs. When the girls were small they would squeal with laughter on her lap. Sometimes they would sit beside her and watch their legs disappear in the mobile sand. But now that they were getting bigger, they'd swim and play until sun and surf exhausted them.

Naturally, on a day like this, there were more people than usual on the beach. We didn't have it all to ourselves as we did that long ago time when we dried the wool for Mamma's mattresses.

Nunziata, Beatrice, and Flaminia built a sand castle. And then when they were bored with it, crashed it down and had a sand fight. Mamma called out for them to stop, but the children were full of enthusiasm, wrapped up in their foolish game, and didn't pay heed. Just then, Nunziata kicked sand into Beatrice's eyes. Peppe told her to wash it out with seawater, but Mamma yelled to do no such thing and especially not to rub it, which is exactly what she did while Mamma ran and got a bottle of fresh water. By the time she arrived at the water's edge, Beatrice was screaming wildly and wouldn't keep shut. Mamma, her nerves fraught whenever anything happened to one of us, slapped Beatrice hard on the backside, saying, "Here's something you can really cry about!"

When Mamma had finished washing out Beatrice's eyes, she cautioned Rina to watch the three young ones more carefully. I saw my sister Rina's eyes grow enormous, then she made a face, but not because of Mamma's scolding. Without having to turn around, I knew just then that dear *Compare* Leo Ranieri, Papà's friend of forever, had arrived. *Compare* Leo wasn't with his wife, Mamma's petite friend, Graziella. He had brought his nephew, Liborio, instead. My father and *Compare* Leo made wine together and hunted together. He and his sweet wife had no children, so when Liborio's parents died and he was left an orphan, they adopted him and raised him as their son. What a sacrifice, having to look at the face, every day, all day long, of the short, fat, pimply boy of twenty who had a long nose and halitosis. I had detested him ever since Lella's engagement party.

Each time I saw Liborio, my stomach somersaulted and I thought I'd heave. I must confess, he was always polite, yet I was unkind because he repulsed me. As I glanced over my shoulder, I thought I'd die. Today was worst of all because he tried to balance—actually juggled—a bouquet of flowers, a basket of wild strawberries resting on moist fig leaves, and another of white grapes along with a bottle of red wine. This kind of offering could only mean one thing. Rina was still too young, although she understood at a glance as I did that he'd come to propose marriage to me. All of a sudden I realized that Mamma must have known and was short-tempered with Beatrice not because of what happened with the sand but what was about to happen to me.

It was a blistering day. Mamma and I wore our loosest-fitting clothing and, naturally, we were barefoot, standing at the water's edge. The spectacle of ridiculousness advanced. I pictured him rutting, a pig in heat, on top of me. The situation about to ensue seemed so outrageously funny to me that I had to bite my cheek to suppress a laugh. Here now approached Liborio, encased, as he must have thought, as a tempting gift package, buttoned up from the cravat around his pudgy neck down to his overstuffed waistcoat, bulging suit jacket, and ill-fitting pants that dropped to cover spats wrapped over his ankles. He looked every bit like a live, overstuffed sausage spilling out of men's clothing.

I shot a look at my mother, a look that spoke volumes though no sound issued forth. I wanted to scream at her, "How could Papà profess to love me and arrange this?" But apparently he had. And was Mamma implicit in the plan? I wasn't sure because Mamma stood there so bewildered that she never uttered so much as "good day" to the gentlemen.

I had to get away before it happened. I couldn't risk the chance of being asked by him, or having to embarrass him with a quick reply of, "No! Never ever!" But where could I escape? I prayed for a volcanic eruption. *Dear God, let the sand part and swallow me live.* They were rapidly approaching. I whispered to Rina to splash me. Who cared if she ruined my new linen dress? She was going to save my life.

Thank God, the girl was fast. Before I knew it, I was soaked, Rina fussing all over me, asking to be forgiven and me saying Peppe would have to take me back home, I couldn't possibly stay in this bedraggled condition.

Oh, and Papà! God bless him, he would have understood if he'd seen the message in Sanskrit. He acquiesced, merely shrugging his shoulders. As I ran past them, I heard my father say to *Compare* Leo and Liborio, appalled nephew/suitor, that there was nothing left to do other than eat the fruit and get drunk. I could have kissed my father, but I was still playing the part.

Mamma scowled, which meant I'd be scrubbing floors instead of doing the more gentile tasks at home. I could hear her saying that she couldn't get anyone this week to do the menial work in the store, and "Ah, Angelica, you don't mind this little penance; after all, you're going to need to get used to it."

Mamma ran for a towel and reprimanded Rina ever so scathingly. I thought all would see through the sham, but I didn't care a bit, not a whit, not one iota.

CHAPTER XXIX

Angelica

IN DREAMS AND AFTER DREAMS

THE FOLLOWING NIGHTS A RECURRING dream frightened me. It was a double-edged fear. I relived the past and dreaded when it might not be a dream but a reality.

Blood everywhere. The soaked mattress.

Rina and Nunziata dressed in babies' clothes were on the floor. Mamma stood at the washstand, spilling water all around, like I spilled water onto baby Concetta's head in the rite of Baptism. Mamma sat on the bed humming, stroking my hair. Hair, I remembered when I awoke, meant treachery. I tried to force it from the dream. Dream of a woman and it's good luck. Never kiss a dead person. Just as I was about to kiss Concetta, who held a bouquet of lily-of-the-valley and purple pansies, Mamma said, "Kiss me instead." Everything moved in slowed time like a marionette show I'd seen in Palermo.

The dream changed. The show I'd seen performed by puppets reenacted itself, but completely different from the story I'd seen about Orlando Furioso. It had changed to a sad tale about "Lorenza and the Merchant," whoever they were. I was transported back to a time that Mamma had told me about in Venice when Jews wore yellow turbans and large letter *O*s sewn on their clothing and the Venetian Ghetto thrummed with bristling life. I heard the entire scene told in my own voice as if I knew the people represented by the dancing *burattini*.

The year that rains came to flood the city,
    When houses were lost and sacked,
There came to the home of Don de Medici
    A merchant named Sem Simonetti.

This Jewish lad had his heart set
    On the pure hand of Lorenza,
The youngest daughter of the household;
    Sweet and fair as she could be.

They were at the dinner table;
    The merchant's eyes caught Lorenza's.
Now guest and daughter both were lost
    In a love world all their own.

Down narrow halls and secret paths
    Love's sweethearts dared meet and kiss,
While thinking all the household slept,
    Were caught embracing one dark night.

The merchant was held with cruel words
    While the father bade his daughter go,
And called his son to come to his aid.
    The quiet household no longer slept.

Don de Medici's voice grew enraged
    As the Jewish man begged mercy
For loving the Christian maiden;
    And asked for her beloved hand.

The father, implored by the son,
    Let the guest go out unharmed
Only to swear a sweet revenge—
    A duel on the following day.

Lorenza's brother (an obedient son)
    Did fight his best friend Sem.

The merchant's blood spilt on the ground;
 He lay dead in his lover's arms.

Lorenza crossed the earth in blood,
 And swore to avenge her betrothed's life.
Then quietly stole her brother's sword,
 And took her life that morning.

The dream played on, and as soon as Lorenza left to commit suicide, the taste of chocolate on my tongue became so real, so bitter. My mother had said she'd get some sugar. I heard running steps on stairs and the echo of my own voice hollow in my ears, asking, "What's this drink?"

"Pig's blood to replace what you lost, but it's unclean."

"Give some to Zia Concetta," I said.

My mother shook her head, tears in her eyes. "I can't . . . can't . . . can't . . ." The words faded.

I awoke in a sweat, then fell back to a fitful sleep. When I dreamt again, Mamma said, "You never knew that all those years ago I had gone into the yard, but I did." Then I saw my mother slit the sow's belly open and reach inside. She held the piglet embryo high in the air and said, "I killed for you, but God forgives me. I'd kill anyone who'd harm you, Angelica." I watched my mother place the piglet on the stone table used for beating the wash. She washed off the embryo with rainwater from a barrel under the apricot tree. "Drink," she said, holding her hands cupped together with dripping blood.

"I drink only the blood of salvation." I awoke a second time, my mouth clamped shut, shaking my head from side to side. The insistent thought in my head: refuse to drink.

⚜

I WONDERED ABOUT THE DREAM of puppets and held it in reserve to ponder later. I had just finished reading Shakespeare's *The Merchant of Venice* and *Romeo e Giulietta* and somehow knew my dream was a fusion of these two plays. Yet I couldn't help rhapsodizing about the words of my dream and feeling sorrow for the star-crossed lovers. It was as if I'd lived vicariously through them. Much the same way that I felt my mother sought to recapture her youth through me. I understood the love the doomed couple shared—such a miraculous sensation.

The Lorenza dream sequence got tucked into a sanctuary of my brain to contemplate when I retreated privately in meditations, vaulted in my heart of hearts.

I recounted the other parts of my dream to Mamma as we strung out the wash. There was a pattern, I realized, but I couldn't remember and told the dreams out of sequence. "You're blessed and cursed with the gift of seeing," she said. Then my mother asked, "You didn't kiss Concetta, did you?"

Mamma hung out a chemise.

"I was about to when I woke up, Mamma."

Mamma looked at me over Nunziata's dress with its loose whisk collar and shirred top. "Never kiss the dead in a dream."

"That's silly, you can't control a dream." I reached into the wash basket and took hold of a corset, shook it out, and placed it on the line, thinking how embarrassing it was to hang this up in plain sight.

"We control everything in life, including dreams. It's the spirit world we can't control. Maybe that wasn't Concetta, but the devil. 'When the devil caresses you, it's your soul he wants.'"

I muttered something inaudible and Mamma lashed out at me, "Too much religion, that's your problem, young lady. Try a little housework for a change, not just cooking and mending. Look at Rina. She's already received two proposals of marriage."

"The one from Ludovica's brother doesn't count. He's a tailor," I said, deprecation in every syllable. "And she also refused the second."

"And you, my precious? "

"I've also received two, Mamma, but who even wants to be reminded of them—and, like Rina, I've had the good sense to refuse both."

"Refused two. *Non ci sono due senza tre!*" She was fond of saying there were never two without three. "Well, what when the third comes? Be careful! Remember not to spit up to heaven that it doesn't come down in your face. My Angelica is going to be a saint, maybe, but get that convent business out of your head. You'll have to find sainthood by living a normal life."

"But, Mamma, every family has a nun or priest."

"Not this family. When I get to heaven I'll explain why. Now hand me

that frock with lace and ruching; no, the other with the *broderie anglaise.*"
Mamma stretched to reach the garment. "Two *mollette* pins, please."

"Don't you want a daughter in the cloister to pray for your soul?"

"I've already got a sister-in-law and a brother in heaven's dress circle
seats. Don't you think that's enough? I don't want to sacrifice anyone else
just yet. Understand?"

"You've changed since we came to Carini, Mamma. You used to be
so sweet in Villaggio Pace." I said this knowing it was unfair as well as
untrue, but I had no better argument.

"When you have six children and have lost six, you'll understand
why. I'm happier here than I've ever been. We have the *bottega* and an
easy life."

IT WAS FRIDAY EVENING WHEN dusk was just about to descend.
I watched Mamma bow and cover her head with a lace veil from Spain
that had been her mother's and her mother's before. She stood in front of
the candles as she always did on Friday evening. Mamma lit the candles,
blew out the match, and wafted smoke toward her in concentric circles.
Her eyes began to tear and she prayed aloud, "Blessed art Thou our God,
King of the universe who has sanctified us with His commandments and
ordained that we kindle the Sabbath light." Mamma closed her eyes.

She was the only person of all our acquaintance who performed this
ritual and I loved it. I loved the prayers Mamma offered for our family
and our dead, and I loved Mamma for doing it. I felt it was something
that belonged to the ages and, happily, I was part of it. This was of the
world I would miss if I entered the convent. Not having a daughter whom
I could hand down this tradition to, I would also miss being able to give
this gift of Sabbath candle lighting to someone I loved, as Mamma had
given it to me.

CHAPTER XXX

Rosalia

RINA'S BETROTHAL

THERE WAS A KNOCKING ON the door. A messenger boy delivered the finest *marron glacé* bespeckled with violet sweetmeats. Rosalia was perplexed when she read the card, which had been addressed to "The Domenico Household." It was signed "The Bonanno Family."

⚜

THE NEXT DAY A DELIVERY boy brought an arrangement wrapped in floral paper from a noted Palermitano pastry shop called *Pasticceria Fiore*. Inside was a pure white confection of excellent quality *biscotti*, dotted with pastel-colored confetti. The card read: "For the parents of Signorina Rina." Signed: "Pietro Bonanno."

⚜

ON THE THIRD DAY WHEN a calling card was left with an enormous bouquet of seasonal flowers, Rosalia's husband's cheeks became florid.

"This is the third day," Nicola said. "What's going on?"

"I'm as much in the dark as you," Rosalia said, arranging the flowers in a ceramic blue and white vase.

"Impossible."

Nicola summoned Rina and read out loud the attached card. Rina flushed the red of cooked lobster.

"Who is this man?" Nicola demanded. "How do you know him? Where does he come from? Who are his people? And how does he have the audacity to call you by name?"

"It's true," Rina said, "we don't know his family, but we all know him. Very well, I might add."

"From where?" Nicola said, pacing the hallway where Rosalia had set the flowers.

"We've seen him a million times in the law offices of Don Ruggero's advocate when we went to sort out the will and the inheritance Zu Vanni left Mamma. And he delivered papers for Mamma to sign on thousands of instances. Why Pietro—"

"Who?" Nicola asked, stopping his pacing and cutting her short.

"The gentleman in question—he was most courteous," Rina said.

"*Disgrazziata!* Have you any idea how this makes me look?" he said.

Rosalia saw that Nicola's pressure was on the rise. With a toss of her head, she summarily dismissed her daughter. "Nicola, I do wish you'd control yourself. You look like you're going into apoplexy!"

Rosalia tried to convince her husband that it probably would be in their best interest to entertain this man. She explained that since Rina had such a rebellious spirit, the girl would most assuredly cause all sorts of future headaches.

Rosalia felt stifled and the heat seemed oppressive.

"Let's walk in the garden," she said, taking him by the arm and leading him toward the door. "Better to marry her off now—"

Nicola stopped short. "She's too young."

"As I was saying, better someone she cares for and save the family grief later. Obviously this young lawyer has serious intentions and good manners."

They took an alley laden with fruit trees and shade, but it didn't seem to alter Nicola's state. He was adamant and kept repeating, "How dare a daughter of mine find a prospective husband without my knowledge?"

Rosalia answered, "Maybe we should thank heaven she's found someone she likes more than the last one you gave permission to come calling. My Lord, she behaved ghastly that time."

At the thought of Rina's last suitor, Rosalia envisioned a scene that would make anybody think her daughter had just escaped detention from a crazy house.

~~~~~~~~

NICOLA, ROSALIA, AND A GUEST had been sitting out on the veranda, awaiting Rina. After many silent pauses, Rina finally appeared looking like spring herself in a light-green silk suit, a bunch of violets pinned at her breast.

"*Ciao*," she said, and right then and there, Rosalia knew they were in for a scene because Rina had boldly used the familiar word with the guest who was a mere acquaintance.

The poor man sat with his legs crossed on a wicker chair that matched his sickly hair, stumbling while trying to disengage himself. Finally uncoiled, he stood to greet his quasi-intended.

Rina did not offer her hand but merely giggled and pooh-poohed his efforts, like shooing away an annoying fly. By the look on his face, he hadn't misconstrued the gesture intended for him. Rina dismissed him further when she told him not to bother to rise as she wasn't staying long. She'd made a previous arrangement with her sister to prepare Communion hosts at the rectory.

Nicola was about to object, but when Rosalia raised her eyebrows, he fell silent. Rosalia thought, *Will she ever find anyone?* But what she said was: "Won't you come here then, my dear, and kiss your mother. I wish to present this young gentle caller."

Rina acquiesced, and as she bent over to kiss her mother, Rosalia pinched the soft underneath part of her upper arm.

"Yipes!" Rina cried.

"So sorry, dearest. Now do sit a minute. This"—she indicated the star-struck buck—"is Mr. Zampone."

Rina sat. "Like a salami?"

"To be precise, it's a big pig's foot," said Mr. Zampone, the words spoken so loudly they echoed and lingered on the air.

Rina smiled. "Would you care for something cool to drink, Mr. Zampone? I'll fetch us some anise and water. Papà will always accept a glass, won't you, Papà?"

Nicola nodded and Mr. Zampone said, "What a delightful idea."

Rina was on her feet again and off to procure the drinks before anyone could object.

When she returned, the drinks wobbled on a beautifully hand-painted Florentine tray that Peppe had given his parents for their last anniversary.

Rosalia could see the young man's doubtful expression turn to one of joyous hope as Rina gingerly set the tray down on a wheeled cart, never once taking her eyes off Mr. Zampone.

Oh Lord, prayed Rosalia silently, *what now?* She didn't have to wait long to find out.

Rina served her father and mother and smiled at Mr. Zampone, who smiled back at her as she spilled the iced drink in his lap.

❦

ROSALIA PICKED A BUTTERCUP AND placed it in Nicola's lapel as he was saying, "I'll ask Rina what the meaning of all this nonsense is."

"She's coming of age, Nicola. There's no use denying it," Rosalia said. "And let's not forget Zampone."

Nicola said, *"Basta!* Enough!"

That ended the discussion for the time being.

❦

A DAY LATER, ROSALIA EXPRESSED her feelings again to Nicola, this time a little more forcefully. The couple had just gotten into bed. Nicola moved closer to Rosalia. She felt his foot upon hers, rubbing the arch. She knew immediately what he wanted and waited until Nicola had finished. Then she broached the subject she wanted to discuss with him, knowing he'd be more relaxed and in a better mood for listening.

"If we aren't careful with her, Rina's capable of disgracing the entire family by running off."

"She wouldn't dare." Nicola turned on his side.

Rosalia pulled down her nightgown and adjusted her position. She leaned over, grasping Nicola by the shoulder. She kissed her husband's cheek.

"I say let him court her," she whispered.

"When?"

"Now. She may even tire of him quickly."

"She's so young. And what about Angelica?"

Here they were again at an impasse. They fell into silence.

Nicola would not consent to Rina's beau calling, especially because he preferred their daughter Angelica to marry first even though, in private, they were beginning to reconcile themselves to the fact that maybe she really was intended for convent life. Angelica had already refused two proposals. For the time being, there were no future prospects in view, but as her daughter was growing into a handsome woman, Rosalia was sure someone would come forward. She only wished there was a way to deter Rina.

AT ANOTHER MEETING WITH RINA a day later, Nicola said, "I'm sending a response to Mr. Bonanno that under no circumstance is he to darken our door. Do you understand? I demand an answer, young lady."

Rosalia noticed Rina looked at him as if he wore a second head. What was she up to?

After a while, Rina said, "Papà, Mamma. What will you have me do?"

"Inform us as to your plans."

Rosalia wanted to contradict him, saying, "You mean, 'Inform us before you ever again make plans on your own.'" But she didn't dare and kept her thoughts to herself.

"Of course I will," said Rina in a haughty tone.

WHAT OCCURRED NEXT WAS SO unexpected that even Rosalia was taken aback. She chided herself afterward when she thought it over and realized it shouldn't have surprised her. It was typical of Rina with all her gay spontaneity to find a professional man to propose marriage with or without her parents' consent.

The next morning as Angelica left for Mass at the crack of dawn, Rosalia kissed her daughter and let the dogs out. She then went to feed the chickens. Something white caught her attention. It was there, under the rock where the gate key was always kept, that she found a sheet of paper with a note scratched in Rina's bold handwriting.

The paper read simply, "I love you all, but I also love Pietro. We intend to marry. I pray I have your blessing."

Rosalia beat her head against the chicken coop, whimpering over and over, "Rina, Rina, *bambina mia*," as she staggered back to the house.

❦

WHEN ANGELICA RETURNED FROM MASS, her arms free of bundles, her mother greeted her at the door and asked her, "Where are the brioche, the *pane*, the *svogliatele*?"

"Last night I gave Rina the money to buy them," Angelica said.

"Why?" her mother asked, unable to conceal hurt and pain in her voice.

"I thought I might be detained at the rectory."

"Why?" Rosalia repeated absently.

Angelica followed her mother into the kitchen. "Oh, Mamma, what is it? You're so pale. What's happened?"

"Rina. She's run off with that barrister." Rosalia sat down heavily.

"And our bread money," Angelica said in disbelief. "She never breathed a word of her plan or I would've jinxed her any way I could've."

Rosalia handed the note to Angelica. "At least she didn't lie. She informed us of her plans. This will break your father's heart." *And fracture mine*, Rosalia thought. *How I'll miss the vixen.*

"Mamma, I can't believe she would have taken the bread money. What if—" Angelica took the *paniere* down from the wall. She reached inside without looking and felt the bottom. Her hand came up with the money and a note that she read to her mother. It said, "Angelica, someday we will all be free to make our own decisions. Kiss Mamma for me."

"Dear God, let him be good to my baby."

"He will, Mamma, he loves her."

"Love," she snapped. "What do you know of love?"

❦

AT ROSALIA'S INSISTENCE, NICOLA HAD contacted Pietro's boss at the law firm. Nicola learned that Pietro had given notice the week after he had started sending favors to the Domenico household. She saw the effect of all this distressing news. Nicola lost weight and was not even able to work with the men till the fall harvest.

Rosalia's heart didn't fracture nor did Nicola's break, although he moped around for weeks, even after the telegram came stating that the newly married couple were honeymooning in Rome.

THE NEXT DAY *COMPARE* LEO CAME to visit with his wife, Graziella.

Rosalia made demitasse and served cannoli. She listened to *Compare* Leo cheer Nicola.

"They'll be fine," *Compare* Leo said. "They're in love."

Nicola answered, his voice located somewhere close to his shoes, "The lawyer quit his job. What will they live on? You can't eat air or, for that matter, love."

"They're young. Believe me, they'll survive. Youth has a way of being resourceful. Don't you remember how it was with you when your Rosalia was a bride?" *Compare* Leo said.

Rosalia made a face that only Nicola caught. It read, "Doesn't your *compare* know I'm in the room?" She started to clear away the coffee service.

Compare Leo's wife tried to signal her husband. Rosalia caught the gesture. She figured his wife wanted to warn him that he was treading on unsafe ground and she was right.

Rosalia cleared her throat and offered the men a moment alone where they could smoke. She informed them the women would retire to the ante-salon.

While the women moved into the salon, the men decided on a walk in the garden.

"Finally, a moment of peace when we can chat privately," Graziella said.

The real burden of this runaway marriage, Rosalia confided to her friend, fell on Angelica's shoulders. "What with Rina married, how can the girl possibly leave home now to enter the religious life she so yearns for?"

"But I thought you didn't want her to become a nun."

"Naturally, I don't. But do I want her to remain a spinster to care for her father and me the rest of her life, especially if she'll resent it and become bitter? I'd rather see her in a convent scrubbing floors than miserable doing what she hates—though I can't admit that to her."

"I don't think you're that selfish, my dear Lia."

"Only Nicola has called me that since Concetta died," Rosalia said. Sentiment fragranced her voice. She patted Graziella's hand.

"You haven't told Angelica this, have you?"

"I can't now. It would kill Nicola."

"Then wait. Time has a way of adjusting all of life's problems. Look at me. I couldn't have children and now I have the love of Liborio, his wife, and soon a grandchild."

Rosalia winced. A sore subject, to be sure. "Did you hear about Peppe's commission?"

"Nicola told Leo and we are thrilled for him, but back to Angelica. I think it wise not to air your thoughts with either her or Nicola. Let's see what the future brings."

At that, Rosalia thought of Gina and the future she had forecast. Casting futures, Gypsy's work. She thought about what Angelica had told her concerning the Gypsy in Villaggio Pace. That sparked the memory of a caravan Rosalia had seen at the crossroad at the bottom of the ravine in back of the old Castle a week ago. She wondered if the camp would still be there. Tomorrow she'd walk near to see. *Non ci sono due senza tre.*

CHAPTER XXXI

Angelica

AFTER RINA'S ELOPEMENT

NOT A DAY WENT BY that I wasn't plagued by questions. How could my lovely Rina do such a thoughtless thing as to elope? Ah, but it was just like her. And me—hadn't I done the same thing when I'd run away to the convent a few months earlier? And didn't Rina know how she made our parents suffer? Hadn't Papà come after me, yanking me out of there, throwing my suitcase onto the cart and telling the abbess to mind her business, not his. Of course, Rina's happiness balanced the scales. Papà was helpless in Rina's affairs.

There were other questions I didn't have answers to and these weighed heavily on my mind. How could I possibly leave my loved ones again, when they needed me so much? Mamma worked in the Enoteca, Peppe was in the military, Rina had eloped, and I had to govern house, hearth, and the growing girls.

<hr/>

MONTHS WENT BY, AND THE only thing that interrupted my thoughts was a surprise visit from Lella, who awaited the happy event of her second baby. Of course Rina was supposed to be the godmother this time, but in her absence, I accepted the responsibility a second time with a gladdened heart, knowing that in so doing, I served both my sister and my cousin well. But I speculated over just how much in life was due to God's will and fate.

Rina had visited Lella in Messina to tell her of the elopement and confide that it was the couple's intention to go to Rome for a honeymoon where an appointment awaited her husband, Pietro, in the new offices of Marchese Montagna.

Lella and I were seated on the terrace. I said to her, "At least Rina had the courage and foresight to marry so as not to shame herself or embarrass the family."

Lella said she'd had a letter from Rina. "Please let me show it to you." I refused for fear I'd burst into tears.

She begged me to write to Rina and showed me her Rome address. She turned the address card over. Rina had written one word that tugged at my heart. "Please!"

Lella said, "Rina wants to be reunited with the family at all costs."

"I don't see how it's possible. She's broken irrevocably, and as for myself, I feel betrayed. She should've told me long before or at least when I gave her the bread money." I realized how petulant this sounded in my own ears and was amazed that kind Lella didn't berate me for it.

"But she couldn't tell you, you know it, and she left you a note with the money."

"And what of my papà?" I asked.

"I've seen how Zu Nicola broods. He misses her so, doesn't he?"

"That's not what I mean," I said.

"What then?"

"If I wrote to Rina, wouldn't that be an act of disobedience?"

"I don't think so because your father never told you not to correspond with her, did he?"

"Are you being deviously clever?"

Lella shook her head.

Her beauty shone around her like an aura, but I became suddenly frightened by a vision of Zia Concetta. Every time a woman conceived she put herself at risk—even if all went well, there was still the pain to reckon with. There was no separating life from pain. Happiness was sorrow's mirror image. The joys of motherhood were always accompanied by hurt and suffering. Could a neonate really compensate for the torture of birth?

Lella was saying something that I'd missed and I apologized. Then I said, "I just wish I had a clear conscience about this."

"Then bring up the subject with your mother," she said, placing a hand on my shoulder.

"Papà has forbidden everyone in the house to speak Rina's name."

"He'll rescind the order. If I know Zia Rosalia, she'll get around him. You'll see. Especially now."

"Why now after so many months have passed?"

"Because now, my dear cousin, your sister Rina is expecting her own child." She took her hand from my shoulder and I thought, *Oh my God, now even dear Rina will lament and experience torment. Is love for a man so strong an emotion that it blocks out the fear and pain? Is that what it is? Is it pain that is responsible for my actions and thoughts? Is it fear that drives this spurious desire for convent life? To elude anything is a coward's way—am I a coward to this point?* I had an urge to inflict injury to myself just then as if that could exonerate me to myself.

"Please," I said and opened my hand to receive Rina's letter from Lella, who smiled.

I TRIED DESPERATELY NOT TO think of the union between a man and a woman that brings forth a child. No matter how much I'd denied my curiosity about it to Rina or Lella in the past, the simple truth was yes, of course, I was curious. Denying it to myself was quite impossible. So there I stood, questions about the mechanics involved in copulation searing my scalp. But how could I ask? How would I have the nerve to utter the words: "How do you make love?" Even though I'd seen two people engaged in lovemaking, it remained mysterious. Was the devil tempting me?

While my spirit and brain argued, my soul was saying, "Be brave, don't ask," my mind was saying, "Be smart, ask." I heard Lella's words, which stopped me cold. "Tell me," she asked, "are you still entertaining thoughts of becoming a nun?"

I listened to myself stammer an answer, so off guard did this take me when the only thoughts I entertained were of the mechanics of procreation. I tried to quell each and every one.

NEWS OF RINA'S CONDITION, ALTHOUGH exhilarating, was nonetheless frightening. Lella and I discussed this some more and decided that, for the time being, it would be better not to mention Rina's pregnancy. In my heart's soul I prayed Rina had not disgraced herself or the family by means of a premarital liaison. That remained to be seen. Who did I think I was, anyway, some sort of judge? In the meantime all I could think about was that she was my sister, that I loved her, and that I must protect her good name and shelter her in whatever manner I could.

All of my good intentions didn't exempt me, however, from that most human of conditions: fear, caused by doubt. I didn't voice my fear to Lella, nor she to me, but I was determined to make a novena to the Sacred Heart and to Saint Jude, helper of the impossible. I started the novena that night, and when it came to the part for my special intention, at first I asked that Rina had remained chaste until her marriage, but then changed it, for what had passed was irrevocable, written in stone. Thy will be done. And so I prayed for her safekeeping and the baby's.

<hr />

WHEN LELLA LEFT TO GO visit her husband's relatives in Palermo, I told her how disappointed I was that she'd not brought my goddaughter and chided her for it.

"Here's a gift for my lovely goddaughter," I said and gave Lella the rag doll I'd just finished sewing. She extracted a promise from me to meet her in Palermo in a week before she left for Messina.

"If only Peppe were here to take me to Palermo. I don't know if Papà is up to it," I said.

"You'll convince him. He adores you."

Lella was just about to leave when I remembered she'd recently been in Calabria to see her mother and Zia Sofia. I asked about them.

"Zia Sofia's failing. The doctors say it's her heart."

"I'll have a Mass said for her and write her soon."

"And news of Silvana?"

"My sister is fine, but I guess you haven't heard her fifth baby died shortly after she was born. So sad."

"Oh," was all I could manage. I wasn't shocked by this news, but by my own accusing thoughts of Silvana. Mamma told me there were many of these almost "instantaneous" baby deaths, where a mother in postpartum delirium accidentally rolled over and smothered her baby.

"Do you know what happened? Was the baby unwanted?"

"I was told the midwife, in her haste, forgot to tie the umbilical cord." Lella couldn't look at me. I understood it was one of those sudden deaths.

I raised her chin with my hand and kissed her cheeks.

"Good-bye, dearest." She hesitated, then said in a voice of the heart, "Angelica, you're not even aware, I suppose, of what a splendid woman you've become. I hope you'll reconsider . . . I'm praying it's just that you haven't met the right man for you. You'll make such an enchanting wife and loving mother. I dreamt of you in a wedding dress."

I don't remember answering her, although the feeling was dreamlike. Was she really talking about me?

From outside the door, she waved and called out "good-bye" one more time. My chance to ask about lovemaking had vanished. Maybe next week.

***

THE HOUSE WAS AS QUIET as church when I spoke to Mamma concerning the possibility of writing to Rina. It was the most convoluted conversation one could possibly engineer without mentioning my sister's name.

"Mamma, I want to write a letter."

"As long as you don't say—" Mamma began to cry.

"Her name." I comforted her, patting her shoulder and handing her my handkerchief.

"Do you want my permission to write?"

"No. I just want you to know I'm going to do it.

"You won't mention it to Papà—not now, anyway."

I nodded. I didn't, however, tell her the news about Rina's expecting. I again fretted, especially because Lella had cautioned me with vehemence not to say anything. I realized in that moment just how genuine a love Lella had for Rina, for me, and for my family.

Instinct also cautioned me to wait for a more apt moment to speak to Mamma about Silvana's baby and the instantaneous death. I looked at my hands. I too had midwifed. I too had the power of life and death.

SO IT WAS THAT A YEAR and a half progressed in the blinking of an eye and we'd all accustomed ourselves to life without "The Pepper Pot," as Papà used to call Rina. I had become an aunt for the first time. It was a relief to know that I had counted an excessive number of months on my fingers from Rina's marriage to the birth date. Rina wrote me that she had chosen Rosaria as the name for my niece. She promised me that her next girl would be named Angela, after me.

BY NOW I'D ASSUMED TWO roles, that of Rina and myself. My father doted, passing the affection of his missing daughter on to me. But what was far more suffocating was that in the absence of Rina, so did Nunziata, Beatrice, and Flaminia.

We received letters from Peppe who was serving in the military and stationed near Naples in a barracks at Caserta. He'd achieved the rank of lieutenant and had announced his desire to propose marriage to Ludovica, the dressmaker's daughter, on his next leave, although he wasn't certain as to when it would be.

MY MOTHER HAD ALWAYS BEEN a fanatic about cleanliness, but now without Rina's help, the entire ordeal fell on me, which included Briciola, the dog. Nunziata and Beatrice called the scamp Crumb because she'd eat everything in sight, never leaving a single crumb. But it was little Flaminia who brushed her and saved her a treat from every meal she ate.

It was a beautiful October day when the sun shone brightly in air crisp as *crespelle*; the persimmons were green balls on the trees, still almost indistinguishable amongst the leaves. But soon, I thought, they'd dangle like Christmas ornaments. In November and December, the reddish globes of mature fruit would hang in a tangle of treeless branches.

"Briciola," I called out, tying two aprons around me—protection from her wild shakes and splashes.

She was clever, though, and went into hiding, just like a street urchin who knew a punishment awaited, or worse yet, had to face a Saturday bath.

"Briciola, my lovey girl, come here to Angelica. I've a luscious bone for you to crunch." I called out several more times, as sweetly as a bird of paradise, but it was useless.

I had the feeling I shouldn't have assembled the brush, the soap, and the wooden grape cask that served as her bathtub.

"Should I prepare the bath water and towels?" Nunziata asked.

"If you do, then I can hunt her up. But how will I capture her?" I said, thinking that by the time I found the lout, the water would be a skating pond.

"She's probably chasing rabbits or squirrels."

"I don't think so. She's in hiding. Or else Flaminia is fussing over her coat somewhere. I'll get Beatrice and search the grounds. When we find her we'll cinch her with this," I said, displaying a strap and halter, strong enough for a pack of Icelandic huskies.

Less than an hour later, a cowed Briciola, soaked and soaped, stood pathetically in the tub. I hummed a song.

Nunziata said, "It's a long time that you don't sing."

"Since Rina left," agreed Beatrice.

The next thing I knew all my sisters were begging me to sing, and sing I did. It felt so good. Like a cloud had been lifted from my soul— with certainty I felt that Rina would come back to us. Just then a cresting wave hit me and I was inundated.

My two aprons served me naught when, at the sight of Peppe, the dog jumped clear out and shook herself free of lather. I, on the other hand, wearing her suds, ran to greet my brother, arms open. In that instant of joy as I embraced my brother, I thought of my parents and how thrilled they would be to hold him once again. And for a brief moment I had the shadow of an inkling of what it was like to love a child and all I would be giving up if I became a nun. In that brief press and release, I decided I would tell my parents that they were now grandparents.

CHAPTER XXXII

Angelica

CHRISTMAS AND RINA

THE CHRISTMAS SEASON WAS ONCE again upon us. My dearest prayer was answered when Rina wrote to say she'd be with us for the holidays. Mamma didn't show the letter to my father.

When Rina arrived, for me it was as if she'd never been away. But for Papà, her return was another matter. He arrived home at midday. Rina ran to greet him. He was stiff and unyielding. I watched my sister take his hands and kiss them, begging his forgiveness. And still he made no move in the foyer and neither her tears nor each kiss she offered melted his cold demeanor.

Mamma came toward the vestibule but didn't enter. She stood crying in silence with her hands covering her mouth.

Rina pulled back from Papà. She wiped her eyes and stared back at him.

"Papà," she said, squaring her shoulders and summoning up courage, "if I were a man, you wouldn't behave so cowardly. You would rebuke me and be done with it. The past is gone. Will you let it go, or shall I put on pants?"

My little sister, standing up to my father! What mettle. How I admired her, and just as I thought my father was reaching out to her, he slapped her across the face. As he moved to backhand her again, she grabbed his hand and shrieked at him, "You've made your point! Enough! I'm asking your pardon. Will you not take in your prodigal daughter?"

"Should I hang you on the wall with the saints' pictures?" he said, his tone menacing.

Rina said barely above a whisper, "No, old man, just let me be your daughter."

Abruptly, he pulled her into his embrace.

⁂

RINA RETURNING TO US MADE the world spin faster. Everything seemed so much more exciting. Her baby was a fat-cheeked darling. Nunziata was totally enthralled with her. Pietro, Rina's husband, was in Switzerland on business. My wild and outlandish sister Rina had learned typing and now helped him with his correspondence in the office. Pietro would be down to meet the family for *capo d'anno* and we were going to have a New Year's party. Rina, Beatrice, and Flaminia were the chief organizers.

Mamma and I couldn't wait to scurry off to the Tuesday market. Since it was so close to Christmas Eve, the market stalls stayed open all day and well into the night.

After we'd completed our morning and afternoon chores, Mamma closed the store early and said, "Thanks be, we're finished."

"Mamma, let's take Rina with us. Nunziata can supervise baby Rosaria while Beatrice and Flaminia wrap parcels. And besides, Peppe is home."

The argument sounded good in my ears, but Mamma immediately found fault, chiding me for always wanting Rina with me. "Don't you remember when she was little? You couldn't stand the way she mimicked you. Then there came the time I couldn't separate the two of you. She's a married woman now and has a baby to care for. She's better off staying with the girls, lest she tires. She'll still be here when we get back," she said, shooing me out the door. "You'll probably take her with you on your honeymoon."

Mamma asked Beatrice to pick six or seven oranges, a lemon, and some cuttings of mint to make *insalata d'arance*. On our way out, she told Beatrice that she'd bring home the coconut, lettuce, and *finocchio*. "Please shell a half cup of almonds and put out the Marsala, sugar, and olive oil. Cut the oranges and lemon crosswise and set these aside. Angelica will do the rest when she comes home—she's got a talent for all things Sicilian, plus a good measuring eye to determine the soul of a dish, giving it a benediction."

Peppe held the door for us. "Angelica's like Goethe and I quote," he said, "'Without Sicily, Italy leaves no image in the soul. Sicily is the key to everything.'" We all laughed and Mamma and I left in good humor.

⸎

THE SKYLIGHT DIMMED AS IF a play were about to begin. Mamma and I walked arm in arm until we reached the market square. Hawkers and criers shrieked their wares for sale. A cold wind stung my eyes, and they were tearing by the time we approached a vendor turning chestnuts on a brazier. We stopped and bought some toasted nuts wrapped in a paper cone. Mamma held the cone while I took two plump ones out and put one in each of my pockets, every once in a while jostling them for warmth. Later when they'd cooled, I peeled and ate them. I fretted somewhat when I looked at my blackened fingertips, which I hastily wiped on the seat of my coat—immediately mortified at having done the exact thing that Peppe would have done when he was a boy.

Old people cloaked in shawls and muffs tramped by in boots. I counted two muffless ladies in fur-trimmed cuffs. Though I didn't recognize the fur, it looked warm and soft.

I had no idea that Mamma wanted to grocery shop. I thought we'd spend our time looking at crèches, witches and candy, or small gift items.

Mamma bought bread. The seller rolled it in brown paper, and she tucked it under her arm. We moved on a short distance, and she stopped again to purchase the missing ingredients for the orange salad.

"Why didn't we think to bring a shopping basket?" I asked, already aware of the answer.

"Because we were so excited and in too much of a rush. And I'd no intention of buying groceries, except for the fennel and mint for the salad, but just look at the diversity of items."

She picked up a tin of imported Cadbury's English Drinking Chocolate and another tin of Earl Grey Tea. Nonno Giuliano had always had these for Christmas. She liked this tea because it had oil of bergamot from Sicily. Doling out *lire*, Mamma promised to make hot chocolate when we got home. "We can drink it with the Christmas cakes." *Cucidata* cakes were overstuffed with dried figs, dates, and nuts, and each one weighed at least a kilo and were impossible to bite without risking one's front teeth.

But they were the only things Zia Sofia knew how to bake and she sent us a huge package of them. I wondered how she'd managed, being so feeble now. The entire family hurled insults upon them behind Sofia's back, but by the Feast of the Epiphany, they'd been devoured somehow, not a crumb or a broken tooth left among us.

We ducked under a canvas tarp ingeniously rigged as a tent, spread above a salami peddler's wares. He also displayed cheeses—some I'd never seen before. Mamma took change from her petit point purse to pay for *soprassata* that she probably made better and some kind of ripe cheese that smelled so strong I felt I'd be sick.

"Why ever did you get this, Mamma?" I asked, holding the package at arm's length.

"Gorgonzola. One of your father's favorites. I'll mix it with cream for gnocchi on San Stefano's."

What a waste of cream, I thought.

"The cream will confuse the taste and put out the fire of the cheese. I haven't made that dish in years."

"We haven't missed it, Mamma."

It started to drizzle, but as we moved along I felt the temperature drop, and the fine rain turned crystal, then white. Snowflakes covered large square umbrellas. Crowds gathered, taking refuge beneath.

We started to collect many bundles so Mamma gave me some change to buy a raffia mesh bag in which to put our purchases. I made a dash for a free sheltered space, accidentally bumping into a man in a pea coat and sailor's cap. He paid me no mind, even when I mumbled an apology. I only saw his Romanesque profile and part of a thick mustache. I didn't get a good look at him until he was some distance away and he turned around. He was the man I'd seen at Lella's engagement party—the one I hoped would have asked me to dance. His laughter rang out, a peeling of joyful merriment as bells, a song that plays itself all day long in your mind and, no matter what tune you try to sing, you always come back to that one. It stayed with me the rest of the night. I kept turning around for a peek, hoping he was tracking me.

Had I ever seen such a tall man? Or one as handsome? I must have been staring because when my mother caught up to me she tugged at my sleeve. "Angelica, come away, you're gawking."

"I've seen him before. Who is he?"

"Which one?" She took my arm and bustled me along.

"The giant man with the sailor's jacket on."

"That's—I think we're related somehow. I'll ask Ruggero next time I see him. He's so good looking and clever. A hard worker. The kind of man I'd love for you to entertain thoughts about—you and your precious nun's habit—but I'm afraid he would be a wrong choice."

"Why, not that I'm at all interested?"

"There's bad blood between your father and his," Mamma said and picked up a small miniature *befana*. The traditional tiny witch held a broom in one hand and a sack of coal candy tossed over her shoulder for naughty children. "Not too long ago, Papà purchased land from his father. Actually, it's his wife, Maria's, property inheritance from her parents. But she had no say in the matter as a married woman."

"You mean it's over her possession, not his?"

Mamma didn't answer and instead held up a yellow box of torrone with beautifully scrolled lettering. *When would women ever be able to handle their own affairs?* I wondered. Somehow I stopped blaming men for being the bosses and attributed our second-class standing as a fault of our own. I'd seen how Mamma manipulated Papà when she wanted to wheedle something out of him. I was guilty of this myself. Why couldn't women just come straight out with things? Were we always to be devious, never straightforward?

The box Mamma held, I saw, had beautifully drafted lettering on it, as if it were an old sacred scroll written in calligraphy reserved for things ecclesiastical. She handed it to me. I scrawled over the writing, making of it a palimpsest with the words: who is he?

She tapped the box. "How about this after Christmas dinner?"

"The girls will love it," I said, picturing the delicious contents of the box, gold-wrapped, individually cut pieces of nougat candy with almonds and the thinnest white wafer covering the top—thinner than the Communion host.

On the way home, we met some carolers. Mamma said, "Revelers. They've had too much mulled wine." We tried to hurry past them.

Instead, they stopped us to ask directions and I noticed they had Roman accents. It was difficult to get the gist of what they were saying at first, so I asked one pretty girl to slow down until my ears became accustomed to the cadence and dialect. Her smile brightened and she said, "If you think my speech is difficult, you should try traveling in the south if you're from the north." She continued saying how our Sicilian dialect was even more incomprehensible, with so many words using *d*'s for *l*'s and *u*'s for *o*'s.

Mamma and I laughed at that. The girl complimented me on my school Italian, and as she departed, Mamma elbowed me in the side to let me know she'd been right all these years insisting we speak properly.

I'd hoped for a night brilliant with stars, but instead we got air brittle with snowy flakes and a sky dulled and chalky, a painted winter landscape.

Nearby there was a public fountain where women did their washing. Ice had formed and children made scratchy figures on it, some trying to skate across. A shattering noise drew our attention. We spun around like toddlers' tops just in time to see a snaking train of carolers slip-slide into a heap.

Lanterns began to fade and soon we reached the hilly, unlit road that led us home. Our footfalls crunched snow, frightening field mice that scampered into the brush.

I told Mamma that I'd hold her to her promise to make hot cocoa. As we crossed the threshold, I glanced backward. I could have sworn the sailor followed right behind because I heard his laughter, which made me smile.

I realized then that Mamma had never told me his name and decided to ask her again when we laid the kitchen table for hot chocolate.

As usual, there was a commotion when all the children gathered around. Peppe had helped them make Christmas ornaments from large mussel shells we'd accumulated last summer. I remembered he saved all the large ones, washed and dried them in the sun, and then painted them with varnish so they shined. I was surprised at how pretty they were because I'd assumed he had no talent for art. My sisters were all eager to show Mamma their work.

Rina suspended one of the handmade ornaments in front of me. Somehow she'd fashioned a tiny angel inside the shell on a tuft of cotton cloud. "This is for my beautiful sister whose eyes are shining brightly tonight," Rina said.

I was speechless. I never thought of myself as beautiful, except the time in my formal gown, which I always thought of as a fluke, and maybe one other time when Lella visited. What's more, I never dreamed that Rina thought I was anything but plain. But ever since I'd seen the sailor,

I'd felt beauty within myself, which reminded me of how much I wanted to know his name. But if I asked now, I'd be teased to death forever and ever, amen!

Since Rina voiced it, I really did feel something different about my appearance. I accepted the gift and kissed her. Then I pretended I wanted to put it away for safe keeping in my room. So I stole upstairs and looked in the mirror. Rina was right. My eyes shone and my cheeks flushed, probably from the cold air outside and the warm blast once inside. I opened my top dresser drawer and fished around till I came upon my revised "Icicles" poem. I read it aloud.

Closing the drawer, Rina's words, almost an echo of Lella's, came back to me. Time passed, but I can't recall how long. Was the angel-in-the-mussel a sign? Was it my angel who had sent me the man's laughter? "What is his name?" I wondered audibly in front of the mirror.

"Giacomo Scimenti," my mother's voice answered as she stood looking at me gazing in the mirror.

<hr />

THE CHRISTMAS SEASON ALWAYS SEEMED a blur in memory, for it passed by faster than a train whistle's echo. Our New Year's party went off without a hitch. Papà was cordial, if a little off-putting with Rina's husband, Pietro, despite all of our efforts. Mamma and Pietro stood off in a corner near the hearth and I heard her tell him to be patient. "All good things come to those who wait," she said.

And then to emphasize that he was now part of our family, she recited an old Sicilian proverb: "*Ricorditi, Pietro, 'Li parenti sú parenti e li stranii sú sempri li stranii,' mi capisci?*" meaning, relatives are always relatives while the others are always the others—in the sense of strangers, outsiders.

Mamma didn't wait for his response but plowed on in hopes of making him understand my father's side of the situation. "Now you too are a father. Put yourself in Nicola's shoes and think how you'd feel toward the man who ran off with your daughter." Pietro shook his head, his face changing to a sympathetic expression. Mamma toasted the New Year with a glass of champagne Pietro had brought and, as was her custom, she dashed the flute into the fireplace to thunderous applause. We all ran to the window and threw out something old to usher in the new.

JUST AS I ALWAYS PREDICTED, this year's *cucidata* were no different from any other and were finished by the Feast of the Epiphany. Soon Rina's departure would be upon us and with my heart so full, it was all I could do to concentrate on her leave-taking to pick up the strands of her newly woven life as wife and mother.

On January sixth, every child's heart understood why the term *wild excitement* existed—it was to describe the joyous beatings of the savage organ, for this was the day in which the three Wise Men, Balthasar, Caspar, and Melchior, adored the Christ child with their gifts of gold, frankincense, and myrrh. They were responsible for leaving gifts for the little ones. These presents of the Magi were, in our family, a tradition like the signing over the doorpost of the main entrances of houses with chalk on the first of the year. The initials of the wise men were marked in capital letters and looked like this: 18 B-C-M 99.

In church, I went to light a candle to illuminate my heart and mind in the New Year as to what I should do to please the Baby Jesus. And there, by the wrought iron candle stand, with a burning wooden stick in his hand, was the man I had wondered about the night before Christmas. Our eyes touched for one brief instant, and I knew his thoughts were embroidered in a fabric elsewhere. I was not even sure if he saw me at all. I left him standing there before an old oil representation of the Adoration of the Magi and went back to my pew, opening my missal at the place where I'd left a red satin tasseled ribbon. There in black and white I read upon the page the words of Isaiah, apparently written one thousand and scores of years ago for me: "Then you shall be radiant at what you see, your heart shall throb and overflow."

I shook, a last-clinging leaf in winter wind. Chasing my thoughts, like elusive shadows, I slammed the book shut and knelt for the remainder of the Mass.

CHAPTER XXXIII

Angelica

FEAST OF THE CRUCIFIXION
CARINI, 1907

IT WAS DAWN ON THE Feast of the Crucifixion. I watched a man walk up the long, winding street toward the village. He stopped by a water fountain. Tossing his duffel bag down next to a twenty-liter *bummolo* receptacle for water, he drank in huge gulps. Then, with the water I knew to be frigid, he washed his hands, face, and the back of his neck. He smoothed his thick mustache and wiped his hands on the backside of his dark-blue suit.

The man was Giacomo Scimenti, who had been in America for a year living with his brother, Neddu. From the gossip I'd heard, he lived like a hermit because of his celibate, lonely existence in a strange new world. He had perfected his English working as a longshoreman on the Brooklyn docks, but felt himself becoming hard and embittered. Neddu had convinced him to take the next ship back to Palermo when news arrived in a letter that their mother was severely ill.

There were many stories about him, about his move to America last year, and years before when he'd been in China during the Boxer Rebellion where he'd fallen in love with Lian, a Eurasian beauty who had been his nurse. I pictured the stark white of a uniform. I knew of the rumor that before he was about to be shipped out, he was going to marry her, but she had died. How tragic. Would it ever be possible for him to love again, to find a wife who would bear him children? Did he even desire that? I had heard that Giacomo could not imagine risking so much to be left to the whims of fate again. That he had decided to be master of his own destiny, making his world spin in the direction he chose. I was very curious about him from the first time I'd seen him at Lella's engagement party and at the Christmas market, but after all this fascinating hearsay, I was determined to find out more about him.

I was just going home after an entire night of service. I had paid a call on a girl; her name was Sofia, like my poor, recently departed aunt, who was carrying an unwanted child of an incestuous relationship. Why did God allow such things? The girl had experimented with hot and cold baths and herbal teas to rid herself of the pregnancy. A mere child herself, the girl had ingested inordinate amounts of parsley, which is poisonous, but none of these methods proved efficacious and that tenacious fetus held tight to its mother's womb. I arrived just in time, her sister told me, for the girl was going to attempt to dislodge the embryo with a knitting needle. And where are the laws to punish incestuous men who take advantage of their own family? I felt unclean and was relieved to be out in the air. I was afraid that she would attempt something even more dangerous and detrimental to her person, but I could only offer her the idea of putting the child in a home run by the nuns with the hope that some kindhearted childless couple would adopt it.

Now, just past dawn on this September morning, the village air in Carini was still cool, but by noon it would seem to have been scorched in a kiln. Two men I didn't recognize picked up the demijohn near Giacomo's bag and carried it away. He watched the men lumbering in the distance and I watched him watching them. After a long time, I could barely make out their shapes through the mist. Giacomo heaved his bag onto his shoulder and walked the rest of the way home, passing houses and cottages laden with garlands of flowers for the procession that would take place at five o'clock. I knew this because I followed him.

Young girls and boys were still collecting flowers with their mothers as I had done so many years before. When I was a girl, we had come to visit Zu Vanni. The excitement I felt the night before with the preparations for the feast was almost as wonderful as Christmas. I had decorated the street and my uncle's home with flowers, much like the ones I saw on the walk.

At one point, Giacomo stooped to pick up a branch of lemon blossoms that had fallen from someone's gathering basket. He inhaled and kissed the small white flowers, tossing the branch in front of a small statue of the *Madonna di Poggio* at the gate of a house not far from his own. A grace. A grace would befall him now. I knew this small act was a sure sign of some little miracle, a wonderment to come because he did it without forethought as if guided by an unseen hand. Would he ever again give a girl a bouquet of flowers? Maybe one never could control destiny. He was *siculo*, after all, Sicilian blood in his veins from the time of first settlers of the island, and who knew how capricious the winds of fate could be!

After he entered his home, I continued on my way, imagining his homecoming. His mother, though aged, was almost fully recovered. I had seen his home once when I was young and my father and his discussed business dealings about a property his father owned. The internal surroundings were comfortable. In the living room there was a piano covered by a silk brocade shawl with long tassels made from the material that Giacomo had brought home from China. On top of it was a photograph of his parents taken seven days after their wedding, as was the custom.

I could sense the joyous mood, almost a physical presence to be touched, warm and festive, especially when the parish priest, dear uncle Don Ruggero, would enter to greet Giacomo, possibly saying, "Welcome home, my son," making the sign of the cross over him. Did Giacomo's thoughts race backward, turning time in his head to years before when Don Ruggero had welcomed him back from Asia, saying, "God will bless you for putting down the infidel and returning to Christ's bosom."

Had Giacomo excused himself, walked through the kitchen into the garden, and cried with thoughts of Lian? The slant of her almond-shaped eyes when he'd said to her, "Nothing is written in stone yet"?

Had Lian answered with fluttering eyelids, "Not even death will separate us. I'll love you always. I was your first love, but your great love is still unknown to you. I'll never leave China; after you're gone, my life is nothing. So be it, by Buddha's hand"?

Where had these romanticized ideas and thoughts of mine come from?

I felt obsessed and oppressed by all this reflection. But my mind had a mind of its own and wouldn't slow down. Another question formed like an image. Had Giacomo just now looked up to see that crow nesting in the venerable lemon tree at the back of his home?

A slight breeze stirred and the fragrance of the small buds was headier than perfume.

I wondered if every one of his memories was enveloped by haze. What shade of black were her eyes? Ebony? Ink? Coal? The passing of time, a descending curtain, covered recollections like dusty props upon a stage.

Street noises broke my reverie. Animals, carts, and people coming and going on the cobblestones made a din. A stablehand led a tethered horse—a roan, decked out in the colors of his *quartiere*. That quarter's colors were lavender and yellow and the horse's silk blanket matched a huge flag to be twirled later heralding the race's beginning. The horse was wide-eyed, but for the race he would wear blinders to keep his peripheral vision in check. The roan was skittish on the cobblestones. The stablehand spoke to him in reassuring tones. Hot puffs of breath issued forth from his black, wet nostrils into the frosty air. He shied from a cat moving stealthily across the road.

The stablehand doffed his beret. "*Buon giorno, signorina.*"

I nodded my head in reply, stopping to watch him pull the horse's head forward, then pass his hand on a knot of nerves and taut neck muscles. Gently, he guided the horse in a turn, patting his flank.

"*Di chi è?*" I asked, curious to know whose magnificent steed this was.

"Don Stefano Scimenti. The horse's name is Aquila di Cinesi."

"*Grazie.*" Something untethered and wild in me wanted to mount him till his bucking threw me or ride him till a tangle of trots became a canter, a gallop, transporting me to another life.

I'd just passed Giacomo's home and now looked up to see if he leaned out the window of the living room to watch the festivities get underway.

The most exciting occurrence today would be the *palio*, a horse race without jockeys. This year the sure favorite was Giacomo's father's horse, Aquila di Cinesi, named because his father purchased him in nearby Cinesi and the horse was said to fly like an eagle. But was the name too close in pronunciation to Lian's country, *Cina*, for him to want to bet on the horse?

From the balcony off the dining room, the Scimenti family had a vantage point to see the race quite well without being in the crush of onlookers. When couples walked by, would he ponder, *What is my life lacking? Someone I can share with, someone to love me, but somebody I can love also, even if I think it's impossible?* He must be so confused and alone, though he's with his *parenti.* I turned around once more as his family came out onto the terrace.

While they stood on the front *terrazza,* perhaps his mother shivered with the aftermath of ill health. As I walked on, perhaps he'd taken her inside, leading her by the elbow, all the while considering asking her to find him a wife. It was still the accepted way. Why should he be any different? Maybe, he reasoned, because he desired not just marriage; he also wanted love. Where had I heard this? But maybe instead he'd ask, "Was betting heavy this year?"

"When isn't it?" his mother probably answered.

✦

LATER IN THE PIAZZA, AS I passed by the tables and stalls laden with candied lemon skins and fruits, caramelized nuts, and candies in the shapes of fruits made from almond paste, I saw Giacomo again. He greeted people he knew and who recognized him. Between handshakes and kisses, he finally managed to get to the betting hall.

I stood a short distance from where I heard him say, "I want to place a bet." What a resonant voice.

"What are the names of two horses other than my father's? Tell me without thinking. Quickly," he said.

"Saracen and Lightning," the clerk answered.

"Lightning it is!" Giacomo said. His smile showed white straight teeth under a black mustache.

"Hurry or you'll miss the lineup. Better go straight away," the clerk said. I stepped back to avoid being seen.

Giacomo didn't answer. Instead, he visited a grotto on the side of the church. I watched from behind a linden not three feet away and heard him thank the Stella Mattutina, the Morning Star, Virgin protectoress of the sea and sailors, for yet another safe return to his homeland. He beseeched her to let his heart open once again, allowing him to love.

Oh, my God. My inner imaginings were truths.

I ducked inside, placed a white lace on my head, and knelt near two nuns. After his prayer, he walked past the open side door of the church.

Looking inside, he glimpsed me in my *mantilla*. For an instant it seemed as though I was caught in a time frame that held. I somehow visualized the watch in his pocket, stalled, to be sure. Perhaps he recognized me as the wine-seller's daughter. But did he think my name was Angela, not Angelica? An unfinished thought about discord between my father and his interrupted my pious attitude.

I wondered if he thought I was going to become a nun. Why would he? Did I really want that life, or was I living a charade I must end? He saw only the nun's profiles in the flickering of votive lights. I felt the pace of my heart quicken. I ran out after him. Jostling people hurried by, but still I felt anchored, my movements slowed to hundredths of milliseconds as one trapped in a dream sequence. By and by, I came out of the church garden, past the round three-tiered fountain, and crossed the street to where he'd placed his bet. He was waylaid by a group of friends. I lost sight of him, though I kept looking over my shoulder before being carried away with the crowd while he walked in the opposite direction toward a nearby tavern.

The bar facing the square was always overcrowded and the tavern overflowing, but today it was worse. My mother said nothing had changed since she was a girl, and as I gazed about the piazza, I saw the same grim men and voluble women. Life was an eternal cycle and here, for the first time in a long while, I felt at home and at ease.

The upward climb from the end of the piazza was steep. The unpaved street curved beneath the baroness' castle and led to the road out of town. Passing by the malevolent-looking castle imbued with history, romance, and murder, I thought of the legend surrounding it, the doomed love of the baroness. Not unlike Giacomo's love for Lian. Would a great love befall him? A Chinese fortune teller-astrologer told him it would; only how did I know?

When you have truly loved, can you ever love like that again?

A carriage passed me on the road, and once again I sensed he was looking at me, the veiled young woman uncovering her head. Was it him? I could have sworn it. He looked at me as if the sun had just shone upon me to reveal a truth he'd only begun to understand.

I stood staring after the carriage for some time. The street was bathed in sunshine but lined with enormous poplar trees whose branches swished with the slightest movement of air. Stepping from the sunlight to catch my breath in the shade, I wiped my forehead and took the shortcut home. For some sky-bound reason, serenity and happiness soared within me.

⸻

TWENTY MINUTES LATER, GIACOMO PARTED the braided and beaded entranceway of the grotto store banked on a hillside. I knew Lightning had crossed the finish line first because, as Giacomo stood in the doorway, it was as if I myself were hit by lightning. He looked with honesty into my face, the face of the storekeeper's daughter. I didn't know if he knew my name, but was only mildly surprised when he mouthed "Angelica."

His eyes touched my unveiled head of dark hair, and then my eyes—eyes that Mamma said speckled with gold filaments when I was excited—saw that he'd seen me without having looked directly in my face.

I was perched on a stepping stool reaching for a sack of rock salt. My skirt rose to show white lisle stockings and a glimpse of ankle. My step down was sure-footed despite the kilo burlap bag in my hands. I did not look away as Giacomo moved from the light into the cave-like store. No wonder the Eurasian had loved him. Looking at him, his eyes drank me in. Those eyes. I could lose myself in those eyes forever. Rebuking myself not to think like this, it occurred to me that he might even be recently married and I hadn't heard.

I moved behind the blotchy travertine counter. Giacomo stood on the other side. He looked at my hand and I at his. No wedding bands. I did not demurely drop my eyes as I had been taught to do, but recklessly locked my gaze into his, and it was as if the immoveable barrier disintegrated. My mother entered the shop seeing, too late, what had happened because she gasped with fright.

"Out of here, this instant," Mamma said to me, shooing me with gentle prodding.

Mamma plucked an apron from a wall hook and tied it around her waist, saying to Giacomo, "She's never in the shop, but I had to tend her sister who has the flu."

I walked out slowly, deliberately so I could hear everything they said.

"I sent Angelica to get me some salt." Mamma sighed audibly and continued, "Girls these days. Please forgive her impudence."

By now I stood on the threshold of store and house. How my mother prattled on without catching a breath! "You must have taken her by surprise . . ." Mamma's words trailed.

I peeked in to see that Giacomo didn't look like he was listening to a word she was saying.

"Are you all right?" Mamma asked him.

"Oh, oh, yes. Yes. Why, yes, I'm fine, thank you. And how is your husband, Don Nicola?"

"Ah! I hardly recognize you. Stefano Scimenti's son, back from America."

"I've come for some wine."

"How much do you want?"

"Two liters of red."

"I hope it's not too dear for your purse," my mother said, her little sarcasm not wasted on my ears.

"My friends want to celebrate the palio. We've all made wages on the race."

Giacomo took out some change from his pocket and placed it on the stone countertop to pay for the wine.

"What joy your mother must feel today to have you back at her table."

He answered, "Angelica has blossomed. I barely knew her. Tell her to forgive me for staring, but I think I saw her in church."

"She wasn't supposed to be in here and I'll tell her no such thing." By way of explanation she added, "My husband—"

Giacomo interrupted, "Is she going to take vows? She looked so religious."

"I fear that isn't a concern of yours. Give my regards to your mother."

I closed my eyes and folded my arms behind me and leaned back against the wall. I must have appeared a mere child when Giacomo had last seen me before he left for China. But I was no longer a child last Christmas in the square, shopping the stalls with Mamma. I had to be just a few years younger than he. Now that Giacomo had seen me, would he be forever shaken from his contemplation of Lian? What a bold idea!

Giacomo's beauty pinched me, as if to say, *Wake up!* But he possessed more than external beauty, of this I was sure, for his eyes had a depth of soul I yearned to comprehend. I couldn't control my feelings. They seemed to be a physical thing—an entity climbing around inside me. It was as though I recognized Giacomo's soulful stare from another moment in time. And for a fleeting second, I agonized, hoping he could blot out Lian's face forever. But he would make his destiny in America. And I would remain alone.

◆

AFTER LUNCH, ALMOST EVERY ONE of the villagers walked to the piazza in front of the Holy Cross Cathedral where the procession would begin. I saw that Giacomo was one of many among the crowd.

I had changed my simple dress and now wore a white, high-neckline blouse, a tight-fitting bodice with mutton-chop sleeves, and a brown taffeta skirt that crinkled with each movement. There was a tiny gold cross at my throat. Giacomo stood a short distance from me obliquely, and in the space between us, he formed an open circle with his hands, middle fingers and thumbs touching each other. Slowly he separated them farther and farther apart. What was he doing? Suddenly I understood that he was measuring—his separated hands shaped the size of my tiny waist.

I stood in back of my father. Mamma was home. My sisters, except for Flaminia who was sick, had gone to ride the carousel with Peppe and Ludovica. Don Ruggero passed, dipped his stick into holy water, and made the sign of the cross over the crowd. I turned and looked into Giacomo's eyes. I heard thunder, but paid it no heed because the sun shone so brightly and portrayed its good humor. His hands closed and he tapped his pointing fingers twice against each other, then brought them to his lips. He dropped his hands to his side.

Mine. And mine alone. From this moment.

What if he thinks I'd be wrong for him? Or that he mustn't try to see me again? That there's too much dissension in our families. Though, dear God, there must be a way.

The priest went from left to right, followed by a scaffold upon which rested the fourteenth-century crucifix carved in cherry wood—the hard wood used to prevent termites from nesting.

Some of the crowd affixed large lire bills to the lace altar cloth covering the scaffold table. Other parishioners threw coins. Many took off their chains and medals, rings and earrings, and attached them next to the money.

Six of the strongest men of the village carried the burden up their winding Calvary. One of the men had a powerful build and resemblance an ox. Strong men carried the cross, men who hefted bales of hay for livestock, hoisted wagons, and boosted upon their shoulders huge, weighty baskets of olives or lemons. Some of these men helped my father with the citrus harvest and some helped him in construction.

Looking at the sky, I heard thunder again. "Did you hear it?" I asked Papà, who was now standing next to me.

"What?" Papà asked befuddled.

I didn't answer. I searched the crowd. Giacomo was lost to me, but so quickly? He'd been right in front of me. I felt my heart plunge.

When I'd seen Giacomo, I'd heard a loud noise, but dismissed it again as distant thunder. But after the procession, when I returned home, I realized what it was and fully understood its portent. I told my mother that I'd heard thunderclaps for Giacomo. It was something I'd scoffed at all my life. Now I couldn't blithely dismiss it. I stood near the stone oven for a moment to catch my breath, walked to the iron pump in the granite sink, and primed it for a pitcher of water. I poured water into a green jelly glass with a raised stamp on it and the words *Four Seasons*. I drank in huge gulps, then I said to my mother, "It's like a faraway rumble in summertime when clouds move fast and gather, but no rain falls. It's love, isn't it? I mean, I love him. It sounds absurd. I feel so foolish, but it's true," I said.

I listened to my mother's answer with my heart pounding.

"Catch your breath. You're not the only woman in the world who's fallen in love without knowing someone. These things are written in the heavens. God ordains them to make up for past errors. My mother, God rest her soul, used to say, 'From another life, another Universe.'"

"You accept it so nonchalantly?" I asked.

"I married your father, didn't I? And I only saw him once when he bought a horse from my father. But that old fool of your father—after what he did against Don Stefano—Giacomo will never be able to make a proposal. There are so many other men. Lina Talese's brother, don't you think you could love him?"

Silently I thanked God that my mother never became a matchmaker for me. Lina Talese—skinny and round-shouldered. Her brother—bad complexion and buckteeth!

"Mamma, what are you saying?"

"I know. I know it's ridiculous. But Nicola Domenico is feuding with Stefano Scimenti. Matters of importance—the dealings of men and women don't interfere. Can I make myself any clearer?"

Shock registered. I shook my head, felt my heart, which had soared to unknown heights only minutes ago, fall from my chest. I sat down as if forced by a heavy weight.

"Why do these men always come to us noninterfering women with their important muddles, messes, and bargains, eh?" Mamma, standing next to me, stroked my head and continued, "Let me think. First, we'll see Don Ruggero. Maybe he can act as intermediary, but no . . . be advised, daughter, that even if bad blood didn't exist between your father and his, your papà will never hear of this. Do I have to tell you how he positively dotes on you, especially now that Rina is married? Anyway, Giacomo lives in America. He's happy there; maybe he'll not want to return to Sicily to eke out a miserable living."

"Why?"

"There's money to be made in America and a future to be etched. With the right person, he wouldn't be lonely, but would you? Without your family? Think, Angelica. Would your papà consider a marriage that would take his daughter across the ocean to a foreign land? But worse"— my mother sat down and continued—"despite the fact that the dispute over the property has never been settled, your father and Don Stefano haven't spoken in close to two years because the Scimenti family feels superior to us."

"Are you sure?" I sat next to Mamma.

"It appears that way."

"Is there any hope at all?"

My mother put a finger over her lips and then motioned me to follow her. We stepped into the laundry room off the kitchen. I looked up at the closet, surprised to see new haberdashery hanging on the door.

Mamma told me to try on the finery. It was the blue of his peacoat. Had his been a physical attraction with Lian at first, or an emotional one due to loneliness in the Orient? Had he loved her because she'd filled a void? Did Giacomo think of her still and the love they'd felt for each other? Would he ever think of the Eurasian girl in the finality of the past? If I had ever been in love with someone, could I forget? Would these questions consume me?

"I think of Giacomo and feel a burning in my chest," I said, realizing that had never happened with anyone. "At the mere mention of his name, butterflies loop in my stomach." I blushed and continued, "I feel like a schoolgirl."

I knocked my hip into the ironing board that was a wooden piece extending from a cupboard next to the closet.

"You must speak to your father."

I sighed. "God help me."

"Tell him you've had a change of heart." Mamma closed the ironing board. "Tell him you've decided to marry and give him grandchildren."

"How can I?" I whispered.

"Because it's the truth."

AFTER VESPERS, PAPÀ, MAMMA, AND I exited the downstairs chapel and walked to the upper floor of the house, coming out onto the back terrace. Mamma and I stood under a leafy-covered lattice. Papà asked for a bottle of wine and some antipasti. We immediately laid the table with caponata, salami, and black olives while my father and Peppe took their places. The girls busied themselves until I called them to table.

"Don Ruggero had to run an errand. He might be a little late for supper," Papà said to Mamma. "It's such a beautiful evening, let's sit out here till he comes."

Mamma said nothing, so I seized the opportunity. "Papà, I have a family matter to discuss with you."

"Speak, my daughter. It's never good to eat with a heavy heart. What's bothering you?" Papà poured wine.

"Today I have seen Giacomo Scimenti three times. If he were interested in courting me, would you allow it?"

My father did not seem surprised that I mentioned a man, or that I might want to be courted. He was focused on something else.

"The land feud has not been settled with Don Stefano," he said. "That old bastard. How dare he continue to slander me when the matter has been agreed upon?"

I had never heard my father utter such profanity.

"If it's a question of money—" Mamma started to say.

"What?" Papà asked.

"We could give—" she broke off.

"You? Insult me at my own table? Confront me with my own affairs?"

"I only—" she began again but was cut short by my father's brusque tone.

"Only what? Because your skinny little filly of a daughter is all smitten now, I have to be assaulted with an onslaught of calumny?"

"Nicola, no one accused you of anything. Be reasonable. I just—"

"Silence!" my father yelled. He slammed his fist on the table. "Am I no longer head of my own household?" Papà pushed back from the table, upsetting his glass of wine that mapped a stain redder than blood.

AFTER DINNER, PAPÀ AND DON Ruggero went for a walk to the piazza. As soon as he left, Mamma explained Papà's wrath to the girls, who were understandably shaken. Mamma let them off from kitchen duty and sent them to play cards with Peppe who had just come home on leave.

When Mamma and I had cleaned up and were alone, we sat outside for a bit. She shivered slightly from a chill and said to me, "Let's go in. There's too much frost in the air."

But it wasn't the cool air that had made her tense.

Once inside she continued, "There's one possibility." She opened the window and pushed out the wooden *serranda* partway for some moonlight. She placed a shawl around her shoulders. "We'll pay a visit to his mother, Donna Maria. She's a cousin of my cousin's wife. Maria and I studied embroidery together in the convent school near the cathedral of Palermo one summer and she knows Don Ruggero. She may be of a mind to marry off her son. And we'll see Don Ruggero tomorrow without Papà, if for no other reason than to ask his advice and prayers."

"Do you think a blessing will help? Did you hear my father's words? He's as irrational as that other old goat. God forbid mentioning his dealings."

I WENT TO BED STRUCK by love's thunderbolt, thinking not the saints in heaven nor the demons in hell could stop fate if it was meant to be. Not Don Stefano nor my father, not even one sworn to make his own future in America, or a girl who had lived for years with thoughts of the abbey.

Somewhere in the depths of my soul, I was afraid I wouldn't measure up—not in the real world where men and women were lovers and mates, but at least there I'd have a fighting chance. Whereas in the protected space behind convent walls, the recesses of my heart had railed, confirming what I'd long suspected. I'd be too tempted by the outside world, which wouldn't allow me to serve God the way a nun should. In that instant of honesty between me and myself before sleep overcame, I realized I'd never be a nun. Then where did I fit?

I will be his wife. I touched the cross around my neck. *Lian will be part of his past, but I'll be with him always. My destiny will be with Giacomo.*

THE NEXT DAY, DESPITE A break in formality, I took hold of my mother's arm for the long walk uphill to Giacomo's house. Donna Maria invited us in and said that Giacomo had told her of yesterday's meetings and that yes, he was interested in seeing me again. Talking to Donna Maria, it was decided that Giacomo would pay call on our household the following day.

IT WAS STILL FEAST TIME and not unusual for visits. Giacomo left his father's beautifully engraved calling card for my father since he didn't have one of his own. Donna Maria had written a note on the back saying that after her son's call, she would like to invite us for a visit the following afternoon, but her husband would send word of the time.

After dinner on the evening the card was left, Mamma handed me the card that was to be returned. It had been ripped in two and moist as if spat upon. I looked at my mother. She shook her head. "Hopeless."

"But there must be a way," I said.

THE CLOCK TICKED AWAY, BUT dawn found me looking out to sea. "I will convince him to stay in Sicily, or if there's no other way, I will go to America with him. What makes me feel so sure? I haven't even spoken to him. Yet I am. But how do I circumvent the biggest obstacle— my father?" This I asked the stars of Orion's constellation. Feeling dumb and inconsequential as Don Ruggero's ass, I continued talking to the stars.

My thoughts, emboldened by need and desire never before felt, made me begin to plot, invading dominions of privacy and respect. I must give Papà my jewelry inheritance that Zia Sofia left me in order to settle the land squabble. Even if it meant losing the respect of my father. This long-standing argument was over pride just as much as money. If my father's debt were paid, he would save face, and doubly so if I called it a loan and he paid me back. I didn't care about the money. Perhaps my father would make an invitation to the Scimenti family if he thought it was to settle this dissension. What was so important about a sheep pasture anyway? Or was there something else? I hoped my mother could get Donna Maria to bring Giacomo along.

CHAPTER XXXIV

Rosalia

WANT AND DESIRE

LIKE ALL THE GOOD WOMEN educated in the nineteenth century, Rosalia never asked her husband candidly for anything she really wanted to obtain. She had learned through experience that the tried and ancient means of allure and seduction were a possible way to get what she wanted. Sadly, this was the only alternative she had. Confronting Nicola honestly might bring about, through male obstinacy, a result opposite to that desired.

Rosalia thought of what she would say to Nicola that night as she reached into the wrought iron match holder nailed to the wall by the stove. She struck the red head of a wooden match along the side of the iron fry pan and the acrid smell of sulphur invaded her senses, reminding her of a story her great-grandmother had told her of the match girl who used to come to light the Sabbath fire. As she lit the kindling beneath the pan, she recalled her mother's account of this same great-grandmother's elopement. It was then that she made the connection between her wild daughter Rina and her mother's grandmother. Rosalia's mother had said, "We are Jews from Spain, but we are now Christian."

When the fire had taken, she stared into it, hypnotized by the flame, until one of the barking dogs startled and broke her trance. When the pan was very hot, she took a big pinch of salt and with it dusted the bottom of the pan. She reached for the large cubes of lamb and chucked in the meat. It began to sizzle and sputter, sending off an aroma of plenty and abundance. It was early Friday afternoon and the family would eat fish for dinner, but she was preparing the meat for Saturday. She never cooked on *sabato*.

❦

THAT NIGHT ROSALIA SLIPPED INTO her sheerest nightdress, leaving the buttons of the shift undone at the neck all the way to her huge breasts. Thanking God she was no longer of childbearing age, she put her Rosary out of sight and removed the scapula from around her neck. Before she approached the bed with the carved headstead, she daubed lemon blossom scent behind her ears, at the hollow of her neck, and at her pulses. She released her hair, letting it fall in waves down her back and blessed herself furtively, quickly. Attired thus, Rosalia's next flurry of activity was a practiced one. Though she herself did not derive pleasure from coupling or commingling, she hoped afterward she'd convince Nicola to take the jewelry and money Angelica had set aside for a convent dowry. She intended to say the offering was to make amends for Angelica's running away last year to the convent and in hopes of settling the Scimenti/Domenico rift.

Next Rosalia would say that the jewelry could be sold, and the sum garnered, along with the dowry, could be a payoff for Don Stefano. Deep within the well of her soul, she knew this sum would never be enough for the payment, but she also knew her husband didn't need Angelica's money. Rosalia would then put into action a second strategy, persuading Nicola not to take it.

She raised the covers and slipped in beside him. She didn't have to wait long before he raised her nightgown, crushing her with his weight, taking possession of her body.

When he was finished, she knew not to move, but rather to speak to him with endearments, and when she deemed the moment right, she proposed her plan.

Again Rosalia said, "You must do it not only for Angelica," cushioning Nicola's head against her soft breasts and massaging her husband's temples. She admonished him with gentleness and soft words to relinquish what was owed to Stefano. She used an almost cooing voice, one that would comfort a colicky child.

Rosalia continued, "But also for yourself, *tesoro mio*, because you know in your heart, *amore*, that this sum added to what you've already paid Stefano comes out to the original agreed-upon price."

There was silence. Rosalia heard the rise and fall of Nicola's breath, and she knew he was thinking over what she had said to him.

"*Caro?*"

She felt Nicola still her massaging hands with a firm grip on her wrists. He drew each in turn to his nose and then let his mouth suck the lingering scent of the perfume till there was none remaining. Reaching behind her neck, he pulled her face around to his, his mouth mastering hers, thus paying twice in one night for a favor that was for his own soul's salvation.

CHAPTER XXXV

Angelica

PAX DOMINUS SIT SEMPER VOBISCUM

THE FIRST INVITATION MY FATHER sent to Don Stefano had been turned down because not enough of a hint at a settlement was made. The second one was not refused when a definite assertion of an agreement was mentioned.

Through my mother's pleading and intercession, I had convinced my father to accept money from me as a loan to finish the argument with Don Stefano once and for all. It seemed a logical solution, once I prompted Mamma to remind Papà that he and Don Stefano had been godfather for each other's cousins. Mamma did not mention, however, the fact that, even with this money, my father had still underpaid for the property. But he flatly refused to pawn Zia Sofia's jewelry.

I tried desperately to conceal my disappointment at not seeing Giacomo. I forced a smile to my lips and made chitchat with Donna Maria and Mamma. How could I have been so stupid to think that the man would bring his son on a social call when this was a matter of business? Wishful thinking. Had love made me a dreamer? But at least the matter was settled between the fathers, and when the old men shook hands, I felt proud and glad, even if my dearest wish that Giacomo might come to the meeting had been foiled.

TIME WAS RUNNING OUT FOR Giacomo. His ship would be leaving in a few months' time. For two weeks I glimpsed him at the six o'clock Mass. His parents must have counseled him to be patient for a time, at the end of which Giacomo could finally leave his own new calling card at our residence. It was at this time Papà answered in the form of an invitation from our family for refreshments the following afternoon.

ICE CREAM WAS SERVED IN Baccarat-cut crystal cups with linen doilies beneath them that rested on small Ginori porcelain plates rimmed with gold. The fruit ices and cream refreshments were served on a veranda covered with philodendrons and ivy just beginning to change ruby red. The terrace overlooked the bay's basin. Bathed in sunlight and reflecting gold along the coastline shone the *Conca d'Oro*, the golden conch. It included the hills that encircled the hollow of the Bay of Palermo.

Espresso was served next. The men took it corrected with Amaro Averna and the women plain or with a drop of homemade anisette. The conversation was jovial and festive, until I saw Giacomo could contain himself no longer and asked for my hand in marriage. Giacomo and his mother sat on a love seat opposite us. My father, flanked by Mamma and me, sat on a wicker settee with chintz cushions. Papà sat stiffly, holding my hand. The propositional words were barely out of Giacomo's mouth when my father looked at me and said, "My first born, my soul. You really want this man?" He dropped my hand.

I did not answer my father but took my eyes from his and cast them down. In that instant, by that simple sign, I let Giacomo know that I had acquiesced to the proposal. I wanted him. And I knew he yearned for me. Why did I want him? My look sported the demeanor—no, wore the eyes of a woman in love. It exuded from the inside like swelling tidewater from an enclosed basin. Was this really happening? Would it be enough to last a lifetime? Then, to my horror, I locked eyes with my father and watched the expression on his face change. I thought he might strike me. The room seemed to spin. My breath caught in my throat. I felt my chest heave with the weight of my lungs, the pulse in my neck—a fly trapped by a closed window.

As the thought of wanting Giacomo as much as he wanted me

flashed over again in my brain, my father grabbed my hand with both of his, brought it to his mouth, and bit it. I perceived his yelp as that of an injured animal. I merely whimpered, though injured physically. I felt my father's emotional pain outweigh and exacerbate mine to such a pitch that he was capable of hurting me. My wound was nothing, diminished, overshadowed by his grief.

Giacomo watched us with tears in his eyes. Papà reached for the bottle of Averna on the wrought iron table in front of him. He dipped the bottle of the dark herb liquor onto his linen handkerchief and wrapped it around my hand.

My darling Giacomo started to get up to protest my father's behavior, but before Giacomo opened his mouth, his mother gripped his arm like a vise and raised her frightened eyebrows. She tilted her chin outward. I saw that it was almost impossible for Giacomo to hold himself in check, the muscles in his neck taut, his hands clenched. Did he feel the blood coursing hotly through his veins as I did? Did he hate my father?

Did Giacomo understand that Papà adored me, that he was desolate at the thought of losing me? Giacomo wore the look of a killer in his eyes. And it frightened me to see that he was capable of murder. I couldn't believe what I saw in his face, but somehow knew he would always protect me. I wondered if even he himself believed what he felt for me. How could I know this? Yet I knew he could have killed my father for hurting me.

Then I saw a shift in his face when doubt invaded reason. Would I leave a father so crushed by his daughter's decision to marry that he bit her hand? How many times in our lifetime would Giacomo's mind stumble into this scene again and again, repeatedly seeing my hand being bitten in slow motion, leaving a mark forever? Giacomo winced.

I saw Giacomo and his mother back away as I wept in my father's lap. Mamma escorted them out, her eyes gauzed with parental ache and confusion. With my last gaze at him, I saw Giacomo bend to kiss my mamma's hand. When he raised his face, he looked Mamma in the eyes and said, "I will never inflict pain on your daughter when she is my wife."

I shook my head, knowing that if love is unbounded, its capabilities are frightening and limitless. A tear fell on my new green silk skirt, shimmering like a leaf on an apple tree, shiny as Oriental jade. For a fleeting instant I felt perhaps Lian had given us her blessing from a world beyond;

in the same way I sensed that the tableau of my father and his daughter remained behind Giacomo's eyes even outside the house as he passed our iron garden gates.

I had sat up and stopped crying by then. Mamma smiled wistfully. She said, "From Genesis, it has been decreed by God that men and women will always be at odds."

CHAPTER XXXVI

Angelica

THE WEDDING

GIACOMO LOVED ME, THOUGH HE had not declared himself to me. I knew. And I loved him. After my engagement had been announced, the bans of matrimony were read aloud in church, and the realization of what I faced set in. I couldn't eat. I couldn't sleep. I obsessed with fear of the wedding night and the possibility that I would become pregnant. I began to think of ways it could be avoided, but Lella told me she knew of only one way: stay away from your husband. Since this was ludicrous, I prayed. Somehow I knew this man was destined to be my husband. A darting feeling in the pit of my stomach came over me whenever he was near, yet even an insignificant thought of him was stimulus enough to provoke the same sensation. I wondered if it would ever wear off, or was I forever going to be a slave to this internal uproar?

Everything happened so fast. I felt caught up in a whirlwind, a leaf aquiver on a mimosa in February. I had no say in anything. We were to be married after a courtship of thirty-three days, barely a word spoken between us, and when we did speak, it was always in the company of a chaperone. Yet I knew a bond existed between us from the intense gaze of his eyes.

Rina had come for the wedding. She went to light a candle after Mass one Sunday. While we waited in the vestibule of the church, I asked Mamma if I'd done the right thing accepting Giacomo's offer of marriage. She blessed herself with holy water from the font on the way out of church. Walking down the steps, Mamma halted, blessed me, and said, "The heart is a safe harbor, one of truth, and—" She gripped my hand and kissed it. "Always follow the footsteps of your heart."

Her words were what I needed. I'd chosen in Giacomo a redemptive lover, an asperges to wash away my past with its iniquity of fear and one in which to consecrate the future. I couldn't help recalling my thoughts as I baptized Concetta's infant. How wrong, how inexperienced, how terrified, I'd been.

Mamma, Rina, and I walked toward the piazza. A scrumptious respite of rain had sweetened the air. My mind circled around like the piazza itself, and I understood that from the first moment I saw Giacomo he had never left my thoughts. I imagined a world without him in it. I recoiled. And what of my immediate world? I couldn't bear the thought of living a life without him. Would it be a life if he were not part of mine? With every step I took, I discerned exactly what it was I was asking myself. What was the meaning of love?

How could I, so untutored in worldly arts, come up with a definition? My brain asked more. Is it emotion? Is it that physical hop and skip your heart takes when you hear his voice? Is it anticipation at the sound of his steps? I was thoroughly attached even to the idea of my loving, which I felt with permanence yet pitied—for it had nothing solid on which to subsist as of yet. I rhapsodized in sync with nature, understanding how even magnolia blossoms felt on a tree bare of leaves.

<hr/>

THERE WERE ONLY FIVE DAYS remaining before the wedding. Mamma, Rina, and I sat at an open-air café. We were having *spumoni* while we listened to the band play. Mamma ordered espresso for Rina and herself, and Martini *bianco* to settle my nerves.

"Music," Mamma said, "is angelic, a heavenly language. It should be a bride's meaningful communication with her groom, and so it should be for you, on your day of days."

This declaration from my mother surprised me, but I was even more stunned when she continued saying, "What better way to speak of choosing love than to select a special accompaniment for your marriage celebration?"

Rina piped in and said, "If I were choosing a musical conversation as a bride walking down the aisle I'd make sure it is not only saying, 'I do,' but sending many other messages to my groom. I never had this opportunity, but I want it for you."

Rina shifted her chair a little closer for more confidentiality. Mamma poured water from a little pitcher into my vermouth and the waiter in a long white apron brought me green olives and salted nuts.

"I like your ideas about original music, but which?" I asked.

"What variations and alternatives to church songs other than Mendelssohn's 'Wedding March' can you think of?" Mamma asked.

"That's traditional, but so common. I'd rather have something meaningful like Schubert's 'Ave Maria,'" I said.

"That's such a religious hymn," Mamma said. "Do you think it appropriate?"

"Absolutely," chirped up my lovely sister. "Wonderful, diverse, and a salute to all women—a marvelous wedding song," she all but gushed. I had thought that her elopement had been daring, courageous, and romantic, but now I felt sorry she'd missed out on all this. I reached for her hand under the table and squeezed it.

Mamma, unaware, continued, "There are many other magnificent musical compositions by Bach, Liszt, and Beethoven . . ."

I fidgeted, tapping my fingers with impatience. I wanted the dialogue over because I felt the way my sister did. I needed words and melody that encapsulated everything. "I agree with Rina. This song sums up all for us and will make my wedding timeless!"

<hr/>

THE SURPRISE OF MY LIFE occurred that night after the discussion of music I had with Mamma and Rina in the piazza. After dinner my betrothed showed up beneath my balcony with a string quartet and my family and I were serenaded. Does every girl not dream of this? Chills made the hair on my arms all but leap off, and Mamma covered my shoulders with a shawl, even though I insisted I wasn't cold. "*Romeo e Giulietta*," I sighed, praying that our love would not end tragically.

After the mini concerto, we strolled in the garden. My parents were just paces behind us. I dared to put my arm through Giacomo's the way Mamma did with Papà sometimes. Giacomo confided that he'd gone to his friend Lorenzo who worked in the Chamber of Commerce to ask for suggestions as to volunteer orchestras and bands. The wonderful serenade group worked for nominal pay. But this was not the only thing my future husband disclosed. We stopped by a small rough-hewn bench, but my parents kept on walking toward another bench farther down the lane. They sat and spoke quietly while Giacomo and I sat gazing at each other. Now was my chance. I asked, "Tell me about China . . . and Lian."

"She said I was a wayfarer, and I was one until now that I've found you." Giacomo didn't tell me anything else about Lian and instead spoke only of the Chinese—the shiny black queue tossed forward before a man's beheading he'd witnessed in Peking; the way people squatted to eat bowls of rice, steamed vegetables, and eel with *fai ti*, chopsticks. The look of peasant women in the northern provinces with no bridges on their noses and how they dressed in pants and straw hats. He spoke of the taste of pomegranates and plump, moist lychee, the touch of a serpent's skin at the open market by the quay in Shanghai, the scent of incense in the temples, and the twanging sound of a zither, reminding him of the Jew's harp he'd played as a child tending his father's sheep at the grotto. He said these things, but was the sound of Lian's laughter in his ears? He was quiet and then I became terrified by the look on his face as he said in a hoarse whisper, "Angelica, I'm not the man you think I am."

His eyes were luminous—almost to the point of feverish. Before he spoke, a lemon blossom struck me on the shoulder. There would never be paradise on earth, for all things are passing and happiness, the most fleeting of all. I thought, if I were reading this in a novel, I'd think it was authorial invention, a manipulation—but it was real life, my life. It happened and so I accepted it as symbolic. The blossom fell to my lap as he took me by the shoulders. "You still have time to dissolve our engagement if you want." His fingers dug in beneath my collarbones. Would he tell me now about Lian? I was afraid my parents would see his hands on me, but it was dark in the shadows and the moon aided us with its coyness of playing hide-and-seek behind swift-moving clouds. He said in a rasping voice, "I'm a murderer. I've killed a man, after I could not save my friend Enrico." His fierce grasp underscored his confession. He shook me as if to wake me from a spell.

"I know," I said. My mind whirlpooled. "I understand."

"No, you don't." There was movement in a treetop.

"Oh, but I do. Sometimes we're powerless or trapped and we react and terrible things are the consequences. I too almost killed a man."

"You?" He pulled me in a tight embrace and I thought he'd smother the life from me, but all I could do was fret about my parents down the lane. I cleared my throat and gave a fake cough. He pulled back from me somewhat and said the exact words I was thinking about the stabbing in the barn. "I never meant to do it."

Gradually he released his clutching hold and I told him about the man in the barn, how I'd stuck him with the knife.

"And I . . ." he said, hanging down his head, "I had to take the life of the man who shot and killed my friend Enrico."

"His name was Ciccio," I said absently, waking from a bad dream.

"Dear God. Are we soulmates?"

"I would hope so. Why?"

"The man I killed—the scum of the earth, a scourge, a filthy bandit— was also named Ciccio."

I wanted to disclose all the ideas I'd had walking toward the barn that day so long ago, especially my notions of virginity. But before I could, Giacomo kissed me. His lips, soft and tender against mine, yielded to passion, becoming harder, pushing into me more forcefully, till I was breathless. The most peculiar thought chased about for me to latch on to—if I'd been gardening a few paces from where we sat, I would've dropped my tools as if I'd heard the master of a manor step lightly on the stones of the patio. A beckoning. I knew I belonged to him. I was not revolted as I'd been with Domenico—in fact, I leaned into his kiss, begging for another, heedless of my parents.

<hr>

NEWLY FORMED THEORIES OF MY life raced through my head as I dressed for the wedding, almost tangible, live beings. In this new venture—this walk down the aisle toward a new life that I'd finally chosen—I would have to go beyond range, beyond cosmetics of the body in order to find my soul and be a good wife to Giacomo.

The dress I had made was silvery and pearl in whiteness and sheen, like the iridescent inside of an oyster, and was made of a fine imported silk brocade. I wanted something stylish, some delicious thing quite removed from a nun's habit, now that I'd made my decision to marry. My wedding dress had a karakul jacket and just beneath the collar would rest an embroidered jabot of *mousseline de soie*. I had sewn a cornucopia of seed pearls on it, spending hours embroidering and dreaming every evening till I finished. I started sewing the jabot on the eve of the Feast of the Crucifixion, never dreaming it would be part of my wedding costume. And now when I needed to attach it, it was missing. How could this be? I looked under the vanity table, on the bed, under the bed, on top of the dresser, on the floor beside it, on the nightstand on Mamma's side, then on the one on Papà's side. I tugged gently, pulling the skirt and petticoats up, and got on my hands and knees and searched in vain. I prayed to Saint Anthony: "Good saint come around, something's lost, and must be found." Then I sat down in front of the vanity mirror in Mamma's room about to burst into tears when Beatrice ran by. I called out to her to fetch Mamma and Rina. They both came in with astonished looks on their faces.

"Whatever are you thinking, Angelica? A bride is supposed to be late, but this is outrageous," Mamma said.

"I left you ten minutes ago and all you had to do was attach your collar," my matron-of-honor, Rina, said. Her eyes were brilliant, and she looked radiant enough in her pink dress to be a bride herself.

"Your eyes are so shiny. Are you pregnant?" I demanded. "If you are you mustn't be in the wedding party. Under any circumstances. I forbid it. Mamma, tell her."

Mamma agreed with me, and I could tell by her facial expression that she was afraid if Rina was expecting and took part in this public display, she would undoubtedly lose the baby. "Of course I'm not," Rina said, exasperation in her tone. "Now, what's this all about? Why aren't you finished dressing?"

"My collar. I haven't got it," I said. "I even said the prayer to Saint Anthony to help me find it."

"He's a powerful saint. He never fails, but did you put a glass upside down?" Mamma said.

I shook my head. She took a glass from next to a pitcher on a tray on top of her vanity and turned it over. "This always worked for my mother," Mamma said.

"Just do without—but what do you call that lace thing around your neck?" Rina asked, pointing.

"That's the inner one attached to the blouse, silly. You know that. I mean the jabot that I worked so hard on."

"Oh no," Rina said. "Oh dear."

"What?" I said, hearing my own voice scratchy and unnerved.

"You can't mean Mamma's handkerchief that I borrowed—the one laying on top of the jewel case?"

"My bridal jabot!"

"Actually, I thought it was a bit rough and so ornate—"

"Oh, Rina, you didn't," my mother protested.

Rina flew out of the room. Mamma went over to her dresser and took out a handkerchief embroidered with initials and dates all over it. She held the frail keepsake as I looked at it.

"Mamma, I've never seen thread like this. What is it?"

"Hair thread from our womenfolk. There have been several that didn't survive, but this heirloom records our family history back to the Inquisition when my great-grandmother's people, Jews from Spain, escaped to Sicily. This was my mother's, her mother's, and before her—all the way back to Toledo. We have in our family tree the name Toledano."

"Does Rina know?"

"You are my eldest daughter. I prayed every Friday that God would tug you by the ear to marry. Remember, once I told you that our holy men study the Torah? They also marry and have families. We do not acclimate well in convents. I knew you'd never enter the cloister."

I was stunned and almost didn't hear the rest of my mother's declaration. "You will give it to your daughter someday . . ." she trailed off. All of a sudden I thought of Mamma covering her hair every Friday before sundown, the only woman in our parish to do so.

"Friday night, the candles and prayers." Recognition of who I was finally hit me, and Mamma read it on my face.

"I light the Sabbath candles in memory of those who have gone before." She handed me the handkerchief and I felt something electric.

My mother gasped, looked at our hands, and said, "Oh, dear God, don't let this be—"

"A bad omen? It won't be. I promise you, it's something blessed." I put the dainty cloth to my cheek. "My ancestors are taking watch over me."

My mother and I heard Rina's approaching steps.

Rina danced in waving the jabot. "Hardly a wrinkle, see?" she said. As she put it on me, she asked about the handkerchief and Mamma said she'd tell her but not now. Rina smoothed down the jabot and attached it at the back of my neck.

I glanced in the mirror and saw the jabot had taken a jaunty little upward pleat at the top of the neck where it was supposed to lay flat. "Oh no," I groaned.

"Not to worry a snippet," Rina said and quickly undid her brand-new cameo brooch with a small diamond. "Here, take it," she said, extending it toward me in open palm.

"No," I said, pushing her hand away. "I couldn't. It's brand new."

"Oh, heavenly saints and souls in Purgatory! Wear it! And you'll need some money for your shoes." Rina fastened the breastpin at my neck. "There," she said, "now you're perfect."

"Angelica—" Mamma started to say.

"You're outnumbered, my dear sister bride. Surrender for once. Please," Rina said.

"Then you must have a coin for the pin." I rummaged around and finally found one in the vanity drawer.

Mamma said to Rina, "Make sure you have Peppe and Papà give her money to put inside her shoes. I don't want her penniless because then I'll have to support her."

⁂

DRIVING IN THE CARRIAGE ON the way to church, I slipped folded lire notes into my shoes. My father and I were much later than anticipated when our carriage pulled up to the church thronged with people. As dusk fell it seemed as though the lighted candles took life from their wicks, burning brighter flames, and I realized I was a Sabbath bride—a contradiction in terms—the wonderful irony of it. I caught a glimpse of Giacomo, but he had not as yet seen me. He stood next to Lorenzo waiting for me, his bride.

Giacomo wiped his forehead with a handkerchief. It appeared that Lorenzo looked nervous. Giacomo leaned closer and whispered something to his best man.

Excitement overwhelmed me. What if he wanted to change his mind and was only going through with it to avoid a scandal?

Lorenzo couldn't answer quickly enough because necks began to crane backward to see my entrance with my father. Music began to play. The wonderful soloist's voice filled the church with poignant mood. The Latin words of "Ave Maria" descended with celestial chords from the organ loft as though carried with the fragrance of incense upon the community.

Giacomo turned toward me. His eyes beheld me in a way that bespoke love. I recalled the bubbly feeling I'd had that morning telling Rina about my love. How love itself insists to be spoken of in natural terms, for it is powerful, a geyser springing from our depths—a munificent blessing, an offering that of necessity must be bestowed.

I adjusted my veil, took hold of my papà's arm, and we began to walk toward the altar. Mamma, dressed in a shade of mourning dove, seated in the first pew, caught Giacomo's gaze. She began to weep and I knew it was from joy, the fullness of emotions exposed on her heaving breast in thanksgiving to a kind God who'd granted her dearest wish.

When we reached the altar, we stopped. After my father raised my veil, he kissed me. I thought of the veil Mamma told me she'd taken from my face when I was born. I knew I existed for this. I squeezed Papà's hands and he gave me over to my groom.

Throughout the ceremony, I did not completely understand all the priest was saying. Words loomed, like the sun downing—they almost shimmered above the candle flames. But I was certain of one thing, so fixed was Giacomo's gaze upon me, his bride, that he willed me to raise my head and face him, to look at him, to see love registered in his countenance.

Giacomo's eyes joined mine, but the expression he might have read therein was almost of annoyance at my being distracted from the ceremony taking place. I wanted him to know it was sheer happiness, so my own eyes vouchsafed a tender beam. How wrong he was if he thought me anything but thrilled, because I also had lost the significance of what was being spoken and wandered astray in his reflection.

I couldn't grasp the service completely, so imprisoned was I pondering my life and where it had taken me. I couldn't comprehend or contemplate what Ruggero was saying because awareness enveloped me, its raw strength building to crescendo until, like the swelling of a musical andantino, it had taken me to another passage. There I dwelt among familiar vales with my loved ones, among the advice, the consent, the emotions of the past thirty-three days. And I was inundated with the significance of Christ's years being the same amount of days as my courtship. And this called to mind the day on the terrace when Giacomo had asked for my hand in marriage—I had been drowning in an emotional flood, but could not speak and merely inclined my head—and it was in that instant all my life changed, when I acquiesced without so much as a word to him. With acceptance, I cut away from the life I had dallied in, entered upon a mutated existence while still remaining encapsulated by the old. Looking back on this time, I realized that it was jubilation tempered by woe. I'd detached myself from the family chain and hinged all of myself—aspirations, dreams, fears, needs, wants—on this man. Totally, completely on him.

Reviewing my old life, I concluded in an examination of conscience that I had been paralyzed by my past behavior and sentiments. They appeared obdurate and unfeeling compared to these new sensations taking possession of me now. I couldn't believe I'd disappointed those I loved, that I'd been baffled by my own ideas and choices, thwarted by inexperience and, to a certain degree, even by religion.

The zenith of my life lay not in back of me but in the morrow. Fright tinged with exhilaration for my new life.

My reflections were curtailed by other thoughts. At the Communion of the Mass, "*Panis Angelicus,*" "Bread of Angels," began to play. The Eucharist was sustenance for soul, much as Giacomo and I would be each other's bread of life through this exchange of wedding vows.

<hr />

AFTER THE CEREMONY, I PLACED my bouquet on the altar for my Zia Concetta. Then we went to a nearby podium with our witnesses to sign our formal documents.

Giacomo and I walked down the aisle arm in arm and then stood to greet our guests. Lella and her husband were the first couple to offer their congratulations. After our receiving line thinned out, Giacomo and

I exited the church showered by confetti—sugared almonds—and I said, "Giacomo, these symbolize the sweet and bitter of life." Some people threw coins, and the adults laughed as the children scooped them up.

When we arrived home, we stopped in the vestibule before making our entrance. I took the cross off my neck and gave it to my spouse. He attached it to his gold chain. It slid next to a Buddha, not quite covering it. Watching him and seeing the strange Oriental jade figure for the first time, I felt my eyes open wide. We went into the garden with our guests.

NOW HERE I STOOD WITH Mamma on the threshold of my nuptial suite. Somehow my head leaped backward in time a month ago to the Feast of the Crucifixion. My struggle to become a nun had been thwarted by my family, my confessor, and myself. Should I or shouldn't I take the veil? I had been saying a novena to the Sacred Heart and each of the nights I dreamed of Zia Concetta. I begged of her a sign in red if I were to become a nun, in white if not.

There had been blight on the lemon harvest, not a complete disaster, but in our garden every plant had dried up. The ninth and last day of my novena, Mamma commissioned me to get a kilo of salt from the store. Before I went to get it, I strolled in the garden. I was dazed by the pungent perfume of *le zagarelle*, yet only one tiny branch had lemon blossoms on it. How could this overpowering aroma come from just one frail offshoot?

I picked the bloom and put it in the top buttonhole of my blouse. I entered the store and climbed up on a stool to reach for the sack of salt. Someone came in. I turned around. I saw Giacomo Scimenti and knew immediately that fate and my Zia Concetta from the *al di là* had sent me the white bloom and this man to love. It felt right. My mamma's words came back to me: *it's what God ordained.* She always reminded me that only now priests don't marry, but Jesus Christ's apostles were ordained three times and each was three men in one—Jewish, married, and a fisherman.

MY MOTHER AND I WALKED into the bedroom. The room had undergone such a transition I thought I'd walked into a magic wonderland. The windows were festooned with garlands of white tulle, ribbons, and flowers. Decorative boughs of lemon blossoms were placed above the lintels. And my bed! I was so surprised when I caught sight of it, at first I thought I'd entered the wrong room. I didn't recognize it, for it looked as though some masqueraded spirits had entered leaving trails of Carnival.

"Where did the lemon blossoms come from?" I asked Mamma, surprise in my voice.

"Don Stefano sent them from his land, *sotto columbrina*. His harvest is miraculously intact, and he promised to help Papà with ours."

A white linen sheet had been laid on top of my bed. I ran my finger along the edge. My bed was strewn with confetti, flowers, and gold and silver coins. My mother said to me, "There's nothing to fear. All you have to do is lie very still and he will grunt and fondle you and then it may hurt for a while. But it's over quickly. Try not to cry. Men don't like crying when they are aroused. And remember—"

We were interrupted so she was never able to finish. Peppe called us down to the garden for a toast with *champenoise* and the wedding cake. Rina had been my matron-of-honor, and Nunziata asked me to save her a piece of the wedding cake, as I had done with Lella's, to put under her pillow so she could dream of her future husband.

As soon as I stepped into the garden I caught Lella's eye and she smiled. Giacomo came over to me. I stood a head and a half shorter, and looking up, I became lost, a seeker of paradise, but astray in his *sagomato* eyes that stunned me. I had the sensation of falling into a labyrinth. I waded among his pupils' sideward rhomboids, almost as tawny as his sun-tanned skin pulled taut across high cheekbones whose ancestral hordes knew each sigh of the wind upon the Steppes. My mind tripped me up, for there, perched bareback upon a stallion in a speed-away game, tossing the head of a freshly butchered lamb, I saw him splendid, wildly Gypsy, nomadic. His eyebrows arched as he smiled only with a twitch at the corners of his lips. His hair ruffled in the wind. Was I here in the garden or in a dream? Did I know him from another life and time? Giacomo's thick hair was in a pompadour that swerved like a turban of lush clusters, blacker than grapes on top of his head. The handlebar mustache beneath his nose matched his hair and hid part of his full claret-colored mouth. My eyes drank him in until I saw him as he was in his vested suit, high collar, and white cravat. He took hold of my hand and ushered me forward. Our three-tiered cake stood on a lace-covered table surrounded by *bomboniere*, wedding favors of five confetti, one for each working day of the week, wrapped in tulle and tied with white satin ribbons.

He picked up a knife and handed it to me. I took hold of it and he clasped his hand over mine and I felt him lock me around the waist. "Make a wish," he whispered. I had wished that on this night of my wedding, I would not be afraid, though I was little prepared. I hadn't understood about the hurtful part, but while we ate our cake and thanked our guests, I had to push away thoughts of his touching my breasts. Before the marriage, I'd been tortured by impure desires, but I didn't confess them to Don Ruggero the day of my wedding. Instead, I made a pact with God. I told Him that what went on in my bedroom was between Giacomo and myself, and no earthly priest would hear of it. Only He by His infinite omniscience and omnipotence would know until Judgment Day.

WE WERE STANDING ON THE threshold of my room—Giacomo took my arms and put them around his neck. "Hold on. You're going for a ride."

He picked me up and pushed the door with his shoulder and carried me inside. I was delighted by his strength. "In America, that's what new grooms do. It's for luck. We don't need luck, we have each other, but just in case—"

With that, he deposited me on the bed as if I were a sack of lemons.

After we were in the lemony-scented sheets, Giacomo kept telling me to let the tension in my muscles go and breathe deeply. He kissed me many times and then began to crush my lips, part my mouth, his tongue a probe that played with mine. I concentrated on not choking, realizing for the first time that I belonged to him, even my mouth's cavity.

He backed away; I guessed he knew he was overpowering me. He became compassionate, murmuring, "Not to worry, everything's as it should be." His kisses now were delicate and gentle.

Without warning, there was a sensation. Never never had I felt anything like it. Not even my crash in the wine shed equaled this one brutal thrust and then the insistent hammering of a railroad spike piercing me. It was the strangest feeling to desire something and yet at the moment when it was attained to want to reject it, throw it off, toss it away. My mind played games. It made me feel as though this couldn't last forever. That this ardor would wear thin and then there would be a moment of extreme peace and fulfillment. However, it wasn't to be. Instead, there was no way I could find a comfortable position that would enable me to accept this penetration. The slightest flexion set my brain waves pulsing and tears started flowing. No control, no caring that this was an embarrassment to me, a lacking of courage.

I despised myself for my weakness. I thought of curses I'd never used to express my inability to be independent of this experience. I wanted my body to be able to serve its purpose, to do what was normal—an everyday, wifely task. But I couldn't. I grasped at something that was beyond me. Why was this happening? What did I do that was so bad to warrant this suffering from God? Had my fall from the horse and on the wine bottles truly left such lasting damage? Wasn't it enough that I suffered so in my dreams when I lost so much blood? What did God want of me? Immediate sainthood? How could I make offerings of my pain for the reparation of sin if I could not cope?

I hated feeling sorry for myself, but that's how I felt. I couldn't manage a breath without feeling the need to cry—a crutch to support the uncomfortable sensations. Weakness, a trait I so abhorred, had overcome me. It washed over me like a wind-swept storm. Never easy on myself, I always pushed to the limit. But not even the numbness of strong desire could make the pain vanish. Even at the conclusion of Giacomo's love-making it still had not subsided. Worthless.

I fell asleep and in my dream I was on the terrace as Lella and her lover had been and it was I who was in the throes of wild passion with Giacomo. I felt no pain, only a longing for him to enter me.

Toward morning fear seized my heart, for there was no virginal blood stamped upon the pure white sheet—the symbol of the consummation of my marriage, the indisputable proof that I had been deflowered by my husband and had never been touched or defiled by another man. Where was the blood to stain the sheet? Why hadn't I bled? Why did I think I would? There was something so horrifically wrong, and all I could do was cry silently. Words would not form on my lips. I had no possible excuse. My mother should be in soon to claim the banner of my maidenhood and hang it from my balcony window for the entire village to see. But would she come, knowing what she did? Had we made a dire mistake in not disclosing my childhood accident to Giacomo and his family? My poor mother, what mental torture did she suffer this night because of me?

The dawn crept through the window heralded by the crowing of a cock while a million spiders webbed my heart, strangling it. The sound of a horse neighing and the slap of a saddle broke the next silence. A rider trotted away. In the semi-dark room I wished for swift death. Now. I imagined a knife plunged into my heart. A heart cut in two by this most terrible trick of Nature.

Giacomo sat up in bed. He leaned against the headstead of bronze putti. "I thought I married a virgin," he said, soft rancor in his voice. Then he turned to me, lifted my chin, and kissed me. "I'm so confused," he said, his tone once again tender.

I never dreamed so precious a thing was rarer than a jewel, I thought, but I couldn't speak.

"Should I feel cheated, or robbed?" His doubt persisted.

How to quell it? "If an angel of the Lord could carry my soul to heaven now, this very minute—God alone knows of my innocence."

"What have you done to beguile my hunger for you and then deceive me so? How could you dupe me like this?"

"When I was a girl, I hemorrhaged due to an accident. It was awful, so much blood. I dream about it sometimes." My thoughts raced. Why, oh why hadn't my mother told him or Don Ruggero? "I swear you've deflowered me. I'm a virgin. Perhaps not in the physical sense but most assuredly in every other—till you entered me last night and made us one. I am yours and yours only. I've never been unfaithful to God, or you, my husband."

"How can I doubt you? Look at your face. Who can understand why fate has dealt us with this low blow? Why do I vacillate? Why didn't you tell me before?" He ran his fingers through his hair.

"And me? How could I have confided this to you? I've been swindled of giving you perfection—and yet, how has this burden come to rest with me? Oh God, that it weren't true." I sobbed into the pillow, wishing it would smother me to the death I would rather face than his accusing eyes. I tried to free my legs of the tangled sheet.

"And the sheet?" I asked in a voice horror-filled and not my own.

Giacomo buried his face in his hands.

"The town will know of this and think me deceived. I will look the fool in everyone's eyes. But you're not lying to me, are you?" he asked, imploring. "I'll have to hang my head with shame."

"I have never been with any man but you."

"Yet . . . you are so beautiful in this aurora half shadow." His kind words were masked by a harsh whisper.

I wanted to feel reminded of his love. But then, like a whip's lash, anguish colored his face. I feared he would strike me. Instead, he punched the pillow till it burst. Regrettably, I understood his ambivalence. What should we do? Goose feathers escaped, drifting midair. Souls from dead bodies. We also yearned to be released from the burning torment of this Purgatorial dilemma, free to seek heaven, yet finding none. Then he wept. I reached for him and pulled his head upon my bosom. My tears mingled with his.

"I, Giacomo Scimenti, have been with a virgin and know what it's like. I confess this now—if only I'd told you before—perhaps . . ."

I wallowed in sorrow, misunderstanding his confession and bewildered by a quiet yet insistent knocking at the door.

Giacomo jumped up and stood behind it in his nightshirt, his hand on the knob.

CHAPTER XXXVII

Rosalia

AFTER THE WEDDING NIGHT

ROSALIA HANDED OVER THE COFFEE tray and said, "Please consent to speak with me now, Giacomo. It's about the bridal sheet." She felt a pang in the pit of her stomach and felt her face go scarlet.

Giacomo asked for a minute to dress. He left the door ajar, and Rosalia watched him place the tray on the small glass table near the window, which had been covered with an elaborate white lace cloth.

Rosalia heard Giacomo say, "I'm going to speak to your mother. Have some coffee." Rosalia heard her daughter gasp.

In the hall Rosalia met Giacomo and accompanied him to her sitting room. Closing the door and without prelude, she began, "In my utter joy at seeing my daughter wed to you, I recklessly overlooked the possible consequences of the wedding night. No, that's not true—I was afraid of the possibility that you would never wed her. Forgive me. When I'd finally worked up the courage to speak to you, you'd already retired, and still I would have been brazen enough to disturb you, if it hadn't been for the last few straggling guests who would not leave. By then it was too late to come knocking at your door. I did you a terrible disservice, Giacomo, and I can only beg your forgiveness."

Rosalia paced up and down the room like a frightened animal with nowhere to run. She motioned for Giacomo to sit, but he didn't, and she watched his every movement, glad that he didn't interrupt or ask questions because she thought she would falter.

Rosalia wrung her hands and began to tell him Angelica's history and how she was thrown by a horse. "My daughter Angelica was pure as her name and the wedding dress she wore when she came to the altar yesterday, you must believe me." Rosalia continued, and when she'd finished she said, "Angelica lost an inordinate amount of blood. I was never sure if it was just being thrown by the horse or because she had played in the wine shed afterward and had a bad fall in there. You know I'm a midwife; I was alone and afraid for the child's life—I did what I would do for a woman who had just delivered a child in order to slow blood flow. Do you understand what I'm saying?"

"Forgive my ignorance, but I don't."

Rosalia indicated a chair. Giacomo sat. Rosalia, not accustomed to speaking to men so freely, knew that her daughter's married life and happiness hinged on what she would say next. She breathed deeply, then sighed.

"I packed her with cloths to stop the bleeding. I'm not sure—it might have been—I must have pushed too—if the accident didn't injure her and break *l'imene*, the marriage seal—then I did, making it appear to you that she wasn't the virginal being she is." Rosalia sat down and put her face in her hands. Through her sobs, she repeated, "I had to save her . . . save her."

She looked up, thinking that perhaps the damage had already been done in the wine shed.

Giacomo's face could have been carved in stone. She heard his voice ask, "How did you know there was no bleeding last night?"

"I didn't sleep all night, and this morning I heard Angelica's weeping and—" Here she faltered. "—and your accusations."

"Signora Domenico, I want to believe—"

"I swear on the life of my daughter."

"I didn't ask you to swear. How could I doubt you when you've had the courage to speak so? But I am distressed—how can you convince a whole town?"

"I don't care about the town. I'm responsible for your faith in my daughter. Your marriage must be founded on trust or it'll never succeed. Besides Nicola and myself, there are two people who know about this. My dear departed sister-in-law, Concetta, and—"

Giacomo stayed silent. Rosalia fell to her knees in front of him, her hands clasped in front of his face, thinking, *Dear, Lord, don't let him be a closed-minded, primitive Sicilian male!* She took in a deep breath. "Ruggero, my brother, the priest who married you, came the day after the accident and I confided to him what happened. He blessed Angelica. I had hoped that he would have told you when he heard your confession before the wedding. He has feathers for brains sometimes. When he should keep his mouth pinned closed, he babbles. Yet I can't blame him entirely. It was a gross misunderstanding. I thought that my husband reminded him. After you had taken leave of the guests, I questioned them, and to my utter grief learned that you had not been spared this agony."

"Ah! A family conspiracy?"

Rosalia was crushed that Giacomo believed this to be a plot. She cried from desperation, "On Angelica's eyes."

"Forgive me, Donna Rosalia. I should've bitten off my tongue rather than offend you. Please forgive me."

Her thoughts raced. *Does this mean he believes me, dear God?*

She could not conjecture any longer and blurted out, "If you will support me in this, I have devised a plan in my wakeful hours."

Giacomo took his mother-in-law by the elbows and raised her from her genuflection as he himself stood.

"Come follow me." Rosalia opened the door.

They went into the yard and entered the coop. Rosalia spilled a handful of corn feed while she stalked a chicken. Once she had it, she took better hold with her hand and twisting it furiously in the air, broke its neck. She carried it to a block under a shed, and there cut off its head and threw it over the fence. She clamped the headless chicken, still writhing, in a tight grasp about its bloody neck. Then she pulled a cloth from her pocket and tied it around like a tourniquet. Her mission accomplished, she dared to look at Giacomo with imploring eyes, eyes that spoke volumes and needed no verbalization.

He sighed and she saw his shoulders heave. He acquiesced with a shaking head. They moved into the house and up the stairs. The household still slept, for it was the morning after a celebration.

Giacomo was about to knock on the door when Rosalia signaled no, just open it. When Giacomo and Rosalia entered the bridal room,

Angelica was standing by the window. The coffee lay untouched. The glass that held anise and water was shattered.

Angelica's hand flew to her mouth when she saw Rosalia step from behind her husband, clasping the chicken. No one spoke. Angelica's other hand held a piece of the broken glass and there was blood on the bed sheet.

Rosalia muffled a scream, all but stuffing her apron in her mouth. Angelica's eyes begged forgiveness. Giacomo ran to her and picked her up and laid her on the bed, her immaculate nightgown tainted with blood. Giacomo raised the gown to expose a gash on Angelica's thigh. He ripped her nightgown and made a tourniquet to stop the blood flow.

"Forgive me," she whispered. "I'd rather die than disgrace you."

Comprehension was total. It was as if all three had agreed to this secret pact.

Giacomo poured a cup of coffee. Angelica's eyes followed his every move. Then Giacomo turned, picked up Angelica, and seated her on the chaise longue near the window. He turned her shoulders so that she looked out and offered her a cup with the tiniest spoonful of sugar. Rosalia saw in profile that her daughter's eyes glistened and knew she would do anything for Giacomo.

She had found God, at last, in love and in him and she adored him. But what if she hadn't been a virgin? Would he be like the Church—easy to assign guilt, yet asking a life of penance for pardon? Would Angelica ever know if she'd achieved the right level of repentance for absolution? *My daughter, my blood. You will know him—his every wart, every thought.*

Rosalia prayed that Angelica's devotion would be reciprocated. Here, now, she felt invisible to them as she observed Giacomo wipe Angelica's tears away with his hand and kiss her cheeks. Her daughter took the cup without hesitation and sipped. He poured himself a cup, as if they were alone in the room.

Rosalia turned her attention to the task at hand. Seeing their eyes averted, she saw Angelica's bloodstained nightdress and thanked God Giacomo had bandaged her quickly. Rosalia was again reminded of that night years ago when her daughter had hemorrhaged. She shuddered and finished her job of defiling the sheet with the chicken blood. Asking God's forgiveness, she knew in her heart there would be retribution to pay, for that is the way of the world. Even if she deemed what had been done a good act, she said under her breath, "No one remains unscathed." Her emotions were great, and she felt her heart would burst with happiness for Angelica, with pride for Giacomo, with sorrow for both of them—this beautiful couple in the soft morning light. She knew that if they loved each other fiercely, they would conquer this and more—they would survive the harsh reversals life offered.

Rosalia slipped from the room, hurried along the corridor, down the stairs, and out into the sun that promised an exceptional day of warmth. She was a practical woman and looked at the chicken; dressing out this fowl for the afternoon meal crossed her mind. She remembered the day when Angelica was eight and found the egg-bound chicken. Rosalia recalled how another time she herself retrieved the chicken out of her neighbor's pot. In that split second she understood that chicken wouldn't be included in her daughter's diet. She decided to pluck it clean and feed it to Nicola's hunting dog. She pivoted and retraced her steps to the kitchen where she placed the chicken in the larder till she could attend to it later.

She set a fresh espresso coffee pot on the tray and carried it to her husband, telling him that she would now knock on the door of the newlyweds. Again she begged forgiveness from almighty God for evading the truth that she'd already knocked once before.

Rosalia rapped loud enough for all the household and guests to hear. When she was admitted, she hugged her daughter, kissing her on both cheeks. To Giacomo, she inclined her head and curtsied.

"Don Giacomo," she said, a catch in her throat, "with your permission I will take your wedding sheet." Her hands trembled as she interlaced her fingers for control. He steadied her.

Rosalia opened the door to the balcony and dropped the sheet over the wrought iron railing for the entire world to see. She observed the young lovers lost in each other. Then she saw Giacomo take hold of both of Angelica's hands and kiss them, his eyes sparkling with tears. Giacomo was no longer a stranger. In her mind Rosalia had elevated his status, and she knew she had another son, one who would be to her on even footing with her own Peppe.

CHAPTER XXXVIII

Angelica

MONDELLO

I BROODED ALL THE NEXT day and closed into myself, a morning glory yet untouched by sun. The result of this folly was that I became Mount Etna ready to explode. Yet why couldn't I speak to him?

He kept at me all day with sweetheart remarks and tender kisses at the nape of my neck when I wouldn't look at him and then, after lunch, we took a walk in the garden. Stock-still, I faced the *Conca D'Oro*. He cajoled, but I wheeled around and faced him, knowing my nostrils flared and my eyes held anger. As Mamma always said, "If it tastes bad, spit it out," so I finally took my courage into both hands and almost socked my Giacomo.

I walloped him, as surely as if I'd been a pugilist.

"Giacomo, you had no right to disbelieve me and I will leave you, so help me God," and here I crossed my heart, "if you ever dare again. Marriage is based on trust." I knew I was exaggerating to make a point and said, "My father never questioned a single action by my mother in all their wedded years, and you must promise you will respect my position as your wife and credit my every judgment, or you'll have this, and not me." With that I twisted off my gold band and threw it at him. My vitriolic words were intended to shock. This relationship was going to be for the rest of my life—I could not chance having him doubt me again in the future. But why had he not caught the ring in midair? How I wished I'd never done it. His eyes were full of tears.

"You're not being fair. You can't dictate how a person thinks. Forgive me. I love you, Angelica, but it's the nature of the beast to strike out when hurt. I could promise you I'll never hurt you again, but I'd be lying. I don't know what the future holds for us."

"The day you came to propose, you promised Mamma you'd never inflict pain on me," I said. "All day long I've felt like the absolute slough of despond—"

"What? I meant I'd never wound you physically—but there are other kinds of aches, injuries we brave all our lives. I won't swear that it won't happen again. I can only try—" He reached down to pick up the ring, sinking to one knee and kissing my skirts till I felt the pressure of his face smashed against my cut thigh. His action took my breath. There was no more need for words.

Then he raised himself and repeated the ring ceremony of our wedding. Crushing my hands in his, he pulled me to him in an embrace that made me understand why I'd married him. He kissed me, smothering me with such passion that I realized why I'd reconciled myself and been able to accept the mental and emotional side of marriage, crowned beyond spiritual. My body responded, tremoring with desire. I'd already submitted once, yet still wasn't able to face the physical side and, worse, the possible result of another sexual union.

I extricated myself from his excited hold, seeing myself in his eyes. What had I done? What had I created in his imagination? Did I see his soul's thoughts? Or was what I saw the shadow of an elusive truth that up until now I had not been able to conciliate? I wanted him to possess me mind and body.

He took me by the hand and ushered me back into the house.

How could I explain my feelings to him, these things I couldn't? I doubted my ability ever to confront him. But didn't I just do that? This dilemma was mine and I needed an ally. I had to confide to someone in whom I had complete trust and who certainly had the knowledge I sought to overcome my trepidation. Mounting the stairs to our room, I thought of my three choices: Lella, Rina, or Mamma. I felt fragmented emotionally and knew I had to calm down and control myself.

I recited the *Memorare* and stopped midway in the prayer, after the phrase, "Inspired with this confidence I fly unto thee, O Virgin of Virgins, my Mother," because it was then that I knew that I must speak to my own earthly mother. But how would I approach her? Where and when?

Giacomo opened the door for me and I passed inside ahead of him, my legs quaking from fear and desire.

BY THE SIXTH DAY OF my honeymoon week, my insides seemed to have settled into place—the hurt and burning sensation quelled by the twelfth bath I'd taken during these days. Without a word of explanation, Mamma had given me a salve to apply after each bath.

Giacomo and I sat on the beach at Mondello under a huge red-and-white striped umbrella. A phrase came to me: "Anguish has taken wing, dispelled is darkness." I struggled to remember where it was from. I took off my laced boots and stockings, rolled them into a ball, and stuck them into the boots. It was so warm that I undid the mother of pearl buttons on my karakul jacket and draped it around the chair. I lifted my black crepe skirt. We walked to the water's edge. Gulls hung in the sky as if appended by clouds that blew away every trace of morning haze.

"Isaiah," I said, pleased I'd recalled where it was from.

"What?" Giacomo asked.

"Oh, nothing."

"But you called someone by name."

"If we have a son, I'd like to call him Isaiah."

"Which son? Not the first or second," Giacomo said. He grinned. "Besides, we've got plenty of time. Our whole lives."

Giacomo looked magnificent in the sleeveless jersey pulled tight across his chest and the snug green-striped bathing trunks that reached his knees.

I walked in the hard sand at the shoreline and watched him dive into the waves, a porpoise like I'd seen in the Mar Tirreno off the coast of Messina when I was a girl.

I couldn't believe that he'd go in bathing, but he did and I called him a "Swiss tourist." They were the only ones who swam after summer. His face soured. I realized I'd displeased him, but didn't know why. Maybe because he'd met a Swiss he didn't like.

After his swim he sunned himself on an enormous towel spread upon a rattan bath mat. I sat in the chair and fanned myself with a hand-painted fan edged with white lace. I felt calmer with him beside me and realized I had been agitated every time he disappeared into a wave.

Afterward he went into the cabana and changed his clothes. I admitted to myself that he was strong and built like a Roman statue. I'd seen many in athletic poses in the Museum of Palermo. I wondered when I'd ever see him nude and blushed at my own curiosity.

He came back to where I was sitting. Then we walked along the jetty rocks. The sun was about to set. Our vigil focused on the orange ball that consumed itself in flame falling into the becalmed sea, a rippling expanse like a silver stream.

The road leading from the jetty, powdered with sand, led all along the quay. As we walked, we talked of his going to America without me. He would be leaving soon.

Giacomo rented a boat at eventide, and we paddled a parallel line along the shore. As he rowed, I watched his powerful arms pull, his muscles surging and diminishing with every stroke. I could barely discern the underside of his forearms or veins, so I closed my eyes to recall the disposition of them, formed like bulbous rhizomes, tree roots exposed to years of weathering. I listened to the creaking oars, the slapping sound they made contacting the ocean.

My hand trailed in the cold water and I inhaled deeply of the sea-censed air. I licked my fingertips free of salt and observed the sun-soft dusk ignite the argentine water as it extended from sea to shore in an erupting cone of froth.

This moment, in the chiaroscuro of evening, etched forever in my mind, a photograph that in the future I'd be able to call upon. This precious tableau would then come back to me, to be relived vicariously.

Giacomo docked and we walked along the shore. I watched other lovers stroll arm in arm and wondered if their lovemaking resembled ours. Did those women satisfy their men? Did they themselves know how to derive pleasure? Would I ever learn the art of lovemaking? A sharp image pierced my heart—Lella on the terrace.

Fishermen mended their nets. Someone yelled that a boat was coming in and we saw the mariners, their shirtsleeves and pant legs rolled up, haul in the nets. Tears streamed down my face, yet I didn't know I had been crying till I licked my lips and tasted salt. I thought I'd die from wanting to hold him. I slipped my arm through his, mimicking what I'd seen.

We crossed the street to Trattoria Bella Vista, sat at a table outside just as dusk took complete possession of the evening. Tiny flames were ignited on the candles of all the tables. He ordered *pannelli* and a carafe of wine.

The fried squares of *cecci* flour paste tasted delicious, and it was thrilling to pour wine from a carafe that I myself had not filled. I thought of the preparation, hefting the heavy demijohns, emptying them into smaller liter bottles, and corking them.

The wine cooled the palate following the hot *pannelli.*

"America is where I live. You're my wife. You must come with me. You have an obligation."

"How can I if you're staying in a rooming house for men? Where will you put me?"

"I'll get a house, or rent a flat. We should have talked about this before we married, but there was so little time and no privacy."

"I can't leave my father. He needs me in the house while Mamma tends the store just till we get a governess for my sisters. And a cook—my father's exigence must be tended to in the kitchen as well as the rest of the house. He's getting old."

"La! This is no way to begin a marriage."

"My love for you is great, Giacomo. Be patient with me, I implore you." I thought, *But it's something I don't know how to reckon with—I've never loved like this, have no basis of comparison.* "I love my father too, but that's different."

"Is it? You won't leave him for me. Come with me, be by my side where you belong. Now."

"Please—just a little time. Then I'll come to you. It would be too much for Papà now. He's so possessive, and it's my fault because of what happened when I was little." I told Giacomo about the overturned cart on the way home from the Messina market and how I'd made my father depend on me, thinking he'd love me more. Then I said, "But then Rina eloped—I never dreamed he'd become like this. Let me have the opportunity to smooth his feathers. Grant me time. Everything was so rushed. Thirty-three days isn't much," the number reminding me again of Christ's age. His suffering too. A separation might even grant me time to over-come my physical fears, if I could first surmount the fear of being able to talk about it with someone!

"Angelica—I just assumed you'd come with me."

I took his hand and stroked it.

I poured him another glass of wine, adding water to mine, and he playfully switched glasses. "I'm relaxed. It's you, my wife, who needs wine."

I knew by his intense look that he desired me.

"My brother must finish his scholarship studies till at least All Saint's Day. Then he'll be able to accompany me to Messina to Zu Nino's— you met him at the wedding—and his new wife. His first wife, my dear Zia Concetta, died in childbirth. He got remarried to a schoolteacher. They're going to live in her family's house in Messina. We have to sell or rent the house they live in now because it's ours. Papà will give me some money, and I'll take the ship to New York."

"You'll not depend anymore on your father. I'll give you the passage money—do you hear?"

I nodded. "My brother will bring me to you. You won't have to come back for me."

"One month?" he asked, reason dominating his emotion.

"At most two." I covered his hand with mine.

"An eternity, but I must get back or lose my job, and I'm up for promo-tion to foreman. We'll be spending our first married Christmas apart."

"We'll have a lifetime of Christmases. And I'll write you every week. It'll go by quickly. You'll see, I promise. In the meantime you can scout the area where we'll live. This will give you time to find proper living quarters and make the necessary arrangements."

Giacomo lifted my hand, upturned it, and kissed my palm tenderly. I knew what he wanted. And I wanted it too. Hopefully this time I could become a willing participant.

"Let's stay the night here. We'll go to a hotel and send word to your parents from there," he said.

I was about to object, saying I had no nightclothes or a change for tomorrow. But somehow instinct persuaded me to hold my tongue and grant him this wish. I would drink a little too much wine and not think about pain this time. But I couldn't help it. If a man's spike felt like this, what must an infant feel like passing through the birth canal? I poured myself another glass of wine. My hand shook and Giacomo teased me, calling attention to my drinking because he didn't want me sick. But neither my shaking hand nor his words stopped me as I tossed back the entire glass.

"Do you need wine to face me? Does it hurt you that much?"

I looked down.

He lifted my chin. "I'll try to be more gentle," he said and looked out to sea, then back at me, his gaze steady. "One night is not a honeymoon, but someday I'll take you someplace and we'll have one . . . maybe the Orient. I swear."

"Our life together will be enough," I said, knowing that life doesn't always deliver what one desires from it. The waiter brought the check and with it a bottle of Amaro Averna and three glasses. Giacomo's eyes locked with mine, and I knew he was thinking of the day he proposed and how Papà bit my hand, then disinfected it with Averna. The waiter poured three glasses and then toasted our happiness. How did he know?

I had never tasted Averna before and made a face at the bitterness of it and the memory it provoked of my bitten hand.

Giacomo drank the rest of mine and paid the check.

THE WINDOW OF OUR HOTEL room looked out at the ocean-front. Giacomo opened it wide and took off his jacket. The only light in the room shafted in streams from outside the window. He sat in a chair and pulled me onto his lap. He kissed me, and when I started to tense, he nibbled my ear, a bunny tasting lamb lettuce. He told me to slacken all my muscles. Start with the tips of the toes, he said. Now the calf of the right leg. Now the left. He talked me into a total abandon of myself. He was master, and I responded like an obedient slave.

He unbuttoned the top button of my blouse and kissed the hollow of my neck. My arms turned to gooseflesh with the thrill of his lips upon me. He continued unfastening, and at each buttonhole loop, he brushed his lips over me. I felt his moustache tickle through my chemise. I wiggled a bit and he pulled my blouse free and dropped it on the floor. I heard the surf crash on the shore. I looked toward the window, but he drew me back with soft words and kisses. Next he tugged at my chemise and it landed in a heap on top of my blouse. I was glad that I hadn't worn a corset, knowing I would've been uncomfortable on the beach. He looked surprised—was it because of my free-falling breasts, which instinct made me cover? Or because I wore no lace-up—I didn't have time to think. He released my crossed arms, stood me on the floor in front of him, and devoured every surface he came upon from my waist to my neck. My skin prickled with excitement. Then he picked me up in his arms and deposited me on the bed. I felt I was losing control and that my body sought to escape my skin. I started to object about the spread not being down, but he silenced me with his demanding lips and probing tongue. He undressed me, with skill and sensitivity, a patience I've never used on myself. Each quiet tug or silky sound seemed instigated by a soft talcum-powdered baby's touch, his breath upon me, soft sunbeams at midday—sweet as innocence, yet sensual as night-blooming jasmine coming in from the window, perfuming the air, overcoming my senses.

He brought my hands to a region of his body I'd never even dreamt of holding. The surprising warmth of his soft parts and hard parts thrilled me till I floated in clouds I'd painted on the ceiling. He stretched his naked body over mine, but did not enter me until I heard myself beg for tenderness and union.

I felt a joyous burst of rhythm overtake me as our bodies rocked in perfect unison. And when I felt a shivering release, I muffled my cry, turning into myself, my chin resting and caressing my shoulder.

His pulsations ceased with mine and he said the strangest thing: "God has given you to me. I have never before felt love for God the way I do now."

I couldn't speak from the emotion choking the breath from my body. Never had I felt so alive and happy, so exhilarated yet peaceful. We fell asleep entangled like the bed covers in each other's arms.

TWO DAYS LATER, ON THE octave of my wedding day, we drove to Palermo by carriage to Donizi Photographer's Studio where our wedding photograph was taken. Giacomo's expression was one of pride mixed with loyalty. Mine must have had the slightly startled look of a wounded doe not knowing where to run. I dressed in black, signifying that our marriage had been consummated.

After the picture-taking session, Giacomo took my hand and kissed my father's scar. He then gave me a pair of white silk gloves embroidered with seed pearls in the form of starbursts and a small bouquet of wild flowers from the field of our fathers' dispute. There was hardly any fragrance, just a slight grassy smell and colors rainbow rich.

⁓⊱⋆⊰⁓

BEFORE WE RETURNED HOME FROM the photography studio, Giacomo and I lunched at a restaurant in downtown Palermo. It wasn't far from the market where my mother used to live and I remembered her telling me the day she got her period her mother had slapped her face, like Mamma had slapped mine once when she thought I'd gotten mine and once again after I had.

It was a poignant experience walking around after the luncheon, remembering the things she'd told me about her youth and her courtship with my father. During the walk in the totally unfamiliar yet familiar environs where Mamma grew up, I decided I'd have that talk with her.

At home, I took off my gloves and laid the feather boa Rina had loaned me on the needle-work tapestry stand she had brought for Mamma. I didn't like feathers and was glad to give it back. The men were smoking cigars or playing bocce, and once in a while their laughter reached the house. Other than that it was quiet except for dust motes falling in the streaming light of late afternoon. It was as if I heard them call out, "Angelica, it's time now."

I cornered my mother, but before I spoke to her, she made me sit down, placing before me a demitasse cup filled with fresh coffee and laced with anisette. She sat next to me, bending close, and asked, "What's troubling you?"

Never taking her eyes from me, she poured herself an accurate amount of coffee in her cup. How did she manage that knack?

I didn't know how to begin. The words were in my head, but before I uttered a sound, Mamma robbed the question from me and answered, saying, "Laudanum."

"What?" I picked up the cup by its tiny gold-rimmed handle and felt the heat exude in waves of steam approaching my lips.

"When a woman can't stand the labor pains, or is fearful of child-birth, they take this."

I sipped the coffee. "Why have I never seen this before? Witchcraft or medicine?"

"It's a tincture of opium that comes from the poppy plant in the Orient."

"How do you know about it?" I asked, trying to look calm, smoothing my hand over the back of my upturned hairdo.

"Giacomo's mother gave it to me," she said. "He brought it to her from the Orient."

She looked at me with such intensity that I knew she hadn't given it to Zia Concetta and a chill stole through my spine.

"Love," she said after a small silence, "is a great panacea for all ills, angel, real or imagined. And not everyone . . . dies from love, or having babies."

"Something else. When Giuseppa died, her twelve-year-old daughter, the one who still lived with the old man, became pregnant, didn't she?"

"Be careful where you go with this. Are you sure you want to know?"

"It was her lecherous father's, wasn't it?" I demanded.

"Fortunately, she miscarried, but not before you visited her. What did you do to the girl to make her lose the baby?"

"Fetus. It was not yet a completely formed infant."

"An unwanted baby was destroyed. How?"

"When I left she was fine. Later when I returned her sister told me the girl threw herself down the stairs."

I finished my coffee and started to remove the cup, but she stayed my hand and with her other poured me straight anisette, saying, "I've wondered a long time when you would approach me. I even feared you wouldn't go through with the wedding. Rushing you to speak, or adding needless worry to your list, would've been worse, I thought. Though, in part, it was neglect on my behalf not to relieve your worries . . . I should've addressed your problem long ago. My neglect is overdue. Is the soreness gone?"

I kissed my mother's hand and she clutched mine with a firm hold, then let go, motioning with her chin that I was to finish what was in my cup.

I sipped, replacing the cup on the saucer.

Mamma said ever so softly, "My world is not merely a generation removed from yours—there are chasms one cannot always bridge. Ask Rina what's important to know. That vixen could probably write a book. And remember, memory only serves up a bitter plate if we let it. Faith can season it, rendering it palatable."

"But, Mamma—"

"Hush now," she said. "Signs written in your face, child, indicate you'll overcome fear because you love him." My mother touched my shoulder as she left the room. So overwhelmed by gratitude for her and safe in the knowledge that there was a way around Nature, I knew my love for Giacomo would come to fruition. Tears of happiness coursed down my cheeks. Why does a person cry from sadness and from joy? A weight had been borne away while a host of angelic beings buoyed me on a cloud. However, even after I'd finished the sweet dregs of my cup, a slight metallic taste, not from coffee, remained in my mouth. Would I ever vanquish fear?

CHAPTER XXXIX

Angelica

REALITY BITES

DURING THE NEXT TWO WEEKS, Giacomo and I moved our residence to the Scimenti household. When Giacomo was not working in the groves, he followed my every movement. When I was in close proximity to him, I felt his eyes watch my every sway. He studied the conformation of my buttocks and I knew he imagined seeing me naked. When I left the room or climbed the stairs, he peeped at my black-stockinged ankles. Once he told me they were delicate and fragile, almost like wrists.

On Sunday, less than a week after we'd decided to spend some time with Giacomo's parents, my skirt and petticoats swooshed in the hall, like the rustle of autumn leaves. I approached him in a taffeta skirt, making sure his senses were awake to my approach.

Apart from that, the house was dead quiet. Everyone attended church service because it was Sunday, except Giacomo who'd excused himself as he was just getting over a cold. I had gone to Mass early so I could attend him.

I sensed he'd been afraid to make any attempt at loving me again since Mondello. He played a waiting game, hoping I'd come to him, desire him. He needed to know that this was so. Was it his imagination or mine tempting him, making overtures? Morning after morning while he faked sleep, I bustled about him, straightening covers, plumping up pillows, bending over him, thrusting my breasts in his face or sliding them along his leg. When he felt them, he became hard with desire. I wanted him to be certain of my yearning, my longing for his touch.

Giacomo inhaled deeply as I entered the room. By now I understood that my jasmine perfume intoxicated him.

I cluck-clucked at the disarray of his bed cloths. My strong hand brushed strands of hair off his forehead. I whispered something he couldn't make out but sounded sweet, like song lyrics.

He moaned and turned away. I asked if I should open the shutters, but he said no. "Let me rest some more."

"Are you sure it's rest you want? Everyone's at church. We have hours. Surely your parents will stop in the piazza to greet friends and the men will have an aperitif while the women buy pastries."

He turned back to face me. I was so close to sitting on the bed that he patted it, and at his signal I sat, my hip smack up against him.

I was endowed by nature with a very prosperous figure. He knew instinctively I would fulfill my duties, but he wanted more from me—he intended to enjoy these gifts nature had bestowed.

I played with the fringe of the pillowcase between my fingers. He took my hand and kissed it. He must have been thinking, *If she pulls away I haven't a chance, but if not . . .*

Just then I leaned forward, feeling my firm breasts against his lean chest through the thin material of his nightshirt. He pulled me down. The next thing he felt were my lips kissing his. I squirmed on top of him, and he turned me over in a tangle of sheets and covers, slipping his hand under my skirt. He touched the sheerness of my stockings and reached the garter that held them in place, and then realizing I wore no bloomers, lurched his hand down to my calf. In no time at all, he learned his hand had a mind of its own and glided back up to my thigh, but this time settled between the junction of my legs. Here, I fought for control of my emotions—I wanted him to understand he was welcomed. I felt warm, moist. It made him sweep my skirts and petticoats up along with his nightshirt. We struggled and he stripped free my clothing in a topsy-turvy swirl. He yanked off his nightshirt, straddling me, and then he blanketed my limbs with his long legs. As he entered me, I thought of a pestle, then tried not to think at all, only to feel.

It was over almost as quickly as it had begun and it was only then, I believe, that he realized I'd been ripe and waiting, a woman longing for this experience.

Giacomo did not lose his erectness. He was aware I hadn't moved, and before either of us could think about if we should or shouldn't try again, we did. The uncontrollable pulsating and heaving lasted longer this time, until Giacomo grunted at the conclusion of this second ejaculation inside of me, his woman, moaning, as I stifled a shriek of joy into the pillow.

IT WASN'T UNTIL DAYS LATER that a change overcame my Giacomo as he learned to revel in the slow pleasures of easy touching and fondling. We were in a lemon orchard near his home one day at the end of the second week of our stay with his parents. Both of us, intoxicated with the sweet pungent essence of lemon blossoms filling our nostrils, sensed the thrill of his manhood bringing me to my first climax.

As a couple, we were drunk on love and the heat of the day. On and off throughout the day. All day. We picnicked in the lemon groves and he told me about his crush on the lovely little Corredina when he was a mere lad in grammar school. He blushed at the remembrance choreographed to falling blossoms. I might have been jealous, but was too happy that he'd shared some of his past life with me.

GIACOMO WATCHED MY EVERY MOVEMENT when he was near me. He particularly loved to watch me sew, and this I did on many occasions while he read something at the kitchen table. Somehow I always found time to embroider, making treasured accessories such as collars and cuffs that would dress up the simplest ladies' cotton or wool haberdashery.

One afternoon after the picnic, Giacomo came into the kitchen while I attended a crostata of blackberries I'd just put into the oven. There was a ball of yarn in a basket on the floor next to my chair. I was knitting. Needles clacked, the only noise until his mother started a conversation. He acknowledged his mother with a kiss and he nodded to me. When his mother wasn't looking, he winked. My own husband, flirting with me. Then he pulled up a chair, straddled it backward, and listened to what his mother had to say about my talented hands. I could see he was proud of me. I felt his possessiveness. Was this an answer to my prayers to understand love?

"Your work and fame is spreading from Carini to Palermo, Angelica, and I'd like to make a suggestion. Perhaps you should start taking your work to stores," Maria Scimenti suggested. "Sell your wares in *mercerie*, the notion stores where you buy your threads and cotton spools for making lace and crocheting."

"*Signora*, I could never—"

"You won't have to sell yourself. Merely show your work and I know it'll be a tremendous success. If you're afraid, I'll go with you. I'm experienced at dealing with store proprietors. And," she said, stifling a cough and making a magnanimous sweep of her arm in her son's direction, "Giacomo can take us. We'll leave promptly tomorrow morning and be there when the shopkeepers open."

"You are too kind, *signora*."

"Tomorrow is the only day I'll be able to accompany you—to instill a little courage. And if I say it's all right, I know my husband, Don Stefano, will agree. Get together some samples of your work."

Giacomo caught his mother's eye. "I can't go tomorrow, Mamma, I'll be helping at *le grote*."

"Leave it to me, son."

Giacomo noticed the embarrassed look on my face. I hoped his mother didn't detect it.

"The sweet smells delicious," he said. "I don't think I can wait till evening to taste it."

I smiled at that, wondering if his mother knew he referred to me and not the sweet in the oven.

⟨⟩

GIACOMO SAW ME OVERCOME MY shyness and, after the first time selling my accessories with his mother at my side, I had no more difficulty. In fact, I took great pleasure in it, and my husband said my eyes shone brightly. On one occasion, I frequented shops near Palermo's Cathedral.

Signora Maria didn't accompany us anymore. Giacomo took me every other day so I'd get used to it. I tried to spend money wisely on articles necessary to make new and different ladies' adornments. When I'd concluded my business, I'd show Giacomo the profit. With the hand-manufactured articles I sold in shops, there came a call for more. The convent nun's and Mamma's instructions and sewing for my reverend uncle came in handy after all.

Giacomo knew I horded my savings, but then one day, with a pock-etful of money, we walked past a jewelry vitrine that caught my eye. The golden trinkets reflected the sunlight, but when I pointed out the prices to Giacomo, I said, "How stupid of me; at first I didn't think they were real gold. But look at the prices."

"Too dear for me," he teased, "or I'd buy you one." He gave me his most engaging, sheepish grin.

"I've a better idea. You've brought me happiness and luck, Giacomo, let me buy you something for good fortune." Before he could argue against my scheme, I took hold of his hand and led him into the musty, dark goldsmith's.

The wizened old man behind the counter looked to be a hundred. When the man stood, his spectacles sloped down his nose. The goldsmith wiped his hands on a long black cloak covered with dust. He showed me many charms.

I selected *un corno*, a horn charm to add to his chain, and although Giacomo protested, I insisted. He was mortified, yet, I noted, quite thrilled at the same time. The item was dear and cost me quite a sum.

"Gold lasts forever," I said, attaching the gold corno to the other charms on his chain.

"Why not get it for yourself?" he said.

"It only brings good luck if it's a gift."

I refastened the chain round his neck and felt his heart ready to spring out of his chest—a praying mantis. I knew he became aroused because he thrust his lower body smack against the showcase in the hopes that neither the seller nor the buyer would notice. Barely above a whisper he said, "Thank you," and flushed apple red.

⸙

ON THE RIDE HOME GIACOMO stopped in a shady glen.

I felt beneath his shirt. "Do you like your gift?"

"It's the most beautiful thing anyone's ever given me."

I realized he'd just lied. I thought of the jade Buddha that also hung on his chain. Was he aware of his deceit? Was he thinking of her now?

"I'm in love with you, Angelica, in a way I never dreamed possible, but there's something I must tell you."

I didn't respond right away but took hold of his hands, then looked deep into the recesses of his eyes. "If it's about the green Buddha—"

"You'll have to know sometime—"

"I'm not ready to hear it yet. And if you have to dream about loving me, maybe you don't."

"What does that mean? I'll love you always from the very core of my being. Don't you believe me?" he pleaded.

No reply came from me. His unanswered question hung in the suffocating air, making it impossible to speak of anything else. He clucked his tongue and snapped the reins. "Let's go."

Apart from the horse and carriage, the only other sound was the high-pitched drone of cicadas.

After a while, as if to break the silence, he began to hum, which lightened the mood. He laughed a little and said, "I must tell you about my friend Bulldog."

"What an awful name."

"His name. His face. His strength. Nothing compares to his heart. He saved my life in China. I'm here with you because of him. You'll meet someday, I promise you," he said, and was about to say something else, but changed his mind and offered nothing more. Neither did I ask, fearing he might veer onto something else about China.

We were again quiet for a long time. I placed my hand on his thigh, but he ignored it until farther along, when the road forked. As we approached the bend before the lane that led us home, Giacomo stilled the horses. He faced me, took my arms and placed them round his neck as they'd been just a few short hours ago in the jeweler's shop, and drew me into his arms. I didn't resist. My tears wet his face. My breasts heaved against his chest. He grasped me tighter. Then he kissed me, a long, slow kiss, parting my lips with his open mouth, exploring the unfamiliar cavern. His tongue played about mine, but he desired more. He unbuttoned his trousers, taking hold of his penis with one hand, forcing my head down upon the waiting appendage with the other, but I wrenched free of him. He wanted to feel my mouth on his erect member. I almost retched and grabbed the reins and whipped the horse all the way to the Scimenti gates.

When we arrived at the house, I ran inside, passing Donna Maria without greeting her.

"What is the meaning of this rudeness?" I heard her say to her son.

I couldn't even imagine the exchange that took place between mother and son. What he told me later was that his mother had glared in her son's direction, a look that read grave disappointment. He was humiliated. And he knew he'd have to make some excuse to his mother concerning me. His brain flurried with the excitement of preparing a lie when all of a sudden he didn't have to. He said, by means of explanation, "We were on the open public road. I was rough and embarrassed her. I forced her . . . to kiss me," though conveniently he left out the destination of that kiss.

Then he added, "I'm so ashamed, Mamma, I was completely out of control." He buried his head in her shoulder and cried, wondering if I'd ever forgive his lust.

Maria had said simply, "Men." She shook her head and then shushed him and brought him into the house. "Oh, don't fret—you'll do the simplest, sweetest thing and she'll forgive you. We women always do."

She's right, of course, I thought and sniffed the nosegay of buds he'd brought me.

Giacomo and I walked in the parts of the garden that were left untended and where nature ruled. There were many cactus shoots of *fichi d'India*, sprawling jasmine bushes, oleander, fire-red hibiscus flowers, and phosphorescent violet and pink bougainvillea grappling for a hold on a dismantled wall of bricks in ruin.

We sat under a mimosa and leaned back against the tree. Giacomo told me that his feelings of guilt about his lust for me swallowed him with sadness. Were all men interested in sex above all else?

I supposed that guilt encompassed much more than his lust, but who could tell him about it? He bent one knee and placed his forehead on it and asked me to consider the differences between men and women.

"Are there no books that instruct about these life problems? Does everything have to be figured out on one's own? Is sex a thing apart from love for men, one and the same for women?" He didn't answer any of my questions. He merely shook his head and wept.

CHAPTER XL

Angelica

THE PARTING

THE WEATHER CHANGED A FEW days before Giacomo departed for America. There was a great deal of rain followed by scorching sun—perfect weather for mushrooming. Giacomo and I hunted wild *porcini* and *ovoli*, but also found other species. Then abruptly it turned cold. It was the day he helped me reinstall myself in my parents' home. I tried to bear up stoically, feeling the double layers of coldness, the wind's assault on my body and wintry blasts of encroaching loneliness surrounding my heart. I had but one consolation, and that was the feeling that I finally belonged completely to him and he to me. He confessed he'd had relations with the woman in China. Revealing his past desire for Lian, he swore it had been surpassed by love for me. I melted into his arms in my girlhood bed. He took me so tenderly in love the night before he left for America that I begged him to continue and he contented me the whole night through.

Both our intimate families, Giacomo's and mine, were present for his departure. We gathered on the pier to see him off, hoping to bring consolation to him and courage to me, his bride. I had insisted on a small party to brighten everyone's heart, most especially mine and my husband's. I'd prearranged to have a large, round table in the ship's dining room set with glasses for champagne and *tramezzini*, small sandwiches of artichoke hearts, tuna, and prosciutto.

Afterward, when everyone said good-bye, Giacomo and I were left alone. "Some honeymoon couple we make. I can't stop crying," I said.

I accompanied Giacomo to his stateroom where he embraced me as the door closed behind us. We kissed and kissed again. I caught my breath and began to cry anew. He indulged me for a minute, handed me his handkerchief, then entreated me to stop, lest he begin.

There was a blaring sound. The first of three that informed all guests to go ashore. I felt my stomach lurch and implored him to go to the upper deck where I could wave to him and watch till the ship pulled out of sight.

He said, "Wave to me and then leave immediately. You'll take a chill. My darling, Angelica, you must be strong for both of us. This is our mutual decision and it's for the best. I can see that now. Take our parents home, don't expose them to the elements. Prepare lunch. Eat pasta, drink wine. Do something joyous for me today."

Although my heart ranted against this plan, I said, "I'll obey my husband."

He smiled, but I could not return it and buried my face in his chest.

"Come now, you'll mess up your stylish hair and if everyone sees you disarrayed, they'll know how upset you—"

His dialogue was interrupted by the second horn blast. "The third one you'll hear from shore. Now go. My heart goes with you."

"I wish you well," was all I could manage and then fought with the door handle till I wrenched it open. I spun around for his kiss and ran down the hall. On the way, I regretted not having told him once more how much I love him.

When I reached my party on shore, my eyes scanned the upper deck for a glimpse of him, but not seeing him in the throng, I began to despair. I felt hot and cold and on the brink of nausea. Then I spotted him. I wheeled about to tell them where he was, pointed to the spot, but in the heartbeat that I'd looked away, I'd lost him again in the surging crowd.

It was Donna Maria who sighted him, with the universal homing device—a mother's love. I took her gloved hand in mine and kissed it, her sorrow increasing mine tenfold.

I will never forget this day, I thought. *If I am ever truly united with my love again, I vow never to leave him, not for all the rice, tea, and Chinese in Asia.* Of all things to come to mind, why that? I promised myself I couldn't afford jealousy for a woman Giacomo said was dead. But couldn't my brain have picked pasta and Italia instead of thoughts of the Orient?

I remembered my promise to him then and told everyone to wave one last time because he wished us to leave and not catch cold.

His mother's eyes. Would I ever forget her look?

We all waved, Donna Maria and I still holding hands. I then bustled our little band of well-wishers away from the docks toward the awaiting carriages, but stole a backward glance. I realized I'd kept his handkerchief and with it unfurled in the wind, I waved one last time.

It was one I'd made him with rolled edges and invisible stitching.

When we arrived home, I didn't let my mother or Donna Maria into the kitchen. I felt nervous wings attach themselves to my scapula bones, for I moved too quickly even for me. I was never clumsy, but I spilled a bowl of salad greens I was mixing with anchovies, oil, and garlic. The overturned vessel crashed beyond repair. I splattered my dress. In that instant, I knew I wouldn't clean it, but would give it to the poor. I never wanted to see it again, or to be reminded of this day.

Naturally, there was a commotion as the old folks wanted to know what had shattered.

"Don't worry, it's nothing. Break something in the kitchen, you break trouble!" I shouted as my mother entered the door.

"Are you all right, Angelica?"

"Fine. Now go and attend our in-laws. Please."

"Let me know if you need help."

"Definitely."

Next I was besieged by Nunziata, who had finally grown an inch, and Beatrice, whom I was sure would be a midget.

"Set the table, girls, and mind the crystal."

"Angelica, do you want us to put one of the silver coasters you got for your wedding underneath the wine?" Beatrice asked, but before I had time to answer her, Nunziata elbowed her in the ribs and shot her a cross look.

My, my, how she'd matured and become sensitive to others' feelings.

"What did I do wrong now?" Beatrice squawked.

"Nothing," I said, and added, "later I'll treat you all to ice-cream cones. Where's Flaminia?"

"Brushing Briciola. I'll get her," Beatrice said.

I stooped to clean up the mess, but Nunziata stopped me. "I'll continue here. Go change your dress."

"Bless you, dear." I almost called her Rina.

My heart overflowed with the sadness I felt because of Giacomo's parting. I ran upstairs to change, happy no one saw me crying.

When I came back, Nunziata had gotten a new bowl, added fresh greens, and remixed the salad, apologizing for taking the one I'd received as a wedding gift. "There was nothing else. All the other large bowls are occupied, I'm afraid."

"Never mind. You did the right thing," I said, feeling the effects of the highly emotional day. My head dizzied. I sat down. "I don't know what's come over me. I suddenly feel ill."

Nunziata asked, "Should I call Mamma?"

I shook my head. "I'll be fine in a minute. Give me the vinegar bottle."

She handed it to me, and I inhaled deeply and felt my head clear. "It's nothing really. I feel better already."

Giacomo and I had picked wild porcini mushrooms the day before. I had laid some in the sun to dry on woven twig trays, the same ones we used to dry figs. The others I made into a garlicky, peppery sauce with olive oil for pasta that night. And what I had left over, I conserved in white wine for today. I made a cream sauce and added some fresh parsley.

When I went to serve it, I drizzled a little garlic oil on top, knowing how much my in-laws liked it, but the garlic aroma overpowered me, and I felt my stomach rush upward, then stop short.

My brain rummaged for a quick excuse. I asked Donna Maria to do the honors and passed the serving dish to her. The second it was in front of her, I sat down.

I might have fooled everyone else with my gracious act, but I hadn't hoodwinked Mamma. She gave me that look, and I raised my eyebrows so she wouldn't question me now.

When Giacomo's parents left, Nunziata, Beatrice, and Flaminia cleared away and did the dishes. I don't remember how I managed to get through the afternoon, but I pleaded with my sisters to let me stay home, gave them money, and sent them for ice cream. Papà said he'd walk with them to the piazza and I was relieved.

The minute they left I tore off my bodice and slithered into my lace-trimmed cotton voile nightgown that had been a wedding present to me from Donna Maria's ex-maid, Anna, who designed and made it. She also had given me a gold *corno* "for luck to match Giacomo's," the card had read. I wondered how she afforded this and how she knew he owned one. She'd been in service at the Scimenti house when he was still a boy. But it was curious that she gave me two gifts and Giacomo none. I thought, *How odd.* And now I was sorry not to have asked Giacomo more about it. It would have to keep. Two whole months. I felt I shouldn't write it in a letter. Something told me I needed a direct look into his eyes when he answered me about it.

Mamma came and tucked me in, just like when I was little.

"The girls helped me a great deal in the kitchen. They'll be good in the house and for Papà when I leave."

"I haven't convinced him that you're really going." She smoothed my covers. "What happened to you at the table?" She took my chin in her hand. "Your eyes look strange," she said and let go.

"A day of emotions. I was suddenly overcome by it all."

"Soon you'll get used to the idea of being a *signorina* again," Mamma said. "Oh, I've had a letter from Zu Nino. I'm so glad he's found a companion."

"What did he write?"

She pulled the letter from her pocket and read me excerpts.

"He's trying to rent or sell the property for us. He brags about his wife, a wonderful teacher." She looked at me puzzled. "Has he seen her in the classroom?"

I laughed. And Mamma's face relaxed with the assurance that I'd be fine in the morning.

"Rest now, dearest child."

I took her hand and drew her back. "Mamma, how can I ever thank you?"

"For a family luncheon?"

"The wedding. And what you did for Giacomo and me."

Mamma touched my cheek. "I'd lay down my life for you, and when you have children of your own, you'd do the same." Mamma blew me a kiss before she closed the door.

I remembered part of a prayer from my childhood that went, "Let nothing affright thee, nothing disturb thee. All things are passing, God never changeth."

CHAPTER XLI

Angelica

NEWS

AS THE DAYS WAFTED ONE behind the other to form weeks, I began to understand the nature of my listlessness. I was petrified, thinking of all the many things that could go wrong. At first I thought I suffered pangs from missing Giacomo, but then other symptoms made it quite clear that I was going to become a mother. This shocked me, but I reasoned, when one plays with a fire stick, she's apt to get . . .

Images of Zia Concetta's travail gripped me, and it was difficult to shake loose of them. I began to pray to my aunt, hoping she would intercede with Christ and the Father. I implored her to ask that her fate would not be mine. My hands were iced yet sweating.

I calmed myself with a cup of rose-hip tea and tried to think of the joyous side of my new situation. My mother came into the kitchen, shattering the interlude just as I rehearsed the words I'd use to tell her my news.

I was frying zucchini. Mamma announced the postman had brought another letter from Zu Nino, who was most distraught because he was unable to rent our house. He demanded Mamma send Peppe with me as soon as my brother finished his studies. Mamma said, "His precise words were, 'Let them come and take care of selling it for their papà. I can't dally anymore over this situation; I'm disregarding the harvest.'" She pocketed the letter.

She huffed. "I'll hazard a bet, it's the influence of his new wife—city girls and their pompous ways. After all we've done for him. Living rent-free all these years and now he won't spare the time to reciprocate the favor to his own brother."

"Mamma, hush, Papà'll hear you."

"He's feeding Briciola." She twisted off an onion from a braid.

I flipped the little wheels of zucchini and oil skittered. I wondered if Mamma would let me go to Villaggio Pace in my condition. I said, "How will Peppe manage on his own without someone to cook and clean for him, Mamma?"

She chopped the onion and set it aside. "I'll think of something, *cara.*" She went to the dry sink and was intent on selecting just the right carrot.

"Oh, by the way, Mamma, I'm having a baby."

"That's nice, dear," she said, preoccupied with peeling the carrot.

She sat down at the kitchen table and began to read the letter again, when she stopped mid-sentence and said, "Angelica, repeat what you just said."

I did and she jumped up, threw her arms around me, and we danced a Mazurka. Unprepared for her reaction of joy, I dropped the fork I'd used to flick the green rounds.

She stopped breathless and made me sit down. I forgot about the vegetable frying and did as I was told.

"I knew there was something different about your eyes. I'm going to be a grandmother again, but this time I'll be close to the baby."

"Oh my God, Mamma. I want to go with Peppe and then leave directly for America."

"Certainly not!" she proclaimed without hesitation.

"Which?"

"Neither." She took the letter from her apron pocket and fanned herself.

"Mamma, I promised Giacomo no more than two months. And I want to see Villaggio Pace again."

"He'll have to understand."

"But will he?" I asked, the scent of burning zucchini permeating the air.

I WROTE GIACOMO THREE DAYS in a row, telling him the news, each time from a different perspective. When I finally received a letter back from him, he sounded disappointed because I couldn't tell him in person. But much worse was that he said it was useless to keep on looking for an apartment and he'd decided to stay in the rooming house and save money. He wrote that he'd been terribly ill and a German woman with red hair nursed him. By the way he mentioned the nurse it made me think he was more interested in her than with my baby news. Was she a professional nurse? Or just a redheaded tart who took care of him during the illness? What else did she do for him?

My elation plummeted, hurled into doldrums. I became frightened at what the consequences of this baby and the separation could mean.

I had kept all of Giacomo's letters to myself, reading only certain parts to Mamma, but this one I handed her to read posthaste.

She soothed my fears, reassuring me it was sensible of Giacomo to stay put. He was thinking of saving on expenses, she rationalized. The nurse was a necessity.

"You don't think he's unfaithful?"

"He was celibate for a year when he was brokenhearted before, why not now?"

"True," I said, unconvinced, remembering our sleepless night of sexual abandon before he left. "I won't deem his letter with an answer—nor grovel for his affections if he's interested in a carrot top!"

"Angelica, *sii prudente*. Not only will you write him, you'll tell him you can't think, eat, drink, or sleep without missing him—anyway, it's the truth." She picked up my wrist and let it fall to my lap. "Besides, you couldn't scare away a crow."

CHAPTER XLII

Rosalia

OBSERVER OF CHANGE

ROSALIA SENSED NOW MORE THAN ever that Angelica needed her family, yet yearned for Giacomo. Because life is difficult, Rosalia thought of it not just as a money issue. She could send her daughter to America, but there was something impeding her. As a mother, she wanted security for her daughter and to know that Angelica could make her own way in the world if she had to. The opposition Rosalia had felt to her daughter's becoming a midwife at the very beginning now changed; she saw it as a way for Angelica to provide for herself if she needed to in a strange and new world. America would be enough of a challenge when the time came; she didn't want her daughter to leave Sicily ill prepared if hardship were to strike the newlyweds' hearth.

Rosalia wanted Angelica to become a midwife in earnest and even earn a living from it, not like the gratuitous work she herself had done. Would Angelica despise her for insisting on not leaving soon? Perhaps. But now, in her condition, should she be exposed to all the problems that could arise from childbirth? Hadn't Rosalia herself been exposed but survived?

After dinner one night, Rosalia sat with her knitting needles clicking while Nicola was engrossed in a newspaper article he was reading on agriculture and the sensible art of crop rotation in America.

Rosalia put aside her work and began to discuss her ideas about Angelica continuing her studies of midwifery. At first Nicola just glanced at her from time to time and then back at his paper, but then the discussion took hold and became heated.

"I object," Nicola said.

"Why? Before you were for it wholeheartedly."

"In her condition? Have you gone mad?"

Their voices became quite loud and shrill, but when Angelica walked into the room, her parents fell silent.

"What is it?" Angelica asked. "What's wrong?"

"Nothing," her father said, snapping the newspaper in his hands as if the sides he held were the reins of his horse.

"Mamma?"

Rosalia got up and said, "Come, Angelica, and we'll make a nice soothing tisane of chamomile for your father."

"No, thank you," Nicola said in a terse voice. He set the paper aside, stood, and blew out the lamp. "Your mother has such modern ideas, why, we'll be getting electricity soon, I suppose."

On the way past the women, he kissed his daughter's forehead and bade her good night.

"No need to go to the kitchen now that he's left," Rosalia said in a ruffled voice.

"Angelica, if you continue to midwife, you'll always have an income even if something happens to Giacomo—God forbid."

"I agree, Mamma. As a mother-to-be I think it would be an advantage." Angelica relit the lamp and sat in her father's chair.

Rosalia relaxed and sat back. "You seem eager to comply—I hope I'm not pushing you."

Angelica shook her head. "Please don't fret. It's what I want."

"I can't get around your father on this. He's overbearing and overprotective. I'll leave that to you."

"Will you contact that physician in Palermo?"

"Dr. Lavinio? I've already written him to ask if he'd take you on as an assistant and could work with him on weekends. But first settle the argument with your father and gain his permission." She unbuttoned the third clasp on her bodice and extracted a folded piece of paper and handed it to Angelica.

"Consider it done, Mamma," Angelica said, taking hold of the letter. "Has Papà ever denied me anything, including marrying a man he didn't approve of?"

"You may be a married woman, but you're under his jurisdiction in the absence of your husband. This is Sicily, not America. Now read the doctor's letter."

Angelica read that most of Dr. Lavinio's duties included work in the overcrowded lying-in hospital, though he did have a private practice and still visited patients at home. He assured Rosalia that her daughter would learn a great deal and at the end of her term of six months as an apprentice she would be a paid midwife.

<hr/>

ON THE FIRST TRIP TO Palermo, Rosalia thought anyone who didn't know her daughter well wouldn't see the subtle changes of beauty taking place. Angelica profiled to get a better view of the gardens of San Giovanni degli Eremiti as they wheeled past and Rosalia saw the singular, fleeting beauty of a woman in love. Angelica's entire face, her cheeks dusted as if by rose petals, eyes large and lustrous as a doe's, declared what Rosalia knew. And when Angelica turned again to look at her mother, Rosalia noted the full lips and smile, which illuminated her heart-shaped face with small dimpled indentations. As her daughter spoke to the driver to ask him to stop for a moment, her voice, rich and throaty, had become mellifluous and mature. Even Angelica's gestures graced her being, emphasizing in each lithe and quick movement that she had become a complete woman. Pride swelled in the mother's heart and she rejoiced.

CHAPTER XLIII

Angelica

THE MIDWIVES

PEPPE CAME HOME FROM SCHOOL to ask if I needed anything in town. I asked him to post a package for me. I sent Giacomo a hand-made sweater. He worked as a stevedore at the Brooklyn Navy Yard and wrote me of the bitter cold on the docks. He'd been in several rows but claimed they were nothing. Apparently Italian longshoremen fought Irishmen. Riots broke out over childish name-calling. I was appalled, told him to ignore it, and prayed for his well-being.

The Christmas season came and went, and winter inexorably gave vent to a pre-spring season. I had become quite an expert under the tutorial guidance of Professor Lavinio. He was kind and gentle and taught with the enthusiasm of one who enjoys learning from students. I was able to continue my apprenticeship because my pregnancy didn't show. I was very lean, and the nursing smock concealed a great deal. My baby wasn't due until July. Dr. Lavinio said I probably wouldn't show for at least another month, possibly a little longer.

Papà decided to leave for Villaggio Pace when the mimosa bloomed in February. He left with Mamma to settle everything concerning our other house, but as things worked out, it was to no avail.

It was decided that Peppe would take over Papà's work and I'd replace Mamma in the store—no argument this time as I was a married woman—

except on weekends when it would remain closed and I assisted Dr. Lavinio. My younger sisters were to undertake all the responsibilities connected with the house. Would that it were never decided so. What a disaster!

I worked the store and gave my sisters careful instructions on what to do at home. Half the time I ended up doing the cleaning and cooking myself rather than explaining what they should do and having to break up their bickering over who should do what. Beatrice came up with a brilliant idea: we should get a servant to help. I said, "Fine. You pay for her."

Mamma and Papà's trip accomplished only one thing. They had sent some furniture that we'd left behind in Zu Nino's care. Papà wanted to give me certain pieces for a house that he still hoped I'd set up in or around Carini. One of these was the piece we'd restored together. Not even the joy of seeing it conquered my depression from these discussions with him. I began not to respond at all when he started one. I became recalcitrant, more so because the intervals between Giacomo's letters were getting longer and longer. I wrote to his brother, Neddu. He wrote me back a short, succinct note. It read: "Come to him. Do not delay. He's beginning to lose hope." But destiny had its own way of thinking.

❧

FOR MONTHS I HAD BEEN panicked, afraid something would go wrong with the birth. Besides the numerous and distinct births that I was involved with at the lying-in, I had brutal nightmares and daydreams filled of snatches of conversation with Gypsies without faces. I begged Don Ruggero to give me Last Rites, but he refused. Preparedness was all I desired, I told him, if God had deigned an eternal visit for me. Still Ruggero refused.

❧

MY PARENTS CAME HOME AT the end of May. As the time shortened, I prayed more and endeavored to distract myself. Bitter thoughts and frightful dreams of pain, birth, and death haunted my nights, invaded my days. A lumbering tortoise, the month of June crept by. On the seventh day of July—and although I had had increased urination in the last few months—I woke up with an urgency that was similar but much more intense.

I felt cramps but paid them no mind at first. As they became more insistent, I thought of the dull aching after my accident. Then I walked the dog, but when I returned home the need to relieve myself had intensified. Around lunch time I felt acute pressure cramps in my vagina and lower abdomen. I didn't want to alarm Mamma, but after what seemed like a long while with no abatement, I called her and told her I was having pains. She helped me undress and clothed me in one of her oldest, largest nightgowns. She teased me, saying I looked like a grandmother, but it didn't help lessen the tension I felt. I was just thankful she didn't tell me to be brave. She propped me up in bed and stuck a book in my hand. "There's time," she said. I was hungry, but she refused me food; I was particularly frustrated that I hadn't eaten breakfast. She gave me tepid water and told me to sip, not gulp.

The window to my room was open, curtains aflutter, and lovely garden scents surrounded me. I started to cough and sneeze and realized it was due to pollen. But then coughing produced another reaction. With each cough, I felt wet between my legs. I tried to suppress my coughing and guessed it was also because of nervousness, not just the pollinated early-summer air thriving in my room.

"What's wrong?" Mamma asked.

"I'm trying not to cough because when I do I feel like I'm wetting myself."

"Shall we bustle you off to the lying-in?"

"No."

"Do you want me to send for Dr. Lavinio?"

"No."

"Why not?"

She tugged the covers aside and examined me, holding up her fingers by way of a measurement, and my mind flew back years to Zia Concetta's bedroom. A chill crawled up my back to my neck. I shook my head to dispel the memory of that and a recent newborn's death I'd seen at a most difficult lying-in.

"I'm sending for the doctor. You're much more open than it seems possible and I think the water broke," she said.

I had ignored all the symptoms. Fear had paralyzed my brain. All of a sudden I was drowning in the realization that my labor had begun.

"Too late, Mamma." *Too late, Lia,* I heard Zia Concetta echo.

She left the room and I heard voices from the hallway.

When she came back I watched her put on her apron and then remove the cork from a brown bottle. "Not now," she said, sternness in her voice, "and only if you absolutely need it." Mamma placed the bottle on the bed stand out of my reach. She'd already explained that if the process was going smoothly she didn't want the drug to interfere or hamper the expediency of the birthing process.

"It's much better not to retard—"

"I know, Mamma. I'm fine." I bit my lower lip. Right then I drew in a deep breath because a sharp pain had lashed my lower back, circling the girth of my large, protruding belly.

"Good girl. Keep taking deep breaths. Now let's see about this position. Then I'm going to hunt up Nunziata to help."

When she'd left the room, my thoughts turned to Dr. Lavinio, how he'd promised to be in attendance for me, and how he'd miscalculated the day, though no one could calculate exactly. I looked at the crucifix on the wall and made a deal with the sufferer on the cross. I felt too strong, too young to think I'd die. My supplication took another direction. *Don't let me show fear—for my mother's sake—I offer this up for the sacrifice You made.* Then I decided to involve the Father who'd sacrificed His only Son. *Of You, Almighty, I ask, please just let my baby be healthy and live.* Some minutes went by and in the middle of my coercing the Third Person of the Trinity, I uttered a little yelp, then smothered my mouth with my hand.

Mamma had heard and I listened to her quickened pace on the stairs. She stayed with me and read to me.

I tried to doze for I hadn't slept well the night before and was cross with myself for having eaten ice cream after dinner. The pains interpolated thoughts, sleep, breath, coming at irregular times. But when I saw Mamma pull out Papà's pocket watch and begin timing, I began to catch their rhythm and knew the contractions were faster, more regular, more powerful, and with little time in between. Mamma wore a puzzled face.

"What is it, Mamma?"

But I knew before she said, "This birth may be quick. Better so. You won't have time to think."

Nunziata popped her head in the door and smiled. "Anything I can do, Mamma?"

Mamma looked at Nunziata a minute. "Bring me two bricks from the shed."

"Angelica, turn on your side." She examined me again and then kissed my hand. "All is fine. The baby's in position."

When Nunziata returned, Mamma rolled me onto my back. She wedged the bricks between the bedstead and my mattress. She made me put the pads of my feet and toes on them, pushing against them, bending my knees.

I had several more strong pulsations, the thrust of an infant very ready to meet his world.

"Let's get you into a slight sitting position," Mamma said. She bolstered my back with cushions. I watched Nunziata's eyes grow in size as Mamma splayed my knees. I was so keen on Mamma's orders that I didn't think of being shy or embarrassed.

"Suck in as much air as you can and then push when I tell you," Mamma said. "Keep that air inside like it's the Spirit of the Holy Ghost and this is the end of the world."

I felt like a helium balloon about to burst.

"Now push!" she said in an explosion of emotion and strength. "Push. Now stop forcing. Let the air out. Slower! Three short puffs of breath. We're fine now." She raised her voice and head toward Nunziata and said, "Get me those extra bed clothes and push them under Angelica."

"Mamma, remember when I hemorrhaged as a girl?" I said.

"You're not going to—"

She turned her head slightly. "Good, Nunziata. Now separate her knees. More."

I watched my sister's eyes grow large from shock and fear.

"Mamma." I started to cry. "If I die like Concetta, save the baby, Mamma."

"You're not going anywhere."

"Aiyee! I don't care if I die. The baby—"

"Don't let go, girl. Hear me now. Listen. Take in a deep, deep breath. Hold on. Angelica, keep your knees apart as much as you can. Nunziata, hold her hand and let her squeeze."

Nunziata came to the side of my bed, relief on her face. She wiped my forehead with her apron and then fanned me with it twice. She let go of her apron and grasped my hand while my other hand flew to the bar of the headstead where I gripped it to save myself from falling down a well.

"Push, Angelica, push . . . a little harder. Again. Harder!"

Mamma signaled something to Nunziata and I thought I'd die from not breathing. "Stop pushing," Mamma said.

Nunziata held my hand and said, "Let go the air now. Slow, Angelica, slow." I felt a gush of warm fluid spill through the opening between my thighs and soak the covers at the same time a hard ball-like shape penetrated, expanding me farther and farther, wider and wider till I thought I might split up and down and burst sideways.

"The head—what a perfect head looking side and down, and oh, Angelica, bambina mia, I'm reaching in and pulling the head clear. Breathe short breaths, quick ones. Let them go. Oh, Angel," she purred. "I'm cleaning the fluid from the nose and mouth, turning the shoulders—no blue here, this is a pure white-skinned birth—I'm pulling out. The infant's free. Ah . . . and here are the legs."

I felt a long corded tube still attached to my baby follow out the larger mass and thought of Silvana's unwanted baby.

"Oh, Angelica," my mother cooed, retrieving my child from my body, "here is your beautiful baby girl."

She held the babe up, still part of me. Holding the baby by her ankles, Mamma smacked the back and got the wail she wanted to hear. Still bound to my insides, my child cupped in my mother's hands like huge scallop shells, we were three generations of Sicilian women. I looked from the baby to my mother. I'd never seen such a radiant smile upon my mamma's face.

"Mamma, the joy overcomes the pain, but I'm so uncomfortable."

"I know," she said, placing the baby awash in my fluids on my belly.

Nunziata, standing next to Mamma, laughed. "What an initiation," Nunziata said, "one I think I could've skipped for a while, ladies."

<hr/>

I PRESENTED MY WORLD WITH a beautiful baby girl, a little ahead of schedule but very welcome. I put pink bows in my hair, and Mamma placed a large pink corsage of tulle with flowing satin ribbons on our front door, announcing the birth of Maria Giuseppa. Giacomo had picked out the name to honor his mother and grandmother.

God and my mother were with me and everything went according to schedule in a normal way. Mamma was right. The minute I held my precious baby girl, all remembrance of fear or any semblance of pain dissipated. I was overcome by incredible joy such as I had never known. A day later, I could do nothing but cry.

⚜

WHEN THE BABY WAS THREE months old, I wrote a letter to Giacomo telling him that as soon as the baby was strong enough we'd come to him.

He wrote back and told me there was no rush. The baby's health took precedence over everything. Besides, he'd only begun looking for a place to live. The other thing he said was that Neddu would also reside with us. This was not an ideal situation or, as Machiavelli would have stated it, the best of all possible worlds. Neither was the sentence in the form of a question but rather a gruff statement, which made me feel quite insignificant. I was also peeved that I'd let him choose my baby girl's name, even though she was named in accordance with Sicilian custom, so I nicknamed her Pina.

I berated myself over and over for not having made the voyage immediately after Peppe finished school like I'd promised. I shouldn't have told Mamma about the pregnancy. "Should" and "would" filled my daily meditations, but the truth was, hindsight makes vision perfect.

⚜

RUGGERO PERFORMED THE BAPTISM. NUNZIATA and Peppe stood in as proxy godparents for Rina and Bulldog.

Mamma organized a party for the baby, who wore an organza dress with tiny pink embroidered flowers. Pink streamers decorated the terrace. Bunches of cut flowers were placed on all the tables strewn with confetti. I had beautiful *ricordini* printed on holy cards of angels. I sent one to Giacomo, to Neddu, to Rina, and to Bulldog. Mamma, Nunziata, and I had crocheted the borders of white handkerchiefs with pink silk thread. When we had enough we set them aside, filled with confetti and tied with pink satin ribbons, for the guests. These were placed in a basket that served as a centerpiece for the banquet table.

When the rush of baptism activities ended, I resumed my work in the shop.

Mamma was pleased with the sales increase in the store and said I was a natural for business. She told Papà, who delighted in the news.

The next time the matter of Papà's house was mentioned, he suggested I accompany Peppe to Villaggio Pace. He assured me that if I went with my brother, I'd be fortunate and sell it. He also promised me half of the sale price. I started going around Carini and Palermo acting as if I wanted to buy a house, or property to build one. Papà was pleased, but I had a different scheme in mind. With information I had amassed on the prospective buyer's side, I would use it to my advantage when trying to sell Papà's house. I explained my plan to Mamma and put it into operation without further delay.

I sat at Mamma's desk and wrote to Giacomo to tell him what my strategy was, inferring that the money I'd earn from the sale would enable us to buy a bigger place for ourselves somewhere in Brooklyn, or possibly to maintain Neddu in smaller quarters of his own.

I felt tired and decided to take a short nap before writing my next letter to Rina. I blanketed myself with a knitted lap rug that was rather light, being made of mohair. Though I felt a bit cold, I didn't want to stir from my comfortable position on my chaise lounge.

I awoke from the nap with a terrible foreboding. I tried to dispel the feeling and I began a letter to Rina. In pouring out my heart to her, I discovered that I'd related the dream. I threw the rug about my shoulders and reread my words, which chilled me to the marrow.

"Rina, the dream was so real, so frightening. Papà was dressed all in white, and though he didn't say it, he seemed like an embodied spirit. I thought, is he dead? We were sitting on straight-back cane chairs, like the ones Zia Concetta used to have on her terrace that overlooked the garden bursting with summer flowers and fruit. We were chatting and I reached to touch him, but I couldn't because of the distance between us and the chairs were extending upward, higher and higher and higher. I had the feeling that Papà earned his height and that he was not afraid. I felt an overwhelming sensation of love for him that I couldn't express because I was unwilling to follow him any higher into the evening sky. My hands gripped the sides of the chair seat like a vise and I looked down. I towered, elevated some enormous distance above the garden, where I was settled, shaking with fright. Somehow I wasn't willing to go where Papà was heading. He looked so comfortable and I've never seen him more content. This aggrieved me, making me all the more afraid. I knew I had other things to accomplish still—how was I going to get down?

"Everything was in my head, nothing spoken, but I knew Peppe would be the one to bring me back to earth from that dizzying height. Papà would be left alone, I thought, as he kept ascending into clouds that covered him while I shook in the chair awaiting Peppe, hoping he had a ladder tall enough to rescue me. Then I woke, shuddering so . . . quaking till I thought the earth had exploded. Whatever do you make of it, my sister? Please do write me soon."

CHAPTER XLIV

Angelica

FOR LOVE OF BRICIOLA

BY MY FIRST YEAR'S WEDDING anniversary, I had stopped all manufacturing of articles to sell in the mercerie. Handmade accessories were for family members only. My hands were never idle for any of my loved ones, especially my little one.

I found myself instead a different kind of businesswoman en route to Messina, armed with techniques I'd gleaned from clever salesmen, and Papà's smartest hunting dog, Briciola, for protection. My father insisted I travel equipped with the tracker as bodyguard, or not at all. So the expedition got underway, the four of us, Peppe, Briciola, the baby, and me.

Peppe had finished his studies and training and would begin work at the Questura, the police station in Carini, in six months' time after his wedding to Ludovica, who had inherited her *sarta* mother's golden hands. He and I made excellent travel companions, now that he had matured into such a fine man. Although he still was a tease, I'd learned to take it better. Briciola would alert us to any possible danger.

THE DAY WE ARRIVED IN Messina we stopped in a lovely copse for lunch so that I could nurse the baby in comfort and rest a bit. We had a picnic lunch of cheese, bread, wine, and grapes the size of thumbs, big enough to peel. While we were napping, Briciola growled at a stranger about to make off with a piece of my luggage. In my periphery, I saw the ruffian Briciola scamper off at a decided pace behind the man, who dropped the suitcase when he looked over his shoulder to see the dog bounding after him. I had a distinct urge to yell, "Attack, Briciola!" But since no theft took place, I decided to let the would-be perpetrator live and called the guard back with an unladylike whistle that Peppe had taught me and which woke him.

WE MADE A FORTNIGHT STOPOVER in Messina to visit Lella, now living there, and Zu Nino and to spread the word about the house for sale. Lella was her usual exuberant self and she played tour guide for us. Peppe and I revisited this unusual city, prominent for its churches. The largest one was the Cathedral, which possessed a monumental belfry guarded by a lion who roared and two nuns who struck the hour at midday. A statue of the Madonna gave her blessing to the onlookers. The belfry contained a miniature church and a skeleton, representing death.

I noted the inside was practically all mosaics in gold inlay and twelve apostles were carved in marble. Zu Nino and his lovely wife accompanied us. She was visibly awaiting a baby, and both of them were in high spirits.

Lella took us to visit Saint Anthony's. Papà's mother was named Antonia for this saint and in turn she named her other son Antonio, though everyone had always called him Nino. I'd never seen this church, which contained the most decorative paintings and fabled religious art one can imagine.

Lella told me about our homegrown Sicilian "Joans of Arc" called Dina and Chiarenza. Names I'd keep in mind for another baby girl. Giacomo would surely name a boy Stefano, after his father. I'd have no say whatsoever in that case. In each church, I made a wish for our safekeeping—mentioning by name Peppe, Pina, myself, and, of course, Briciola, until we were once again reunited with our loved ones.

AFTER A WONDERFUL SOJOURN WITH our relatives, Peppe and I departed with heavy hearts and made our way to the *casa paterna* with mixed emotions.

Peppe said, "It is so difficult letting go of one's past."

"We never really do. We march on toward the future, memories tucked into the pockets of our hearts," I said.

I adjusted the precious bundle in my arms to accommodate her. The baby, my little imp, was voracious at the breast and so I nursed her. When she finished, I put her on my shoulder and patted her gently on the back. She gurgled contentedly, so I placed her in a traveling crib at my feet where she toyed with her blanket till the clopping horses' hooves, music in her ears, brought her gently to peaceful slumber. Peppe unlocked the gates and swung them open. They groaned and creaked from disuse. He mounted and drove us through the gates. Driving down the viale canopied by huge trees brought to mind games and chores of my youth—the nostalgia of which brought tears to my eyes. But I wiped them away quickly at the sight of the house. It was like seeing a friend who had aged terribly in our absence.

"Sad, isn't it?" Peppe said, robbing my thought.

<hr />

IN ONE MONTH'S TIME, I'D received three offers on the house, but none of them close enough to conclude a deal. I'd almost settled on the last bid, just to be done with it, but I telegraphed Papà, who answered to hold off until I got my price. When I got back from the telegraph office, we had a wonderful surprise visit from Zu Nino. "I didn't bring my bride," he said, shyness in every syllable, "because of her condition." He unloaded supplies with Peppe and stayed for lunch. We talked into late afternoon, which rolled and tumbled into dusk, a joyful child down a grassy knoll. Zu Nino stayed the night. I put Pina to sleep in the enormous bottom drawer of a dresser. This functioned as her cradle.

Early morning ushered in a violent looking sky of red and purple. It settled on a violet gray, the color of a mourning dove, which tranquilized me. The colors reversed themselves that evening as I prepared the meal. Peppe ate with gusto, and I left him comfortable, seated with Pina in his care, talking to Zu Nino.

I walked the dog, in need of attention because she'd acted strange all day. Briciola usually played hide-and-seek with me. Her manner was impish. She loved to prankster about, giving me a hard time going back in the house. Dusk was her favorite hour. She'd chase rabbits, birds, and field mice.

However, all this day I'd found her in the oddest places as though she sought refuge. This evening I called her many times before she finally slunk up to me, her tail between her legs. We started to walk and she nipped at my heels, like a sheepherder. She yanked my skirt in the direction of home.

"Whatever is wrong with you, moose of a dog?"

There was no way of keeping her outdoors, so I gave in and went back to the house. Instead of crouching on the kitchen floor near the warm oven, Briciola raced upstairs. I called her, but she refused to come.

I searched the upstairs floor. No Briciola. Had she snuck up to the attic? Sure enough, I found her coiled upon the top stair. I tugged, but she was cemented and wouldn't budge. I was too tired to argue so I said in my sternest voice, "Just for tonight, rascal, because you seem out of sorts."

Peppe and I walked Zu Nino to his cart and I gave him a set of crocheted collar and cuffs for my cousin Letezia, and one "for your bride," I teased. We watched him for a spell and then he turned and waved. A wave of inexplicable sadness hit me as I envisioned him drowning in a sea of mud. I shook my head as if to clear cobwebs.

"What is it, Angelica? You're white as a communion host," Peppe said.

"Nothing. It's been a long day."

Then I wished Peppe good night and took the baby from his arms. I kissed her and laid her down in the makeshift cradle. Then I crawled into bed. Two hours later, I checked on the baby and fed her. When I put her down again, she was already asleep.

As sleep almost overtook me, I was roused by a high-pitched yowling. Then I heard Briciola's breathing close to me. The stinker had crept into my room. "Out, this instant!" I said, pointing toward the door so she'd get the direction straight. She left the room, but minutes later she was barking mad in the doorway.

I hushed her, called her over, and stroked her behind the ears. She quieted. "All right, you win. If I'm to get any sleep at all this night, you may stay in my room. Go sleep under the rocking chair. Go on." Again I pointed. She went.

Before long there was a frightening howling and sick-sounding mewing, a discordant chorus of farm animals and pastured sheep bleating nearby. The night turned very warm. I thought perhaps a freak storm was on its way. I jumped out of bed and ran to the window. Just then Peppe came running down the hall, asking me if everything was all right.

"What on earth do you think it is?" I asked.

"An electrical storm. I heard a rumble of thunder in the distance."

Briciola paced, a caged tigress finding no peace. She yipped and barked at my brother and me till she woke the baby. There was no silencing her with the scratching-ear trick. I could have beaten her, I was so angry. The outside animals calmed and Briciola went under the rocker, cowering, her snout covered by her paws. I took her posture as an apology and said, "You're forgiven."

I picked up the baby who was testing her lungs and my patience. Peppe patted my shoulder and said to let him know if I needed anything.

Shooting a cross-eyed look at Briciola, I said, "Sorry, girl, you're out for the night. Would you mind putting her outside, Peppe?"

"Sure. Get some sleep."

"I'll take the baby in bed with me."

I grabbed her blankets from the drawer and carried her into bed. I rocked her a little, but her eyes were wide open. I knew that if I didn't nurse her she'd never sleep. And neither would I. "What a fat one you're going to be," I said, pulling my breast free. I hummed a song that Mamma used to sing to me and watched my darling little girl's feathery eyelashes flutter, then close.

I placed her next to me and made a fortress out of extra pillows on the other side of her so she couldn't roll or fall. I heard barking somewhere outside but fell asleep anyway, only to be awakened again by a horrible shaking. *It can't be the baby,* I thought, *it must be Peppe.* "Peppe, whatever do you want? What is it?"

I reached over the baby and patted the bed. I sat bolt upright. Peppe wasn't next to me, he was running down the hall, screaming, "Earthquake! We must get out!"

I seized the baby. In my haste to put on my slippers, I stumbled, kicking them clear under the bed. I bent to retrieve them, but Peppe jerked my arm hard, yelling, "No time!"

Then it happened. We dashed out of the room as the dresser where the baby usually slept keeled over. I heard glass tinkling. The handblown Venetian chandelier in the upper hall swung like a trapeze artist's bar. Running underneath it, we saw the intricate lamp pick up momentum. We were well out of range when it crashed to the floor, an explosion of writhing glass in flight. We ran faster. The shaking almost seemed to subside. As we neared the head of the staircase, the tremors stopped. Within seconds there erupted a veritable sea squall, taking place in waterless waves of splintering furniture and smashing glass beneath us. The staircase jolted, and with a tremendous vibration, crumbled right before our eyes. In a matter of seconds, the banister collapsed with me suspended in nothingness on the third step. I reached for Peppe, who hurled me up and we staggered backward. We got separated in the melee, thrown apart, sailors without sea legs, bouncing off walls. Peppe seized my hand again, yelling, "Watch the glass."

We raced down the hall from where we'd just come. The baby was screaming, and so was I.

"What are you doing? We must get out," I said, my voice frantic.

"Let's try for the attic, then onto the roof."

"Mother of God! Peppe, is it safe?"

"Too late for safety!" he shouted. "Should've escaped when the dog warned us."

"Briciola!" I cried, as if she could hear me in the noise of the house crashing in on us.

Our footing gained purchase. We made it to the steps, but fear seized my heart when I saw that an antique wooden laundry press and wardrobe blocked our passage.

Peppe let go my hand and, with Samson strength I'd never seen him demonstrate before, heaved the blocking furniture as if it were a mere featherweight clear across the landing. "Go up!" he screamed, shoving me. "And don't look back, no matter what, for God's sake." I obeyed my brother with a sinking feeling in the pit of my stomach and climbed upward toward the attic. Clutching my precious cargo to my breast, I tripped on my long nightgown, ripping it underfoot and stumbling on the top step.

The house shuddered and groaned, a living mortal in the throes of death. Moving toward the window, I glanced over my shoulder to see the stairway disappear. No sign of Peppe. Not a sound from him below.

Only the baby's cries in my arms. Nothing else except the crunch and crack of a tree's spine, felled by lightning, splintering deep within a forest, which echoed and reverberated throughout my innards. I forced myself to remember what Peppe had said. In confusion, I looked back, still not recalling exactly what Peppe had said. Then instinct took over.

With one free hand and power I didn't know I possessed, I picked up an old baby high chair and smashed the attic window. Shards of glass stuck out at the sides, but my body seemed impermeable to pain as I shot through the opening I'd forged onto the roof. My steps were inaccurate and everything inclined or pitched at such a strange angle that I almost slid off, but I crouched, anchoring myself with my free hand in time to observe a freak of nature as the ground below opened, exposing the bowels of the earth. Yet the house didn't collapse entirely. Almost to the edge of the roof, I made my way carefully across, a blind man without a cane, to the pigeon coop, where I squatted and held my baby tight. I rocked and crooned as much for her as myself, hoping to ease my panic. I don't know how long I crouched there. Panic was replaced by a raging fear. How long? I only know that when everything stopped quaking, I continued to shake, like the last leaf on a persimmon tree in December wind.

Cold and dread. My nightgown stuck to my upper arms. My nostrils filled with the sweet, nauseating smell of my own blood. My arms, scissored and sliced, oozed. I ripped the bottom of my already tattered nightdress and somehow managed to tie armbands, using my teeth to pull the ends of the strips that colored instantly. My feet hurt and were bleeding. I pulled two shards of glass out of my left foot with a fleeting thought of the wine shed.

As dawn crept toward me, huddled with the child, I heard a yapping bark and immediately recognized the pitch of urgency.

"Briciola, you lovely hound, where are you?"

I slid down as far as I dared to the rain drains and peered over the roof ledge. There she was, as if she'd spent the night like a bitch in heat, muddy and disarrayed, indeed in want of a shampooing. I laughed out loud to think of the absurdity of that at a time like this. I thought perhaps the night wind had blown away my brain.

"Briciola, go find Peppe. Peppe. Go get him. Bring Peppe here." I issued the order like an impervious general and knew my trusted and faithful underling would not disappoint me if it were possible. But was it? The sun began to warm and the baby cried for milk. I had enough nourishment for now, but how long before I needed more to make milk for my little one? And how could I descend from this height? I recalled the dream of Papà and me ascending to great heights on chairs, and of my fright, though I'd known that Peppe would come for me. But that had been a dream. I wasn't so sure now. Another thought plagued me and I began having all sorts of terrible visions of my mangled brother, buried under trash and debris.

<hr />

TIME PASSED. I MUST HAVE dozed. Briciola returned, but there was no sign of Peppe, who surely would have tried to make it out from the second-story floor, which had been collapsing. Much of the building was crumbling by the time I'd reached the safety of the attic, supported by huge pillars and stanchions. When I thought about that, it seemed ludicrous to climb rather than descend, but Peppe had been right. Dear God, where was my brother?

"Briciola, run, fetch Peppe. Go fetch."

She slunk off, tail between her legs, like she'd disappointed Papà by not bringing in a felled duck or a shot jackrabbit or a brace of birds. I lost sight of her. But I heard her and, it appeared, she was under the house. I looked out at the horizon—where my world had been, now swallowed by earth. A huge stretch of land from our house to the gorge below lay devastated—deep crevices and ravines replaced immense structures and trees where only yesterday these had stood serenely. The earthquake, God's wrath, had unleashed Sodom and Gomorrah. I began to laugh hysterically and my frenzied laughter woke the baby. I held her to me and sobbed. I needed one of Mamma's slaps—somehow that thought calmed me.

I tried to gauge my surroundings, but wasn't sure of time or space or place. After what seemed like hours later, my feet were stabbed by pins and needles. Muscle spasms. Contractions and forced releases pulsed in my legs and I was having stomach cramps. Massaging legs and feet with my free hand, I did a desperate thing. I couldn't sleep and there was no satisfying the baby. I had to get down from the roof, but how? I hauled the pigeon coop near to the chimney, forming a V. I tucked the infant in that pie wedge. Knowing she was safe, sandwiched in, I was free to explore my options. The house listed to one side. What if I tilted it with my moving, throwing it off-kilter?

I heard wild panting from below. I sat and slid down as far as I dared to see Briciola digging furiously in a pile of rubble that should have been, that could have been, where my bedroom had been situated.

When I spoke to the poor animal, Briciola hunkered down and whined as if her heart had shattered. Her tongue protruded a kilometer. She caught her breath and I watched her unearth debris, stones, and masonry. She scratched and pawed as if she'd located something, someone. I screamed, "Peppe! Peppe, can you hear me?"

There was no response. Only my echo.

What if I jumped? I might break an ankle or leg, but worse, how would I rescue my baby? What if the fearful fate I dared not imagine for my brother had become reality? I ranted at our cruel kismet. Thrusting my fists toward heaven, I shrieked, "God! God! Are You deaf to my cries?" Then I whimpered, "Forget me. Save my brother who has never known love. Dear God, have mercy, I entreat You!"

"Don't wail, Angelica. God has heard your plea," my brother, Peppe, answered, sounding apocryphal. He looked up at me from the ground below, a ghost who'd seen Purgatory. He stood half naked, white with the dust of a century-old house covering him from head to toe.

"Briciola dug me out," he said in a hoarse voice.

All I could think of as I cried with joy was, *Briciola, you darling mutt, if we ever get out of this horror, I'll give you a steak, no, an entire lamb!*

My ingenious brother got us off the roof after he'd fashioned a ladder with broken pieces of wood that he'd hammered nails into with rocks. It was rickety, but it worked. We surveyed the devastated land, hushed. In that silent moment, I knew God loved me.

My mother always read from the Old Testament because she said her mother did, and I remembered Mamma telling me to listen to the small silences. A quote came to me like chalked words upon a child's slate. It was from Kings, "After the earthquake a fire; but the Lord was not in the fire: and after the fire a still small voice." I'd chosen the right path to please Him. I was never meant to be a nun—the maternal instinct, handed down to me from Mamma, was niched within me beyond reach into the very filaments of my soul and I could never wrest free of it.

CHAPTER XLV

Angelica

AFTERMATH, ENDINGS, AND BEGINNINGS

IN THE WEEK THAT FOLLOWED the earthquake, despite the aftershocks, somehow we'd managed to keep body and soul together. Peppe built us a lean-to extension onto the kitchen, where we cooked, ate, and slept. We knew that if anyone could get through to us they would come. Our prayers were almost answered when Lella and Marco came to us a week later when the roads were somewhat manageable. They brought us supplies, told us that Messina lay in ruins, but before Lella was able to give us the brutal truth, I shrieked, "Zu Nino *é morto!*"

"He was killed, buried alive in a mud slide," Lella said. "The shock of his death brought on the pangs of childbirth for his new wife. Zu Nino's son will carry on his name."

Peppe choked over his repeated, "*Dio mio, Dio mio.*"

❧

THE AFTERMATH LEFT THOUSANDS HOMELESS. Thousands more had been killed because the earthquake erupted at night when so many were caught sleeping. God had spared the rest of our family, and we said a prayer for our departed uncle and rejoiced with *cin-cin* for Zu Nino's baby boy with a raffia-covered bottle of wine that Lella brought.

Later, when we'd finished drinking, we used the bottle as a candle-holder. Lella spoke softly, telling me that the twelve apostles I'd admired so much only two months ago were entombed under the Cathedral. Now the entire city was a mass of open graves and buried ruins. Looters had ravaged the city. What remained were buildings razed to shambles.

⟨ ⁂ ⟩

PEPPE AND I DECIDED TO stay put, even though Marco was against the idea. We had plenty of deep well water, which we assumed was uncontaminated but boiled for safety. In fact, much of Messina had a problem with water, so we sent water back with Lella and Marco, who visited us again a week later to leave us what staples they could. Disease ran rampant in the city, we were told, and I was glad we'd decided to remain. Lella informed us that news of Messina and its environs had gotten through to other parts of Sicily and the mainland. Red Cross ships and other organizations, even some private ones, carrying stocks and supplies, arrived daily in Messina. We breathed more easily, literally heaving sighs of relief from time to time, knowing our parents would come for us.

⟨ ⁂ ⟩

TWO WEEKS LATER, PEPPE AND I knew we'd done the right thing as Mamma and Papà, dressed in mourning, Nunziata, Beatrice, and Flaminia pulled into the gaping space where our gates once stood.

Embracing our father, words failed us, as if words mattered when our eyes bore our sorrow for his loss. After a tearful reunion of more embraces and kisses we all settled down. Mamma told Peppe and me that they'd left the store in the charge of Ludovica and her mother. Giacomo's father was tending our land and groves. Mamma handed Peppe a letter from his fiancé, and to me she gave a packet of Giacomo's letters tied with a leather thong. As I accepted them, I fought to push back the envelope of unexpected loneliness. I imagined Giacomo and I once again together, united in body and soul the way we should be, the way we were, married in the mystical body of Christ. I longed for him the way a mystic saint yearns erotically, ecstatically for the love of God. I thought I'd rupture within from wanting him.

Mamma was speaking and I tore myself from my thoughts back

to the reality of the minute. La Letterina, the train that ran along the northern coast of Sicily, had been totally derailed in Messina. Otherwise, our parents would have come sooner. Provisions were being made to rebuild the railway station.

I kissed my husband's letters and put them in my pocket to savor at a more appropriate moment. Papà shouted orders. Briciola danced round, her tail in a fury, barking like she'd just discovered his voice. I just hugged my mother and sisters and cried till Papà shoved them all toward Peppe. Then he took me, cradling Pina, into his powerful arms. He hoisted us up, a doll holding an infant doll, and swung us around like a whirling dervish. I giggled and cried and begged him to put me down, and when he did, I kissed my papà smack on the lips.

He cried out, "La! Take that, Giacomo, foolish man in America who left my little angel behind." He turned and put his face into mine. I heard him say that he'd promised himself if the baby and I had remained unharmed throughout the earthquake, he would give me passage to America. "Mamma and I will remedy that. We've written to your Giacomo and procured your passage—" He couldn't finish, his eyes brimmed with tears and so much emotion, I feared it'd kill him on the spot.

"Papà, what are you saying? I could never leave now." It was only then that I saw my trunk and belongings piled onto the wagon.

I repeated over and over, my own voice fraught with emotion, "Oh, Papà. My dear, dear papà. Not now. It's impossible."

"Angelica." He pushed my shoulders down and sat me on a crate. "Not only is it possible, it's what you'll do."

"No, Papà. I can't leave you like this." I swept my hand around at the devastation.

"Your place is in America now with Giacomo." He bent over me and with his face close to mine, said, "No parent wants his child to leave the hearth, but if the bonds are strong enough, separation is nothing— not permanent. We overcome death by talking to the spirits of those departed, so you'll have your mamma and me with you in every household chore you do."

Peppe started a bonfire of broken furniture and tree branches. I knew then the acrid smell of burning wood and leaves, the sight of curling smoke above a fire, would be a reminder of this moment for the rest of my life.

MY PARENTS HAD BOUGHT ME a first-class ticket, which I
exchanged the minute I could. They wouldn't take the difference I'd saved
by purchasing a second-class fare. Papà said to keep it to buy shoes for the
baby. Peppe would have accompanied me before, but now money would
be tight and we could no longer realize anything from the sale of the house.
We could only sell the property, but certainly this was not the right time.

From that moment until the morning I boarded the S.S. *Vulcania* for
New York, everything blurred, a picture out of focus. I only remembered
one frivolous moment—laughing—the effect Giacomo's letters had on
me. I brightened in spite of the sad reality of my imminent leaving. My
husband had found a house and Neddu might not live with us after all.
Praise God.

I wrote to Rina, giving her the ship's itinerary. The *Vulcania* would
make one layover on the mainland and two more stops in Portugal, one
in Lisbon, and the other in the Azores, then sail straight for New York.
The ship would not stop in Rome, but make port in Naples for three
days, docking time 5:45 a.m., three weeks exactly to the day of my letter.

I asked Rina to arrange to come and meet her goddaughter and to
organize a Baptism party at the Hotel Metropole on the waterfront. I
wanted to walk along the Via Carraciolo that Giacomo had told me so
much about and where he'd spent time with Bulldog after their time in
the Navy. I requested Rina contact Bulldog, honored godfather to our
Pina, who had saved Giacomo's life in China.

THE DAY OF MY DEPARTURE arrived. My whole family saw me off.
I knew exactly how Vespucci or Cristoforo Colombo felt setting out on
discovery. I thanked God I would have the baby to distract me.

My family went ahead, Nunziata taking charge of my little one while
Peppe—wearing a black armband out of respect for my uncle—and I
checked to see that my trunk and luggage were boarded safely. My brother
had the good sense to match the tickets I held with those attached on
each item. He tied Italian tricolor ribbons on all my belongings for quick
recognition when I reached Ellis Island. He did the most unexpected

thing. My brother gave me a tiny box. I undid the grosgrain ribbon and opened it. Inside on a tuft of cotton lay the Trinacria, the three-legged heraldic symbol of Sicily, since the time of medieval Norman dominion and said to represent the island's three points. Speechless, I rubbed my finger over the head—the center that is the head of Medusa.

"For my niece Pina," he said. "Never let her forget this island of her birth."

I threw my arms around his neck, wishing him many blessings for his upcoming marriage to Ludovica. "You do forgive me for not waiting for your wedding?" He nodded his head.

AIR SCUDDED ABOUT AND AROUND my skirt hem while I stumbled along the roped lane as fast as I could to catch up with my parents. Leaves skittered along the pathway, and I thought of how I was always noted for my punctuality. Why had I delayed? In the deep reaches of my heart I knew, but was afraid to think, to breathe.

I saw two lovers kissing farewell. Recollections of other silhouettes. Two eclipsed bodies invaded my morning space—the peace with which I'd kept control of my misgivings about leaving.

The simple chore of controlling my suitcases and belongings was obscured, a gloaming of nights long ago. Lovers on the terrace. Lovers in a Mondello hotel room. Everything in my mind fused. I was late because each action had been assaulted by shadows and afterimages of physical love. I had lost time, moving slowly trying to obliterate them, forcing myself to concentrate on the duties at hand and a different kind of love that I was leaving. How many kinds, Mamma? How many kinds of love exist?

PEPPE AND I FINALLY CAUGHT up with the folks.

When the last horn blared its mournful sound, I kissed everyone, my parents last. Then I hugged Beatrice and Flaminia and took the baby from Nunziata. I faced my parents and Peppe and said, "Thank you for everything in my life and for all you are and all you've done for me."

Then I handed Mamma the baby. My inner core assured me I'd see her again. But a chill ran through me, through the entire curve of my backbone, when my father took my hands in his. We embraced, holding on to each other, never wanting to let go. A niggling fear that I'd never see my papà again wormed its way into my heart. I stood apart from him, gazing at his strong bronzed face, memorizing every feature, each worry line I'd caused him. He blessed me.

"I love you, Papà," I mouthed and broke free of his grasp.

I kissed Mamma again, taking my precious daughter. Only recently had I begun to understand what I meant to my own mother and today that feeling intensified.

Mamma said, "Hold still, Angelica," and reached for something in a box Beatrice held.

Mamma was getting shorter, I noticed. She pinned a corsage of *zagarelle* on my suit lapel, saying, "This is your heritage, my sweetest blossom."

I inhaled the perfume of the tiny white lemon flowers, certain she'd picked them from a tree in the grove where I'd been born. My eyes thanked her. Mamma caressed my cheek.

I climbed the gangway, convinced I'd never see Sicily again. A new life awaited me across the ocean in America with Giacomo.

A wedded life. A family life.

FINIS

ACKNOWLEDGMENTS

HOW DO YOU THANK SOMEONE who has given you the thrill of love, the joy of family, the excitement of world travel, the time to read, study, and write, the friendship and strength to sustain you through the difficult times life hurls at you like a hailstorm? Humbly. And that is how I thank Felipe, my husband.

There are so many people I would like to acknowledge for this novel, but who are no longer earthbound. My father, John, who told me about his life in Sicily when he was a boy; my Aunt Jay, who told me how her grandmother was a mattress-maker; my mother, Marie, who was my first reader of the early drafts; my brother, Bud, who listened to me read scenes and chapters.

I want to thank everyone at Turner Publishing, and everyone who has read any part or all of this book through the writing of it.

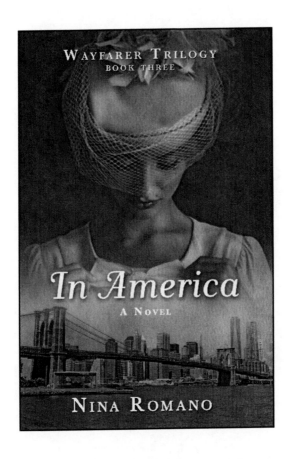

Available July 2016

FROM

TURNER
PUBLISHING COMPANY

CPSIA information can be obtained at www.ICGtesting.com
Printed in the USA
BVOW05*0957220116

433903BV00013B/138/P